Help!
Wanted

Tales of On-the-Job Terror

Edited by
Peter Giglio

Help!
Wanted

Tales of On-the-Job Terror

Edited by
Peter Giglio

New York

Other Books by Peter Giglio

Anon
A Spark in the Darkness
Balance (forthcoming)

With Scott Bradley

The Dark (forthcoming)

This book is dedicated to Melissa Mia Hall. Rest in peace, dear scribe.

Table of Contents

Editor's note: British English spelling was left intact for stories by Stephen Volk, Adrian Chamberlin, Trevor Denyer, and Craig Saunders.

The Chapel of Unrest

Stephen Volk

There is a man frequenting a certain public house in Yorkshire, who, for the price of as many pints as it takes to tell, will share with you this story:

There is one question I cannot answer. Given the choice, would I have chosen a different profession? The business was my father's, and his before him. Mine was the name above the door, and somehow I knew that from infancy my destiny was to be fulfilled therein. By the time I was old enough to question, I was too old to change my ways, and there it is.

The profession of funeral preparation necessarily separates its acolytes from everyday society. Apart from the solitary nature of the work, there is some suspicion on the part of a public satiated by centuries of folklore, that such a practitioner may somehow be privy to some dark knowledge best left alone, some occult sensitivity merely by dint of his contact with the dead. It is a view one must grow accustomed to tolerating. People brand us as carriers of melancholy and gloom merely because our station requires a modicum of dignity and respect. I became used to being treated as an outsider, as everyone in my trade must. I also became used to my own company, for the same reason. I have only had three friends in my life, and two are dead. I buried them both. The third will bury me, I suspect.

But we are needed. Why? Because people fear the dead. It is a dirty job, and people do not wish to do it themselves—they would rather entrust their dearest ones to a stranger. It is peculiar, and I will never understand it, but it is true.

People imagine a corpse to retain something of the nature of the living being that preceded it. However, in my experience, there is no such ambiguity. The dead are sad objects. Their souls have passed on. We deal only with the husks, and it is our function therefore, not to attend to the needs of the deceased so much, but the living—by providing sympathetic services to help the process of grief. That is our function, and no more.

One thing changed my mind. One thing happened to make me question all the certainties I have just expressed. One thing made me begin to approach my job with increasing—unease. Even, yes—caution.

It was a day in April. I remember because one of the boys made a joke about April showers. The sun shone brightly on pavements like glass. It was a miserable day. I had stayed in my office all night, pondering my accounts. My father had died seriously in debt, and however I juggled the figures, it always came out the same—I owed his creditors several hundred pounds. I could not even afford to pay them pennies. The resolution that greeted me with the dawn was the only possible one: with a heavy heart I decided to sell the business.

These thoughts were foremost in my mind as I received a message from Dr. Frith that a death had occurred up at the Big House to the west of town. (It had been called "The Big House" since my childhood, though its true, unremarkable name was Pryne Hall.) In a miserable stupor, I took the hearse whence I was bidden, and found myself ushered into a death-bed tableau no different from dozens of others at which I had been present over the years.

The owner of the house was a tall, thin man with a stooped back, and a jutting chin supported by a wiry neck. His eyes were pale and clear for one of such advanced age, and his head was adorned with white hair as insubstantial as melting snow. He gestured with the cordiality of a nobleman, and spoke, which he did infrequently, with the merest hint of an accent, though his English was nothing short of impeccable.

He sat immobile in a cushioned chair as the doctor and I conversed, all the while his eyes fixed with a kind of deep suffering upon the pitiful figure in the bed. Occasionally his eyes darted sidelong, nervously, or he would blink, or twitch, but always his eyes would return to rest on the deceased.

She was his daughter, a woman of some forty years of age. She lay as peacefully in death as if she had been arranged there, like the composition of a Pre-Raphaelite painting. Her hair was dark and lustrous, and lay thickly on the white waves of the pillow. Yet I saw no tears in her father's eyes, merely numb and staring eyes set in a wan and haggard countenance. But grief takes many forms, and I thought no more of it.

The doctor signed the death certificate and I transported the cadaver to my Chapel of Rest. At the door the old man hesitated, as if to say something, then declined, and shut the door. Only upon leaving, and hearing the bolts thrown from inside, did I notice that every one of the windows of Pryne Hall was barred like a prison.

Preoccupied by my troubles, I could do no more work that day. Instead, I confined myself to my office. I even drew the drapes to block out the mocking happiness of sunlight. Once more I pored over the books, and once more could only come to one conclusion: sell the business. I paced, stamped, cursed. I prayed to God: give me a way out of this mess! There was no answer.

I had just taken my coat from the peg to go for a brisk walk to work off my frustration, when a visitor was announced. I had him shown in, though I was in no mood for company.

It was the old man I had met earlier in the day. His name, I had learned, was Gaetano Prelati. He wore a heavy coat and had his hands stuffed firmly in the pockets. Against the darkness of the material, his pallor seemed almost grey. He refused my handshake and as he sat his head sank into his collar, bird-like.

"I have come," he said in his perfect English, "to discuss"—he hesitated—"*arrangements.*"

"Very well," I said. "Have you spoken to the vicar, sir, or would you like me to take care of everything? Naturally, you will want things taken care of as soon as possible. Perhaps we should strive for a Friday funeral? I'm sorry—I have not asked if you are—er—Church of England, Roman Catholic...?" His unemotive manner was flustering me.

He shook his head. "Whichever."

I coughed. "I see. Well, we have a rising scale of prices; perhaps you would like to see that?"

"No."

"There is a wide range of caskets available: oak, mahogany, satin black—plain, velvet-lined—with gold furniture or bronze. Let me see if..."

"I am not interested in the quality of the coffin," said Mr. Prelati.

"Then what have you come to discuss, sir?" I enquired with what politeness I could muster.

"The preparation of the dead."

"You would want our full treatment, sir? Yes, we can do that. Naturally, we can do that. The normal health and hygiene processes..." I used the usual euphemism for embalming, of course.

His pale eyes were unblinking as he produced an envelope from his pocket and placed it in front of me. "I wish my own treatment. I realise my request is unusual, and when you read it, you may well have extreme reluctance to carry it out. I can only say, however, that my daughter's *condition* necessitates such action, and if you will not comply, I shall find another who shall."

I held the envelope in my hands, and let out a light laugh. This all seemed over-dramatic: why didn't the old man merely *tell* me his instructions? Why the secrecy? Why the warning? What could be so—*objectionable*? I was soon to learn, and as I read the enclosure my fingers began to tremble, and a cold sweat rose up my body.

After reading it, I flung it down. I stared at him.

"In the name of God, man!"

My first instinct was to throw the fellow out. Had he not been so old and frail I may have dealt him a blow. As it was I just stared, and he stared back with limpid blue eyes.

"There is no purpose in explanation," he said. "I could tell you the truth or I could give you one of many lies, but I have no intention of either. You accept the work, or not, as your feelings see fit."

"What kind of monster are you?" I blurted, able to keep my silence no longer. "This goes against every law of God and Man. It is the foulest of all deeds to abuse the sanctity of the dead!"

He sneered with awful bitterness. "You do not need to lecture me about the sanctity of the dead. I have my reasons. Religious, philosophical, call them what you will. I need your co-operation, and for the use of an hour of your time, and your guilt, I am prepared to pay—let us say—substantially."

I looked at the paper again. "Nothing can pay for—this! This—abomination! Good God, she was your daughter: does that mean nothing to you?"

"It means everything to me," he said quietly. He took out a cheque and laid it on the desk before me. Upon it was my name. He said, "One thousand pounds. In your pocket—or another's. Nobody will ever know. The grave cannot speak.

I was struck dumb. My thoughts spun, my head swam, no longer with disgust but with—interest. The rest of the conversation

I cannot, will not, remember.

I poured myself a brandy, and to my horror found that I had poured two, and before I realised it we had raised the glasses and made a toast for which, to my eternal horror, I was, in that moment, eternally grateful.

———————

Time was the monster.

I lay on my bed, fully clothed. The clock in the room ticked like the workings of an infernal machine, each passing minute reminding me of the first two words of Gaetano Prelati's abhorrent instructions.

Before sunset.

I turned on my side, closed my eyes to block out the room, but could not block out the thoughts. I felt unclean. I felt as if I had been complicit in a Faustian bargain. My body churned inside—my professional ethics flung asunder, my soul felt like a sacrificial lamb, terrified, bleating, yet unable to escape. To do this—to succumb— for greed. Where was the dignity of death? Where was the dignity of life? Would I ever have it? Could I ever truly *live*? Oh God— help me.

Before sunset...

It was madness. My humanity does not have a price. There are more important things. No. I shall not do it. I shall resist. I respect the dead.

Why?

What are they? What is it? A husk of flesh and bone. It isn't alive. It's a thing. It can help me. If it knew what I needed, perhaps she would have said in life—yes, do it. Do it if you need the money. Do what he wants you to do! Who are more important, the living or the dead?

Before sunset.

No. I can't. I have to resist.

Yes. Do it! Now, quickly. Don't be weak, have strength for once in your life. Do it and build the business again, or if you don't you'll go under, you'll be destroyed, *you'll* die.

Suddenly in an instant I became aware of the lengthening shadows in the room. The sun was setting over the far rooftops. I sat up, rigid. I took in a deep breath of air. Even so, I swayed giddily, heady with the responsibility of a decision I had now to make in a moment.

Why?

Why before dark? What nonsense was this? Bugaboo tales? Would an hour make such a difference? Does it have to be *now*? Couldn't I have an hour, a minute, to think, to ponder, to *decide*. I laughed, but the air was chill. I was cold. Evil, feverish cold fell over me, and I shivered 'til my teeth chattered.

Obey them to the letter, he had said.

Before sunset.

I stood, determinedly. I went to the telephone. I rang Prelati's number. But before it began to ring, my mind had begun to think of the money again. The madness was mine: what did it matter *why*? Ask no questions. This is no murder, no one will come to harm. Why am I even questioning it?

It goes against God. But where is God in *my* hour of need?

I took up the paper again, and read it.

Before sunset...

Yes, yes. I picked up the box on top of the wardrobe which contained all the equipment I needed. It had not been taken down since my mother had died. It seemed faintly sacrilegious even to touch it—but I dispelled my fears. I took the crucifix from the wall above the "Home Sweet Home" emblem.

The shadows were like a thick wash of seaweed at a shoreline as I waded along the landing and, in the silence now, not even comforted by the ticking of the clock, I descended to set about my grim task. Moonlight imbued the passage downstairs with a church-like serenity, filtering as it did through the stained-glass of the front door. For once I wished that my profession did not regale in the trappings of Christianity. The Christ portrait stared with accusing, watchful eyes as I entered the Chapel of Rest.

My hand twisted the handle of the door.

In the ante-chamber, coffins were stacked in rows, one on its end, its lid half-open. I used one arm to part the scarlet drapes that led into the Chapel itself, and the candle-lamp that I had brought from upstairs lit my path with a flickering, beeswax glow.

The Chapel was not a catacomb. It was not shadowy, nor sepulchral, nor even eerie. But the silence of the place seemed designed to catch any whisper—even the unsaid whisper of a guilty mind. I was afraid even to breathe.

The coffin lay on its bier, without a lid. I paused for a moment, looking down at the pallid figure of Alba Prelati. I thought it must have been the intensity of my emotions, or the ambiguity of the candlelight, but for an instant I would swear she had the face not of a forty-year-old woman, but of a girl of less than twenty summers.

I could not shy away now. I had come too far. Then it must be done without faltering, quickly.

Holding my breath, I placed the crucifix from my bedroom wall in the corpse's limp right hand, closing the fingers tightly around it. Strangely, they were not yet stiff with rigor mortis. In fact they were curiously warm and clammy. Hastily removing a second crucifix which I wore around my neck, I placed this one in the palm of her left hand.

Place a crucifix within each of her hands.

I turned and went to fetch the large, leather-bound Bible from the lectern that faced the pews. I placed it upon the dead woman's breast, the cross embossed on its black leather covering her heart.

And a Bible upon her heart, the Trinity to bind her to the place, the weight of the Lord's might to hold her down...And in penance for her Sins, in Hell for all eternity.

I opened my mother's sewing-box. You cannot imagine how long it took for me to thread the needle with thick black twine. The perspiration more than once blinded me. I licked the end of the cotton a hundred times into a tiny point, but still it would not thread.

Before sunset...

The needle finally threaded, I leaned over the beautiful face beneath me. The beauty of the dead had not been lost on me, the sadness of a perfect child, the pity of beholding the full bloom of womanhood cut off in its prime: but here was something altogether different. Something inexplicably different about the upturned nose, the full lips, the almond-shaped eyes.

I touched her lips. They were dry as parchment. I puckered them together between my forefinger and thumb and began to sew. I had seen my mother sewing the Christmas turkey, pricking the pale flesh with the needle, forcing it through, pulling, stitching again, yanking the twine until the whole was a tight, immovable scar.

...the mouth must feed no more, and let her hunger...

The twine criss-crossed the mouth, pulling it shut, dragging the entire face into a grimace, drawing hideous wrinkles across the once-perfect cheeks. With the black outlines, it seemed she had the grinning teeth of a skull. I bent down and bit off the twine, and knotted it.

And now. My breath was tremulous, but echoed around the Chapel loudly. The stone angel stared with unseeing eyes, blind but all-knowing. Oh God. I must finish. Finish and go.

...and let her eyes not open...

I took the needle to her left eye, and beginning at the inside edge, I inserted it just under the tear-duct, and through the inside of the upper lid, out, and in through the lower lid again. I made in all seven stitches to seal her eyelids together before beginning on the other eye.

Suddenly it opened.

Like a glistening pearl it shone in the darkness, with the same steely blue as her father's. But staring, bulging, terrified, darting to and fro.

With a scream wrenched out of my intestines I fell back, spewing the contents of the sewing-box over the tiled floor of the Chapel, needles and cotton-reels and buttons tinkering in all directions.

In an instant I was out of the place, falling against the staircase, using my arms desperately to claw my way up the carpet, rebounding along the walls to the sanctuary of my room. I flung myself on the bed, at once rising to lock the door, and place a chair against it, and for an hour sat on the bed, shivering and gibbering like a lunatic, my eyes never leaving the door-handle.

———————

I woke at two in the morning, as if from a nightmare. I prayed it was. A brandy bottle lay upended on the floorboards. My head was throbbing. The chair was propped against the door.

Wearily, I forced myself downstairs, one hand gripping the staircase as if for dear life.

I entered the Chapel of Rest to find that the coffin was empty.

"Dear God!" I said to myself, almost collapsing with horror. Within minutes I was in Pryne Hall, screaming my horror at the perpetrator of the crime himself. "Dear God!" I cried, pacing so that it shook the house. "You are *evil* as well as perverted! You deceived me! You lied to me! That you wanted to do this—this disgusting ritual—was bad enough, to a dead body! But she was *not* dead! I saw her, she looked at me! Dear God! May God have mercy on you! She was *alive!*"

Gaetano Prelati said nothing for a long while. He seemed in a dark reverie, a prisoner in the book-lined library in which we confronted each other. Beside him was a side-table on which a pair of wooden glove-stands sat in an attitude of prayer.

"Your daughter is alive!" I screamed again.

"No," he said, and for the first time his voice quivered with emotion. "Alba is dead. She died fifty years ago."

I was overcome with rage and for a second time wished to attack him, but found myself instead uttering a laugh that seemed somehow to come from elsewhere.

"And she is not my daughter," he pronounced softly. "She is my sister."

"That's impossible!" I said angrily.

"There are many impossible things in the world," he said. "All of them real..."

"I'm leaving. I've had enough of madness. I am going to the police."

"Wait," he said. I turned back and saw an old man in need of the confessional. "If you go you will never know the truth."

I took the seat opposite him. The room was lit by gas from the wall-hangings, but darkness separated us like a black river. His voice was a croak, as if his throat protested against the tale he told.

"Before you were born—some half century ago now—when my sister and I were approaching our twentieth year, our father provided us with the means to travel. It was his belief that we should see something of the world, as he had done as a sailor before making his fortune. Alba was a spirited, rebellious child, and I was the quiet, studious one. My thoughts were for a career in the priesthood, hers only for excitement and laughter. You see me trembling? It is because I have not heard that laughter for fifty years! Please..." Prelati fidgeted in his seat, head nodding like a bird towards the side table. "Please, light the hookah. There are substances within to ease my pain."

I did as I was asked, rapidly, impatient for him to return to his history. He took a deep inhalation of foul, pea-green smoke and spoke with slow modulation:

"In Alexandria, I became incapacitated with severe sunstroke, and was confined to bed. Alba was not a good nurse, and I told her to travel onward, that I would meet her in Ushpur. My fever became worse and I was delayed much longer than I thought—and when I was strong enough to lift a newspaper, I was horrified to find that Khudi brigands, religious fanatics, a devilish horde, had invaded Ushpur, and that all Europeans, together with thousands of innocent women and children, had been flung into the vile pits of Ushpur prison.

"In a state of panic, I accompanied a contingent of English troops, only to find the city in a state of siege.

"It was four months before the Khudi were routed by the massed armies of our allies. We found the prison in a condition far beyond our worst nightmares of human degradation. Hundreds upon hundreds of people had been confined in utter darkness—and left to starve. I helped clear the many dead bodies. I sorted the living from the dead. I touched living and dead hands. Black and white. I dug through near-skeletons in the dark. Many had been mutilated as if by pestilential vermin. As for the living—their pitiful eyes looked up at me, but my only thought was for Alba.

"I found her, a withered shadow of her former self, a tiny stick-puppet cowering in the dank dungeons of Ushpur amongst the slime of faeces and decomposition that surrounded her like a bog of inhumanity. She could neither speak nor move.

"I returned with my sister to our home in Paris. She was nursed to health. Or, more correctly, what I believed to be health. It became clear to her family that her mind would never be the same. She stared out of the window, took no joy in the scent of flowers or beautiful music. She ate little, to begin with; then ate nothing. And yet she was no longer losing weight. In fact, she began to show a glow in her cheeks that the Alba before Ushpur never had.

"She slept erratically. More than once I woke from my own fitful slumber to hear an unfamiliar voice echoing throughout our family home—a voice neither Ushpuri nor Khudish, indeed approximating no tongue I had ever heard before. A voice racked with the anguish of sheer physical torment, the voice of a lost soul howling in the dark. One night, I was so agitated I went to her room; but the bed was empty, the bedclothes strewn around, the window open. I found her a street away, walking blindly. When I called her name, she stopped, and, suddenly aware of where she was, began weeping. I carried her home.

"I became curious as to the cause, purpose, or intent of her somnambulation. Perhaps, like the doctor and nurse observing Lady Macbeth, I could perceive some answer to her peculiar malady by a nocturnal vigil. This I decided to do.

"I entered her room, fully dressed, and sat in a corner far from her bed, an oil lamp at my side. For an hour nothing happened. Even the streets were chillingly quiet: no Parisian chatter, no far-off music, no dogs. Just the silent eye of the moon. Finally, my sister began to toss and turn. Her long fingers clutched at the sheets, pawed at her belly and throat; then she rose from the bed and slowly, like a wispish phantasm, drifted to the door and out, into the night.

"I followed.

"She descended the cobbled path towards Montparnasse cemetery, and I watched her scale the locked iron gates like a cat. Once inside, she became ever more like a stalking animal. Her eyes, glazed in half-sleep, fastened upon a small marble tomb in the corner of the graveyard reserved for poets. With a quiet intensity she set to the door, which, even though split, must have been incredibly heavy. Nevertheless the urgency of her task imbued her with supernatural strength, and the slabs were cast aside as if they were cardboard. I..."

Gaetano Prelati took another long suck on the hookah pipe before he could master his emotions. "You can have no idea, no man can have *any* idea—what I beheld when I looked into that—that *ravaged* sepulchre. She stood over the open coffin with the hideous substances of the grave staining her chin and breast. The inhabitant of the long box was naked, a man, decomposed, or mutilated, half lifted out, and his head tilted back, his sagging jaw dropped almost to his chest, no eyes in those dark orbits. Alba had his arm lifted in what I first took to be the act of kissing—of running kisses up the corpse's festering arm. But the sounds...the sounds, you see! The sounds, they were of crunching, they were of breaking, they were of gnawing, chewing, *swallowing*..."

My heart was in my throat. I could not believe what I was hearing.

Prelati waited. He moved his eyes in arcs around the room, as if moving us through time—as if passing over the years of pain, murmuring the names of other cemeteries in the city. "Pere Lachaise, Ivry...Paris was in the grip of a defiler of tombs. The staunchest efforts of the police could not apprehend the evil-doer, who seemed to roam with impunity, like a theatre-goer choosing an entertainment. Countless graves—their contents scattered—shrouds torn to the wind...

"There was no vermin in the dungeons of Ushpur," he intoned with insufferable melancholy. "Or if there was it had two legs, two arms, and the face of a beautiful woman."

I tried to comprehend the horror he was trying to force on to me. My mouth gaped, unable to respond. His mind seemed to wander uncontrollably.

"In the age of Plutarch, the daughters of King Orcommenu of Boetia were imprisoned in his palace. Soon they were overcome, unable to resist an insatiable urge, falling upon the young Ippasus and devouring him. You look dumb! Do you still not see? Do you still not know?

"Perhaps you have read the *Arabian Nights*? The 'Story of Sidi-Nouman' in the 'Encounters of Haroun-AI-Raschid on the bridge of Baghdad?'" I shook my head. "Amina, the wife of Sidi-Nouman, nightly deserted the marital bed to feed upon the dead!" Gaetano Prelati looked to the book-lined shelves. "Each of these books contains the legend! Hoffmann told the same tale to his Serapion Club in the form of 'Aurelia: Vampirismus.' Same story. Same creature. It comes from the Slavic word *ogoljen,* you know—meaning 'mortal remains.'"

I stared at him, dumbfounded and more perplexed by the minute. He saw the mystification in my face, and leaned forward.

"Ghoul," he said precisely. "Eater of the Dead! Vessel of Demons! Being of the Night! You see? You understand? In the dungeons of Ushpur, those who survived did so by one means alone—by *cannibalism*.

"I see your visage grow pale. I am beyond the horror now. But I have learned, to my pain, that such a thing is not beyond human endeavour—or taste. The Scythians and Bretons devoured their dead. The Carthaginians, ancient Gauls, and Sioux Indians of North America consumed the blood and flesh of their enemies as a way of assimilating their courage into their own bodies. The Brahmins and Estonians began the practice of draining blood from meat before eating it. In hot countries this became the norm, until final vindication came from the voice of the Hebrew God: 'Be sure that thou eat not the blood: for the blood is the life...' In Ushpuri legend, a cannibal in life will become a ghoul in death—and be condemned to eternal purgatory on Earth. You see! I have done a lot of reading! I have learned many things!"

I decided to humour the old man.

"What happened after you found your sister in the cemetery?"

"I need not tell you the thoughts that raced through my mind as I followed the *necrophage* that was my sibling back to our home. I did not sleep, but in the morning resolved that my family would not be made to endure further horrors. The bespoilings of the graveyards were already public knowledge, and for them to be linked to our noble house would destroy my parents, I was sure.

"Instead, I said I wanted to take over a wine importing enterprise in England, and I wanted to take Alba with me. I imprisoned her here, this was to be her tomb—and mine. For the first years, I was dominant and she was the prisoner, but then gradually as I became older, she began to inflict her horrifying will. I began to see her waste away with apparent consumption, and, unable to withstand that, I began to give her offerings—God help me, *I* became the grave robber!

"But she demanded more and more. It became like the addiction of a drug. Alba could derive pleasure from nothing but the consumption of human flesh. The Demon within her tormented me as it did her. I felt that I might lose my sanity unless I found her some escape. I read, I read...Filippo Raimondi's *Dissertazione*, Horapollon's *Magie*, Dom Calmet, *De Daemonialitate et Incubis et Succubis* of Liseux, Juan de Lobkowitz Garaamuel's *Teologia Fondamentale*—everything; searching, desperately, in some old grimoire, in some folk-tale, for any recipe to rid me of my hideous tyrant.

"I found it in Stefan Hock's *Die Vampyr sage und ihre Verivertung in der deutchen Litteratur*: the destruction of the *ogoljen,* the ghoul. And the instructions therein were precisely those which I specified to you in such detail—to be administered whilst the monster was in satiated slumber. For the ghoul, like the vampire of legend, once it has outgrown normal human age and attained its preternatural maturity, reverses the biology of life, sleeping during the day and hunting, scavenging by night..." He took again to the hookah, and its copious smoke enveloped him like a ghastly fog of unreason.

"There is a question I must ask," I said. "If you believe all this..."

"Believe? What is there to believe? I believe in nothing without the evidence of my own two eyes. And I have it. The evidence of my own two eyes!"

"Yes, I know," I said, hesitating. "But—why did you come to me to begin with? Why could you not carry out the instructions yourself?"

Prelati sat back in his chair so far I thought he might melt into the shadows. From the dark I heard a whining laugh that had no humour in it. It stopped as abruptly as it started. He said: "Oh but I did. I did. I took the equipment in hand, I visited her bed. I stood over her. I took the needle towards her eyes. I hesitated, you see, and I was lost. I could never do it again. She made sure of that."

I felt a lump in my throat. "She—made sure of that?" I queried in a whisper, almost too afraid to hear his reply.

He lifted his arms from beneath the shawl that covered his knees, and I saw that they ended in blunted knobs, severed at the wrists. The glove-stands were not glove-stands, but wooden hands.

"Yes," he breathed. "She *ate my hands*."

I ran from the house with the madman's insane and pitiful cries in my ears. He implored me to stay, not to leave him, but I ran without looking back, like a child running from a haunted house.

———

My conviction that Gaetano Prelati was quite mad did not diminish with the passing of time. My conclusion was that I had been cruelly duped by a sadistic creature who wished to exact an awful torment—of being both *disfigured* and *buried alive*—upon his innocent sister. The thought of having been a pawn in such a bizarre and insidious game filled me with self-loathing, not least because it made me see in myself aspects of personality more odious than I would have imagined I possessed. Whether I would recover from having been a participant in such a horrifying enterprise, I did not know.

But I did tear up the man's cheque, and burn it. Financial stability is not worth the price of one's humanity—or soul.

However, within the week, I was visited by Sergeant Opie. It was not unusual for our paths to cross, since the constabulary are often amongst the first on the scene of a death. But the body that he delivered to the Chapel of Rest that day was more of a surprise.

"Suicide," said Sergeant Opie before I turned back the sheet. "We received a letter telling us when and where to find the body.

Poison, it was, Dr. Frith says. Some exotic stuff. In a room with a locked door. Locked windows, too. Don't make much sense. And he had a letter on the table addressed to you, in person."

The body was Gaetano Prelati, and the face, remarkably unaltered, showed an expression of aching peace.

When Sergeant Opie had gone, I opened the letter to find that it contained a note with three words written upon it: BURY ME DEEP. I stared at the cadaver in stunned, wordless dialogue. Prelati's tale went through my head—that mad tale—and I listened to his voice and those final, pleading screams as I had run away. Pleading with me to finish my uncompleted task.

I set about cosmeticising the body, without delay.

With my thumbs I forced his staring blue eyes closed. I combed his cotton-hair. I used mortician's putty to fill the sunken cheeks, and fixed the jaw closed. With foundation, rouge, and cochineal, I worked to give his pale visage a mask of health it never had in life.

The funeral was arranged for Monday, and I was pleased to be able to give his body three days' solace in the Chapel of Rest before going to its final resting place. Each morning and evening I visited it and paid my own respects, and gave my own prayers, to a man who, I now believed, was not mad after all.

The funeral was attended only by me, and a boy apprentice I had taken on the week before. He was the son of my new partner. Now there were two names above the door, and the debtors were on the retreat. Why did I not feel more at ease with the world?

Walking back from the cemetery, the boy seemed concerned that we had been the only ones to pay respects. I mumbled an explanation, not too far from the truth: that Mr. Prelati was a foreigner, and as such had no friends here, and that he shouldn't worry on such account.

"Was he never married?" said the boy.

"Not that I know of," I replied.

"Then who was the woman?" said the boy.

"Woman?" said I.

"The woman who came yesterday. She was all in black, and skinny. I thought she must be a relative, in her widow's weeds and that. She didn't say nothing, even when I asked, like she was a dumb tit, but I supposed she'd come to pay respects. You were out, so I showed her into the Chapel of Rest. I stayed and waited, because she was strange. She just stood there, didn't pray or nothing. Just stood as still as anything, never saying a word. Then she raised her veil to kiss the body on the cheek and..."

The boy paused, blushed.

"I know I shouldn't have looked, sir, but...she dropped her veil when she saw me staring. But I couldn't *help* staring, sir. Then she went. Turned her back and was gone. But I saw it. Her mouth and eye, sir, all stitched up closed, sir, and this one eye, sir, staring. Just one eye, sir—and it was weeping..."

Stephen Volk is the creator/writer of the British TV paranormal drama series *Afterlife* and the notorious BBCTV "Halloween hoax" *Ghostwatch*. His latest feature film, *The Awakening*, stars Rebecca Hall and Dominic West, while his other credits include Ken Russell's *Gothic* and *The Guardian*, which he co-wrote with director William Friedkin. His first collection of short stories, *Dark Corners*, was published by Gray Friar Press in 2006. More recently his novella *Vardoger* earned him a nomination for both a Shirley Jackson and a British Fantasy Award.

Another Shift Change

David Dunwoody

It's cool, not cold, but uncomfortable nonetheless. The A/C's Freon fingers reach down from the ceiling to tickle the hairs on his arms. They snake up from the floor into his shorts. It's nice first thing in the afternoon, when his shift starts, but seven hours in he feels sick from it. Against all reason, sweat begins beading along his hairline.

His underarms are already damp. It's just that he hates it so much. Every second he spends in this chair with its sticky rubber armrests and prickly cushioning, every form he enters into the computer—God, those forms, pages so light and smooth he can barely separate them, and with an ultra-fine layer of some dust or powder or *something*, probably just paper fiber but it makes him nauseous to feel the invisible stuff coating his fingertips. The sun has gone down and the blinds behind him have been drawn. Now it's just the fluorescents overhead, which seem to intensify, and the sight of the contrast bleeding out from everything around him, that makes him sick, too.

The others in his row—mostly middle-aged women—somehow don't notice the hell they're in. He supposes they've been numb to it for a long while. Lifers. Their vacant stares only flicker when they laugh at a cruel comment about someone on the next row. He hears all the comments, despite the sweat-clogged headphones he keeps on his ears at all times. The whispered junior-high gossip and the furtive shifting of seats when a manager walks by—he hears all of it, every day. Because he has made himself a shade, a non-entity, they prattle on shamelessly around him. He hears them sing sweetly to one another's faces and spit venom once backs are turned. They're the dead heart of this place.

They must talk about him too, because they talk about everyone. *He never says a word. He barely looks at people. Probably thinks he's better than everybody. Probably lives alone or with his mother. Can you say*

Psyyyyychooooo? I'll bet he's a pervert, bet he thinks about us the way our husbands used to. Or maybe he's not into women. That would make sense.

The grandmother of seven who sits directly behind him taps his shoulder. He pulls off his headphones and she tells him, "Some of the girls brought cookies for Linda's birthday. They're on the table behind Rosie's cubicle."

"Oh, cool. Thanks." He turns back to his monitor. Linda was gone last Friday and this Monday. She took an early birthday trip with her sister to Phoenix. Grandma back there had spent both days telling everyone what she'd heard about Linda and her "miscarriage," which went in air quotes because everyone apparently knew it had been either a fake pregnancy or an abortion.

His palms are growing sweaty now. His fingers stick to the keys and come away with the feeling of rubbery crud on them. The day-shift person who uses this terminal probably wears those finger things to separate the forms. They probably leave some grotesque residue and now it's gumming the spaces between the ridges of his fingertips. Sweat gathers in the crease of his neck and shoulder. Between his thighs. He needs to go to the restroom. Just needs to sit in a stall for a few minutes and clear his head. He rolls back from the terminal.

His fingers stick fast to the keyboard. They won't come away.

He can't get up.

His elbows are fixed to the armrests now. He looks from them to the keyboard, plants his wrists on his ergonomic gel strip and tries again to pry his fingertips free. Their skin is pulled thin and white. So are the keys. *So are the keys.* His hands go slack and he watches the keyboard's surface flush pink. He presses down on the spongy keys and he can feel the threads of bone beneath. He can also feel the pressure of his fingers from *within* the keyboard.

It's in me. I'm in it. I don't know.

He tries again to pull out of the chair. His back and arms refuse to cooperate in the slightest. After all, one can't just pry oneself in half like that.

His monitor flickers and goes dark. Everything is flickering. It's his vision. His periphery is fading and his hearing is muffled. He tries to scream. There's not a mouth anymore where a mouth should be. Something jostles and tugs in the cavity behind his fused lips.

The activity of the people around him is a dull murmur, but he can feel their tittering. They see. They know. It has to be them doing this, and why? Because he refuses to set roots in this place? Because he doesn't paste family photos to the sides of his monitor and doesn't air his bare feet beneath his desk? Because he won't have any of Linda's cookies? Because he hates his job like a normal person?

His spine and the chair's are one now, and they're moving. It doesn't hurt, the blocks of bone stretching his flesh and scraping over one another. That only makes it more terrifying. He wants to be in pain, torn and rendered and invaded—not *part of the thing*. He can't be! He still has a name. He still has a mind.

The monitor hums to life. His name appears beside the winking cursor. Then:

Favorite color—*Green*

Favorite movie—Naked Lunch

Favorite drink—*Coca-Cola*

He stares blankly at it. He has no choice. Meanwhile his stomach has calcified and is beginning to push out from his belly. Flesh recedes in sheets from his torso and slips through the panels in the floor. His sternum softens and pulls apart like taffy.

Favorite band—*Post-Gabriel* Genesis *(says it's* Arcade Fire*)*

 # Books of poetry owned and displayed but never read: 3

Most frequent masturbation material—*Kendra Billings (best friend from high school and college—never slept together, was an usher at her wedding. Most recurrent fantasy involves taking her in her wedding dress)*

Their laughter shakes his bones. He can't struggle. There's nothing to struggle against. He is the chair. He is the terminal.

 # Times beat up at school: 21

 # Times fought back: 0

Fantasizes about violence against tormentors: Weekly

Listens to while throwing air punches in studio apartment: Post-Gabriel Genesis

His head is vibrating as they howl. Thick spurs of bone, like gear-teeth, have emerged from his front and back and bottom. The chair moves slightly backward with a rumble.

Favorite high: Ambien

Most embarrassing memory: Wet pants during sixth beating by Dan Galli

Most shameful secret: At sister's twelfth birthday party

His viewpoint is jerked up and away from the monitor at that second, and he's at least glad for that, though he isn't spared the gasps and quiet chuckles.

The entire terminal is moving now. The spurs in his back have joined with those of the grandmother behind him, and he is rotated on a pelvic axis until he is parallel with the floor. His head is now just another gear-tooth; it catches between two of hers with a dull clunk. He starts to move again, and the sounds in his head fade as he's lowered into the floor.

He is alone in Freon-cooled darkness. Once again level with his gaze, the monitor is blank, save for the cursor.

It flashes and tells him, *Data entry shift complete.*

I don't clock out for another hour, he thinks.

A mechanical snarl pierces the air. He jostles, and this time there is pain, the pain of separation, and then he's falling and then nothing.

———————

The next day a warehouse employee pulls a palette stacked high with boxes into the data entry department. Inside each box are five hundred new forms to be entered. Each is coated with a fine dust which sticks to the fingers, just as the forms stick to one another, as if desperately clinging.

No one really pays attention to what they're entering into the computer. Something like highway hypnosis sets in what with the ceaseless clatter of keys and the same fields over and over again. Most carry on conversations about other things while their fingers fly. The forms' names and personal information don't really register with anyone who handles them, not even if it's the name of an employee from their row who was promoted just the day before.

Work flows. Freon flows. The girls titter. The job sighs contentment.

David Dunwoody is the author of the zombie novels *Empire* and *Empire's End* (Permuted Press) as well as the collections *Dark Entities* (Dark Regions) and *Unbound & Other Tales* (Library of Horror). Dave lives in Utah and can be visited on the Web at daviddunwoody.com.

Face Out

Lisa Morton

"There should be no difference between selling a book and a bar of soap, and if you're in this because you love books, then get out."

Megan Barlow snapped the point on her official FinnBooks pencil.

She'd already bristled at the first two hours of the FinnBooks management seminar. She'd endured everything from rah-rah motivational speeches to sales pitches on the company's new Fook e-book reader (version 2.0 included built-in text-to-speech, full-color graphics, and five free downloads of current bestsellers) to dressing-downs on how sales had slumped over the last quarter (because, of course, that had to be the managers' fault). But the bar of soap comparison was finally too much. *Portrait of the Artist as a Young Man* was not a bar of soap. *The Shining* was not a kitchen appliance. *Dune* was not a can of soda. The pencil point left an angry black hole torn in the FinnBooks notepad, and Megan almost rose right then. It would have been so easy to walk out, to tell the smug, blandly-handsome District Manager to stuff it, that she thought books were more than toiletry items, that she'd go off and start her own independent bookstore and show them how it was done…

Except the economy was tight, unemployment was over 10%, she was hardly paid enough to have accrued savings, and she needed the health insurance. So she forced herself to sit, and endure, and nod, and pretend to take notes. And when it was over (God, when *would* it ever be over?), she'd shake the District Manager's hand and tell him she looked forward to his next visit to her store and she knew the re-tooled Fook reader would turn things around, yes, sir.

And that night, she'd crawl through traffic to head home, where she'd promptly get just as stinking drunk as her salary would allow.

"That bad, huh?"

Megan looked up from her tumbler of cheap rum and coke as her roommate Delilah walked into the living room of the tiny two-bedroom house they shared. Megan nodded, then took another swallow before speaking. "Did you know books were exactly the same as bars of soap?"

"They really said that?"

"They did."

Megan gazed at the bookcases lining the living room wall. She and Delilah had traded off: Megan got three bookcases, and Delilah got an entertainment unit with a large-screen TV. The cases were already filled, though, and Megan had begun stacking them up in her bedroom on the floor until she could get a new case in there. She gazed at her books fondly, at her novels and Celtic history books and movie star biographies and graphic novels, then giggled. "I've sure got a lot of soap."

Delilah laughed as well, then went into the kitchen and came back with her own glass full of fizzing cocktail. "Hope you don't mind if I join you."

"Misery loves company."

Delilah plunked herself down on the far end of their slightly tattered couch, then pulled out her smart-phone. "Hey, remember my cousin Ralph? The one down in Louisiana?"

Megan was sure she'd heard her roomie mention the name, but right now her brain was too clogged with alcohol and irritation to bring the data up. She settled for a lie. "Yeah."

"He sent me the craziest shit today. Y'know, he's into voodoo, magic, all that stuff. Look at what he sent me."

She brought up her email, scanned messages until she found the right one, then opened the attachment and held the phone up to Megan. Megan squinted through her drunken haze and made out a complicated symbol of some sort. "What the heck is that supposed to be?"

"He says it's called a 'veve,' and that it calls down some spirit or something. This one is a big secret or some crap. It's supposed to be a…" Delilah scanned the email, then smiled, "…a 'loa' of vengeance. He claims it really works. He set it loose on a girlfriend he broke up with and he says she was just killed in a car accident."

Normally Megan would have laughed and asked Delilah how the rest of her day had gone, but tonight she was drunk and not normal and found the notion of revenge against FinnBooks very appealing. "Really?"

An hour later they stood beneath a print-out of the veve, finished reciting the words Ralph had sent with the drawing, and then waited.

After a few seconds, Megan reeled away. "I think I'm going to be sick."

She fled to the bathroom, the spell already forgotten.

Three nights later, Megan was preparing to close her store. It was five minutes until 9, the parking lot outside was largely empty, and she was very ready to go home. The District Manager had just sent around some new guidelines, and FinnBooks was emphasizing faced-out stock more than ever, since they believed that covers (not content) sold books. On one of his visits last year, the D.M. had written her up for not facing out enough books ("but our customers like that we have more stock, and that doesn't leave room to face every title out," she'd complained to deaf ears), but with the new rules she'd be forced to pull a lot of books for return. Last time, just before the D.M.'s bi-monthly visit, she'd actually pulled books, boxed them, and hidden them in the basement until the D.M. had left; the store had an inexplicable, huge, unused basement—someone told Megan it'd been built in the '40s and was intended to serve as the neighborhood bunker in the event of air attacks—and no one ever looked down there.

Megan knew some of her regular customers would be disappointed by the diminished selection. She and her staff were on a first-name basis with a lot of their clientele, and she knew what they liked. Megan prided herself on her store's customer service, and thought it was the reason her FinnBooks routinely placed in the top sales figures for the chain. None of which seemed to matter to Mr. By-the-Numbers District Manager, who only cared that she met all of the chain's carefully-defined standards for the perfect FinnBooks store.

FinnSoap was more like it.

At 8:55, Megan heard the door open. She'd sent her part-timers home early tonight, and was closing alone with her assistant manager, a rangy kid with funky hair (and interesting literary tastes—he liked Kathy Acker and Chuck Palahniuk) named

Damon. When she heard the door, she looked up, about to tell the new arrival they were closing—and her gut clenched when she saw who it was.

Eric. Her least favorite regular.

Eric was a fat bully who never bought a book, but liked to gloat about the latest technological gizmo he'd acquired. When FinnBooks had introduced their first Fook e-reader, he'd been positively ecstatic at having something new to complain about. He liked to grin as he told Megan she worked for a loser company, and that she'd be better off as a secretary; oh, and by the way—why didn't they go out some time?

"Eric, you know we're closing," Megan told him, trying to sound firm instead of merely weary.

"So, have you got the Fook 2.0 in stock yet?"

"They came in yesterday."

He laughed and gestured. "That's it, then. All this paper shit will be gone in six months. You know that, right? Soon you're gonna be managing e-book downloads out of some office, 'cause paper books are *dead*."

Megan sighed. "We'll see, Eric. A lot of our customers still love a real book."

"And a lot more don't care—they'll read their bestsellers in whatever form's cheapest, right?"

She hated to admit he was right. "Maybe."

"So can I see this Fook 2.0?"

"Eric…"

He held up his hands, talking fast. "Look, you can close out while I look at, okay?"

She knew it was against company policy, and she knew he would never buy anything, but she didn't care tonight and was too tired to fight him. "Okay, but five minutes is all, got it?"

"You're a good girl."

She ground her teeth at the patronizing comment, but waved him to the kiosk at the side of the store where the Fook Readers were displayed. Then she locked the doors, walked over to join Damon behind the front counter, and began the close-out. It took them less than ten minutes to count out the registers and run the credit card settlement, then they stashed the receipts in the safe and looked up. Eric was nowhere to be found.

"Eric," Megan called out, now well and truly pissed off. "C'mon, time to go."

There was no answer.

Megan and Damon exchanged a look. "Freak," Damon muttered.

"I'll get him. You double-check the back door."

"You sure?"

Despite his odd tastes in authors, Damon was a sweet guy. Sometimes Megan thought it was almost too bad he already had a girlfriend. "I'm fine. Eric's just a dick, not a crazy."

Damon nodded, then walked away from the front counter.

Megan made her way over toward the e-reader kiosk. "Eric, let's go, c'mon…"

Still no response.

Then she saw the shoes sticking out from the end of an aisle. What the hell was he doing on the floor? "Eric…?"

Megan swallowed back a rush of anxiety and moved around the edge of the aisle.

Then she choked back a scream.

Eric was prone in a pool of blood, there on the carpeted floor between the self-help and legal sections. He was obviously dead, with large cuts and swellings on his head and arms. He looked like he'd gone three rounds with a meat grinder. One eye was covered with blood, but the other was open, already glassy, staring straight up in wide fright.

And he was surrounded by books. There must have been dozens, many now soaked in his blood, their spines cracked and pages creased.

Megan's breath jigsawed in and out as she backed away. *How could this—he wasn't alone that long—whoever did this—*

My God, they must still be here somewhere.

Megan turned and ran. She collided with Damon as he walked out of the stockroom, and this time she *did* scream, a quick strangled sound that cut off when she saw who it was. "Megan, what—"

"We have to get out of here, Damon—NOW."

She half-tugged him toward the front door, her fingers trembling as she fiddled frantically with the keys. Finally the door was open, she and Damon were through, and she pressed the keys into his hand as she grabbed at her cell phone. "Lock the doors."

"Okay, but—"

She ignored him as she dialed 911. "There's been a murder at my store—"

She looked up then to see Damon staring at her in disbelief.

––––––––––

The police came and kept them up all night. They answered questions and waited while detectives and coroners and photographers and forensics experts all went over the scene endlessly.

The next day Megan called the District Manager and reported on what had happened. She promptly received a written warning. Eric, of course, should not have been in the store during closing. There was no "sorry you had to go through that" or "we'll give you some extra money for security until this thing is over," just a mark on her report and the District Manager's reminder that she had a sales quota to meet this month.

Fortunately the killing didn't hamper sales; if anything, it brought more customers in, including those who merely wanted to see a murder site. It took two days for the cops to finish with their work, and another day to replace the crimson-splattered carpeting, and a fourth day to write up all the books that had been damaged.

In some ways, that had been the strangest part of the whole thing: Megan had looked at the books before they'd been bagged and confiscated as evidence, and she couldn't quite understand how so many had ended up around Eric. Surely she and Damon would have heard that many books hitting the floor, wouldn't they? Granted, the Fook Reader display and the aisle he'd died in were probably sixty or seventy feet from the front counter, but Eric had been surrounded by at least 100 books. Why had he pulled so many books down as he'd fallen? Or had the killer for some reason pushed the books down onto him?

And the big question, of course: Where had the killer come from, and where had he gone? She and Damon had already done the final walk-through that night, and the store had been empty until Eric had come in.

The cops were clueless, in more ways than one. The detective in charge of the case, a middle-aged woman with tired eyes, skin the color of stained sheets, and the last name of Washington, told her they had nothing—no fingerprints, no footprints, no DNA, nothing. Granted, there'd been plenty of folks who hadn't liked

Eric ("including *you*," the detective had said, pointedly, while peering at Megan), but nobody likely to have committed a crime this bloody and vicious. "Make sure you never close alone," was all Detective Washington had said to her by way of advice. So Megan kept her full crew on every night until after closing, and they huddled together nervously after nine like hens stalked by the fox.

But after a week they began to relax. Business returned to normal—the crime-scene fans dwindled, the sales stayed steady— and Megan tried to forget about Eric.

Until the night Detective Washington showed up at the store and asked to speak to Megan in private.

It was after 7 p.m., a Tuesday night, and foot traffic was light. She was back to running a small evening crew, and so she called Damon over and told him to look after things while she and the Detective spoke. He frowned, but nodded and told her he'd handle things.

Megan led the way to her tiny closet-sized office in the back stockroom. She took her seat behind her cluttered desk, indicated the only other chair to the detective, and tried to quell the adrenaline coursing through her, especially when Washington closed the door and stood, glaring down.

"I gotta tell you, Ms. Barlow," the homicide detective began, "this is one frustrating case. We've got nothing except you and Mr. Watkins out there—" she waved a hand in the general direction of Damon, "—telling us there was nothing to get. You didn't see anyone, you didn't hear anyone, and you can't think of anyone who could have done this. Can you see why that might bother me a little?"

Washington stared down, her baggy eyes wider than usual, wider in anger, and Megan gulped back anxiety and thought, *Jesus God, she thinks I did this!*

"Detective Washington, I'm just as bothered as you, believe me."

"Well, see, that's the problem," Washington said, pushing aside a stack of books—some classics Megan had recently pulled for herself—to sit on a corner of the desk, a gesture Megan found annoying, "I *don't* believe you."

Well, there it was. Megan was a suspect. She bit back an urge to laugh hysterically, to say there were times she wanted to kill Eric, sure, but not like *that*, not like...dead.

"Do you have anything you'd like to tell me, Ms. Barlow?" Washington said, leaning in closer. "You could make this easier on all of us."

"I…" Megan's throat was suddenly too dry to produce sound. She swallowed enough to squeak out, "No."

"Are you sure?"

Washington leaned in closer—

The stack of books fell to the floor.

Megan jumped at the sound, but Washington had another reaction, a strange one. She looked down at the books—and frowned. "What the…"

Then Washington gasped, cried out, and fell over.

Megan rose halfway out of her chair, then stopped in disbelief at the sounds she heard: There was Washington, making stifled cries of pain and terror, but mostly it was the flapping noises, boards slamming together, the riffling of pages…

Edging around the desk, already knowing what she'd find—impossible as it was—Megan was still stunned when she came into full view: Washington was on the concrete floor, trying to defend herself from…

The books. They smashed at her, their hard spines making soft thuds against Washington's head and shoulders. They flapped back and forth like disembodied jaws, and somehow the detective's skin was sundered with each closing. The titles from Megan's desk—*The Catcher in the Rye*, *Lord of the Flies*, *In Cold Blood*—were joined by coffee table art books that leapt from a box of damaged returns that had been forgotten in a corner. A huge barbecue cookbook battered Washington's ribs, while a collection of Van Gogh's paintings dug into the soft flesh of an ear.

Megan stood paralyzed, mesmerized; some part of her knew she should try to help Washington, but she feared the power of the books. "No," she cried out once, but she bit back on her protest as she realized that Washington had been right—she *was* responsible for Eric's death. Because she suddenly knew that living books could only be magic, and she had enacted the magic, the night she and her roommate, both stupidly besotted, had invoked a vengeful spirit that had somehow taken up residence in the books. And now she was being protected.

In the few seconds it took her to put it all together, Washington was dead. The concrete floor was awash in blood and torn pages. The books were inanimate again.

Megan's mind started spinning. There was no way she could report this to the police—they'd arrest her immediately. Her only chance was to try to hide the body, but where…?

Of course—the vast, unused basement. It had brick walls. They'd even joked once, she and Damon, about what might be behind those walls—perhaps a real-life "Cask of Amontillado."

She took a moment to calm herself (spotting a copy of a Dr. Seuss book in the corner helped somehow), then she stepped out of the office, closed the door behind her, and walked out into the store. Damon looked up from behind the front counter. "How's it going with Mrs. Columbo there?"

"Oh," Megan said, trying to wave a hand in what she hoped was a breezy fashion, "we're done. Hopefully that was the last of the questions."

Damon looked around. "Did she leave already?"

"Yeah. You didn't see her go?"

"No. Well, no big loss there."

At 9 p.m., they closed the store. Megan told Damon she had a few last items she wanted to work on, and she'd probably be late. He left, she locked the doors behind him, and then returned to her office, half-wondering what she'd find.

Nothing had changed: Washington was still on the floor, dead, bleeding from dozens of wounds, while the books waited, seemingly inanimate.

"So," Megan said, feeling vaguely silly, "are you really alive?"

There was no obvious response, but Megan shivered, as if there were a charge in the air.

"Will you help me with her now?"

The books twitched, stood up, and fastened onto various pieces of Washington's clothing. They began to drag the body across the floor; other books sopped up the blood, efficiently, leaving no trace. In fifteen minutes the body had been dragged down to a far corner of the basement, where Megan used a hammer and crowbar to carefully dismantle part of the brick wall. She removed Washington's cell phone and smashed it, then she sealed the corpse in bubble wrap and packing tape, and the books helped her place it carefully in the narrow space behind the bricks.

Tomorrow she'd pick up mortar at a hardware store, but she was done for tonight.

"Now, what do I do with you?" Megan asked the books, their pages stained crimson, the edges worn and corners bumped.

The books piled into the wall around the detective's body. Megan found herself crying softly as she realized that they'd sacrificed themselves for her. She hadn't even read *The Catcher in the Rye* yet, but she already felt a kinship with Holden Caulfield.

"Thank you," she murmured.

———————

She finished bricking in the wall the next day, and she began to wonder more about the books. Did they come to life at other times, when she wasn't there? Did they stay alive once they left the store?

That question was answered a few days later when Mrs. Forrest, an elderly customer who'd once taught high school English and who now celebrated her retirement with three new books a week, came in and told Megan about something that'd happened.

"I don't think I should read any more of those horror novels," she said. "Last week you sold me on that new one, *Malediction*, and I started reading it, and it was very good, but I had the strangest dream last night: I dreamed that a spider had tried to crawl onto my bed in the night, and the book had come to life and crushed it. And you know, it's the darnedest thing: In the morning, I found a smashed spider in the pages of the book. Isn't that curious?"

Megan agreed that it was. But secretly, she was delighted to know that the books were protecting others who loved them.

———————

A week went by. Megan received calls and visits about Washington's disappearance, and she even allowed the police to search the bookstore, but nothing was found. The books had done a good job of cleanup. And no one bothered to look much in the forgotten basement

On a Tuesday morning, Megan pulled up to the store fifteen minutes before opening—and felt her stomach lurch as she saw the District Manager standing there already, waiting for her.

"You're late, Megan," he said.

She eyed him—God, she hated his stupid boring haircut and his cheap suits and his round face that looked like it'd been stamped out of a machine labeled DISTRICT MANAGERS—and then said, "We don't open for fifteen minutes."

"Managers are supposed to be here twenty minutes before opening," he said.

Megan turned her attention to unlocking the door. "Sorry, but—why are you here? I thought the usual inspection wasn't for another month."

"It isn't," he said, blowing on a cup of overpriced coffee, "but this isn't an official inspection. I'm a little worried about you and your store, frankly, Megan."

She opened the door for him, hoping she didn't sound as nervous as she felt. "Because of the murders?"

"Has there been another one?"

She cursed herself—she'd have to remember that the world only knew about one. "I thought I heard something on the news the other night about one in a…" she struggled for a second, then blurted out, "soap factory."

The D.M. grunted, then followed her in. She locked the door behind them.

As Megan headed for the light switches in the back, she saw him critically examining her shelves, already facing out more books.

She'd almost reached the switches when she stopped, realizing: This would be better done in the dark, wouldn't it?

"What's the problem with the light?" he called from up front.

"Sir, would you mind coming back here? Maybe you can help me with this."

He followed her voice, sipping his coffee, glancing around. "Need to face out a lot more stock than this, Barlow. We need to move these things now. Since we brought the new Fook out, our e-book sales have skyrocketed. These things are going to go the way of the dinosaurs. You know that, right, Barlow?"

"Dinosaurs…" Megan had been wondering about which section to lead him to.

"What?"

"Over this way, sir."

The section on paleontology was in a far back corner of the store, and it was dim without the lights on. "What's going on? Why aren't the lights on yet?"

Megan was glad he couldn't see her smiling. "Oh, I think the lights *are* on, sir."

"What are you talking about?"

He struck a shin in the gloom and cried out. But Megan heard another sound over that: The anticipation of books flapping, of large volumes on ancient creatures thudding across the floor as they left their shelves. Thunder lizards of paper.

"You see, sir—the dinosaurs are still alive. In books, that is."

The District Manager shouted out as the first book struck his ankle, and Megan stepped back, giving them room and thinking about how much she hated soap.

A rare Southern California native, **Lisa Morton's** career as a professional writer began in 1988 with the horror-fantasy feature film *Meet the Hollowheads* (aka *Life on the Edge*), on which she also served as Associate Producer. For the Disney Channel's 1992 *Adventures in Dinosaur City*, she served as screenwriter, Associate Producer, Songwriter, and Miniatures Coordinator. For stage she has written and co-produced the acclaimed horror one-acts *Spirits of the Season, Sane Reaction* and *The Territorial Imperative*, and has adapted and directed Philip K. Dick's *Radio Free Albemuth* and Theodore Sturgeon's *The Graveyard Reader*; her full-length science fiction comedy *Trashers* was an *L.A. Weekly* "Recommended" pick. Her short fiction has appeared in the books *Dark Voices 6: The Pan Book of Horror, The Mammoth Book of Frankenstein, The Mammoth Book of Dracula, Horrors! 365 Scary Stories, Dark Terrors, After Shocks, White of the Moon, The Museum of Horrors, Dead But Dreaming, Shelf Life: An Anthology of Bookstore Stories, Dark Terrors 6, Dark Delicacies: Original Tales of Terror and the Macabre, Mondo Zombie, Dark Passions: Hot Blood XIII,* and *Midnight Premiere,* and the magazine *Cemetery Dance.* Her chapbook *The Free Way* was published by Fool's Press, and in early 2010 her first novel *The Castle of Los Angeles* was published to critical acclaim. She has also written numerous episodes of the animated television series *Sky Dancers, Dragon Flyz* and *Van-Pires.* Her first book, *The Cinema of Tsui Hark* was published by McFarland, who also published *The Halloween Encyclopedia* in 2003 and *A Hallowe'en Anthology: Literary and Historical Writings Over the Centuries* in 2008. Her television movie *Tornado Warning* was chosen by the Pax cable station to launch their 2002 fall season, and 2005 saw the release of three horror films, the vampire thriller *Blood Angels,* the mutant shark story *Blue Demon,* and *The Glass Trap,* about genetically altered fire ants. Lisa was awarded the 2006 Bram Stoker

Award for Short Fiction for her story "Tested" (which first appeared in *Cemetery Dance* magazine), and the 2008 Bram Stoker Award for Nonfiction for *A Hallowe'en Anthology*. For the first anthology she edited, 2009's *Midnight Walk*, Lisa received a Black Quill Award for Best Dark Genre Anthology, and she won the 2009 Bram Stoker Award for Long Fiction for her novella *The Lucid Dreaming*. In 2010, she received her fourth Stoker Award, this time in the First Novel category for *The Castle of Los Angeles*. She is also a two-time recipient of the President's Richard Laymon Award, presented by the Horror Writers Association.

Carpool

Gregory L. Norris

The idea came to Sebastian on the third day of the new job while he brooded behind the wheel of his car, mired in gridlock morning traffic. His heart pounded in his chest while watching other cars race through the carpool lane, the rapid cadence aggravated by too much coffee and no breakfast. Somehow, he would find a way to join them. The only flaw to his plan was simple numbers.

"One plus one equals two," Sebastian grumbled. He shot a look at the rearview, but was unable to face his own reflection. His gray-blue eyes darted toward the windshield and the line of inert cars blocking his way, then back to the little green numbers on the dashboard's clock.

The car in front of him crept forward several inches. Sebastian followed its lead. Somewhere lengths behind in the game of leapfrog, a horn honked. Then another bleated angrily. To his left, a black SUV raced freely down the carpool lane.

Sebastian wandered to the edge of his reflection in the rearview mirror. His was a handsome, young face by all accounts, but growing steadily uglier around the edges. His mouth was clamped hard enough to make his teeth ache. And his eyes—Sebastian wasn't aware that he'd stopped blinking until they started to burn. He switched on the radio and stabbed at buttons. Morning talk. More morning talk. An irritating song played to death during a summer years ago blasted out of the speakers, a one-hit wonder from a loser band that would now loop through his thoughts all day, thank you very much. He killed the radio, huffing a swear under his breath.

The monotonous game of watching for the brake lights of the cars ahead to wink out in a domino effect only to surge on again a yard later resumed. The waste of gas was maddening. And it was September, a gray September day in a month when the days were growing noticeably shorter. Compounding the stress of the new job was that first nagging taste of seasonal depression. Sebastian closed his eyes and willed his galloping heart to slow.

The deafening bellow of a horn shocked him back to the moment. His car, one in a long line of dominoes, had failed to creep ahead that extra yard. Sebastian resisted the urge to flip his middle finger at the offending driver and eased his foot off the brake. A yard forward, a second or two later, another car barreled down the carpool lane.

The elite, those business people who'd swarmed together, mixing their perfumes and colognes and deodorants and the aromas of their expensive designer coffees, had been awarded a sacred privilege: speed.

Another step forward. Brake lights. Entropy.

Sebastian imagined the white paint of his sensible two-door economy car soaking up the grime and the fumes of the muffler ahead. The expense of the wasted gas. The merciless numbers of the clock, semaphoring closer to the time he was due at Baker & Sullivan. His third day there. His third day late.

On the fourth, he would take the carpool lane. After all, it was only basic math, and Sebastian Hearst was something of an accountant. That was a glorified way to describe being a Customer Service Wiz but, after all, didn't he field orders over the phone and complete transactions? He knew how to make one plus one equal two. *Two*, the minimum number of bodies required to travel in the carpool lane. Basic math.

Taking a heavy swallow, Sebastian found that his mouth had gone painfully dry. He choked down the ball of desert heat that had desiccated his tongue and tipped his eyes at the rearview. His gaze lingered briefly, drinking in the gray-blue shade of his irises, the square, cleanly shaved jaw, dark hair, slightly spiky on top, all of it adding together into proof of decent genes. Yes, he was handsome, almost painfully so, as one ex had put it. But Sebastian's eyes again darted away, because the face staring back could not be trusted nor forgiven. As handsome as his reflection was, it was also tainted by guilt. Guilt for a crime not yet committed.

I'll find another body, he thought. Someone else to share the long, tedious drive into the city. That way I can hop onto the carpool lane and avoid this bullshit.

———————

He would store her body in the trunk once he reached the parking garage on Congress Street. And he'd get away with the crime, Sebastian thought on the elevator ride to the fifth floor of the Ross Stanton Building, which housed Baker & Sullivan.

He was twenty-three minutes late and caught holy hell from Miss Beckwith for it.

"I know, it's the traffic," Sebastian said sheepishly, taking his seat and pulling on the earpiece.

Miss Beckwith flashed a sharp smile. He attributed the *Miss* part to the harshness of her expression and the severity of her hair, yanked back into a bun, more than to the enormous butt carefully disguised by her frumpy pinstriped business suit. "It can't happen again, Mister Hearst."

"It won't," Sebastian promised. Even her scent was jagged. A trace of cloying cinnamon or cloves bit into the lining of his nose and settled into the soft tissue, where it fermented.

No, it wouldn't.

At six-foot-two, Sebastian towered over Miss Beckwith by nearly ten inches, but he tilted his head to avoid her small, mean gaze and slumped into his seat, dragging his big loafers along the floor guard. He stabbed the winking button on his phone to take his first call of the day while his criminal plan silently simmered at the forefront of his thoughts.

More gridlock greeted Sebastian on the highway. He briefly considered jumping onto the breakdown lane and gunning the gas, but was relieved he didn't give in to the temptation when, several long miles later, the blinding telltale of silent blue police lights confirmed his idea wasn't wholly original. He'd seen half a dozen cars pulled over by the cops for doing the same thing since the start of the hellish week.

An hour later, just when it started to rain, he pulled into the driveway of the dilapidated apartment house, mentally exhausted.

She was born after supper, which had consisted of boxed macaroni and cheese and two hot dogs fried in margarine, washed down with chocolate milk.

Sebastian stretched across the old sofa, thumbing the remote control. Channels flipped past, none occupying the screen long enough for anything to register. He was tired physically but worse his soul felt drained. The makings of an exquisite headache pulsed at his temples.

The hollow creak of the spare room's door drew his gaze away from the television. Sebastian hit the remote's mute button. How long he stared at the door with the chipped beige paint, now standing partially open, he didn't know. But it was enough time for the last act of a sitcom to play out, he realized, when he kicked his legs off the sofa and stood, killing the tube altogether. The wind, Sebastian thought.

A gust of brisk air swept in from the open kitchen door, supporting the theory. A house this old and rundown was prone to swaying doors, hiccupping pipes, and leaky faucets, the same voice in his head reminded, proclaiming the words between mildly painful drumbeats.

The wind's whisper kissed Sebastian's cheek, unleashing the ripple of a shudder down his spine. He rarely entered the spare room, though his mind had wandered beyond its builder-beige door numerous times since returning to the apartment from his lousy day at work. He placed a palm on the cracked paint and pushed. The door swung most of the way open before snagging on the old carpet, groaning as it did. None of the doors in the ground floor apartment were completely plumb with their frames. The floors creaked, especially the one in the kitchen. What had started as a small crack in the ceiling plaster above his bed was now a root-shaped lightning bolt whose tendrils snaked halfway across the room.

A rush of stale, bottled air greeted him. Adding to its stagnancy was a hint of musty cardboard and the dregs of the previous summer's heat, which the room had baked in for months, its two windows covered in heavy, dusty panels parted in the middle. Murky gray daylight now oozed through that gap.

Though he hadn't entered the room in months, perhaps years, Sebastian knew its topography with near photographic recall. As second bedrooms went, it wasn't a small room; it sat wedged between the kitchen and the staircase leading to the upstairs apartment. The staircase had been walled off decades earlier when the drab New Englander was converted into apartments, though he still heard his upstairs neighbor's comings and goings, especially when she wore heels.

The room's closet had been built under the slant of the staircase and covered the entire wall. The rest of the room contained unopened cardboard boxes. A futon. A dress form and sewing machine. Sebastian's old 10-speed bike and a post lamp.

Two of the lamp's three bulbs had burned out. He turned the light switch until the metal shade on the top flared to life. A warm, stale odor filled Sebastian's next shallow breath, the result of dust cooking on the bulb.

How long had it been since he'd set foot in the room? Winter? But not necessarily the most recent winter. Sebastian had lived in the apartment for the last seven of his twenty-seven years. He knew what most of the unpacked boxes sitting slumped in piles contained. Most of them.

He crossed to the closet door but hesitated from opening it. Instead, he passed a shaking hand across the fur stole draped around the dress form's shoulders. Not for the first time that day, he attempted to swallow, only to gag on the dry heat that had gathered into a ball at the back of his throat. Even more unsettling, Sebastian realized that, for no obvious reason, he'd gotten an erection.

He slid a hand into his still-belted khakis and adjusted himself. The sensation was electrifying. He left his fingers to play there while reaching the others toward the closet.

The door opened with a sough, not a groan, its motion releasing a hint of lilac perfume. Eyes half-closed, Sebastian inhaled deeply, held the scent in his lungs, and then released it. For several minutes, his breaths came raggedly in shallow sips, but he wasn't aware he'd stopped releasing air until burning erupted in his chest.

In the poor light filtering through the windows and the dull glow of the floor lamp's lone lit bulb, Sebastian made out the shape of a rigid, naked body. A body with waxy, pale skin, perky tits, and a seductive, frozen smirk set beneath wide open eyes.

He would call her Ms. Juggles. Sebastian always did.

The rain stopped falling, but the morning dawned with overcast skies and there was a serious bite in the air that hadn't been there before the storm.

Sebastian dressed her properly for the chilly weather, in a periwinkle blue turtleneck and tweed slacks. He rolled wool socks onto her stiff ankles, then slid her thin feet into a pair of lady's loafers. He had set her hair the previous night, combing it back, fixing the lush auburn locks into a tail with a tortoiseshell chignon.

That morning, he'd carefully touched up her foundation and applied a soft shade of magenta lipstick. Lastly, before carrying her out to the car, he gave her a spritz of the lilac perfume hidden on a shelf in the spare room's closet.

His heart thudded in his chest on the short walk from his front door to the car. A brick wall crawling with wild ivy separated the apartment house from its nearest neighbor, and they kept all of the shades drawn on the side that faced him. The woman upstairs worked nights; he'd heard the familiar clip-clop of her heels while he'd masturbated in the shower, so by now he imagined she was fast asleep.

Cradling Ms. Juggles in his arms, Sebastian fumbled the car door open and set her on the front passenger seat. He strapped her seatbelt into place and when his movement stirred a ribbon of lilac scent he gasped, brushing his lips along her ear and briefly melting into the wonderland between her rigid lobe and neck.

The final bit of window dressing was a fashion magazine stolen out of the upstairs neighbor's mailbox. Using tape, he opened the rag and fixed it to her hands, lending the illusion that she was reading.

Then Sebastian drove off, headed for work.

The area of bad highway loomed before him. About three miles before the expected bottleneck, an additional left lane appeared, marked by a traffic sign that read:

CARPOOL LANE: MINIMUM TWO-PERSONS REQUIRED FOR USE.

"That's me and you, one plus one equaling two," Sebastian sang the words. He reached over and patted Ms. Juggles on the thigh, feeling bony hardness beneath the tweed fabric of her slacks.

He withdrew his touch, clicked on the left turn signal, and crossed into the carpool lane.

The smooth, less-traveled pavement streaked beneath his wheels. Sebastian felt no guilt when, those few miles farther along the highway, he passed the same gridlock that had captured him in its web a day earlier. His heart leapt into his throat after he drove beneath an overpass where a state trooper sat like a troll or a trapdoor spider lurking in wait for a victim—the first vehicle with a lone body inside that dared to break the morning commute's cardinal rule. She and he equaled two. The cop remained under his bridge, and his cherries stayed dark.

"I love you," Sebastian growled.

He again reached over, dipping his hands into the v-shaped region between her slender, rigid legs.

"I love you, too, Sebastian," he thought he heard her whisper back.

———————

Sebastian made it to Congress Street forty-five minutes early and was parked in the garage with half an hour's time to spare.

"I'm sorry, Ms. Juggles," he said out of the corner of his mouth. He reached behind her and pulled the tartan wool blanket off the back seat, tossing it over her before exiting the car. The garage was crisscrossed with security cameras—it wouldn't look good for him if a security guard saw him placing a woman's body in the trunk, no matter the explanation. Even if the body was made of hard plastic.

Sebastian fumbled his key into the lock and popped the trunk. He carefully eased her body in, smoothed out the blanket, and professed his love a second time along with his atonement. Then, Sebastian slammed the trunk shut.

He turned in the direction of the elevator. A few steps later, Sebastian swore he heard a single, muffled thunderclap at his back, what sounded to his ear like a fist pounding against metal. Standing frozen in place, he closed his eyes and wished the vision away. It was only an echo from somewhere else in the garage; hell, likely the reverberation of his trunk slamming down, bouncing off a distant concrete wall. That was all.

Sebastian willed his feet into motion and continued on his way to work.

———————

The caustic heaviness of cinnamon perfume invaded his senses, giving Miss Beckwith's closeness away before Sebastian actually saw her. She leaned down and her scent grew. Sebastian fought the urge to gag, but another image invaded his head, and that one wasn't as easily quelled. *Embalming fluid.* That dry, cinnamon thickness conjured thoughts of desiccated Egyptian mummies.

"Glad to see you on time, Mister Hearst," she said, her thin, sharp lips forming a harsh little smile around the statement.

Sebastian smiled back even as he shrank from her eyes, which never seemed to blink. "I left at dawn," he said, hoping the joke would sound funny. It didn't, but her smile persisted.

"Good. Things for you are definitely looking up."

She patted his shoulder. Sebastian went rigid. He felt her stubby, too-warm fingertips through the fabric of his boring blue button-down dress shirt and the white tee beneath. His stomach, already queasy from too much coffee and not enough breakfast, pulled into knots.

"Do you have lunch plans?" she asked.

A rush of nauseating heat billowed through Sebastian's insides. As though it had been timed perfectly to the moment, one of his phone lines lit, accompanied by a muted chirp.

Sebastian thumbed the button. "Good morning, customer service. This is Sebastian speaking—how may I help you?"

Had the person on the other end of the line spoken, Sebastian likely wouldn't have heard a single word. He flashed another smile at Miss Beckwith, mouthed *Sorry*, and turned away from her.

Relief flooded over him as her hand slipped off his shoulder. He waited another maddening second, just long enough to see her pinstriped caboose wander up the line and away from his station, before returning to his call.

"I'm sorry for the delay. How may I be of assistance?"

Dead air poured out of the receiver, followed by the plaintive toll of the dial tone.

At one-thirty, it happened again.

". . . is Sebastian speaking. How may—"

Before he could finish, a breathy, aroused sigh teased Sebastian's ear.

"Who is this?" he asked.

The line went dead. Sebastian glanced around the bullpen, and his only relief came in seeing that Miss Beckwith wasn't present. Likely, she'd taken her lunch alone.

"I know you didn't like being trapped inside the trunk, any more than you liked being left in the closet. How many times do I have to apologize? I feel guilty enough, so don't bust my balls."

Sebastian slid his hand across the seat, only to receive a hard slap.

"Don't touch me," Ms. Juggles admonished.

He had driven most of the distance home in a fog, completely oblivious of the details, going on instinct until his exit rose up. Half an hour later, she had thawed, and they were naked in his bed making love.

"I don't like that Miss Beckwith," Ms. Juggles said.

"That makes two of us." Sebastian rolled onto his back, spent. He was high on the scent of her lilac perfume and feeling absolved enough to broach the touchy subject. "Did you call me at work today? Twice?"

Ms. Juggles didn't answer, and Sebastian remembered that, as had always happened before, her lack of a response *was* the answer. Yes.

He turned back, stirring the smell of their stale sex and his even staler bed sheets, and a hint of lilac perfume. But the bed was empty.

She had returned to the closet under the stairs, where she had lurked for so very long.

"Work is very stressful right now," Sebastian grumbled. He sipped the coffee in his travel mug, a caustic blend heavy on the sugar, light on the cream, a mixture he could never seem to get quite right. "I need you to think about that, and about us, and not add to it."

Ms. Juggles didn't comment. The air sweeping in through his cracked-open window ruffled the pages of the upstairs neighbor's stolen fashion rag clutched between her hands.

"Just try to remember that I do love you and you've got nothing to fear from that Beckwith bitch, so no matter what, don't go doing something crazy. Okay?"

Sebastian received a tisk from the passenger's seat, that sound of the tongue clacking in frustration against the roof of the mouth that people make when they're on their last nerve. It was followed by an angry puff of breath. Ms. Juggles was not pleased.

"I mean it, honey. No tricks this time."

"Don't lock me up. You know I don't like it when you shut me out."

"We have to. We need this job."

Sebastian pulled onto the carpool lane, aware that his heart had quickened pace. But its cadence wasn't for the fear of being pulled over by the cops. It was the tone of her voice that caused it to race; that conjured a shiver from the short hairs on the nape of his neck and sent it tumbling down his back.

———————

Silence, pregnant and ominous, crackled over the phone line.

"Who is this?" Sebastian demanded.

A woman's breathy moan poured out of the earpiece and into the cup of his ear.

Sebastian tore off the headset and slammed it against the keyboard. He jumped out of his seat hard enough to send the office chair into the half-wall behind him.

"Jesus, Sebastian," groused the man who sat next in line.

For a week, Sebastian had remained barely conscious of him; he'd buried his eyes in the long blonde mane of the college girl seated in front of him.

"Where's Miss Beckwith?" Sebastian demanded.

The man, a balding older dude with a big gut, narrowed his eyes. "Calm down."

"*Where is she?*"

"Last time I checked, I wasn't her social secretary," Tubby fired back. "How about you try her office?"

Sebastian righted, realizing every eye in the bullpen was locked upon him. He excused himself. Hands shaking, he shuffled down the long carpeted hallway he knew would play hell with shocks come the dead of winter.

A cheap brass plaque identified the correct door. It read: *Miss C. Beckwith*

Sebastian reached for the knob and turned, but found it locked. He steadied his right hand by making a fist and pounded.

"Just a minute," Miss Beckwith's angry voice filtered through the door.

Tense seconds later, the door *whooshed* open. Miss Beckwith's large red face filled the gap, but her angry expression quickly morphed into one of happiness at the sight of her caller.

"Sebastian," she cooed in a slippery voice. "Come in."

She opened the door, unleashing a wave of smells. The cloying heaviness of cinnamon pooled at its greatest concentration within the perfectly square box of her office. But also present was the bitter tang of sweat and something more. A woman's most private scent.

"Well, don't just stand there, come on in and close the door."

The concept of obeying her order terrified him. "No," Sebastian said.

Miss Beckwith fixed her hair. As Sebastian stood at the threshold, his wide eyes drank in the framed photographs of a plump Bassett hound on her desk, set beside a Bassett hound statue and cheap looking fake flowers in a cheap looking vase. He also noticed the feelers of her headset poking out of the mess of her hair. She'd been on the phone.

"It's you," he growled. The thick scent of her female sweat lay heavy on his tongue and burned in his throat. "You're the one who's been calling me!"

"Me?" she feigned innocence. "I don't know what you mean."

"I'm not interested in you, don't you get that?" he spat, his words striking her face with the power of a backhanded slap, strong enough to remove that arrogant, aroused look, replacing it with one of shock. "Not in you, not in any woman besides *her*!"

Sebastian's stomach lurched. He turned away and doubled over, half expecting to vomit, the little food inside him feeling like shards of broken glass. He willed his guts to calm and was only partially conscious he'd dropped to his knees on the carpet, which he knew was even now building up its energy reserves, charging like a battery so it could deliver painful zaps indiscriminately to any who dared navigate its course come winter.

Some unaffected sliver of his scattered senses heard the sharp crack, immediately followed by the sound of a bulky object falling across the floor behind him. Sebastian caught a shadowy flash of movement at the corner of his eye, the kind of phantom that would vanish just as soon as he turned to focus on it directly. He did, and it was gone.

Quite clear, however, was the image that greeting him: Miss Beckwith slumped on the carpet, a gash on her forehead bleeding trickles of crimson. The Bassett hound statue was in two pieces on the floor beside her.

There was one other element worth noting, this one not so concrete. A hint of sweet lilacs had cancelled out the pungent stink of cinnamon and mummies. The confusion and horror Sebastian had been at the mercy of evaporated. Nobody saw him smile or heard him whisper *her* name as he turned and marched toward the elevator.

"Ms. Juggles," he said, lisping the words in a girlish falsetto.

———

She was waiting for him in the car. The fashion magazine belonging to the upstairs whore had slipped from her delicate fingers or had been tossed aside during her campaign to deal with the nasty bit of work up on the fifth floor. She was the most divine creature he had ever laid eyes upon.

"You're the only woman for me," Sebastian sighed, reaching for her.

This time, she allowed his touch.

"I love you. And I have loved you for so very long, Ms. Juggles."

"I know," she said, her voice musical, hypnotic, like that of a mythological Siren, he thought; a creature who lured men to terrible deaths against the rocks in ancient Greek fables. Or the legendary Celtic Banshee. Or the irresistible kiss-song of the succubus. "Do you remember?"

The vision, however brief, forced Sebastian's back against the car seat. In it, he was an observer to the memory, standing in the shadows, even though he was watching a much younger version of himself. That Sebastian stood half-hidden in a rack of women's clothes, transfixed by the figure of a true goddess. She was tall, lithe, and supernaturally stunning. She stared back at him with haunting, unblinking eyes. Then, as now in the car in Sebastian's present, she had given him an erection. And then, as now, he'd grown so stiff it hurt.

Another woman hissed his name.

"*Sebastian*! I know what you're doing. You disgusting little man! With a stiffy, and you're staring at that mannequin's *juggles*!"

The woman grabbed him by his arm and, though he was twelve and tall for his age, she was still taller and stronger.

"I'm ashamed of you," she babbled beneath her breath. "What you're doing is wrong. Evil. Don't you see? *Evil*!"

As his mother spun him toward her, unveiling the guilt of his excitement into the open for all to see, her movements stirred the fragrance of the lilac perfume she wore; a scent that often caused his imagination to wander to places both wonderful and wicked.

Sebastian sucked in a greedy breath and held it until it boiled in his lungs. The air in the car was sweet from lilacs, but the vision of her, the only woman he had ever truly loved, helped to wall up the ugly memory of how they'd met behind new layers of mental brick and mortar.

"I love you, Ms. Juggles," he said.

They embraced.

She gave him a happy ending handjob on the ride away from the city, teasing him, edging him closer to orgasm, only to release him just as he neared climax.

"You bitch," he chuckled.

At one point, he actually saw the highway's center line tear beneath the car and thought, *She's excited me so much, I'm weaving from lane to lane. But I don't care...*

And, at first, he didn't really care when the telltale flash of blue lights strobed in the rearview mirror.

The face staring back from the mirror was not his own. Nor was it hers, not entirely. Sebastian gaped at the image of smudged rose-colored lipstick. He was wearing her hair; black spikes of his own showed through the auburn wig scrunched haphazardly over his head. The reflection belonged to both of them.

"Oh my god," Sebastian huffed as clarity again swept over him. He turned the wheel sharply to his right and hit the brakes. The car skidded to a stop on the shoulder. The state police cruiser pulled up behind him with its siren blaring.

Sebastian rolled down the window. The storm trooper wasn't even his height, but talked with that tough-guy, tin-god manner all cops use when they nab you for breaking the law.

"Do you know why I pulled you over?" the Statie demanded, more rhetoric than actual question. "That was some erratic driving, *Ma'am*. How about you show me a license and registration."

Sebastian tipped a glance at the policeman and solemnly nodded. He reached for his wallet, then the glove box where he kept his registration.

Leaning over, he saw the department store mannequin with the vacant gaze and naked skull. It now appeared to be nothing more than cheap, aged plastic. It had given up the ghost.

"You mind telling me what's going on here, Mister Hearst?"

"Sure," Sebastian said, peeling off the wig—*her* wig—and choking down a painful swallow. "She's back. God help me, she's come back."

Gregory L. Norris is a full-time professional writer, with nearly 4,000 individual publication credits to his resume, most in national magazines and fiction anthologies. He is a former writer for Sci Fi, the official magazine of the Sci Fi Channel, and worked as a screenwriter on two episodes of Paramount's modern classic, *Star Trek: Voyager*. He is the author of the handbook to all-things-Sunnydale, *The Q Guide to Buffy the Vampire Slayer* (Alyson Books), and, in 2009, saw two of his paranormal romance novels for Ravenous Romance reprinted as special editions by Home Shopping Network for their "Escape With Romance" collection—the first time HSN has offered novels to their customers. Stories of his, both short and long, are forthcoming from Pill Hill Press, Simon & Shuster, Library of the Living Dead, Grand Mal, Raven Electrick, and Cleis Press.

Grist

Zak Jarvis

Vivienne needed to disembowel her specimens before the winds died or the atelier would stink for days. She had two corpses at hand and they were still warm. Though you could never trust what the Mill said, they were definitely young. Both female and about sixteen. With skill and a very sharp blade she separated skin from fascia in long strips.

Outside, time gusted through the city, pushed by a particularly bad storm. Rain sluiced from facades and cascaded over buildings both present and long past. Hundreds of years ago a mortar had leveled the block. She checked her clock and saw she had five minutes before the city's faint memory shook the building again. Vivienne worked faster.

Her timing long since perfected, she paused just before the explosion. Its bright fury engulfed the atelier, sending the peg-boarded tools rattling and the bare lights swinging. Rats scurried out of the dancing shadows, trying to find stable darkness.

She didn't know what her client was up to with this deception. Whether a flattering lie or a political machination, Vivienne didn't like being complicit. She did know, however, that when they put this work on display, her career was over. Before she'd let them take her to the Mill, she'd hook herself up to the bleeder.

She doubted the ghosts had the imagination for any other retaliation.

"I'll pay you no more than fifty for the two of them," Vivienne said. "Their hide doesn't match. I'll have to bleach the darker one."

"No, no. Viv. These are quality. No scars and so plump; lots of skin. Just look at them. Their stretch marks are so fine they're like expensive linen," Carnelia said, gesturing to the girls without looking at them. "They were born in the Mill and lobotomized at puberty. Only two breeding cycles each, I guarantee. Bleaching is no problem for an artisan of your skill. I'll part with them for no less than eighty."

The shorter girl stared at her hands. The taller one looked straight ahead and drooled ceaselessly. It left a streak down her naked body and pooled underfoot. They both wore lot numbers on bright red ear-tags.

"Fifty-five," Vivienne said without looking at what she was bartering for. "It's a vanity project. If I don't make her look good she'll send me to the Mill. Just the clothes for this one are costing me a fortune."

"Clothes? You're talking about clothes with these fine girls right here? You get the best discounts in town on clothes. You must go through more than anyone. Everyone knows. You think you'd get such fancy clients otherwise? Seventy-five. It's already less than I spent on their feed."

"And everyone knows how you gouge architectural clients. You can easily afford to give them to me for sixty," Vivienne said.

"Seventy-two and I'll throw in a boy they sent me by mistake."

Vivienne considered for a moment. "What's wrong with him?"

"He's little. Young I guess. And," the merchant stammered, drumming her fingers on the desk, "well, someone at the Mill damaged him. He's no good for breeding."

"What? What am I to do with that?"

"It's free skin!"

Vivienne sighed. "I have no male clients or place to keep product. Sixty-two. Just the girls."

"Viv, Viv, Viv. Are you trying to hurt me? Do you want to come home with me and see how my husband cries when I tell him I can't pay for his treatments? I can't go lower than seventy."

"Sixty-eight. I shouldn't even buy from the first vendor on my list. Dimitrios might have some merchandise that fits my specifications."

"You've done it, you cunning harpy. Sixty-eight. Will you at least pay market rates for my husband when he dies? It won't be long with the money I make from you," she said, scowling. "Besides, I got you good money for your wife."

"You should know better."

"I don't mean to be so difficult. It's getting hard to get quality product. Ask Kokudza or Dimitrios. Bad times are coming."

Vivienne turned to look at the drooling girl. "Coming?"

Carnelia clicked her tongue and dove into the forms for the transaction, leaving Vivienne to examine the office. Nothing moved in fifteen years, everything in its place. Just like the two of them.

While the girls were draped for city travel, Vivienne checked her watch against official time and surveyed for storms, marking up her map with a grease pencil tied to the clock.

Before she stepped out the door, Carnelia called her over with a conspiratorial wave.

"Be careful, old girl. Somebody told me they'd seen a blanker lurking about just before that big raid."

"Probably saw the vampire mayor of Central, too. The people you talk to are superstitious."

"It never hurts to be afraid, Viv."

Vivienne leashed the girls and stepped out onto an empty street. Even ghosts didn't want to be so close to the Mill.

On an unseasonably clear day Vivienne waited for her client. Constellations of dust danced in the path of the sun through Vivienne's office. She sat at her desk, palms patient against wood. The room—tidy as a politician's—smelled only faintly of chlorine and meat.

This one came from so high in the government that Vivienne couldn't hear the name of the district. And she was old, this client. Very old. Vivienne held tight as she waited.

After twenty minutes her jaw hurt. After an hour everything else did too.

The client came in off the wings of a distant storm, flickering across the room several times before fully manifesting a few centimeters above the chair. A light breeze that belonged only to her ruffled her clothes. With no cues of rank Vivienne could only offer the basest of obeisance.

She lay face down beneath her desk.

"Oh please rise," the client said. "I want you to think of me almost like an equal."

"I'm honored," Vivienne said, pausing for the client to offer an honorific that didn't come. "Your lady."

"You wouldn't know me," the ghost said. "To now I have had secretaries prepare my disincarnations. But you are famous and I have a very special occasion."

Vivienne climbed back into her chair, knees popping loudly.

"What can I do for you?"

"You can do what you always do *Vivienne*," she said. "Make a corpse in my image."

"Do you have pictures I can work from?"

"If you agree to the job, I will take time to sit for you."

Vivienne put on her best smile.

"I can be ready any time that is convenient for you. It only takes a few moments."

"Excellent," the ghost said, doing something like standing up. "Look for me sometime next week."

Out of habit Vivienne committed the ghost to memory.

———————

Carnelia's office nested just beyond the neon signs and clothes lines of the city's most desperate living quarter. The bright colors masked the purpose of the Population Center and the men who waited outside it for an empty breeding chamber. While the main street was stable the corner was not. Sometimes it was the modern Vendor Street, but Vivienne and the girls stepped onto the older Peccary Square. Towering buildings blotted out the sun, some present and solid, others smearing the sky like smoke from the distant past.

Other than the men waiting at the Population Center there were no living on the street. The sidewalks teemed with ghosts though, dignitaries and war-planners, the cultural elite, and an uncountable mass of the unmoored waiting—perhaps forever—to be immigrated.

Looking at her watch, Vivienne struck out for her atelier. The streets shifting, she and the girls passed empty shops burned out, re-boarded, then emptied again. A block to their west a storm blew thundering explosions and the screams of atrocities no one would ever prosecute. With four blocks to go they had to take refuge in an alleyway.

With twenty minutes before a clear path opened, she upended a packing crate and sat down to examine the girls. The noise and false-fury of the surrounding wars terrified them. They hugged each other so tight she had to pry them apart to lift the tarps and look at their skin.

As Carnelia had said, they were in very good condition. Much better than most of the poor, scarred things that came from the

Mill these days. But in brighter light the tonal difference was even clearer. She wouldn't have a choice but to bleach.

Vivienne hated using the bleaching vat. The vapors were probably giving her cancer.

The old ghost, when she deigned to arrive, quickly changed herself to look like a long-dead cinema heroine. Vivienne pretended not to notice and worked the camera in silence. She hefted the first plate so the client could see.

"What an astonishing device."

"I'm very grateful to be allowed to use it."

"Oh yes," the ghost said, coughing out a little laugh. "I'd forgotten we proscribe their use."

"The government is probably far too lenient to us," Vivienne said, repeating a common radio-screed.

Disapproval flickered over her face before the ghost turned to face Vivienne's desk.

"I know you're just telling me what you imagine I want to hear. Your services are essential no matter what the others say. It's why the breeding program is so important."

Vivienne caught herself before she disagreed, but the surge of adrenaline left her hands trembling.

"Ah," the ghost said, gesturing toward a very particular portrait on Vivienne's desk. "I know her. Wasn't your wife used for that disincarnation?"

She knew the answer. They all did. Most likely it was why Vivienne was their favorite. She would have burned the picture if it hadn't been such an extravagant and public courtesy. Instead she put it on her desk where clients could see it. None before had felt the need to comment. The ghost turned to offer her profile to the camera.

"She was."

"A shame, it wasn't up to your standard. You should have done the work yourself."

Vivienne was trying to find some response, any response, when the old ghost continued.

"You know, I saw her quite recently."

"She is a very important woman."

"No she wasn't," the ghost said.

Vivienne closed her mouth with an audible clack of teeth. She was accustomed to the callousness of the dead, but even she could be surprised.

The ghost turned to see her then laughed. "You thought I meant your *client*. That is so funny. No you silly little thing, I saw your *wife*."

"Aditi has returned?"

"Oh yes. It's quite common really. She can stay huddled with the unmoored. No need to ever immigrate her."

"Truly," she said. "A blessing I never expected."

"So sad that you can't benefit from it in some way. Really though, you were lucky to have her at all. One like that, they'd usually send directly to the breeding program. Anyhow. Is the next plate ready?"

Vivienne never left Aditi's side. Not when the cancer disfigured her, or when she spent her every waking hour screaming in pain, or even when the agony gave way to a silent, twitching coma. Vivienne waited until all heat of life had gone.

Her client asked her to do the work, to dismember the woman she'd loved, but no matter how much influence the ghosts could bring to bear, Vivienne could not see Aditi as meat to be cut. Her status allowed her to decline. She turned down all work for months, then finally got the papers to leave the city. To clear her head, she'd told them.

Past the refugee camps, the road led up into mountains. There she found the ruin of a resort picked over by the bone gatherers.

Thick pads of moss coated the remnants like rotting velvet stuck to the armature of a child's automaton. Pine trees pushed apart concrete and macadam. The air was clean, cleaner than Vivienne had ever known it. Away from the city, wind had no effect on time. She felt it on her skin and expected to see things around her change. Trees swayed, her hair moved, and the world remained solid. Vivienne pulled her leather jacket closed.

After the shock wore off she recognized the place—a building facade there, the stump of a dead tree there. They'd filmed old pabulum dramas there when the world belonged to the living. She had no way of knowing how long it had been dead, but the town left bones as surely as any person.

She camped in a ruined building for a night, thinking perhaps that she'd press further along the road the next day.

Dreams put her back in her childhood home. The apartment high above the city smelled of rotting meat. Her father senselessly rustled butcher's papers, unable to perform the final, small tasks he'd been given. Senility turned him into a corpse long before he stopped moving. She woke with his empty, glinting eyes on her.

The absence pressed her thin, filled her with nothing. It ached. When death came to her father it was a relief. When they took her brother to the Mill, it meant no more teasing. But when Aditi died, she could not bear the thought of the body without the person.

For the first time in her life, Vivienne—wrapped in her leather jacket in the midst of a dead resort—wanted someone to come back for her.

Outside the city the invisible spaces between each moment had the weight of a corpse. In the morning Vivienne turned around and went home. In her time she had amassed enough money that she would never need to touch a corpse again.

After a month of burning savings she took her first client since the death.

She had no talent for aimlessness.

———————

Vivienne bustled the girls into her workshop. They'd been crying for far too long, and the popping and swaying of the atelier did nothing to quiet them. Ancient explosions from unnumbered wars silhouetted buildings against the night, a night that brought with it an angry chill.

Vivienne hated it when they cried. She fixed papaver tea and made them drink it.

Making work until the drug took effect, she began prepping the workspace.

Into the cutting tray went two boning knives to get at the joints, four scalpels for the skin, and her old standby butcher's knife for stubborn viscera. She gave them all a few strokes on the hone, testing with the lightest touch of her thumb until the edges had the tacky-grab of a sea anemone's tentacles.

The girls quieted down.

Using a wide leather belt bolted to the wall, she stropped the edges down to surgical precision. The rhythmic sound calmed her, and—she liked to think—helped calm her specimens. She tugged the restraints on the work tables, ran water through the bleeder lines, and finally returned to the girls.

They stared at the wall, lost in whatever dreams came to the ones processed by the Mill. Vivienne stood them up and took off their tarps. The drooling girl had returned to drooling, so much like her father. Vivienne began with her.

She took off the ear tag. She guided her to the table. She pushed her down. She strapped down her arms and legs. With a deft hand she punctured the inner thigh with a long needle, then switched on the machine.

It hummed and the lines spiraled blood up, out, and down into the floor drain.

The room filled with the smell of it.

The girl turned pale.

Her lips grayed.

She shivered violently well after her eyes had closed.

The shivering slowed to spastic twitches.

Finally, her muscles relaxed and she fouled the table, adding a new stink to the room.

Vivienne grabbed the water hose and gave the body a thorough blast to clean off the piss and shit. She turned to the other girl, quietly cursing that she hadn't run them simultaneously. The drooling distracted her.

She shook her head and picked up the needle.

Hand on girl's thigh, fingertip brushed by pubic hair, she had to lean down to put enough force into the push. The girl laughed faintly and all the associations changed.

For just a second it was another time, another thigh, another laugh. This fragmentary instant coincided with the needle puncturing skin.

Two intimate moments merged. It felt just like killing Aditi.

Vivienne clenched her jaw and watched the girl bleed out. The anger pulled her up, out of the top of her head, to watch from the ceiling.

"No more," she said, her voice an echo inside her skull.

The ghost had some purpose to having the corpse made to resemble that dead actress. Vivienne didn't need to know what the ghost wanted to do. What Vivienne did know was how to make the corpse look like the client instead of her cinema heroine.

An obscene metastasis of flowers sweetened the air to syrup. The field of the Memento Ossium glowed in permanent, false sunset. Towering grave markers sent bright knives of light careening off the wealth of who-knew how many worlds. Vivienne had to shade her eyes from the reflecting gold and silver. This place, a small city unto itself, held all the power of the ghosts. They lavished it with attention, held parties and dinners and fundraisers here.

On the other side of the city was the small memorial for the former-living. The oldest names were pried off and melted down to make plaques for the most recent. Aditi's name had been gone for a year.

Vivienne stood with a small group of the living, well away from the main ceremony. The ghosts clustered around her client in foggy dunes, only their glinting eyes to hint at numbers. There were more ghosts attending the ceremony than there were living in the entire city.

The old ghost wore the actress face from the top of her monument. She lectured them in a language Vivienne could barely hear. She pointed and gestured. Hours passed before Vivienne was called to open the coffin.

The ghosts moved icily through her and mobbed the body.

They pawed at the flesh with impotent hands, their murmurs and exhalations almost sexual. At some point the old ghost had faded back to her own face, but Vivienne couldn't tell if it was before or after they'd begun fawning over the corpse.

The ghosts lavished her with murmured awe, more even than usual. Her disgust and anger melted into pride of workmanship.

They still expected her to help dig the grave though, and dispose of the previous coffin. Most of her clients held ceremonies once a year, she had the muscle for it.

This was the second in a month for the old ghost, and the coffin they'd dug up reeked. It was a rookie's mistake. Cleaning all the viscera before reassembly was the only useful thing her father had taught her.

The old ghost found her after the living finished tamping down the grave.

A smile snagged on the ghost's teeth.

"I'm afraid I had no choice but to tell the others this was your doing."

Vivienne hadn't been in a fight since her teens. The old fear reared up and chased her pulse into a frantic gallop. She fought the urge to put her hands in front of her face.

"They were *so* impressed," the client said. "No one has your skill with a corpse."

"I don't know what to say. Thank you," Vivienne said.

"Oh, no need for that. You'll be hearing from someone soon about your next job. I'm certain of it."

The ghost vanished.

Vivienne stopped in one of the new districts on her way back from the abandoned resort. The last scheduled storm for the day was just blowing out and it left the scent of roasting meat nearby, savory and spiced with rosemary and garlic. Long beams of sunlight passed between towers that blued into the distance like a forest. Only a few unmoored ghosts walked the streets, oblivious to the modern world. They carried tiny pockets of time with them.

This was the only home she could imagine.

Before going outside, she considered joining one of the refugee groups that trickled out of the city.

Vivienne smirked to herself at the irony of finding the outside world too dead.

As she stood watching the retreating storm, she noticed a ghost a half block away. Long black hair blew in wind from another time and little spots of color floated in her wake. Vivienne's breath caught in her throat, certain she was looking at Aditi returned. Unware, she bit her knuckles down to blood and stepped forward.

The ghost startled at an unheard sound and turned to face her. She was just another ghost; no one she'd ever seen before. Vivienne's arms fell to her sides and she sat down hard on the empty street.

The unmoored ghost she'd mistaken for her wife turned and walked away.

The door shut with a clatter. She slid the bolts and closed the transom as though it could keep her safe. Vivienne sat at her desk. The photo of the client who'd taken Aditi's body faced her like an accuser.

In the lower drawer was a bottle that had come with the photo, some kind of amber-colored liquor older than empires. She poured it into a water glass, drank it down, then paced her office waiting for the alcohol to hit her blood.

Hands trembling, she picked up one of the lines for the bleeder and held it like a talisman. That snagging smile of her client made the Mill a much more tangible prospect.

Vivienne wasn't too old to breed.

Her defiance—so easy when assembling the composite corpse—could not be summoned, even with the alcohol flooding her veins.

It took exploratory jabs to get the needle into a specimen's artery, doing it to herself would hurt. Somewhere among her things there were several smaller needles designed for arteries closer to the surface. That she could do.

The room went cold enough for her to look up to see if any of the windows were open. They were all sealed and covered.

Movement made her turn.

Standing in front of the closed door was a ghost. It stood silently, featureless and gray as slate. A blanker, real after all.

"You intend to take me to the Mill," Vivienne said.

The ghost didn't move. It had no eyes, no mouth, nothing of a face.

"Get one of the others to butcher me, but I won't go there."

She pulled the long needle off and attached the smaller one, holding it up like a threat.

In response the ghost lifted something, something impossible to see, an emptiness, like a face cut out of a picture. Through the thing she could see sky.

Trying to look at it hurt. Full body, flu-sick pain washed over her until every articulation in her body moaned.

With her left hand she raised up the line to the bleeder and pushed the needle into her neck just behind the jaw. The pain flared bright but she kept pushing until the tube filled with blood.

As the ghost moved toward her, its eyes opened. They opened and opened until there was nothing but eyes.

Vivienne frantically switched on the bleeder. It tugged in her flesh, pulling inside her like a fish hook.

"You're just a ghost," she said. "You can't touch me. I'll be dead before anyone can get in this room."

The smell of blood filled the air.

With the thing raised up, the ghost closed the distance between them. It slid the empty thing into her head.

And then Vivienne was on the floor. She couldn't move.

She watched the door burst open. She watched herself dragged into the street and thrown onto a cart. She watched Dimitrios shaking his head over her. She watched someone cutting her.

She could feel everything. They dressed her for a client, and she could feel the other's skin covering her like wet cloth.

Even after she'd been buried as someone else, Vivienne never stopped seeing.

Zak Jarvis is a writer and artist living in southern California. He has stories in *Werewolves and Shapeshifters: Encounters with the Beast Within* and *Demons: Encounters with the Devil and His Minions, Fallen Angels, and the Possessed*, both edited by John Skipp.

The Interview

Adrian Chamberlin

"The decision to terminate my employment at Fairlight Hospital was a mutual one, agreed between myself and the hospital board." I swallowed noisily as I answered, and fresh sweat broke out on my neck.

James Quinn looked up at me with narrowed eyes as he considered the answer I had given him. I knew he recognised it as a lie, knew what he was thinking. *Mutual decision to leave—in other words, dismissed. Sacked.* His eyes flicked back to my resume that rested on his imposing rosewood desk like a futile peace offering. I squeezed my knees anxiously as I waited for his reaction, suddenly aware that the heels of my shoes were drumming against the plastic base of the swivel chair where I sat. I forced my feet to stop. I had shown too many nerves already.

Quinn's eyes narrowed suddenly, and he leaned over, peering closely at my resume like some scavenging animal searching for signs of life in a road kill victim.

I stole a glance out the window to my left. I know it's bad form to gaze around a room during a job interview, but I needed to divert my attention from this rapidly deteriorating scenario. I had to remind myself there was an outside world, to fool myself into thinking my future didn't depend on this young man's opinion of—and ultimately, decision on—me and my abilities.

A beautiful May morning. Sunlight kissed the grounds of Nemeton Hospital, the neatly mown lawns and well tended rosebushes a perfect picture of early summer freshness. Only the high red brick walls in the distance reminded me this was a secure hospital, and the long term patients treated within were in effect prisoners.

Just like I—no other avenues to consider. No other company dared consider my employment applications after the media blew the Fairlight scandal out of proportion. This interview, for the position of clinical psychiatrist within a newly formed company, was my last hope. And the first question I had been asked I answered with a lie. Did I lie because I was nervous? Or was I nervous because I'd lied?

Truth told, I'd nearly thrown the invitation letter away, believing it nothing more than a cruel joke. Almost a full year had passed since Fairlight. After the enquiry, the threat of legal action, and continuous harassment from the media, I had given up hope of finding employment within the mental healthcare profession. My application had been halfhearted—one last grasp at my former glory before I succumbed to thoughts of suicide. I hadn't seriously expected a reply.

But there I sat, in front of an interview panel that, strangely, consisted of only one. James Quinn looked at least twenty-five years my junior, probably fresh out of university. I was surprised that the personnel manager was one so young. His sharply cut suit and flashy tie, combined with stylishly cropped and gelled blond hair, bore more resemblance to a sales rep than a man entrusted with such an important position. However, his youth reflected that of the company. Nemeton Hospital had only recently been built. The office I sat in still smelled of fresh paint and newly laid carpet tiles, and I noticed the filing cabinets behind Quinn were still covered in the protective polythene routinely used during transit. Things seemed to have been set up in rather a hurry. Even the letter inviting me to attend the interview had arrived less than a week after I posted my application. Why the urgency?

James Quinn steepled his fingers, a strange gesture for one so young, then leaned back. The sound his high backed chair made told me the black upholstery was leather, not vinyl. This company had money—or credit—to spare.

His eyes lingered over my scuffed brogues, my crumpled—and outdated—double breasted, beige suit. The trace of a sneer played at his lips.

"Mutual decision," he murmured. "You disappoint me, Mr. Hughes. We do read the papers here. And we read the report made to the Mental Health Commission. We know *exactly* why you left your last job."

I groaned and closed my eyes. Quinn's continuing words seemed muffled and distant.

"You lost your title. You were dismissed from the position you held for twenty-six years. And yet, oddly, you escaped criminal prosecution—much to the anger of those related to the six young patients who expired in your care. I believe a certain tabloid waged a protracted but ultimately unsuccessful campaign to bring civil prosecution against you. They succeeded in ruining your personal life, though. Hate mail, death threats, and so on. Not long after, your wife left you."

I choked back a sob and slumped in my seat.

Rachel.

The door on thirty years of marriage closed. It hadn't been the malicious letters and suspect packages, the obscene graffiti sprayed on our walls, the smashed windows…it had been the moment I sat her down and told her everything I'd done at Fairlight. What I had to do, to ease the suffering of those poor youngsters. She couldn't understand. I'll never forget the way she screamed at me, her fists pummeling my chest, her tears…so many tears. The ring I'd all but moved heaven and earth to pay for in the lean, early years of our relationship, torn from her finger, thrown at me. The door slamming and rattling in its frame, the Volvo screaming out of the garage…

She lived in Australia now, with our daughter and her parents. After the divorce proceedings I heard nothing more from them. I was truly alone.

"You've had a rough time, Mr. Hughes," Quinn said with some sympathy. He glanced down at my resume again. "And I see you've been out of work ever since Fairlight. I think it would be safe to say that our company is the sole entity interested in retaining your medical expertise."

I couldn't speak. His words had opened the last twelve nightmarish months of my life like a wound. But his last sentence offered a crumb of comfort.

…interested…

I held onto that morsel, a bandage for the wound.

"Your methods of psychotherapy were…unorthodox—"

"But effective."

Quinn smiled knowingly. "'Drastic' was the how the Fairlight board of inquiry colored it. 'Murderous' was the media's adjective of choice."

I sighed. "As you know, Mr. Quinn, I made it quite clear to the board that drastic measures were needed. Those six teenagers suffered from a disorder never before seen in the history of clinical psychiatry."

"So you say. A unique form of paranoid schizophrenia." He flicked open a square cut folder next to my resume and scanned the first page. "The usual symptoms were there, disorganised speech and behaviour, social withdrawal, hallucinations…but it was the hallucinations that marked this disorder as something new. According to your reports, they shared identical visions. Visions that drove each of them to quite horrifying acts of violence and self-mutilation."

Quinn turned a page, then another.

"They each felt they were being tormented, possessed almost, by…well, demons is the word they all used. A shared hallucination?"

"Understand," I said firmly, "None of them had met each other before admittance. And none of them met once inside. They were completely isolated."

"And traditional psychotherapy proved useless. Drugs merely aggravated their condition, and ECT only had a short lived calming effect on their rage. That's when you applied your new therapy. That's when the deaths began."

I cleared my throat. "I came to the conclusion that the only way to cure them was to make them part of the solution. In their more lucid moments they each spoke clearly to me. They insisted that the only way to rid their minds of demons was to cut their bodies. 'Hurt myself to get the pain out,' was how one girl described it to me. And it made sense…in her eyes…in their eyes. Hurt the vessel, the host, and force the demon out."

"So you supplied them—or rather, granted them—unofficial access to the necessary surgical equipment. The inquest grudgingly accepted that since your patients were prone to self-harm, they were ultimately responsible for their own deaths, which is why you were only charged with gross negligence." Quinn closed the folder and rested a hand on it. He fixed me with a knowing smile. "That wasn't all though, was it, Mr. Hughes?"

I didn't answer.

"Rumours circulated. Ward assistants and nurses fed stories to the press about how they witnessed you cutting patients yourself. Stories denied by the hospital board and the Trust. Stories you and I both know to be true."

For a moment I wondered if this was a trap, set up by one of the damned tabloids. Silent cameras and hidden microphones waiting for me to incriminate myself. But the look in Quinn's eyes told me otherwise.

"Direct intervention, Mr. Quinn. Some of my patients couldn't cure themselves. Their demons had too firm a hold. Increased pain and bodily destruction were the only answers—that which no human could possibly administer without assistance. I was only too happy to be their...savior."

"And the treatment was effective?"

I spread my hands. "Their suffering ended. And their demons—if you believe such things—are gone forever."

"Demons..." Quinn smiled thinly and gazed out of the window. I followed his gaze. A bank of heavy cloud rolled in from the east. Sunlight began to fade.

Quinn turned his attention back to me. "Mr. Hughes, Nemeton Mental Healthcare is a rather unique institution. We are privately funded and have no official association with the NHS or any of its Trusts. We specialise in the more extreme maladies that those Trusts are unable to remedy. We have been contracted to take on these cases and apply our own methods, with priority given to the disorder that you so correctly diagnosed.

"This disorder is more widespread than first realised, and cases are becoming more common every day, which will keep us quite busy. Provided we meet all government targets, ours shall be a very lucrative contract. Unfortunately, we are thin on staff with experience vital to our success." He took a clipboard from the desk and stood up.

"Would you follow me, please?"

I stood up shakily, my nerves beginning to return. I felt very uneasy as I followed him out of the interview room and through the spacious reception area. We passed the young blonde with the painted smile behind the reception desk and went through a door behind her labeled *Staff Only*.

Before us lay a short corridor and a staircase that led downward. As we descended, our heels ringing loudly on metal steps, Quinn spoke in hushed tones.

"As you can understand, these special cases must be kept from view. Our contract with the government is dependant on our discretion. We are in the unfortunate situation of being...*deniable*."

We came to another corridor that was longer but not as well lit or clean as what I'd seen of the rest of the facility. Shadows took on added depth, thanks to dirty walls. A strong scent of disinfectant lingered in the air, almost, but not completely, masking the stench of bodily waste. The corridor terminated at a heavy steel door. Secure locks and deadbolts, with a mesh grill at eye level instead of a window, told me this portal led to a secure room. Just like the secret rooms of Fairlight.

Quinn unlocked the door, released the bolts, and pushed our way into a small cell. The sloping tiled floor was bisected by a large drainage channel. Secured with rubber straps to a bare cot on the far side of the tight space was a young man in his late teens. He twisted his head to stare at us as the door slammed shut. His hazel eyes were glazed and unfocussed from whatever tranquilisers he had been given, but possessed that singular look I had seen in the eyes of the poor souls at Fairlight.

Quinn knelt down and reached under the cot. He withdrew a pair of stained, white overalls and a small vinyl briefcase. He passed the overalls to me. The stains were red and recent. Who else had been interviewed?

"Welcome to the practical assessment." Quinn waited for me to put on the overalls before opening the briefcase. "I would like you to demonstrate your direct intervention technique. Use any instrument you require, but I must inform you that you *will* be timed. You have one hour."

I stared at the glittering array of surgical instruments nestled within the briefcase's packing foam, their sharp edges glinting seductively. One hour? How could I perform my therapy with such a limited supply of time? I previously took days with patients.

I selected a scalpel and a bone saw, turned to my patient who was unaware of the events unfolding around him, and went to work.

I was nervous and it showed. Several times I fumbled with the scalpel, so the removal of the nose and ears wasn't up to my usual standards, and the bone saw slipped out of my hands while I was cutting into a kneecap. I heard Quinn scribbling something on his clipboard. I knew it wasn't complimentary.

But as the hour progressed, my nerves faded and my former expertise returned. I managed to cut, saw, and slice into areas that brought about the most pain possible within a short space of time.

As I removed the overalls, Quinn complimented me on my decision to cut out the boy's tongue at the end of the operation, rather than at the beginning, to ensure a constant flow of screams.

"We may go to a second interview, though," he warned me as he led me back to the reception area. "And a second practical assessment."

I smiled. I wouldn't be as nervous next time. I possess that special quality that a young company like Nemeton Mental Healthcare needs.

There's no substitute for experience.

Adrian Chamberlin's works have appeared in Guy N Smith's *Graveyard Rendezvous* and the websites Spinetinglers, Great Scribblers, the British Horror Novels Forum, and the DF Underground, and most recently in the March issue of Lovecraft Ezine. Published and forthcoming works can be found in several anthologies. He's a founding member of Dark Continents Publishing and his first novel *The Caretakers* was released at the World Horror Convention in April 2011.

The Tenure Track Lottery

Ellen Herbert

1. Type each tenured faculty name in 14-point Times New Roman font.
2. Cut the names into one-half inch strips, standard letter paper width.
3. Fold each strip five times in one inch sections.
4. Place in the urn.

My dear mentor Mac, author of the list, was nothing if not precise.

On this the eve of my third lottery here at St. Peter's, a small Catholic college perched on Maryland's Calvert Cliffs overlooking the Chesapeake Bay, I complete these steps and remember Mac, Dr. McKinnon, once chair of the English Department. Tonight as I celebrate my first lottery without Mac, I feel his presence in all that I do.

Mac was always straight with me, a rare quality in academia. Yet on that afternoon in late August eleven years ago when he offered me the job here at St. Peter's, he was intentionally vague about my *special* lottery duties. Pressing his trembling finger to a line on the academic calendar, he'd said, "Note the third Saturday in May, three years hence, Ned."

I scanned the dates.

With doddering effort, Mac came to stand, leaned over the desk, and brought his gnarled, spotty hand to the paper again. "This event occurs every four years."

"Like graduation," I said, naive as a newborn.

"You'll have special duties that night, Ned, duties you will learn about in due time," Mac told me, each word as slow as a Georgia porch swing

If Mac had handed me a syllabus outlining my possible lottery duties, I *still* would have accepted the position here. I was desperate. By the time I interviewed at St. Pete's, I had been looking for a university job for over a year, ever since I finished my doctoral thesis in poetry of the Pacific Rim. I longed to stop delivering pizza and start being called *Doctor*.

And as the young always believe: I was certain St. Pete's was a stepping stone to a bigger, brighter university. I wouldn't be here long, I told myself after Mac assured me that I could never get tenure at St. Peter's. "All your degrees are from state colleges, Ned, and not even name state colleges. Alas, our faculty must have degrees from the Ivies, Stanford, Duke or Hopkins."

And once I taught my first class, I began to understand why I could not be tenured. You see, St. Pete's, like many small colleges today, struggles to stay afloat financially and must accept almost any student who can rustle up our substantial tuition. Not that our students aren't sweet kids and the few intelligent ones masquerade as supernovas in our very "milky" way. Only our faculty's credentials and the fresh blood that comes from a steady turnover of tenure-track faculty members keeps us from being completely mediocre.

Tenure means a professor has a job for life, but at St. Pete's there's a catch to it. Of course if our tenured faculty retired when normal people do, there would be no need for a lottery. But alas none of us, including the great tenured ones, can afford retirement. If not for the lottery, our entire faculty would soldier on into their eighties or nineties, wearing Depends, shuffling to class on walkers, where they would wind themselves up, cut off their hearing aides, and lecture for whole class periods.

———————

As I emerge from the brightly lit stairwell onto the shadowy Columbus Center's roof, lit only in fairy lights, a hush falls over the crowd gathered here, faculty and deans of the School of Arts and Sciences.

Never do I, a lowly term appointment, enjoy such deference from these dignitaries, so I slow my movements in order to savor the moment. At the same time, I listen to the slosh of the mighty Chesapeake abusing the rocks a thousand feet below. A portion of the Columbus Center's roof hangs over the cliff like a diving tower over a pool.

In the fading dusk, all eyes remain on me or rather on the thing I carry, the urn, as in "Ode on a Grecian…" Except ours is faux, made of Styrofoam, painted gray in order to appear stone-like.

"Couldn't we get a new one?" I asked Mac before the last lottery when I discovered a hunk of Styrofoam had fallen off.

But he just shook his shaggy gray mane. "The funny old thing was here before me and will be after."

And he was right about that.

The evening is cool for late spring and as the light seeps away, an almost full yellow moon hangs low like a watchful eye over the roof, large and flat as a dance floor. It was probably built as an observatory for the astronomy classes we offer, which combined with geology form the freshman science requirement students dubbed "rocks and stars," slightly less objectionable than their nickname for abnormal psych, "nuts and sluts."

"Stir those names very, very thoroughly, Ned," Riley, tenured in history, jests as he pats me on the back and moves off, his girth rolling side-to-side, into the crowd forming a semi-circle around me.

I have an evil thought: I would not want to have to scrape Riley off the side of the cliff, something I had to do when Dr. Sam Adler was chosen at my first lottery. Instead of making a brave leap, Sam had to be forced off the roof by a faculty stampede.

At my interview, Mac had shown intense interest in my hobby, rock-climbing, and had questioned me on my rappelling skills. I understood why when I spent the evening after my first lottery, scaling the cliffs below to find Dr. Adler's body parts and send them into the Bay to feed the fishes.

Although Riley is a friend, I give him a solemn nod. Some of the faculty, especially the men, act light-hearted, but it's all bravado.

I take my lottery duties seriously and never joke about what we're about to do.

Amber in a snug white shimmering dress, so unlike the black tents most faculty women wear, comes to my side. "Neddie," she whispers in my ear and looks up at me big-eyed, teetering in high heels like a fawn, all eyes and legs.

"Don't stand too near the edge, darling," I say, for I love her and am glad neither of our names is in the urn. Tonight I rejoice that I am not an Ivy Leaguer or a Dukie, for only the names of tenure-track faculty are in the urn. We lower echelon folks, adjuncts, term appointments, such as myself, and graduate teaching assistants like my Amber, are safe.

Stroking the hair of my knuckle, Amber whispers, "You think Snyde will be okay, right?"

I shrug and tell her, "There are no guarantees except for us."

I secretly despise her boss, Dr. Snyder Carrboro, who I believe is trying to sleep with her. She's often at his condo late at night, helping him edit his latest opus, a pop historical account of the Battle of Little Bighorn. I wouldn't be surprised if it isn't mostly plagiarized, a practice in vogue with historians nowadays. Nevertheless, like his other books, this one will probably be made into a PBS special.

I've suggested to Amber that the way he treats her verges on sexual harassment, but she is not the type to make waves, nor is St. Pete's the kind of place where that sort of charge would go far.

Still I seethe inside after walking into his office last week and finding Amber with her hand up Snyder's shirt. "His back itched," she explained later. "He asked me to scratch it."

Funny, I thought, I too have an itch I'm about to scratch.

I check my watch. Five of eight. Almost show time. All the tenured have become silent and pale. Only the adjuncts are chatting now, exchanging reviews of the latest book or restaurant. "I've discovered a delightful little Cambodian place," says Reese, the most senior adjunct, a wealthy retiree, a wicked twinkle in his eye when he meets mine.

I'm not sure why Reese or any of the other adjuncts come to this proceeding. I attribute their presence to schedenfreude, the pleasure derived from seeing the great ones squirm as their herd gets thinned by one.

Snyder Carrboro, the star of Arts and Sciences, the biggest fish in our little pond, makes his grand entrance, his graying hair moussed to perfection, wearing a black close-fitting jacket and black t-shirt, trying to achieve Upper East Side but coming off as resoundingly bridge and tunnel.

He comes right up to me and pats my balding beige corduroy. "Ned, my man," he says, "another lottery. How swift the passage of time."

I give him a curt nod then sigh with agreement. At St. Peter's, semesters flow into semesters, punctuated by graduations, summer sessions. University work is like quicksand, hard to find but once you're in it, hard to get out. After my first gruesome lottery, only Mac's assurances that seldom did a professor resist as Sam Adler had, and the fact that I had gone to the Modern Language convention resume in hand and gotten not a nibble, convinced me to stay.

Now Amber keeps me here. Our goal is for her to get a term appointment, too, so that we can afford to get married. I fear she thinks she has to sleep with Snyder to make this happen, but there is another way.

At 8:00, I nod at Dr. Marrianna Von Hoff. Now that Mac is gone, Marrianna is the oldest faculty member of the School of Arts and Sciences, so she will officiate. She is a woman of regal bearing except for her height. At 4'10 she's technically a dwarf and looks it tonight because wisely she's chosen not to wear high heels.

As she moves toward me with the good book under her arm, I recall the last lottery when Mac drew his own name. By that time his shaggy mane was gone, and he was bald as a newborn. Of course Mac, ever the considerate gentleman, put his slip of paper into his jacket pocket, ran to the edge, and leapt straight into the Chesapeake Bay, so there would be no need for me to rappel.

Afterward when I sat in his office shredding the names, step eleven on my laminated *Lottery Duties* list, I realized that Mac, having been seriously ill for a few years, had pulled a fast one on me. His name was still in the urn. He had made his own slip then dropped it out of his sleeve like a magician.

"Welcome all to St. Peter's seventeenth lottery," Marrianna says in a croaky voice that does not project.

I fear she sounds like this in the classroom, as well. St. Pete's may sneer at us state college grads, but at least we had to take courses in public-speaking and teaching methods.

"We're all a bunch of old bores," Mac used to say, "sawing on about Chaucer or the Peloponnesian Wars."

Marrianna reads the scripture about a time to sow, a time to reap.

I place the urn on a small table always used for this purpose and stride to the edge of the roof, where there's a gate in the wrought iron balustrade.

As I open the gate and secure it to the balustrade, a brisk wind rises from the Bay, ruffling my hair. I avert my eyes from the immense darkness below, but I can hear the water's slap against the cliffs' base as if there were a monster down there hungry for the blood of a tenure track one.

I return to the urn.

Marrianna, who may be remembering that Mac drew his own name last year, has begun to shake as if she's chilled.

I never told anyone the truth about Mac. "The integrity of our lottery must always be maintained," Mac often said to me. I would dishonor his memory to do otherwise.

"It is time to draw the name," she says in a voice little more than a whisper, but I can tell that everyone on the roof hears her.

I lower the urn to her.

She reaches in and pulls out a name. Her hand is trembling uncontrollably.

She offers the slip to me, while her other hand goes to her throat as if she's been stricken with laryngitis and can't speak.

I sense Mac in the wide sky above me. I can almost hear him say: *When you take the C out FACULTY you get FAULTY.*

How displeased he would be with Marrianna for mucking up our sacred ceremony. Academia has a caste system as strict as that of India. I, a lowly term appointment, ought not to be the one to read the name of a tenure track faculty member.

Still I proceed.

I take my glasses from my inner pocket, carefully unfold the slip of paper, and proclaim, "Dr. Snyder Carrboro." At the same time, I will myself not to grin.

The crowd gasps for he is the department's star.

Amber shrieks and throws her arms around his neck.

He peels her off and hands her his jacket. Turning, he begins to run toward the opening in the balustrade.

Amber follows him at a slower pace, wobbly in her heels.

My heart thumps into my throat. "Amber, don't," I call.

"Snyde, Snyde, what about Little Bighorn?" she yells. "May I finish your manuscript?" My girl is ambitious.

Just before leaping into the darkness, he appears to assent.

She turns her ankle and grabs for the wrought iron railing.

"Careful, Amber." I rush to her, afraid she might topple over into the Bay.

I put my arms around her and kiss her deeply. She pulls away and gives me a reproachful, "Neddie."

I understand. Faculty romances are frowned upon. We here at St. Peter's adhere to a strict moral code. After all, we're a Catholic institution.

But I keep my arm around Amber as we turn to face the group. It is a moment of pure happiness and triumph for me. My rival is gone. No longer can he call her from our bed to proofread his opus.

Everyone is murmuring about how brave Snyder has been.

"Dr. Carrboro was like his hero, General George Custer," Amber tells the crowd. Many nod in agreement.

"Hear, hear," Charlie says.

In my hurry to get to Amber, I jostle the table. The urn turns on its side, and some of its slips of paper fall out. A gust of wind lifts the papers into the air above our heads.

People grab at them.

"I need all those back," I yell. "Do not open them. I repeat: do not open them!"

As usual, the adjuncts, the department's loose cannons, don't listen. Reese and several others begin to unfold the papers as if they are fortunes inside cookies.

"Hey, this one says *Dr. Snyder Carrboro*," Reese says.

"So does mine," Riley says.

Others chime in.

Amber lets out a shriek, steps away from my side, and turns on me. "Ned, how could you?"

I begin to walk backward toward the edge of the roof, my eyes on the faculty, who are coalescing into a fighting unit, coming together as they never do in faculty meetings when they argue endlessly about university by-laws governing tenure, raises, and their health insurance co-pay.

I've seen them like this only once before when they stampeded Sam Adler off the roof.

I'm at the edge now. In thirty seconds they'll rush me. I squat and drop down, holding onto the bottom of the wrought iron railing.

There is a ledge below the roof, known only to those who have scaled this cliff. My right foot slips as I try to balance on it. I'm wearing old loafers, their soles so thin they have no grip whatsoever.

I kick them off. They make a sound far below as they hit the rocks. I release the railing, slink down beneath the roof, and crouch on the narrow ledge, glad for my slender boy body. My fingers find rocks I can hold. Darkness covers me like a blanket.

Faculty members gather directly above me at the railing.

I am so close I could reach up, take hold of someone's ankle, and yank her or him into the abyss. What fun it would be to do that, but I restrain myself.

"Anyone actually see Ned fall in?" Riley asks.

"I heard something hit the water," Reese says.

Marrianna clears her throat. "With Snyder's departure, you're head of history, Riley."

Riley thanks her and accepts congratulations from others.

I hear the whine of the gate being closed. They bid each other good night and walk away, grumbling about losing their star, Dr. Snyder Carrboro and his PBS specials.

I lift my head slightly and see that two shadows remain. The two exchange whispers.

Riley clears his throat. "You've had a tough night, Amber, honey. Let me just unhook you here and give you a little massage."

I hear the rub of fabric and prepare to lift myself back up to the roof, where I'll flatten Riley that big fat letch.

"Don't," she says in a tearful tone. "I can't go on without Neddie." With that she flings herself over the railing like a shooting star, a flash of shimmering white, here then gone.

I must…join my love, so I leap and begin my descent to join the woman who gave her life for me.

Falling through the air, I hear Amber's voice above me from the roof, "Now that Ned's gone, you'll be hiring another term appointment, right?"

At that moment I meet my end, directly on top of the white shimmering dress Amber tossed, a picnic blanket on Styx's last port of call.

I should have known. She always was an ambitious one.

Ellen Herbert's personal narrative essays have been published in *The Washington Post* "Style" section, *Sonora Review, The Rambler, Alimentum,* and other journals. One of her personal essays, "Orphaned Alligators," won The 2006 *Flint Hills Review* Creative Nonfiction Prize. Her short fiction has been published in *First for Women, The Sonora Review, The Iris,* and other literary magazines and has won over 10 awards including a PEN Syndicate Fiction Prize and a Virginia Fiction Fellowship. One of her stories was read on National Public Radio.

Words, Words, Words!

Gary Brandner

Hamilton Baxter sat behind the table piled with fresh copies of *Mischief Afoot*. It was his latest book and featured a nice garish dust cover and his name spelled correctly. The dozen or so youngsters across from him in the bookstore were not a Stephen-King-size autograph line, but they were, he supposed, better than nothing.

Baxter pulled his long, lean face into what he hoped was a convincing smile. When one of the young wannabes presented a book he scribbled his practiced autograph, adding some meaningless dedication if requested. Most of these kids, he knew, were English majors hoping to someday see their own name on a book cover. They had sat patiently through his reading aloud of chunks of his prose. It was a drill he hated, but which seemed to be expected. At the end of the day maybe some of these dipshits would actually come up with the $24 to buy his overpriced hardcover.

Amid the babble of fawning praise and trite questions from the fans, Baxter waited patiently for the inevitable "Where do you get your ideas?" While other writers, *real* writers, groaned at this chestnut, Baxter enjoyed it. It gave him a chance to bloviate and pontificate all the meaningless slogans and shibboleths spouted by writers since, well, probably since Plutarch. All the crap about using your life experience, writing from the soul, distilling the one true word from random thought. Empty words, but they ate it up, these writer groupies. So on this occasion when he opened his mouth to lay some platitude on the eager young faces, he was as surprised as any of them to hear what came out.

"Where do I get my ideas? I steal them."

There followed a moment of stunned silence in which it seemed you could hear the non-ringing of the cash register. Then the laughter began as the group of youngsters concluded that the semifamous writer was making a joke. A beat later Baxter joined the general merriment, hoping his own laughter did not ring as false as it was. For what he had just told the assembled fans was the truth. He was a thief.

It was in his freshman year at one of the California state colleges that Hamilton Baxter discovered his knack for taking the work of other writers, changing some of the words, restructuring a few sentences, and rearranging paragraphs. He could then present the piece as his own and be assured of an acceptable grade. As his skill at word thievery grew, Baxter sailed through college and graduated with a degree in English without producing a single piece of original writing.

On graduation Baxter discovered the career opportunities for English majors were severely limited. He had but one real skill, and he concentrated on some way to use that in making a living. It did not take long for him to settle on fiction writing. There were untold millions of stories in long-forgotten books just waiting to be lifted. Baxter was careful never to use the work of an author whose name people might know, or a story too familiar to the public. He haunted the back shelves of used-book stores and the dusty stacks of unread works in the library. He avoided the Internet as a source because there were too many ways an inquisitive geek could nail him there.

For fifteen years now he had made a comfortable, if not sumptuous living, using the words of others. He was content to be a midlist writer, never breaking into any bestseller list, winning no prizes, selling his work moderately and occasionally playing Author for small groups like the one at the bookstore today.

Shaken now by the inadvertent blabbing of the damning truth to his young fans, Baxter excused himself, pleading a meeting with his publisher. No such meeting was scheduled, but he felt the need to escape before he revealed any more embarrassing facts.

An hour later, in his library refuge, Baxter inhaled the bookish air as a diver might suck in oxygen on emerging from the depths. The smell of the pages, the bindings, and the words themselves invigorated him. The building was new and bright, but the warm musty smell was as old as literature. The friendly middle-aged woman at the desk greeted him with a smile.

"You're later than usual today, Mr. Baxter. No problem, I hope?"

"No problem, Claire. I had to stop off and sell a few books. The artist's curse."

The woman laughed dutifully as Baxter headed for one of the little cubicles at the rear. He was relieved to see that his favorite space was not occupied. He laid his worn briefcase on the desk between the shoulder-high partitions and headed back among the shelves. He was to begin a new book today, and he planned to search among some old material for inspiration. He picked out a volume of stories from long-out-of-print pulp magazines. The writing was rudimentary, but those old penny-a-worders came up with some solid plot ideas. A volume of twentieth-century biographies would provide background for a cast of characters. Play scripts from the 1920s and '30s would juice up his dialogue. An anthology of pretentious fiction from obscure literary magazines would impart a touch of class.

With an armful of stealable literature Baxter returned to the cubicle and settled in. He opened the first book and snatched his hand back with a yelp of pain. A fresh paper cut sliced his forefinger. Damn, on his writing hand, too. He sucked at the wound, blew on it, swore at the drop of blood that oozed out and plopped onto his shirtfront.

Baxter looked around quickly to see if he had disturbed any of the other patrons. Not that he cared, but in his position it did not pay to attract attention. He was relieved to see that no one had looked in his direction. He picked up the book for a closer look at the page that had cut him. Puzzled, he frowned. The paper was old, soft, and pulpy, not the kind of slick linen that inflicted a cut. Whatever the cause, he had a deep nick in his finger that throbbed in time with his heartbeat.

With his left hand he opened another of the volumes. Emitting a strange grunting sound, the heavy cover slammed shut on his hand with bone-cracking force.

"Ow, goddammit!" He tried to pull back, but the book kept his hand clamped where it was. Only when he jammed the book under his right arm and pulled did his hand come free and let the book snap shut. He examined his bruised knuckles and looked around. Again, no one took notice of his outburst. These idiots had to be dead, or too immersed in their own stupid reading, or maybe they were deliberately ignoring him. Baxter found himself unreasonably angry with these people for not acknowledging his irritation.

All right, to hell with them. Get some work done.

Baxter opened the book, cautiously this time. He was relieved that no page sliced his finger, no jaw-like covers snapped shut on him. It was just an ordinary old book. Relaxing a little, he turned to the title page. The letters there blurred as though he were trying to read through Vaseline. Automatically he touched his temple to be sure he was wearing his glasses. He was. He took them off, huffed on the lenses, and wiped them vigorously with a clean handkerchief. He replaced the gasses and looked down again at the page. No longer blurred, the letters stood out in bold black type:

jzsopkn jsrekk poknjjnsd
mw
ljkhodss pnn sijemdoj

"What the holy hell?"

Baxter realized he had spoken aloud, but he didn't care. Nor, it seemed, did anyone else in the library. Had he somehow picked up a book in some foreign language? No, those random letters looked like no earthly language. He flipped through page after page. Nothing on them but the apparently random scattering of letters, sometimes in wordlike clumps, sometimes in solid blocks down a whole page. Not a bit of it made sense. Crazy.

He pushed the book away like some venomous creature and opened another. It held the same meaningless jumble of letters. The remaining books were just as indecipherable. Baxter sat back in the plastic chair, sweat seeping through his shirt at the armpits. He had carefully chosen each of these volumes from the shelves, checked their pub dates and flipped through the pages before selecting them. Everything was as it should be. There were real words on the paper that had formed themselves into meaningful sentences and paragraphs. Now nothing had meaning.

Baxter closed his eyes and forced himself to draw in four deep breaths and hold them as he had learned to do while plagiarizing a book on relaxation. When he looked again at the pages they were the same incoherent mess.

He lurched up from the little cubicle and stumbled back into the stacks. At random he pulled first one volume then another from the shelves, riffled through the pages, and dropped them one after another to the carpeted floor. Not a one of them was remotely readable. *Am I going mad?* He thought. *Or am I the victim of some dreadful cosmic joke?*

Something nudged him from the rear. Baxter spun around, his shoulder slamming against the opposite steel shelf, which had been a comfortable distance away when he entered the aisle. With a grinding, growling sound the tall, heavy shelf edged closer to him. A horrifying vision swam into his head of his body caught there, crushed until his bloody entrails spilled over the books.

He squeezed out from between the shelves, barely escaping before they clanked together. The bright and airy library had darkened as shadows crept in from all sides. The pastel walls now looked like gray stone; the ceiling was lost in murky darkness. The people at the tables and in the cubicles were hunched over their books; silent and unmoving as stone images. Baxter stumbled toward the front desk.

The graying head of Claire the librarian brought him a flood of relief for the sheer familiarity. Something was definitely wrong here, but Claire was an anchor to reality. He coughed, trying to clear his throat.

Claire looked up. It was her face, but it was not the face she wore minutes ago. Something in the eyes was wrong. Very wrong. The heavy brows slanted down in a deep V. Her mouth stretched in a smile. And stretched. And stretched. Until the terrible orifice spread literally ear to ear. Brown and broken teeth protruded from suppurating gums. Baxter staggered back, his own mouth hanging open.

A rasping croak rattled from the ghastly mouth of the librarian. Nothing resembling words came out, though there was a rising inflection suggesting that this hag was asking a question. She extended a clawlike hand toward his face.

Abandoning all attempts at composure, Baxter leaped back and bolted for the door. Through the glass he could see the outside world where the sun shone on soft green grass, cars rolled past on the street, ordinary-looking people strolled on the sidewalks, pigeons pecked at the remains of a popcorn bag. A boy ran happily by playing with a black and white dog. Baxter fought for composure. Once he was back out there in the familiar world of reality everything would be all right.

He hit the bar with both hands to open the door, and bounced back. The bar was fixed in place; the door did not budge. He tried again with the same result. Whimpering, he pounded on the heavy glass with his fists until the pain shot up his arms. He kicked at the door with all his strength. His trendy jogging shoes made no impact.

Crying openly now, Baxter threw himself against the glass. He rebounded, blood dripping from his nose. As he gathered himself for another lunge a heavy blue-clad arm barred his way. The arm was attached to the powerful shoulder and uniformed chest of a security guard. The man was well over six feet tall with a broad, clean face. Baxter had never seen him here before, but on this nightmarish day he seized on the man as a savior.

As panic seized his throat, Baxter tried wildly to pantomime his distress and the need to get outside the heavy glass doors and away from the nightmare world his library had become.

For a moment he thought he had at last found an ally. The guard looked down at him with an almost sympathetic expression. Then the smile began. As with Claire the librarian, the terrible grin stretched and spread across his cheeks, up and back, until the corners of his mouth met his ears. The revealed teeth were long and sharp, not human at all. The ghastly maw gaped wide and a series of short growling sounds spilled out.

Baxter jerked his arm away from the guard and ran back past Claire, still wearing the hideous grin, past the silent lumpish patrons, past the tall murderous shelves filled with gibberish, to the tiny cubicle where he had left his briefcase and the four dreadful books that had kicked off this terror. He fumbled through the briefcase, found his cell phone, popped it open, and thumbed the button to activate it. The familiar tinkly tone came through, but Baxter scarcely noticed. He was staring at the logo on the tiny screen. It read:

womzilj

That was certainly not the name of the company that manufactured his phone. Nor was it any word in any language Baxter knew. He was not even surprised when the short list of names for his frequently called numbers made no sense. It fit with the bizarre world of non-words he had somehow fallen into. Gripping the little phone with one hand he stabbed at the numbered keys with his split forefinger. After a couple of fumbled tries he hit 911. An almost comforting electronic buzzing ring sound came through immediately. A clock sounded as a female voice answered on the other end and said…

What the hell *did* she say? There were only crackling, meaningless syllables in his ear. Baxter flung the instrument away from him and turned to the dark interior of the library. There the lumpish people at last began to move. As in slow motion they rose from their seats and turned toward him. He opened his mouth to scream at them, get their attention and plead for help if there was a sympathetic soul among them. Then as they came at him he saw their faces. Oh my God, their faces!

The sounds he made were the burbling prattle of an idiot child. Try as he might, Hamilton Baxter, who liked to say, "Words are my business," could not form a single intelligible utterance. He fell back in the plastic chair and let his head bump forward on the surface of the desk. He heard the shuffling sounds of the others advancing on him. He cried like a baby as his world exploded.

———

The two men in white uniforms eased the gurney with its motionless burden down the steps of the library. The shorter of the men, who steadied the front end, said to his partner, "Did the doc say what killed him?"

"Who knows. Sometimes they just go, poof, like that."

"They say he was some kind of writer. Sitting there surrounded by books. I guess he died happy."

Gary Brandner, born in the Midwest and much-traveled during his formative years, has thirty-odd published novels, more than 100 short stories, and a handful of screenplays on his resume. After surviving the University of Washington, he followed such diverse career paths as amateur boxer, bartender, surveyor, loan company investigator, advertising copywriter, and technical writer before turning to fiction. Since his breakthrough novel *The Howling*, he has settled into a relatively respectable life with wife and cats in California's San Fernando Valley. He is currently involved in a movie project as writer/co-producer.

Team Player

Patrick Flanagan

Don't fuck this up. Firm handshake. Mark grabbed the man's hand and shook it. *Firm enough, but not too firm. Don't overdo it.* "Mark Mellon," he said in his store-voice, "Grocery and Pet Care." The VDPO favored him with a tight semi-smile and a nod, and moved on to Carla (DVD and Music). Hugh (General Store Manager), an old hand at Home Office visits, shadowed the dignitary at a respectful distance of three steps back, one step to the right, and remained equidistant as the two of them glided past the assembled department heads. Mark willed himself not to sweat or tremble. He didn't want to attract attention or arouse suspicion.

The new VDPO had introduced himself as Fred Paull and confided in them that—if they hadn't already known—he was Really One of Them! He'd started out doing exactly what they did, sometime back in the early Neolithic, stocking shelves and riding registers Just Like Them. Of course, the prices may have been *just a little cheaper* back then. (Ha ha, hee hee, smile and nod.) But now that he was VDPO he wanted the boys on the front line (and gals, too!) to know that They Had a Friend in the Home Office.

Mark dutifully gave an exaggerated sigh of relief and stood "at ease" along with his coworkers. Permission to relax! (Sort of!) They, in turn, moved about slightly and relaxed their posture—their body language dropping Gs that were replaced with irreverent apostrophes—but otherwise remained in place, as if to tell His Eminence, *We feel free to go elsewhere in this store, but we choose to remain here, listening to you. You've won our respect.* And they waited patiently as the visiting suzerain rifled through his mental Rolodex of anecdotes, corny jokes, and small talk, looking for just the right comment to really put a button on this introduction.

It was unbearably mild in the store today. Mark noticed a fluorescent tube high overhead. Goddamnit. If he'd told those nimrods once, he'd told them a hundred times—*Cool* White, *Cool*, not *Warm*. Warm White emitted a vaguely malevolent glow. Sure, it was twenty feet up. Sure, most of the cart-crawlers were too busy keeping track of their grubby brood or surreptitiously staring-without-staring at the tits or the ass of a sixteen-year-old store associate while pretending to browse. But *he* noticed. It stood out like a trapdoor or a hidden compartment in some Saturday morning cartoon, painted a brighter color so that the animators wouldn't lose track of it. Mr. Paull was saying something about the local sports team and comparing their relatively good current record to the relatively poor current record of his *own* local sports team (ha ha, hee hee, smile and nod), and Mark willed the VDPO *not* to look up, *not* to notice, *not* to see the incongruity flickering over his head.

Mr. Paull favored him with another sidewise glance again. *Lock onto his nervous system! !!!D*O*N'*T//L*O*O*K//U*P!!!* Mark felt his brain matter throb and ooze blood from between its folds as he tried to force the man not to look up.

Cool White. Not Warm White.

Please.

Don't.

Look.

Up.

"Don't you agree, Mark?" Mr. Paull asked, about whatever it was.

"Yes, of course," Mark said, looking up at the ceiling.

Fuuuuuck.

Mr. Paull took a step closer. His eyes peered right through him with a penetrating squint. *Did you think I didn't notice the Warm White bulb, Mr. Mellon?* they said.

I saw it the moment I crossed over the threshold.

And *the asymmetrical pyramid of Sprite 24-packs in front of Aisles 7 and 8.*

And *the incorrect pricing on the sale items in Aisle 22. Pet Food*—your *bailiwick, Mr. Mellon.* He was saying something out loud and his expression looked pleasant and bland enough, but Mark was listening to the man's eyes. *Iams dry dog food. Purina ONE cat food. Purina Puppy Chow. ALL. Wrong.*

Did you think I wouldn't notice?

Did? You?

Mark's face turned to wax and began to drip off of his skull in thick, milky rivulets. Every snide remark he made to his friends about how much he *hated* this job. Every bashful smile he gave when people told him he was *wasting* his time in a dead-end career. Every day that was so mind-numbingly, soul-wrenchingly *abysmal* that he punched his fist against the employee break room wall, choked back tears, went for hours without speaking a single word to his employees. It was all bullshit. All of it. $29,800. Twenty-nine *thousand*. And eight hundred. Dollars. He needed that. He was just barely keeping his head above water, it was a struggle month to month, week to week, day to day, but he *needed* this job. His stomach churned, his hairline receded, his teeth ground together at night over the fear, the constant anxiety, never too far from his conscious mind, that one day he'd get that call over the PA. That buzzing, crackly command to report to the GSM's office. Not "when you get a minute." Now. He'd walk in and they'd be waiting—Hugh behind his desk, probably Nancy as well. They'd have Something They Wanted to Talk to Him About. They'd hand him the clipboard with the pink forms. The pink forms you signed, agreeing to your own execution, agreeing with their unspoken accusations that you were a fuck-up, a slacker, a saboteur, and a no-good piece of shit stealing oxygen from the lungs of *REAL Team Players*. Press hard for the carbon copy beneath please. Goldenrod. The goldenrod was the copy of your own death warrant, which they handed to you in exchange for your namebadge, your store keys, and your dignity.

Don't stare back. Don't whimper. Don't make him remember you.

"Yes!" he said, just a little too loudly. And then he nodded spastically, like a drooling idiot, at whatever it was the VDPO was saying. It didn't matter what, it was clearly right.

Mr. Paull pulled Hugh aside for a whispered conference as the inspection broke up. No obvious victims so far, although Paull might want to let people marinate for a while as he turned up the temperature of the crock-pot. Gene (Auto Maintenance) was the first to test the waters, slowly ambling back to his corner of the store, looking back every few steps to see if he was being watched. He disappeared around the corner and then the rest of them began to drift off as well.

"Mark," Hugh said. He waved him over.

"Yes, Hugh?" Mark said eagerly. But not too eagerly. But not with insufficient eagerness. But not—

"Fred here," and all three of them instantly knew that first-name usage had been a mistake and did their best to ignore the awkwardness, "Mr. Paull would like to follow someone around a bit, get a feel for How We Do Things Here." *And for God's sake, keep him isolated to one section until I can come up with something in the office to bombard him with.* "Just go over your daily routine, maybe generate some Smile-Power." A weak grin as he thumped the button pinned to Mark's purple store vest: SMILE-POWER!!!

Mark felt a rattlesnake slither over his intestines. "Sure, Hugh," he said. "Happy to help. Did you want a tour of the store, Mr. Paull, or—" But the VDPO was already off and running, and Mark had to take long strides to keep up.

"A bit" turned into "all day." Hugh and the others had splashed pig's blood on him and thrown him to the wolves. Mr. Paull wasn't just an Interrogator, or a Watcher, or a Critic. He was all three combined. *Move these bookracks a few inches back. We need to reposition the cereal shelf—you've got all the brightly-colored boxes on one end and all the earth-tone boxes on the other, there's an imbalance. Same goes for the milk; get all the 2%s together, then all the 1%s, and so on. Move these bookracks up a few inches, they're too far back now. You've got the wrong plasma-screens on display, you need the even-numbered ones playing, not the odd-numbered ones. Now, this bug-zapper here—it's not going to sell many still in the box, is it. Try to get some flies to feed to it, so people know how it operates. Talk to Custodial about that. We're going to need to talk about waxing these floors; all this constant shoving the bookracks back and forth is leaving scuff marks. Why can't we try and minimize that?*

And on. And on. And on. "Yes, sir." "You're right, sir." "I agree, sir." The rent. The cable bill. The car insurance. "That's a good idea, sir, we should've been doing that all along."

After four hours Mark's desperation had begun to taper off. Only ten minutes left until his shift ended. He did his best to dawdle and coast to the finish line, but Paull showed no sign whatsoever of losing interest.

"What next?" Mr. Paull said after their hour-long inspection for broken cookies was done.

"Well," Mark said, trying not to smile, "it's about four o'clock, so my shift's done. It's been good getting your advice and feedback on How We Do Things Here. I can take you back to Hugh's office now. Have a safe flight back!"

Or, that was what he intended to say, anyway.

What he got out was, "Well, it's about four o'clock, so my shift's done. It's—"

"So we're heading home," Mr. Paull said. "Where are we parked?"

Mark blinked.

Goldenrod.

He knew he should just put his foot down. His time was His Time.

Maybe he just wants to walk me out.

Mark wanted to smack his forehead. Of course that was it. Duh.

"I'm out in front here, near the first tree," Mark said.

"Sounds good," Mr. Paull said. "You need anything from the locker room?"

"Uh," Mark said. "Uh, n-no, no, not really, no. Did you…you know, want to see Hugh…?"

"Nope," Mr. Paull said. "After you, then."

"Okay?" Mark said.

————

"No," Mr. Paull said. He turned the radio dial away from 97.9 (classic rock) and eventually settled on—ugh—92.1 (Christian contemporary). He also took the liberty of killing the A/C, even though it was about ninety-two degrees out. "Pass this guy," he said, nodding at the Celica in front of them.

Mark passed him.

"Going kind of slow, aren't you?" Mr. Paull said. "And that rattling. Explain that."

"Just started the other day," Mark said, pressing down a little more on the accelerator. "Haven't had time to—"

"Make the time," Mr. Paull said. "Pass this car, here."

"Yes, sir."

"What's waiting for us at home?"

"I, well, I…just, just, j-just…"

"Something wrong?" Mr. Paull said. It sounded like a question, but it was more of an accusation: Why *is something wrong?*

"Just, just dinner with my girlfriend," Mark finished. "I think, um, I think tonight's lasagna…"

"Not too soft," Mr. Paull said. "The pasta has to be firm. That's key. Go easy on the ricotta, and don't be stingy on the meat."

What? You're not invited, and this is really
(Goldenrod.)
…

"Well she's probably already making it," Mark said, "and maybe you'd rather eat out, like, maybe your *hotel*, or—"

"We'll just have to make do," the VDPO said.

Abby is gonna be pissed, Mark thought, desperately hoping for a flat tire or a burst radiator. The car defied his will, however, and held together during the drive home, and Mark soon found himself standing in his kitchen with his girlfriend and his boss's boss's boss, racking his brains for an explanation to throw at Abby before she pounced.

To his relief, she forgave him with a look, even as she graciously endured Mr. Paull's cornball jokes and set a place for him at the table. When Paull excused himself to wash up she gave him a half-hearted chuckle.

"…just got in the *car* with me," Mark mumbled. Abby shushed him.

"Whaddaya gonna do?" she said, giving him a peck on the cheek. "He's a VIP, right?"

"Yeah," Mark said. "Hugh was pretty anxious about the visit. Oh, shit, I guess I should call him."

"Hey, it's okay. I'll make you suffer for this another night, I promise."

"You're aces, kid," Mark said, throwing her a lopsided grin. He snuck past the bathroom and darted into the bedroom, quickly shutting the door before Paull opened his. He vaguely heard Abby making small talk as he stabbed Hugh's office number into the phone.

"*No, that's fine*," Hugh said to his annoyance. "*Tell you what, we can even reimburse you for the cost of the groceries, if you've got a receipt. That's a nice touch, the home-cooked meal.*"

"Hugh…don't you have a problem with any of this?" Mark asked, trying to keep his temper in check.

"*No, we can petty cash this sort of thing, it's no problem at all. Just need that receipt, like I said—*"

"What? No, not the food..." *Don't blow up. Don't blow up.* "Hugh, he just *got in my car.* Is that normal? Why is he here?"

Now it was Hugh who sounded confused. *"He's...here to see How We Do Things Here. Didn't I go over this at the store?"* Mark could almost see him run a hand through his thinning gray hair. *"Just wants to follow you around, see how the routine goes...why? Has he said something about me?"*

"Uh, no, Hugh, but—"

"Because if he..." And Hugh's voice trailed off. Mark crept to the bedroom door, opened it a crack. He could see Mr. Paull, sitting grumpily at the table, waiting for his promised lasagna.

"I haven't mentioned this," Hugh said, *"to anyone at the store. But apparently there's a List going around. I haven't seen it yet myself..."*

Mark's tongue began to sweat. "Wh-what, what kind," he asked, "what kind of List?"

"It's never a good List, Mark," Hugh said bluntly. Mark knew he was right. They never sent around Lists of Presents or Surprise Parties. Either Cuts, as in staff, or Closings, as in stores.

He had a sudden stark, vivid, screaming image of twenty-nine thousand, eight hundred dollars piled high on a table in crumpled up dollar bills, doused in gasoline and set on fire.

"He might be here to decide who lives and who dies, Mark," Hugh said. *"You cannot show fear. They can smell that. You can't let him know what you know."*

"But I don't know *anything*," Mark said. He watched Paull rifle through his Lazy Susan.

"Good, go with that," Hugh said. *"Just don't act nervous, don't question anything he says. You know how the economy is right now, Mark."*

"Yeah, I know," Mark said. The panic was rising in his stomach again. "So...so do I...after dinner, I should...?" He waited for Hugh to fill in the blank.

"Yes, exactly," Hugh said, giving him no help whatsoever. Hugh seemed very nonchalant about the whole thing. Had it just been expected that he'd put the VDPO up for the night? Maybe...Mark mulled it over...maybe it was normal? Expected?

He wound down the phone call with Hugh, hung up, and went to rejoin the dinner party. He hoped he could summon at least a modicum of Smile-Power.

———

Mr. Paull's buzzsaw snoring drilled a hole through their bedroom door and kept them awake most of the night.

"Dinner went pretty well," she said.

"I sure hope so. Was he going over the recipe with you?"

"Yeah. I think he wanted to make sure I was doing it right."

"I'm really, really sorry about this, babe. I had no idea Hugh was expecting me to put him up."

"Can't they afford a hotel room for their bigshots?"

"Hugh said—" *Don't mention the List. No need to worry her.* "Uh, he said there's been some cost-cutting going around."

"So they're even making their…their what, VPs?"

"VDPOs," Mark said.

"Even they have to crash on somebody's couch?"

"Guess so."

Abby snuggled against him. "Maybe that's reassuring," she said. "Makes him just like you." *Just Like You!*

"We've Got a Friend in the Home Office," he recited.

"What?"

"Nothing, sweets. Go to sleep."

"'kay."

"He'll be gone early tomorrow."

"'kay."

————————

Mr. Paull was not, in fact, heading to the airport that day. He was heading back to the store. With Mark. By the end of the day, Mark had cleared off and disassembled every shelf, reassembled them (because "the screws needed tightening," Paull said), then carefully redistributed each shelf's load so as to maximally disperse the weight, to reduce wear and tear. "Shelves eventually collapse from stock constantly being thumped down on it, with no regard for balance," Paull had told him sagely, about three hours into their efforts. "Over time, the shelves begin to bow on one end from the cumulative effect. Taking the time to properly distribute shelf loads could add weeks to each shelf's life, saving countless dollars for the store's bottom line."

Mark hadn't even been able to mumble a "Yes, sir," to that one.

Hugh was nowhere to be seen that day. During a merciful break when Mr. Paull had stepped into the employee bathroom, Mark caught up with Nancy (Assistant Store Manager), who told him that Hugh had called out sick that day.

"Is this something that happens a lot?" Mark said, pointing his thumb at the bathroom door.

Nancy gave him a funny look. "Depends on what he eats, I'd say," she answered.

"Har har. You know what I mean. He's...he's been with me for over twenty-four hours straight now. Just came home with me last night. Is that normal?"

Nancy laughed. "What did you expect him to do, sleep in the store?"

Mark was dumbfounded. *I expected him to get a fucking hotel room, or maybe just go home instead of riding my ass for two days in a row!* He didn't think this was something that had to be said out loud. But Nancy, like Hugh, just stared at him blankly, as if he were the one being unreasonable.

(Was he?)

"Do you think he'll be here for much longer?"

"I couldn't say. I haven't actually spoken to him yet, he's been with you all day if you haven't noticed." *Oh, I noticed...* "Looks like he's a fan of your work." And she smiled at him. And Mark picked up a strange vibe from her.

She's...jealous?

Is this a good thing, Mr. Paull's constant attention? Was he, who knows...grooming him for something bigger and better? Was Hugh on his way out? Nancy's smile was ever so slightly out of sync with the rest of her face, like a glitchy digital photograph. Was this how things were handled? Some kind of weird corporate hazing?

And then Mr. Paull emerged from the bathroom and sauntered over. Nancy politely made herself scarce. "Your debit card," he said simply, not looking up from his legal pad (which by now had been thoroughly tattooed with endless notes on their activities and inspections).

"What?"

Mr. Paull swiveled his eyes upward. "Your," he said calmly, "debit. Card."

And he kept looking.

And Mark looked back.

(It seemed crazy, but the three employees in his field of view stopped what they were doing and stared at him.)

And Mr. Paull said nothing.

(So did the six shoppers in their vicinity. Carts clattered to a halt, heads turned, hands froze mid-way towards cantaloupes and bunches of grapes.)

"Is there a problem?" Mr. Paull asked.

"N-no," Mark said,

(*Go. Leave the store, now. Slap your keys down and walk out.*)

taking out his wallet,

(*You are not doing this. You are* not *fucking doing this, Mellon. Get out. Get the fuck out of here.*)

and handing the VDPO his ATM card.

Mr. Paull took it and went over to the nearest ATM.

"PIN!" he yelled from thirty feet away.

"I…" *Don't just yell it across the store, jag-off.* And he trotted over to Paull's side and said, "Five oh five eight."

The man had wanted him to just shout it out for the whole world to hear, but he had refused. He'd held his ground.

In a way.

"Here, give me your wallet," Mr. Paull said. Mark handed him the wallet. Mr. Paull stuffed withdrawn twenties into the billfold, tucked the ATM card in its slot, and put the wallet in his pocket. "Okay, let's take a look at that bathroom," he said.

Mark stood there.

At least five employees had seen that. At least five. One of them was a department head like him. None of them said anything.

Why?

(Was it just him?)

Why hadn't anyone reacted?

(Was this expected of him? Was he doing something wrong? Was his name on the List?)

Mark hustled into the bathroom, doing his best to mash the uneasy thoughts against his dinner plate until he couldn't recognize them anymore.

———————

At the end of the day, Paull followed him to his car again but stood by the driver's side. Waiting.

"I'll need the keys, young man," he said patiently.

"Right," Mark said.

He hadn't even buckled himself into the passenger's seat before Paull backed out of the parking slot and barreled his way out of the lot. He drove like a maniac, weaving in and out of the passing lane and cutting off at least three cars, earning them back a round of laudatory honks and extended middle fingers. Five minutes from home, a police cruiser peeled out of nowhere and hit its siren, and Mr. Paull cursed under his breath and pulled over to the shoulder.

"License and registration, please," the faceless officer (from Mark's position, anyway) said. Mr. Paull reached across and popped open the glove compartment, grabbed Mark's registration and insurance card, and handed it to the officer's gloved hand. And then he reached into his pocket, pulled out Mark's wallet, and handed Mark's license to him. The cop examined all three items without comment.

"Huh," Mark said.

"Do you have any points, Mr. Mellon?"

"No, sir," Fred Paull answered.

"Did you realize you were driving fifty-three in a thirty-five?"

"I'm afraid I didn't, officer," Paull said. "I was just in a hurry to get home, my girlfriend is making dinner for me and my boss here, and I must have leaned on the gas a little too heavily."

"I see," said the officer. And now he leaned in to look at both of them, and clearly, clearly at this point, he had to see that the driver's license photo was of him and not the man driving. There was just no doubt whatsoever. The game was over.

"Wait here, please," the officer said, returning to his cruiser.

They waited in silence. The officer seemed to take about seven years to return back to Mr. Paull's window. He handed Paull a ticket.

"I'm giving you a ticket for display of unclear or indistinct license plates," he said, "on account of the dealer's frame you've got around your rear plate. It's a forty-seven dollar fine, but no points. Just ease up on the gas going forward, okay?"

"Wait. Wait a second," Mark began.

"Mr. Paull," Mr. Paull said, "I appreciate what you're about to say, but the officer here is doing me a favor."

"But…"

"Really," Mr. Paull said.

Mark looked at him.

"All right," Mark said, "Mark."

Well, that was it.

Mr. Paull started the engine again and slowly pulled out. "They're not too bad around here," Mr. Paull said. "If you don't give them excuses they'll usually go easy on you."

"I see," Mark said.

He wanted to look around for the camera or microphone that had to be hidden inside the car, recording him. Recording his every reaction. Waiting for the moment when he would blow up.

He wouldn't give them the satisfaction.

The corners of his mouth twitched upwards, as if trying to smile.

"We almost home?" he said. "I'm starving."

"Almost, sir," Mr. Paull said.

"Your girl makes good lasagna," Mark said, smiling fully now. He had done it. He had crossed through and was now In On It. It was going to be all right.

"I think so, too," Mr. Paull said. He turned into Mark's development.

Abby kissed him at the door, smiled at Mr. Paull, and waved them both in. She had already set a third place at the dinner table for him. By now, Mark was suspecting that she was In On It too, and the realization was an immense relief. They had a very open and honest relationship—it was one of their strengths—and he wouldn't have been comfortable pretending or concealing something from her.

"That," Mr. Paull said afterwards, "was maybe the third best meatloaf I've ever had in my life." Mark smiled and Abby giggled.

"Oh, really? The third?" she teased. "Do you keep a meatloaf journal?"

"Of course," Mr. Paull said solemnly. He waited a second before winking, earning him some major league Smile-Power from Abby. Mark grabbed a broom and swept while Mr. Paull did the dishes.

Abby stood, staring at them. "Such liberated men I've got here," she said, kissing Mark's cheek.

"Hey," Mr. Paull said, tapping his cheek. "Don't leave me hanging here."

"Oh, of course not," Abby said, hopping over and planting one on Mr. Paull's cheek. Mark rolled his eyes theatrically as Mr. Paull slipped his arm around Abby's waist.

"Same plan for tomorrow?" he asked the VDPO.

"I only wish," the man replied. "There'll only be time for a quick stop in to confer with Hugh, and then it's off to the airport. Flight to Cincinnati leaves at five after noon." (*That's it! You've made it, Mellon, you've fucking made it! You've won the Game!*) "So it's off to bed for me."

"Moi aussi," Mark said. He was almost giddy with relief.

"You mind taking the couch?" Mr. Paull said. "I've got some lumbar issues."

"I insist," Mark said. "Let me just grab a pillow and a blanket." And he bolted to the bedroom, came out, and began to set himself up on the couch. Mr. Paull hung his suit jacket up on the coat rack near the door and retired to the bedroom.

"You're awfully chipper," Abby said, taking his hands. He loved when she did that.

"Honey," he said, "it has just been one bitch of a week." He kissed her lips, gently and longingly. "I really appreciate you being such a good sport. I mean it."

"Of course," she said, looking into his eyes. They kissed again, deeply, and he felt a fluttering in his chest. She smiled at him and pecked his cheek. "Night!" she called over her shoulder as she bounced towards their bedroom and shut the door.

(*Wait*)

Mark kicked off his shoes, shirt, pants, folding them neatly on the recliner in the corner

(*Wait, hold on a sec*)

and flopped down on the couch, laying back on the pillow. He was still too wired to sleep. Maybe there was a game on

(*Wait, hold on, think about what's hap*)

or something.

He fell asleep ten minutes later, the remote control still in his hand.

––––––––––

Someone shook his shoulder. "Sir, excuse me," he heard. "We don't want to be late." He blinked himself semi-awake. Mr. Paull—was that Mr. Paull? Yeah, it looked like him, but it was damn *early*—was standing there with a glass of orange juice in each hand. He sipped one and handed him the other.

"Be careful," Mark said, sitting up. "You don't want to spill that on your uniform."

"What? Oh," Mr. Paull said, wiping a few drops of orange juice off of his namebadge. *HI! I'm FRED*, it said, *Grocery and Pet Care*. "Thanks," he said. "Uh, Abby was up early and ironed your clothes for you, they're on a hanger in the bathroom."

"Oh, thanks," Mark said. He pushed himself up off the couch with a groan. "Getting old," he muttered. He stumbled off towards the bathroom and emerged fifteen minutes later, showered, shaved, and as presentable as he could manage.

"Ready to go?" Fred asked.

"I think so," Mr. Mellon said. Fred kissed Abby goodbye and the two of them headed out to the car.

"It was nice meeting you," Abby called to him. (*Really playing it to the hilt.*)

"You as well," Mr. Mellon said grumpily. Probably shouldn't be too friendly, right? He got into the passenger side as Fred started the car up and pulled out onto Johnson Street. Mr. Mellon found himself looking around, curiously wistful. *Weird to think that you're leaving a place you'll never see again*, he reflected to himself. He took in as much as it as he could, the Petersons' crooked red mailbox, the overturned tricycle on the Patels' front lawn. The car pulled away and they all receded from his sight. Vanishing in the rearview mirror.

They walked into the store ten minutes after opening. Mr. Mellon took note, as he always did, of how everyone stood up a little straighter and was just a little more focused on the task in front of him as he passed. Every store he visited had a touch of Potemkin village to it, which was sad, in a way. He never *really* got to know a store's employees. Not even Fred.

Fred swung his arms back and forth jauntily as they strolled down Aisle 5, towards the stairs leading to Hugh's office.

Hugh met him at the door, a stack of folders held out as an appeasement. "My apologies for taking so long on this," he said, turning his head and hacking up something wet and disgusting. He looked like hell. So his sick day yesterday had been legit after all.

Mr. Mellon took the manila folders and thumbed through them, pretending to examine their contents. "Looks good," he said.

Hugh stuck out his hand, and Mellon shook it.

(*Hugh, standing in the street, getting smaller and smaller in the rearview mirror.*)

Given the turnover at the Home Office level, that was probably a good guess. He'd probably never visit this store again. They'd rotate him to another region, or bump him over to another department. Or can him.

Mr. Mellon—Mark—felt very frightened all of the sudden.

"Fred," he said, "I…I wonder if you could walk me out."

"Sure thing," Fred said. "I'll be back in a few, Hugh."

"Safe flight," Hugh said, already closing the door on them.

They walked down the staircase, slowly.

"I don't want to go," Mark said.

Fred nodded, not entirely without sympathy.

"I'd like to stay here," Mark said. "I, I like it here. I like my job." He felt it starting to happen and he desperately tried to stop it, tried to stop the blubbering. "It's, I, I need this, I like this job, I know I talk a lot of shit but I *don't want to go*." A single tear slipped embarrassingly over his cheekbone and dripped off his face into oblivion.

"Mark," Fred said. "This is a Big Promotion. This is a Great Opportunity." Something twisted in Mark's stomach, like a kneecap popping out at the bottom of a quarterback sack. He wanted to throw up, but all he'd had that morning was orange juice. "We're looking for *REAL* Team Players here. We need you to step up."

"This isn't fair," he said, petulantly. His tone surprised him. "You're just…you're just *using* me. To get out."

Fred smiled.

Said nothing.

"I'm expecting big things from you," Fred said, clasping Mark's shoulder manfully. He was already looking a little younger, Mark—Mr. Mellon—thought. Just a little bit. And a little bit more tomorrow. He reached into his pocket. "Oh, Hugh took care of your rental, it's parked out in front." He slapped the key into Mr. Mellon's hand.

They looked into one another's eyes one final time.

Mark tried to summon some kind of resistance. Something. Anything.

Fred's eyes were ice-blue walls.

He crumpled, sinking back inside his suit. Fred gripped his hand and shook it vigorously.

"You have a good flight home, sir!" he said loudly. Mark watched himself return the handshake.

"Yes," he said, trying to think of something appropriate to say. "Yes, good luck to you, young man." He didn't have to look around to know that the employees, the shoppers, everyone, everything inside the store was looking right at him. Making sure he was on board. Making sure he was a *REAL* Team Player.

He was.

Mr. Mellon shuffled down the rest of the stairs and took that long walk down Aisle 5. Past the mouthwash and toothpaste and dental floss, the shaving cream and razor blades, the hairbrushes and nail polish. Then it was out past the girl at the register ("Goodbye, sir!"), out into the sweltering morning heat, and behind the wheel of the rental car.

Traffic was light, and he got to the airport sooner than expected.

Patrick Flanagan was born, he grew up, he has five previous writing credits (with Grand Mal Press, Library of Fantasy Press, Living Dead Press, and Sam's Dot Publishing), and, well, that brings us up to date.

Agnes: A Love Story

David C. Hayes

13

His wife, Maddy, didn't believe he was actually working late. In some sort of delusional, two-lines-of-coke-a-day, suburban housewife paranoia, she actually thought he had a lover on the side.

Him!

Jack Feinberg, partner of Feinberg, Feinberg and Johnson does not have time for an affair. Jack Feinberg doesn't have the patience to put up with another woman.

The partners of Feinberg (Jack), Feinberg (Jack's brother, Tim) and Johnson (Tim's wife, Arlene, under her maiden name) were the only employees of the firm that kept cocaine up Maddy's nose and the payments on their fashionable house under control.

The three of them graduated from University of Michigan's Law School in the mid-eighties (Jack and Arlene one-year ahead of Tim) and quickly became dissatisfied with the state of the legal profession. A few years as a corporate lawyer apiece was sufficient to, in one stellar, drunken Thanksgiving dinner in 1996, draw the three of them together to change direction. To help people.

Maddy would have disapproved, had she been awake and not passed out in a wine and drug coma.

The three quietly left their corporate jobs a year later and founded the firm. To their disappointment, the partners of Feinberg, Feinberg and Johnson quickly realized that those they intended to help, the people that truly needed it, couldn't always pay. Taking the bull by the horns, Jack founded the personal injury and bankruptcy division of the firm, solely to keep them in business. With a steady stream of deadbeat dads claiming financial hardship as they signed over checks for thousands to the firm, and elderly women who waited to enter stores until they saw some hapless stock boy mopping the floors, the firm was able to stay afloat. Everyone got a new chair, a new desk, a used photocopier, and Jack, for all his efforts, got an ulcer. As Arlene and Tim championed the people with pro bono, humanitarian work, Jack Feinberg dealt with the shadiest people he had ever encountered.

12

His marriage hadn't always been traumatic.

Maddy was, at times, a very good wife. She was pursuing an undergraduate degree in Economics when she happened to attend a party at Jack's fraternity. Maddy never finished her degree program, but it didn't seem to matter at first. She loved him, and he loved her. He became a highly paid corporate lawyer and she became his stunning, showpiece wife.

Jack believed that it was the perennial boredom that first attracted Maddy to recreational drugs. A snort here and there, in between skim lattes, went a long way to supplanting the need for a workaholic husband. She actually tried to clean up for awhile when Jack and Maddy attempted to have children. But between Jack's schedule, and Maddy's skewed ovulation patterns from the boozing and "relaxing," they weren't able to conceive. Then Jack's already limited free time was cut even further by the creation of the firm, then the need to keep it alive.

The accusations of infidelity were nothing new for Jack. Maddy had screamed philanderer for months, without even the barest of reasons.

He would leave for the office at seven every morning.

She would wake up around noon and badger Mrs. Alvarez, the poor unfortunate woman that cleaned their home, and then call Jack at the office, demanding to know where he'd spent the previous night. Never once did he arrive home drunk, smeared in lipstick or smelling like another woman's perfume, but that seemed immaterial to Maddy. If it was an attempt to draw them closer through mutual aggression, or fever dreams she had after passing out, Jack didn't know.

He worked far too hard for far too long to deal with her daily ramblings. The caller ID that he had installed at the office helped a great deal.

11

And, yet again, he found himself at the office nearing 9 p.m. Nearly Maddy's pass-out time, he noticed with a great deal of apathy.

Jack stared down at the case he was working on, the files swimming together. He leaned back in his chair and rubbed his eyes. The squidgy sound the rubbing always made never failed to sicken him a little, but it worked like a magic wake-up call. With a sigh, he gathered the documents in front of him together and headed over to the bargain photocopier. The client had requested all documentation from the case, and paying customers, even surgeons who amputate the wrong leg due to a hangover, got what they asked for.

The tiny office didn't provide for a long walk to the photocopier, but during these 10-second trips, Jack never failed to envy Tim and Arlene. While they were off stopping the gentrification of culturally historic neighborhoods or stopping the executions of innocent men, he toiled away in the basement of the legal profession. The hardest thing to cope with was that his brother and his sister-in-law were desperately in love with each other. The last seconds of the walk always brought a flash of anger that was quelled by knowing they needed him.

The ugly gray photocopier stood before him. Mottled here, speckled with toner stains there.

The day the firm had enough money to buy the ancient monolith from a closing convenience store, Tim and Jack lugged the thing into the freight elevator themselves then proudly set it up at the rear of the office.

Arlene, with a strange holdover from her childhood that required her to name everything, decided to call the copier Agnes after a nun from her Catholic high school days. "Sister Agnes was a big gray box, just like this machine," she said with a giggle. We'd all laughed. And the name stuck.

A coin deposit slot jetted from Agnes' wounded side, and the yellow, triangular *5¢ Copies* sign was still plastered on her. Jack snagged a handful of nickels from the jar next to the copier and dumped them into the coin slot. At first, he found this practice immensely annoying, but learned to enjoy the rhythmic song of the nickels as they plopped into the machine's belly. He removed the coins every Friday and put them back into the jar to start the process all over again.

As the first coins fell, the display screen lighted with a strange, pea-green color, blinking a familiar message to Jack: *Warming Up.* And with that message came the deep rumbling hum that, perversely, made Jack smile as if he was engaged in an affair. He couldn't remember the last time he'd warmed Maddy up or heard her hum like Agnes. A small laugh escaped him when he realized he was paying Agnes for her services.

Jack stroked Agnes' cover as her hum faded.

The display changed to *Ready to Copy*.

10

Jack scanned the first document to be copied and winced. It was the initial medical report about the young woman whose leg had been amputated. Her right leg slated for the chopping block due to cancer, she had the misfortune of falling under the blade of Dr. Morgan Braun, full-time alcoholic and part-time surgeon, and lost her left leg in the process.

Anger welled in Jack as he placed the document face down on the scanning plate. He slammed the cover down, getting angrier.

A flurry of thoughts:

How dare Braun call himself a doctor?

Why am I doing this? I'm fucking complicit!

What the fuck?

Jack's mind became a whirlwind of doubt, anger, and frustration. Thoughts of his do-good partners swirled through his psyche, pierced by flashes of a drunken and stoned Maddy.

They all did their part to create his horrific reality: maniacal doctors that smelled of bourbon and blood, attacks from dogs that were beaten regularly, crying children that wanted nothing more than smack free mothers who made them grilled cheese sandwiches and kissed them before bed…it went on and on like an afternoon talk show.

Jack's teeth gritted as his finger slammed the green *Start* button.

Agnes hummed, bringing a small amount of relief to Jack as she put on a light show for his benefit. She spit a copy into her tray.

Jack snatched her still warm offering, the burning scent of fresh toner invading his senses. He flipped the page over to make sure everything had copied properly.

Jack's eyes widened in disbelief. Shaking his head, he pushed the *Start* button again, and waited…and waited.

Finally, she spit out another piece of white, recycled paper.

Jack reached a trembling hand down. He lifted the paper gingerly—it felt even warmer this time—and flipped it over. He read the message on the paper over and over again.

It wasn't the medical report.

Dearest Jack, it read, *I appreciate you—Agnes.*

He smiled nervously.

09

Jack let his hand drop to his side as he stared at the machine. He gently laid the message from Agnes on her cover and rubbed his eyes again, not caring about the disgusting squidgy sound. With a sigh, he picked up the paper and read it again. Nothing had changed, no medical report, just an endearing letter from an inanimate object.

Slowly, Jack lifted the cover and picked up his original document. The medical report in all its grisly detail was unaffected.

Jack pulled the next document to be copied from a tall stack. It was a memo from the firm representing the young girl in her malpractice suit. The avatars of justice at Fariman and Capelli were demanding a cool three mill, as well as the revocation of Dr. Braun's license.

Jack slipped the page onto Agnes. The scanner's glass was still warm to the touch, and Jack felt a little electric thrill as he touched it. He laid the cover down and pushed the *Start* button again.

Hum. Light show.

Jack, his hands trembling again, picked up the new copy from the tray and slowly turned it over.

Dearest Jack, You are needed. You are a vital part of everything that happens. I appreciate you—Agnes.

Jack read the message over and over.

The short walk back to his desk was uneventful, his thoughts completely commanded by Agnes, or his own delusions. Jack looked up and back at Agnes.

She clicked loudly and began a sort of reverse hum that softened by degrees.

Jack cowered into his chair, visualizing her standing up and eating him, her scanner cover flopping up and down like a huge mouth.

She's just going into standby mode, he told himself as he slowly stood, knees shaking like yogurt. He rested his head in his hands, sweat dripping from his furrowed brow.

Without so much as a glance at Agnes, Jack snatched his suit coat from the back of his chair and headed out the door...firmly believing he had a fever from working too hard.

08

Jack walked into the house at 11:30 p.m. and flicked the television off on his way to the bedroom. The unusual events at the office took a backstage to the disrepair of his home. Strewn about the kitchen were empty liquor bottles. Shards of Maddy's mirror were scattered on the food preparation island, and a rivulet of blood ran from one of the broken shards in a weaving, stumbling line to the sink.

Serves her right, he thought with a smirk.

Jack considered cleaning up the mess, but wanted Mrs. Alvarez to adopt another reason to hate his wife. He breezed from the kitchen, prepared to sneak into bed.

 Lights blazed through a crack in the bedroom door. Jack hoped she's simply left the lights on, but the ball in the pit of his stomach told him differently.

He pushed open the door to find Maddy naked, her bloodied hand wrapped in one of his shirts. Sprawled on their bed, she groggily lifted her head from the pillow and stared at Jack as he slogged into the room. She smiled like a victorious cat, droplets of blood peppering her mouth, likely from an attempt to stem the flow of blood.

He shuddered as he removed his suit coat and loosened his tie.

"How's your hand?" he asked.

"Fuckin' fine. How's the bitch you just fucked?" Her smile grew wider.

Jack tried to bore holes in her head with an intense stare. He opened his mouth to tell her, as loudly as possible, that he didn't cheat, then he sucked in a deep breath, ready to unleash, and inexplicably changed his plan.

Calmly. "Fine, darling. She's quite a lover."

As soon as the words fell from his mouth, he wondered why he'd said them.

Maddy's eyes mimicked his, attempting, it seemed, to burn two bloody holes in his chest. She struggled up and out of the bed, wobbling. She splayed a hand on an antique chest of drawers to steady. "I knew it! Bastard! I fuckin' knew—"

Maddy's hand slipped from the dresser, and she dropped face first to the floor with a thud.

Jack walked over to Maddy's prone body.

Her ragged, gurgling breathing indicating that she wasn't dead. A pool of blood, seeping from her nose, grew.

Jack smirked, then slipped on a bathrobe and headed into the living room to fix a drink, half hoping Maddy would never wake again.

Who needed her? Not Jack Feinberg! He was the guy that held things together.

Even Agnes could see that.

07

Jack arrived at the office a little after noon. His neck was still stiff from a night on the couch. Unfortunately, Maddy was still alive.

He'd awakened at 10 to the sound of her stirring in the bedroom.

She gave no response to Jack's "Good morning, darling!" other than gurgling. *A gurgling curse*, Jack mused with a smile.

Tim and Arlene were already in the office. Both were on the phone when Jack entered. Each waved hello. Jack sat at his desk, staring at Agnes, waiting for one of them to get off of the phone. Tim was first.

"Tim? Have you had any problems with Agnes?"

"Agnes who?" Tim had never accepted the name like Arlene and Jack.

"The photocopier," Jack shot back.

Tim threw an askew glance at Jack. "Bad night with Maddy?"

"Forget her. I was wondering if you had any problems with the…photocopier." Strangely, it felt wrong not to call Agnes by her name.

"Uh, no, Jack. Not really. I mean its old, but it works pretty well."

Jack winced at the word "it."

"Why?" Tim asked.

"No reason, forget I mentioned it."

Arlene had hung up the phone in the middle of Jack and Tim's conversation and sidled up to the brothers, shaking her head. "Jack, you okay?"

Jack answered without looking at her. "Never better, just fine, thanks."

Tim and Arlene began collecting materials for court. They shared a glance, then Tim nodded in Jack's direction. Arlene shrugged.

"Jack," Tim said, "Arlene and I have to stand before a judge in twenty minutes. But if you need anything, page us, okay?"

"Don't worry, I'm fine."

"You sure?" Arlene asked.

"I'm sure."

"Fair enough. Wish us luck." Arlene said, not taking her eyes off Jack as she and Tim headed for the door.

Jack waited until he heard the click of the door.

Voices, probably talking about him, lingered for a moment before fading away.

He turned to face Agnes.

06

Jack slowly rose from his chair, grabbing a random piece of paper from his desk.

The walk to Agnes was oddly joyful.

He was alone with her, with Agnes.

She appreciated him.

She knew how important he was.

He was the fucking guy who held things together.

Jack grabbed a handful of nickels and began dropping them into Agnes' slot.

He took his time, caressing her coin slot each time he fed a new nickel into her.

Warming Up…

The deep, rumbling hum. Seductive. Wanton.

Jack lovingly gazed down, eager for her invitation to proceed.

Ready to copy…

An electric thrill ran up his spine as he grabbed the handle of her cover and lifted it high. He slid the document onto her glass, then slowly, lovingly, closed the cover, and ran a gentle, reassuring hand over her hood. His finger hovered over the *Start* button for just a moment. Then he plunged his finger down hard.

Agnes' hum reached a fever pitch. The light show spilled into the room, and her internal paper feeder churned and grinded.

A page spilled into her tray.

Jack leaned over, picked it up. The warmest page he'd ever touched.

Dearest Jack, I am the one for you. There must be no more thoughts of Maddy. There must be no more Maddy. I appreciate you—Agnes.

He was horrified by the implication of the message.

Jack slid his back down the side of Agnes and slumped into a sitting position on the floor. He held the message in front of him, staring at it, contemplating his next move.

Jack rested his head against Agnes' 11x17 compartment, feeling her click and hum into *Standby*. He held his cheek against her body, comforted by little vibrations that lulled him to sleep. Smiling, he closed his eyes…

…and dreamt about Agnes…

…and the proper disposal of an insolent wife.

05

As Jack maneuvered the Volvo into the driveway he sincerely hoped Maddy had done the deed herself.

Too much gin and a drunken plunge into the corner of the coffee table. Clean and tidy.

But all too easy.

He laughed. Maddy never did anything for him that didn't also benefit her. And this wouldn't be an exception. With his luck, she probably checked into rehab today.

Jack became nauseas when the stale stench of cigarette smoke slammed into him like a freight train. He peered into the hazy room and filled with hope when he saw the glass coffee table shattered. A trail of carnage—toppled furniture, Jack's clothes strewn about, and a collection of empty wine bottles—led to the bedroom. Jack followed the path of detritus, then opened the bedroom door.

Maddy lay face down on the bed, naked as usual and snoring like a diesel engine.

Jack slid into the room, taking off his suit coat and letting it drop to the floor. He lifted the large porcelain lamp off the nightstand and leaned his mouth to Maddy's ear.

"Maddy," he hissed.

She continued snoring loudly.

"Wake up, Maddy," he shouted.

Maddy grunted and rolled onto her back. A line of blood and snot ran from her right nostril to her upper lip. Maddy opened her mouth to take in a large gulp of air, and a glob of blood-snot fell into her mouth.

Jack stifled a giggle and bent to her ear again.

"Wake the fuck up, Maddy. Agnes says hello."

Maddy grunted as her eyes cracked and fluttered.

Jack straightened above her, raising the lamp over his head. He stared down at Maddy, waiting for her eyes to completely open.

"Don't fire 'til you see the whites of their eyes," Jack mumbled.

Maddy's eyes fluttered again.

Remembering his father's instructions on wood chopping, Jack spread his legs further apart.

"S'what the fu…?" Maddy managed, her eyes now wide. She attempted a weak grin but her mouth contorted into an expression of revulsion. She brought a hand up to wipe her lips and—

Jack slammed the wide base of the lamp into her forehead, then backed up and prepared for another swing.

Maddy turned a cloudy gaze on him, life fading fast from her eyes.

Jack let the lamp drop to his side as he stared at his work.

She burped a bloody bubble that quivered on her lips. The bubble popped in a spray of red mist, and her eyes rolled back in her head.

Jack studied the incredible dent above her brow as blood trickled from the corner of her mouth.

He brought his shaking index finger to the soup bowl that was formerly his wife's head and touched the interior of the crater, feeling the cracked skull beneath rapidly bruising flesh.

Exhausted, he lay down next to the corpse.

He fell asleep quickly, thankful that Maddy couldn't snore the night away.

04

Jack woke up at 10 a.m., having slept late two days in a row. It was unlike him. Maybe Tim and Arlene would think he had a life outside the office. Or maybe they'd worry about him. He hoped not. He'd never felt better. Certainly he was better than Maddy.

He showered and dressed slowly, taking his time for the first time in years. He made a pot of coffee and sat at the breakfast nook, sipping as he read the morning paper. His home was quiet, and he intended to relish every beautiful moment.

No torturous hangover tantrums. No screeching questions. Nothing.

At 11:30, he decided to go into the office. He made a quick stop in the bedroom and gave his wife a kiss goodbye for the first time in years.

03

Jack walked into the office, beaming. Arlene was out, at court no doubt, but he could hear Tim puttering around. Jack flopped his briefcase onto his desk and walked back toward the front door, shucking off his coat.

"Jack, that you?" Tim called out from the rear of the office.

"Yeah, any news that's fit to print?" Jack hoped Tim would recognize his good mood. Tim probably hadn't seen him smile since they were kids.

Jack flung his coat at the first available hook. It dropped to the floor and he left it with a smile. Nothing could bother him today, nothing. He made his way toward Tim's voice.

"Dr. Braun has been calling every ten minutes, says he didn't get any of the documents you promised him?"

Jack was about to tell Tim that Braun was a drunk, disfiguring bastard. But as he turned the corner, everything he wanted to say stuck in the back of his throat. He fell against the wall, his mouth wide in shock.

02

Tim was crouched in front of Agnes, his hand deep inside her, rooting around. Jack heard the scraping of nickels as Tim fished another handful and dropped them in the jar at his feet. As soon as his hand was empty, Tim plunged into Agnes again, scraping the bottom of her bin, grabbing every nickel he could scrounge.

Jack felt himself moving in slow motion. He stood, continuing to stare down at his brother...*his brother!* His own flesh and blood, elbow deep inside of Agnes, violating her like a drunken surgeon might.

His Agnes!

Jack's vision washed out in reds and pinks and he felt himself moving closer to his brother. He bent over and lifted the nickel jar by the brim.

"Hey," Tim said, not bothering to look up, "you want to put that back? I haven't finished cleaning the machine out."

Jack bristled as Tim's arm shot in and out of Agnes. The bastard thought she was only a machine. Just a "machine."

Jack felt the nickel jar swing back, then sweep at his brother's head.

Tim turned as the jar hurtled at him. And his playful brother-banter look vanished in a flash.

The jar connected with a thud, like the lamp the evening before. Tim fell backward, his nose mashed into his head. A fine spray of blood arched upward as Tim's body thudded against the floor, his lips drawing back into a sneer that showed off a row of broken teeth. His eyes were frozen wide, staring at the ceiling or some ethereal world unseen by Jack's eyes.

Jack placed the bloodied jar in its proper spot on top of Agnes, then stroked her cover reassuringly.

01

When Jack removed Tim's arm from Agnes' bin and closed her door, she began to hum.

He smiled.

Even with all of Tim's prodding and thrusting, Agnes responded to him alone. He grabbed a few nickels from the jar and slipped one, then another, then another slowly into her slot. He pressed himself against Agnes and felt her warm vibrations pour into his body.

Jack kicked Tim aside, making a little more room in the cramped copier area, then lifted Agnes' cover slowly. He laid his head on her glass and felt the change in her hum that told him she was ready to copy.

Agnes no longer needed to spell out her needs. The two of them existed in perfect synchronicity. Jack moved his hand along a row of her buttons. Careful not to push, not yet, he gave each button the briefest caress.

Jack sighed as he pressed the *Start* button.

Heat spread across his face; her light show never brighter. He pressed *Start* again and again, each time a new sensation, a new pleasure.

No Maddy.

No backstabbing brother.

And soon, no sister-in-law.

Only Agnes.

OO

Job finished.

Ready to copy.

David C. Hayes is a genre actor/writer/producer/director. Most recently he has starred in *A Man Called Nereus*, *Machined*, *Reborn*, *Orville*, *Sportkill*, *Jackrabbit Sky*, *The Death Factory Bloodletting*, and *Dark Places*. He produced and appeared in the films *Predatory Instinct*, *Blood Moon Rising*, and *The Frankenstein Syndrome*. David has written multiple feature films, including *Closets*, *Blood Guardian*, *Back Woods*, *Vampegeddon*, *Riverdead*, and *Shower of Blood*. He has also written several comic books/graphic novels, including *Rottentail*, and *Tranquillity*, and is the author of *Muddled Mind: The Complete Works of Ed Wood, Jr.* His feature film screenplay, *Executive Privilege*, was a finalist in the 2010 Bridge International Screenplay Competition, and his stageplay, *Swamp Ho*, was a finalist in the International Cringefest. He teaches screenwriting, film production, acting, and rhetoric.

Work/Life Balance

Jeff Strand

On my nineteenth anniversary with the company, Mr. Swanson called everybody into meeting room 4D. He seemed to be in a cheerful mood, so I didn't think this was a "Guess what? You're all *fired!*" kind of meeting. In fact, I suspected that he might be summoning us in there for cake, even though nineteen wasn't exactly a monumental anniversary.

The dozen of us sat around the mahogany table in our suits and ties (dresses for the ladies) and waited expectantly. I didn't see a cake, which made me mildly sad.

Mr. Swanson smiled. "Don't worry, this is going to be quick because I know you're all busy. I just wanted to let you know that from now on, you have the choice of taking the usual one-hour lunch, or you can take a forty-five minute lunch, in which case you can leave fifteen minutes early."

A murmur of pleasant surprise went around the table. I never really needed the full hour anyway, and leaving fifteen minutes early would help me miss some of the traffic. As much as I enjoyed corporate-sponsored cake, I enjoyed receiving this news even more.

"I could have just sent this as an email, but I thought it would be nice to bring everybody together. This is part of our new commitment to employee work/life balance. If you could all be so kind as to send me a note saying whether you've selected the one-hour option or the forty-five minute option, I'll mark it on the sign-in sheet."

We all left the meeting quite pleased. Even my five co-workers who were going to stick with the hour-long lunch plan and whose lives were thus unchanged were happy to at least be given the option.

A week passed, and the new lunch length worked out quite well, saving me nearly seven minutes in traffic each evening. But when Mr. Swanson called another impromptu meeting, my first reaction (after "Oh no! We're all going to get fired!") was that maybe the new plan hadn't worked out so well, and he was about to rescind it. My precious seven minutes were about to be taken away from me, and we'd only just met.

"Good news," said Mr. Swanson. "We're instituting a new policy of Business Casual Fridays. That means that on Fridays, suits and ties are no longer required. You may wear a much more casual shirt; for example, a polo shirt would be completely acceptable. No tee shirts and nothing with logos or phrases on it, unless it's our own, but feel free to dress down a bit on Fridays. You've all earned it."

Gerald raised his hand.

"Yes, Gerald?"

"But today is Friday."

"Obviously this new policy takes effect next week."

"Oh. Good. Thank you."

Well, to say that I was excited was an understatement; to say that I was very excited would be much more accurate. Business Casual Fridays! I'd heard that such a thing existed at other companies, but I'd never imagined that it would make its way into my own workplace!

The following Friday, I came to work in a tasteful but slightly playful sweater, and though I can't honestly say that it was the best day of my life, it was a definite improvement over wearing an itchy, strangling tie.

And then, three business days later, we got an email with the most shocking development yet: *flexible starting times*.

The amount of time we were to work each day had not shortened or lengthened. It was still eight hours, plus the forty-five or sixty-minute lunch. But now we could start *any time we wanted* between the hours of seven o'clock and nine o'clock.

For example, if I chose to arrive at seven, I would then proceed to work until three forty-five. Somebody who chose to arrive at nine would work until five forty-five, unless they'd previously selected the hour-long lunch option, in which case they would work until six. But I could start at seven-thirty, eight-fifteen, eight-thirty...the options were limitless! Well, perhaps not limitless, but they certainly made *my* mind boggle!

Though I ended up sticking with the eight o'clock arrival time I'd had for the past nineteen years, I truly appreciated this new flexibility.

And over the next few weeks it was as if a floodgate of freedom opened for us. Business Casual Fridays turned into Business Casual Mondays and Fridays, and then, on one amazing day, it became an *every single day of the week* change. No more suits! No more ties! (Unless, of course, you had to meet with an important client, but that was understandable.)

In another meeting, we all gaped at Mr. Swanson in slack-jawed astonishment as he described the new procedure for a compressed workweek, where we could work ten hours a day, four days a week. And we could pick the flex day! Monday! Tuesday! Wednesday! Thursday! Or, yes, even Friday! Yes, there were restrictions (after all, you couldn't have the entire department gone every Friday) but I still felt myself tearing up and almost had to ask to be excused from the meeting.

I picked Wednesdays. Wednesdays were now my favorite day of the week. Tuesdays now carried the excitement of a Friday. Admittedly, Thursdays now had something of a Monday feel, but it was worth it.

We all chattered excitedly in the break room each morning, wondering what might be next.

Casual Fridays! We could now wear *jeans*. At *work*. Not jeans with tears or smudges or rhinestones, but still...*jeans!* The comfort was almost unimaginable. And tee shirts! We could wear tee shirts! Again, they had to be in excellent condition and could not contain text or images inappropriate for a professional environment. As an example of a shirt that would not be acceptable, we were shown a photograph of somebody wearing a Hooters shirt. (Not the uniform worn by waitresses, but rather a gentleman wearing a shirt advertising the restaurant.)

Their commitment to our work/life balance didn't end there. Exactly six months after we were given flexibility in our lunch lengths, Mr. Swanson announced the new work-from-home program, where once a week we would be allowed to do our job from the comforts of our own home! On many occasions, my co-workers and I had discussed how so much of our jobs involved sitting in front of our computers, and how we could basically do it anywhere, but we never imagined that this option would actually be presented to us!

There was, of course, no dress code at home, and I gleefully completed my first day in pajamas. I did, of course, complete all of the same cleansing and hygiene activities that I would have done if I'd gone into the office. Working from home didn't mean I needed to become a savage.

I have to admit, I started to wonder if things had gone too far when every day became Casual Day. Shouldn't we dress in professional attire at least once a week?

Some of my co-workers began to abuse the freedom. On occasion Gerald would show up as late as nine-fifteen or nine-twenty. Yes, he'd stay later to compensate, but still, with two hours of flexibility surrounding our start time, why did he need to push it further?

Mr. Swanson sent out an email, explaining that these changes were privileges, not rights, and that it would be in our best interest to follow the rules. Gerald did not show up late anymore.

On the day of my twentieth anniversary, Mr. Swanson called us all into the meeting room. I smiled. Twenty years with the company meant cake for sure, along with a fancy certificate, and Mr. Swanson would read a very nice note that had been signed by the CEO.

But there was no cake in the room. Mr. Swanson smiled as we took our seats. "Aside from a few small instances, these changes have worked out extremely well, don't you all agree?"

We all nodded our agreement.

"So, effective today, public displays of affection will be permissible."

Everybody glanced around at each other, unsure if he was kidding or not.

"Obviously, I'm not talking about insertion, but kissing and groping, as long as the work gets done, is perfectly fine. Remain conscious of the dress code, but if you wish to simulate certain acts, by all means go ahead and do so."

Everybody was silent for a moment.

Helena, who was sixty and an unofficial mother figure to us all, raised her hand. "Is this a joke?"

"It is not. You've all proven that you're mature enough to be given additional freedom and still perform your job duties, so this is the next step in the work/life balance."

"I'm sorry, but this is a part of my life I'd like to keep at home."

"I think you're misunderstanding," said Mr. Swanson. "I didn't say that this was *mandatory* public display of affection. Rest assured that I would never demand that you dry-hump a co-worker. Goodness, no. I'm saying that if you felt the desire, and both parties consented to the act—or even three or four parties; we're not judgmental of lifestyle choices here—it would be okay. Stress relief is very important to the work/life balance. But of course nobody will ever ask you to cheat on your husband. I promise you that."

"Oh. Okay. Still..."

"This is just in the testing phase. We'll try it for a week or two and see what happens."

"It's not something I ever want to see."

Mr. Swanson frowned. "If you all object to progress, it won't be a problem to return to our old methods. I was perfectly fine with the eight-to-five workday in the office and the hour lunch. I was simply trying to make things more pleasant for my employees."

"No, no, I appreciate that," said Helena. "I apologize. I agree that we should test out this new policy for a couple of weeks to see if it works."

"Excellent. And now, somebody in this room has a very special anniversary!" said Mr. Swanson, winking at me as his administrative assistant brought in a tray full of cupcakes.

The next two weeks were uneventful. Despite the new freedom, very little happened. At one point my two youngest co-workers, Charles and Lori, made out in the break room while I was getting a cup of coffee, but they quickly became uncomfortable and stopped.

I saw no groping of any sort, though it's possible that some happened while I was working from home.

The next meeting was on a Monday, and those of us who worked from home on Mondays were told that we had to switch our scheduled work-from-home day that week. That wasn't an issue. We'd been told when the program began that there would be instances where this might happen, and it was perfectly reasonable to expect to have meetings where everybody in the department was in attendance.

As we walked into the meeting room, there was a long hunting knife on the table in front of each one of the chairs. We took our seats and said nothing, though of course everybody looked at the knives.

"Nobody abused the public displays of affection policy," said Mr. Swanson. "I'll be honest, I thought for certain that I would have to reprimand somebody for penetration, but it didn't happen, and I think we're all happier with the policy in place. And I'm pleased to inform you all that violence is now acceptable."

Everybody was silent as Mr. Swanson picked up one of the knives and stabbed at the air. "I shouldn't even have to say this, but of course any fatal wounding is *completely* forbidden and will result in immediate disciplinary actions, up to and including termination of employment. If you're going to stab, stab an appendage, such as an arm, and not a torso. Let's not let this get out of hand. A rule of thumb is to ask yourself 'Can my co-worker continue to perform his or her job duties?' If the answer is 'no,' then stop stabbing. Any questions?"

Helena raised her hand.

"Helena?"

"Can we opt out?"

"Of being a stabber or stabbee?"

"Both."

"Well, nobody is going to *make* you stab anyone. That's simply not the way things operate around here. But, naturally, with this new policy some people are going to get stabbed who don't want to be. Nobody is going to *voluntarily* get stabbed, right? That doesn't make any sense."

"I want to opt out."

"Sorry. If you opted out, then everybody would opt out, and then we'd have a new policy with nobody participating. It was extremely difficult to get this approved by Human Resources, and they don't like to think that they're wasting their time. Just give it a try for two weeks."

We left the meeting, taking our knives.

"Ow!" screamed Gerald, as Charles slashed him in the back. "You can't do it when I'm not looking!"

"Mr. Swanson didn't say anything about that."

I had to admit, seeing Gerald get slashed like that did improve my morale, and everybody was in a cheerful mood for the rest of the day.

The next day, Gerald stabbed me in the arm. It hurt, and I wished he hadn't done it, but I saw the joy it brought to my co-workers and realized that sometimes the happiness of one person is not as important as the happiness of the group.

And then there was an incident. Charles and Lori had a spat, and she stabbed him thirty-two times using three separate knives. He was taken to the hospital, but it was only a token measure, because he was quite clearly dead when the ambulance arrived.

We were called into the meeting room. This time Mr. Swanson was not smiling.

"I'm very disappointed," he said. "Particularly in you, Lori. There always has to be somebody who ruins it for everybody else, doesn't there?"

Lori wiped some blood from her cheek and looked deeply ashamed.

"Clearly you can not be trusted with this much freedom, and so, effective immediately, we are returning to the old ways. I apologize, but the responsibility rested with you."

And now we work eight-to-five every day, in the office, in our suits and ties. Everybody is a little sad. You can sense it in their expressions, their eyes, and the way people suddenly burst into tears for no reason.

I feel almost chained to my desk, like a prisoner.

We had so much, almost too much, and now it's gone.

Though, admittedly, I get a lot more work done now.

Jeff Strand is the author of a bunch of novels, including *Pressure*, *Dweller*, and *Graverobbers Wanted (No Experience Necessary)*. He is amused by authors who quit their day jobs to write full time and then pretend that they've never worked harder in their life. Uh-huh. Right. You can visit his Gleefully Macabre website at www.jeffstrand.com.

Monday Shutdown

Vince A. Liaguno

The mind slips as the nameless company drones surrounding me
click across keyboards in a staccato rhythm of terrifying efficiency.
Their faces are rendered featureless by too much artificial
    fluorescence,
corporate versions of children of the damned.

We sit centered between the razor-sharp outlines of cubicle cages,
tethered to the technology like one of Gacy's crawlspace boys.
Wires and cords and plugs wrap around our ankles like groping,
    grabbing zombie hands
trying to pull us down into the corporate graves dug by our own
    digits each day.

I'm color-blinded by all the black and white but mostly gray,
grateful for the occasional spray of red across the pavement down
    below our glass tower.
Another manic Monday rises from the beauty of the weekend
like a fire-spewing Godzilla looms over a shoebox-version of
    Tokyo.

I'm slowly being choked by the colorless, odorless air shooting
    through slatted vents,
the noxious remnants of the synthesized souls of a thousand
    terminated employees.
I can feel their presence everywhere, spectral spatters of the
    unemployed that
haunt and taunt and flaunt their disembodied potential all around
    me.

There is much to fear in this bland corporate land,
from the iron fist of the supervisor to the iron lung of the office
    itself.
Even paper shredders and thumbtacks have taken on an ominous

countenance
in the wake of that unfortunate business with the garbage
    compactor and the intern.

Occupational hazards abound in surreptitious forms all around us.
From the dangers of toxic gossip to the terrors of office politics,
the slithering supervisors watch and wait for our fuck-ups and
    fumbles.
Like werewolves in tailored suits and Armani neckties, they hunger
    to pounce on their prey.

My officeland is but one strain of the corporate American disease,
an amalgamated outbreak of greed and ambition,
like bird flu and leprosy thrown into a blender and served over ice
in matching sterilized mugs emblazoned with the company logo.

So monstrous is this disease of mad mercantilism that hushed
    whispers
of "Don't drink the Kool-Aid" waft over and above the burping
    water cooler.
I've seen the aftereffects of Kool-Aid consumption;
the ugly transmogrification from automaton to robot wrangler.

Staple-sort-file, stack-collate-pile,
these are the monotonous rhythms and repetitions of our shift
    work sentences.
Shackled by this snarling corporate beast by the necessity of living,
my fellow droids and I survive to subsist on meager stipends doled
    out like crumbs to ravenous gulls.

Monday begins the cycle that never seems to end.
I'm drifting deeper, deeper into stupor from the strain of stress and
    the stress of strain.
I fear this land and its shuffling occupants, minds and hearts
    hollowed out and empty
like the insides of pumpkins at Halloween.

My head dips and there are introductions: Chin, meet chest. Chest,
    chin.
My eyes blink like lazy camera shutters, half-heartedly committing

the images of officeland
to some floating piece of reluctant memory chip in the nether
    regions of my mind.
My eyelids flutter, then flicker out like the lights of a fog-
    enshrouded Antonio Bay.

I'm lost to the abyss of the Monday shutdown, spiraling into a
    stream of unconsciousness
where the horrors of officeland are muted and filtered through a
    heavy gauze
of self-preservation and delusion and fairytale clichés that evoke
    blissful hallucination.
Behind my mind's eye, I'm emancipated from this corporate
    murder set piece.

Deep within the Monday shutdown, I'm Laurie Strode with a
    knitting needle;
I'm Alice with a machete to swing. I'm every final girl rolled into
    one,
with lung capacity to spare and lucky four-leaf clovers and an
    arsenal of chainsaws
to castrate the faceless slasher of my officeland nightmares.

But like Laurie in the bedroom doorway and Alice in the canoe, the
    work week jumps up
for one more popcorn-in-the-air surprise. And like Nancy in her
    dream state,
my officeland Freddy finds his way into my Monday shutdown,
with a glove full of cold corporate blades to cut out my heart and
    slice at my soul.

I'm a defeated dream warrior now, with veins sliced out of weary
    arms like strips of bacon
that my corporate master uses to jerk me around like a puppet on
    strings.
Even in the repose of the Monday shutdown, there is no escape
    from this cruel life sentence.
Through vacant eyes, I cling to the hope that it's five o'clock
    somewhere and pray for Tuesday.

Vince Liaguno is the Bram Stoker Award-winning editor of *Unspeakable Horror: From the Shadows of the Closet* (Dark Scribe Press 2008), an anthology of queer horror fiction, which he co-edited with Chad Helder. His debut novel, 2006's *The Literary Six*, was a tribute to the slasher films of the '80s and won an Independent Publisher Award (IPPY) for Horror and was named a finalist in *ForeWord* Magazine's Book of the Year Awards in the Gay/Lesbian Fiction category. His latest editing effort, *Butcher Knives & Body Counts* (Dark Scribe Press, 2011), is a collection of essays on the formula, frights, and fun of the slasher film.

He currently divides his time between Manhattan and the eastern end of Long Island, New York. He is a member of the Horror Writers Association (HWA) and the National Book Critics Circle (NBCC).

Author Website: www.VinceLiaguno.com

Accountable

David Greske

Etched in the smoky glass of Allied Brokerage—a goliath of shining steel and polished granite—was the motto *We Never Make Mistakes…Ever.* The statement was carved into the marble floor of the lobby, painted in bold, gothic lettering across the walls; it was even on the bathroom stall doors where anyone doing their business couldn't help but see it.

Carter Beck, an immaculately dressed man of thirty-six with ocean-green eyes that made the women swoon and the men jealous, pushed open the weighty door and walked across the lobby toward the elevators.

"Good morning, Charlie," he said to the guard.

Charlie gave a monosyllabic grunt and didn't bother to look up from his paper to acknowledge the greeting.

The guard's chilly reception surprised Carter. Charlie was always in a good mood, sometimes annoyingly so. "Have a great day, Charlie. We'll see you later."

"Hope so," Charlie replied.

Carter rode the elevator with two guys from Compliance. Although he thought Hank and Brent were boneheads, they always tried to include him in their conversations. This morning they stopped talking and stared at the floor, averting eye contact with Carter when he entered the cab. They even seemed to move away from Carter as digital numbers ascended.

Electronic security kept the doors to the work area locked, and magnetic keycards were needed to enter the premises. Carter set down his briefcase, fished the ID badge out of the side pocket, and touched it to the plate next to the door. He waited for the flashing light to turn green. It didn't.

"Huh," he said, furrowing his face into a mask of confusion.

He touched the ID card to the plate again. Still the door wouldn't unlock.

The elevator pinged behind him and the doors slid open.

"Hey, Ken," Carter said, waggling his ID, "can you key me in?"

"You know we're not supposed to do that," Ken pointed to the etching on the glass. *PIGGYBACKING IS A MISTAKE. REMEMBER: WE NEVER MAKE MISTAKES...EVER!*

"Come on, Ken. Everybody does it. I saw someone let you in last week. Don't make me go to Property Management just to get a temporary card."

"That's a risk I'm not willing to take."

"You've got to be kidding?"

Ken shrugged, stepped in front of Carter and placed his badge on the square plate. The door clicked open and Ken glided into the office.

Just before the door closed, Carter stuck his foot in the jamb. A jolt of pain radiated through his ankle causing him to wince as he staggered into the office. "That's the third time in the two weeks my card hasn't worked. You think they're trying to tell me something?"

No one looked up from their work to reply.

Carter shook of the pain and made his way through a conglomeration of cubicles like a bee weaving across honeycomb, saying "good morning" to those he passed. He slid behind his desk, turned on his computer, and realized not a single co-worker had returned his greeting. Even Paul, his cube-mate for the past five years, kept his head down.

Carter leaned forward and whispered, "Paul, what's going on? It's like a morgue in here and everyone's acting weird."

Paul peered up from his work, glanced over his shoulder, and whispered back, "The boss got a call from a client last night. A mistake was made."

Carter's eyes widened as the Company's motto slammed into the front of his brain. *We Never Make Mistakes...Ever!* "A mistake? Who made it?"

Paul was about to answer when Carter's phone rang. The sudden, shrill chirp made everyone jump, and, although it seemed impossible, the room grew even quieter. Carter looked at the name flashing on the LED screen just above the dial pad. It was the boss.

"Thank you for calling Allied. My name's Carter. How may I help you today?"

"Beck. My office. Now." The line went dead.

Carter hung up, swallowed hard. "The boss wants to see me."

"Good luck," Paul replied.

Carter pushed himself away from his desk, stood, and meandered to the boss's office. He felt the stares of co-workers as he slowly moved, heard their whispers and even a couple of nervous laughs. He took a deep breath, said a quick prayer, and, opening the door, stepped into the chief's domain.

The office was a square space with a large window facing the east. Blinds were drawn to block out the morning sun. Consequently, a pattern of dark shadows cut across the room, making it look like a secret chamber from an old black and white horror movie. The single potted plant in the corner was in dire need of water and transplanting, its large variegated leaves drooping to the floor. A guest chair stood next to the dying plant, but the ratty and lumpy cushion needed replacing.

Jeffery Hansen, the boss, sat behind a gigantic oak desk. Exotic, erotic, and mysterious designs and symbols carved into the wood appeared to move and sway in the dimly lit office. A plate of green-tinted glass covered the desk's top. A black phone sat on one corner of the desk; an ancient adding machine on the other; and a computer monitor in the center. When Carter entered the room, the boss pushed himself away from the desk and stood, and Carter swore he heard the chair give a sigh of relief as three hundred pounds were lifted from its springs.

"How long have you been with us now, Beck?" Hansen asked. He was an egg-shaped man with eyebrows resembling a pair of wooly caterpillars above a pair of rat-like eyes. Except for a crown of wiry gray hair, his head looked like a cue ball that had spent too much time in the sun. Jowls hung from his cheeks like raw steaks and they shook every time he moved or spoke. A bulbous nose sat above his pencil-line of a mouth.

"Five years," Carter mumbled.

Hansen leaned forward, cupping a hand around his ear. "Speak up, boy. I can barely hear you."

"Five years," Carter snapped.

"Ah, five years. And in those five years what was the most important thing you learned?"

"That we don't make mistakes. Ever. Sir."

"Very good, Beck. *Very good.*" Hansen applauded in a condescending manner. "When you first started here I thought you weren't trainable. My bad."

"Thank you, sir…I think."

Hansen stared at Carter as he ran his sausage fingers through his crown of fibrous hair. "Tsk…tsk…tsk."

Sweat formed on Carter's upper lip and forehead. He headed for the guest chair, needing to sit before he fell over.

"Who gave you permission to sit, Beck? I want you here, standing in front of me so I can see you for what you are, a real piece of…work."

Hansen opened a desk drawer and took out a bright red folder. He slapped it on the desk and spun it around so Carter could read the heading: *Performance Issues—Carter Beck.* After giving Carter a moment to digest the heading, Hansen spun the folder again, opened it, and removed a single sheet of yellow paper.

Carter recognized the form immediately. The Company used it to log complaints.

"I received a phone call from a client just after you left last night, Beck." Hansen raised the document above his head and shook it. "According to the information I have here you were the one who assisted her. But what you told her was wrong. Needless to say she was *not* happy, and if a client isn't happy they may seek services elsewhere. If they go somewhere else they take their money with them. If they do that we lose revenue. And that makes me unhappy. So, Beck, tell me again, what is our motto?"

"We never make mistakes. Ever."

"Yet, you made one."

"I thought my advice was sound," Carter said.

The boss stared at Carter a heartbeat longer than necessary then sighed, "I imagine you did." He put the complaint form back in the folder and took out a multi-page document. A staple in the upper left corner secured the pages. Hansen jabbed the document at Carter. "Do you know what this is, Beck?"

"Looks like a contract."

"That's exactly what it is. This is the contract you signed with Allied Brokerage five years ago. Do you remember what it says?"

Carter shook his head. "No, sir, I'm afraid I don't."

"Well, let me refresh your memory." Hansen flipped to page seven of the contract and read: "'Any employee who knowingly or unknowingly provides incorrect advice, suggestions, or answers in any form to The Company's internal or external clients and/or partners shall be subject to immediate termination. There are no exceptions to this rule.'" He looked up from the document and gave Carter a snaky smirk. "Ring any bells?"

"I'm sorry," Carter said.

"I imagine you are." Hansen dropped the contract on the desk, reached in the drawer again, pulled out a loaded Beretta M9 and pointed it at Carter.

Carter's eyes grew wide. He stepped back until he felt the door behind him. Reaching behind him he found the knob, gave it a turn. The door refused to open.

"I'd like to take a moment and thank you for giving the last five years of your life to Allied Brokerage," Hansen said. "Your contributions to the Company have been duly noted in your personnel file—though I hardly think you'll be applying for any other jobs. Unfortunately, it is with great regret—well, not really— that your services are no longer needed. I have no other choice than to terminate your relationship with Allied Brokerage—"

"Please, Mr. Hansen, give me another chance. It won't happen again."

Hansen took aim.

Carter Beck closed his eyes and took a deep breath.

Click.

No blast. No searing pain.

His eyes shot open and he saw the boss struggling with the jammed firearm. If any chance of escape existed he needed to act now.

Spinning on his heels, Carter grabbed the knob with both hands and threw his shoulder against the door.

The door swung wide. Off balance, Carter nearly fell.

A quick glance around the office—employees sitting stoically at their desks, keying information, taking client phone calls, chatting amongst themselves.

Business as usual.

Carter, juiced on adrenaline and fear, scurried between cubicles like a rat in an experiment.

Elevator doors loomed.

Escape!

Carter's breathing grew fast and ragged.

Jabbing his finger into the call button, Carter turned.

Hansen's fat form stood in the doorway of his office, a corpulent finger pointed at Carter. "Get him!"

Heads swiveled in unison, eyes staring daggers at Carter.

Employees rose from their seats.

Ding!

Elevator doors whooshing open, Carter sped into the waiting car.

His rapid-fire finger working the Lobby button, Carter watched a throng of co-workers approach. A sea of eyes blazed with purpose. A new directive.

"Go back to work," Carter pleaded.

Then he noticed their hands, clutching desktop items. Staplers. Pencil sharpeners. Letter openers.

Just as the group reached him, elevator doors clanked shut.

Trying to fix the Beretta, Hansen dropped into his chair, rivulets of sweat trickling down his fat face.

This wasn't good. Not good at all.

From the depths of his mind a voice spoke:

What about Carter Beck?

"It's fine. All under control." Hansen turned the pistol over in his hands and popped out the clip.

The voice chuckled. *You've sent your staff to take care of your business? Are you . . . crazy? What about productivity?*

"Don't worry. I'll work them harder this afternoon." Hansen snatched a handkerchief from his pocket with a trembling hand and mopped his brow.

Smells like overtime pay to me. Unacceptable.

"I'll make it work. I always make it work!" Hansen looked in the gun's chamber—clear and clean.

Do you remember the Company motto?

Hansen nodded.

We might overlook one mistake, but—

"I'll make it right, I promise," Hansen pleaded.

Of course you will. You've always been a company man.

Carter felt like Frankenstein's monster pursued by angry villagers—pitchforks and torches replaced by office equipment.

Holding a hand up to an approaching car, he dashed across the street.

Animal cries vibrated from the approaching horde, hooting like wild animals.

A few yards separating Carter from his Prius, he reached into his trouser pocket, yanked out his keys, and pointed the fob at the vehicle.

Click. Click.

Reaching for the door handle, he could almost taste freedom. He'd make a few well placed phone calls to the *New York Times*, *The Washington Post*, letting the world know—

A calloused hand grabbed his shoulder, pulling him backward.

Carter's head met asphalt with a reality shattering *crack*, two bloody teeth springing from his mouth. Forcing himself onto his knees, his heart pounded and he couldn't breathe.

Thwack!

A stapler struck his head. He fell again.

Crunch!

A coffee cup shattered against his face, and he rolled over on his back, wincing from the pain.

A letter opener pierced his chest, and a bloom of bright blood spread across his crisp, white shirt.

On his back, every nerve in the unforgiving clench of agony, Carter stared up at the monolithic building…

…and watched Hansen fall seventeen floors through a spray of glass.

Carter smiled through the pain.

Hansen smashed through the hood of an illegally parked Monte Carlo.

Car alarms erupted like psychotic invitations to Hell.

Carter's world falling away, hazy voices penetrated the gloom…

"Say Paul, aren't you up for a promotion?"

"Sure am. Guess my first order of business is to call All-Glass and get my office window replaced."

That's my promotion, Carter tried to say. But darkness had already seized his soul and dragged him into the ether.

Raised in rural Wisconsin, **David Greske** grew up watching the Saturday afternoon creature features. He has been writing horror stories since the age of seven and one of his first literary endeavors was a rip-off of a Dark Shadows episode. Many years later his stories have appeared in *Black Ink Horror*, *Back Roads*, and *Thirteen*. Whiskey Creek Press published his three novels, *Anathema*, *Night Whispers*, and *Retribution*. Most recently, his chapbook *A Fistful of Zombies* was issued as an illustrated, signed and numbered limited edition from Sideshow Press Publications. He lives in Minneapolis, Minnesota.

The Gardeners

Amy Wallace

She wanted to scream. They were at it again.

"I *hate* you!" she hissed. "Fuckers."

"Sally?"

"I can't work! I can't *write*. It's those goddamn leaf blowers, Julio!"

"Oh, Sally—"

"They're against the law in California. Why doesn't somebody do something? I bought these great rakes—did you see those, Julio? Out by the garage? Six rakes!"

"That's a flock of rakes. A herd. A convention. How do you say it in English? In Argentina we say—"

"Stop it."

"Sally. You know these poor guys are underpaid. Imagine what they make! They're just taking orders! Who knows what the company tells them to do? Can you begin to guess what conditions these guys—"

"Are you saying I'm a racist, Julio? Am *I* a racist?"

"Well…"

"How *dare* you. I—"

"Listen. The noise stopped."

Julio looked out the upstairs window. "Hey, Sally, how do you call it here? The roach coach has arrived."

She stared at his sculpted profile. "Wow, you even picked up 'roach coach,' huh?"

He turned and wrapped his arms around her, kissing her neck. "Chiquita, I want you. Look at you, my baby." He pulled her to the bed, away from the window, and unbuttoned her skirt with one hand, clasping her wrists behind her back with the other. In his eagerness he might have torn off her clothes, but he had great respect for her expensive taste.

Afterwards he was sulky. He was often that way after sex, and she never totally understood why, except for the obvious: Severe

Catholic Guilt. After all, he wasn't from a social hub like Buenos Aires. He was from a town so small she could never remember its name, known primarily for its production of an excellent dessert made with *dulce de leche*.

He'd come to L.A. to make it in the movies—a goal absurd to Sally, even laughable and sad since he hadn't the slightest clue what was involved and had very little self-discipline.

She tried to believe in his dream with him. Besides, quirkier successes had been made in this Alice-In-Wonderland town. His beauty kept his foot in the door for auditions, but all he got were odd modeling jobs, mostly for nude gay 'zines, something which troubled him immensely, though it still fed his ego.

He scraped by financially, mostly with carpentry jobs. Now and then he got work as a gaffer's assistant, which at least gave him the thrill of being on a set.

He let Sally buy him fabulously expensive clothes from the best shops in L.A., even suits from Barney's. She'd been eager to support his dreams in a careless, hopeful way, because she thought she loved him. He was indeed very bright—surely that, with the clothes and a general *gravitas* (which she was learning was really stubborn pride), could count for much. When he hinted that he wanted a Reverso watch he'd spied in a window in Beverly Hills, she looked at the price and said, "Whew!" And he sulked profoundly. Sally broke down and surprised him with it a month later. *He's not getting Phippe Patek*, she'd thought firmly. She wanted to say something, but kept the thought to herself.

Guadalupe, her Columbian maid, took Julio's measure and said little. Sally and she were pretty friendly despite the language barrier, and she suspected that Guadalupe thought Julio was a gigolo. Sometimes, when Sally needed help communicating with her maid, she asked Julio for assistance, which seemed to make him uncomfortable. Sally knew he came from the same kind of poverty Guadalupe did, or nearly. But unlike the maid, he tried to pass for rich.

He had the kind of body which, as the cliché went, looked great with any old thing thrown over it, but now he had acquired a *real* wardrobe thanks to Sally. Guadalupe watched his growing acquisition of clothes and Italian loafers, and when they came back from their shopping trips, she hung them carefully in the closet.

Though she and Julio didn't live together—they weren't that committed yet—he was there a lot. In his shitty little car, he drove to the west side from Koreatown, where he lived squashed in with six Argentineans who barely spoke English, in a very clean, very claustrophobic apartment. Six of them shared one bathroom. Sally's house had four bathrooms, one for each bedroom. When she spent the night with him, in his tiny, neat room on his single bed (she thought that was sexy), his roommates treated her with quiet awe, partly, she suspected, because of her Jaguar. They knew he got to drive it.

When Sally bought the fancy house with the pool in Westwood, she knew she was in for a lot of expense. The pool guy, the chimney sweep, the gardeners . . .

The Gardeners.

There wasn't much in the way of a front yard—a few big trees and some boxy bushes that separated her from the neighbors. The pool took up the back.

Still, the gardening was lackluster. She approached her neighbor, Fran, a pear-shaped housewife with an absent husband and a noisy teenage son.

"Hi, I'm Sally. Fran?"

Smiles, handshakes.

"I was thinking of hiring a gardener. Do you know anyone?"

Fran looked uncomfortable. She looked over Sally's shoulder, avoiding eye contact.

"We all use the same gardeners. Great price—fifty dollars a month," Fran droned.

"Fifty a month! That *is* good. But…I'm no gardener, and I was imagining something a little more…colorful."

"Well. *We've* never used anyone else."

They saw the head gardener standing off in the distance and waved to him. Fran addressed him in rapid-fire Spanish that seemed to have its origins in "How To Speak To Your Maid."

That seemed to close the conversation. Any efforts to discuss the gardeners with other neighbors went the same way: a shrug, a frown, a dismissive wave.

The first week she moved in, she and Julio were woken by a tremendous noise. Leaf-blowers screeched, garbage cans clanked, hedge-clippers reduced the bushes to the same, square shape.

She went outside to meet and greet. The head gardener was Signor Manuel, a tall, stooped man with a shaggy moustache and a heavily lined face. He wore sunglasses. In fact, they *all* wore sunglasses; which, while it made sense, looked a little unusual. Other Mexican gardeners didn't all wear shades. These guys were kind of odd. And she never saw their truck arrive or leave. Sally shrugged. So they were eccentric. She was born and raised in California where eccentricity was the norm.

She had one conversational gambit in Spanish.

"Hola, senor."

"Hola, senorita."

"Com esta usted?"

He shrugged. "Muy bien."

"Oh, well…mucho trabajo…poco dinero!"

(Much work, little money.)

"Si!" His mouth curved in a smile, showing a row of brown, broken teeth. A few were missing and the front two were lined in gold: the old-fashioned Mexican fillings called "windows."

"Heh. Si, poco dinero!"

She guessed they were going to be, if not friends, not…she bit her lip…*enemies*. What a weird thing to think.

The other gardeners—five of them—pretended not to watch this first meeting between the mistress of the manor and El Jefe.

But they did watch from behind their shades as they wiped sweat from their brows and wielded huge, rusty hedge clippers. The illegal leaf blowers never stopped.

"Eh, Senorita—we take out tree for you." Senor Manuel pointed to an overgrown Ficus that threatened to take over the yard. Scary looking roots humped up throughout the lawn.

"Oh. Well. That sounds expensive. How much?"

"Fifty dollars."

"Gosh! Okay."

"Weh. Good price."

(*Weh?* Maybe this was some Toltec dialect she'd never heard. *Weh.*)

"Um, senor, does that mean you take out the stump, too?"

He looked at her blankly.

"El stump," she said, stifling a nervous laugh. "Um…el *cut?*"
She made slashing and lifting motions.

"Si! We take care of tree. Tree no good here."

When she told Julio everyone on the block hired them for fifty dollars, he took to calling them "The Mafioso Gardeners." When she told him they would take out the horrible Ficus for only another fifty, he looked impressed.

A few weeks passed in a chilly truce with the gardeners, Sally's nerves growing increasingly worn by the noise.

The tree was still there.

And then the awful thing.

Her roses…

They were the first things she'd ever planted. At her favorite nursery she selected Passion's Pride, Snow White, Moroccan Morning, English Cream, and Pale Fire. After a long, dirty afternoon—happy, scratched, shoulders aching—she sunk into a perfumed bath and luxuriated for a long time, proud of her efforts, anxious to enjoy the fruit of her labor.

She made a cup of tea when she got out of the tub, but before the first sip, she fell asleep.

The late nap became an early bedtime.

She woke at dawn, excited as a kid on Christmas morning, and ran outside barefoot in her pajamas to look at her roses.

They were wrong.

All wrong.

Someone had taken shears to them, a hacksaw, she didn't know. They were cut down to fat, raw, one-inch stumps. The tips had been shaved by hand, making her vividly recall the first time she'd seen an amputee change his prosthesis—a raw bulb where a child's elbow should have been.

She looked around wildly, at the grass still wet with dew. When? *Why?* To what purpose had they been mutilated? Leper roses.

Her leper roses.

"Julio…?"

"Uh…whozat? Hmm…?"

"Julio, its Sal. Oh, baby."

"Whssit? Sal? Oh, wow, it's 6:30—you okay, babe? Something is wrong?"

He hated to be woken.

"Yes. Something's wrong. Julio—I bought roses and they're stumps."

"What? You bought stump-roses?"

"No. I bought Passion's Pride, Pale—never mind. Healthy roses, with flowers. And they're mutilated. Mut—"

"Sally, I thought someone had died! Dios! Take a grip! You're confused. For fuck's sake, they're plants, not people."

Tears stung her throat. "That doesn't help—I mean, someone's doing it, Julio. Someone is. They're doing it! Don't make fun of me…" She burst into tears.

"Hey, okay, I'm sorry. It's early still, and my shoot went late last night. Look, no one's doing anything to you…"

"But how can you explain—"

"Look, let me shower and grab a bite. I'll be over by nine, okay?"

Sally couldn't look at the roses again. She tried to sleep, but only managed to sob into a pillow.

At 7:30 the gardeners arrived. The noise was unbearable. She stole a glance out the window. Right beneath her, a thick dark man wearing a wife-beater, his face scored with wrinkles, stood huddled like a sherpa under his leaf-blower, its great metal body strapped to him like an insect's carapace.

A single leaf did a helpless dance through the air.

For a moment there was silence, then she heard the voice of Signor Manuel. He spoke quietly, addressing the heavyset man. "Ka su…Mnu feg." It sounded like he spoke with a leather tongue.

Then, peeking out further, Sally saw the tongue's tip protrude. Black like a reptile's tail, it dallied within the inflamed gap between two front teeth.

The other man nodded, scratching his belly. "Ka." He looked up at the window, and Sally ducked down. She could barely see out now.

The man laughed and made the crude outlines of a woman's body with his hands. The gardeners laughed in unison.

At nine she heard Julio's car. He let himself in and found her upstairs in bed staring at the ceiling. He looked hassled, and worried, too.

"Do you still love me?" Sally quavered, red-eyed.

"Still? You're regressing, babe. I love you, you know that. We've been over this." He spoke gently. "You should go talk to them." He shrugged one perfect shoulder toward the window. "They're as scared of you as you are of them, mi bebe."

"You know I don't speak Spanish." The plea was loud in her eyes.

He looked away. "You should learn."

Like an automaton, she threw on sexless clothes: an over-sized T-shirt and Julio's sweat pants. On the way out, she encountered Guadalupe cleaning the downstairs toilet. Guadalupe, who had a big heart, burst out suddenly, "Miss Sally! He no nice to you!"

Had she heard our slightly raised voices?

"Oh," Sally replied vaguely with a sick smile, "it's okay."

Guadalupe sniffled.

"What I'm really worried about is, well, *the gardeners*. You know, Signor Manuel—" she waved ineffectually toward the outside.

"Ay!" Guadalupe crossed herself and looked away, back at the toilet, and began to scrub fiercely.

Sally tried to say something, but the maid wouldn't meet her eyes. She thought she heard Guadalupe muttering, "No good, es muy mal . . . pericoloso . . ."

Fleetingly, Sally wondered if she was now able to voice her true opinion of Julio, but in the same fleeting moment, he seemed…*less, so small*…compared to what was outside. Confused, she headed for the door…

The gardeners looked at the ground, avoiding her eyes like they always did, grinding, mowing, leaf-blowers raging. "Inside-out vacuum cleaners," one of her friends frequently called them.

She approached Senor Manuel, who was methodically dismembering a small bush with his shears.

"Buenos dias, Senor. I—"

"Eh?"

She pointed to what had been the roses.

All the machines stopped at once.

"Why…are…they….not…?" she made some lame gestures with her hands, snipping at the air.

He looked over at one of the other gardeners, a squat young man who grinned back at them. He was missing all his front teeth.

"Quem," Senor Miguel whispered confidentially. Then he grinned, too. Or was it a leer?

Sally backed into the house, past the lurid stumps of her roses.

Julio was ferreting around in the refrigerator, addressing a beer as he heard her come in.

"See?" he announced. "Like I told you. They're people too. We're all just people. Chica. I don't know how to say this, but you come from…well, from money, let's face it. You had privileges. You had servants! First the black people, then—" He faced her, waving a bag of tortillas. "—Latinos! Now I'm not saying…" He fished out a jar of salsa.

"Julio. You…call…the company."

"And tell them what?"

"About the roses. Tell them the gardeners are fired for destroying my roses."

"Oh. Yeah. Well, I think you should call. It's your house."

He wasn't going to man up about this. She sighed—she always did the hard things herself, anyway. This was just one more. Sort of. But what about all those jobs? All those families? And she did want the Ficus gone. Maybe she shouldn't do it. She looked out the window once more…and what she saw decided her.

It was wrong.

Far too wrong.

"Julio, look—outside there. At the truck. Something strange is—"

"I'm reading the paper. Carajo, Sally. A truck is a truck. Let me tell you something. These people have poor families. Look at my jeans, the hole here at the knee."

"I can fix that if you want."

"No! In Argentina when the jeans have a hole we don't buy a new pair like here—"

"But—"

"I send them to my mother and grandma."

"You send then to your mother? *Really?*"

"My mother! She is fantastic! Wonderful. And my grannie sews, and then they send them back—"

"I guess. Listen. About that truck. Have you noticed how we never see it come or go? Same with the workers' truck."

"Dios mio."

"Okay, that's a coincidence. But—the spelling on it is all wrong. I mean, I thought it would say Tacqueria or something. But it looks like Greek, not Spanish."

"Greek tacos? *Mmmm.*"

"No. 'Atoque…Tormii…Herk…Em.' That's all I can make out."

"So?"

"Julio, they're bringing the food back and sitting down under the Ficus. I can see everything."

"Sally." He folded the paper loudly. "Should they eat standing? What?"

"Look at the food. It's not regular food."

"Right. What kind of food is it?"

"It looks like, um, moss. Moss with beef and some bloody sauce with…maybe some hair in it. They hardly have to chew it…it slides right down."

"So maybe they drink wheatgrass."

"You know they don't." She wondered if she was starting to hate Julio.

He peered out the window. "I don't see much. We'd better go down. Besides, I'm hungry."

"You're scared," she said. It wasn't an accusation; she saw it for the first time.

He was stung.

He was proud, very proud, and he was extremely angry. At times like this he looked so fierce that he reminded her of a bullfighter. But what was he going to fight today? *Mossy carnitas?*

They went down together.

When Julio approached the truck the gardeners pulled together like a football team in a huddle.

"Hola" he tried in his deep tones.

The group of *them* shifted together, hiding something.

Julio walked up to the truck's order window, pretending nonchalance. A fat woman moved inside the truck. Julio studied the list of foods, a stupefied expression sweeping his face. Next to words, in a language Sally didn't recognize—*must be a dialect*—there were pictures.

Some of the pictures were whimsical, or at least unlikely. She felt a sudden and strong throb at the base of her spine, as if something wanted to get out. And right then she was hungry.

Julio looked repulsed by the menu, though, she thought, there was enough red meat on it to satisfy the average Argentinean. *Of course*, she thought with a sigh, *he's very fastidious…*

She turned her attention back to the menu. And her hunger grew so strong that, for once, she forgot about Julio.

A side of meat, probably a beefsteak, on a bed of moss, a melon, a sandwich decorated with dewy rose buds, the grilled paws of an unidentifiable animal in a sloppy sauce, and a small bird that looked as though it would be all bones, like a quail, also surrounded by rose buds.

The buyers pulled money out of their pockets and pushed it through the window. The side dish was something white or gray, like jelly, which the gardeners greedily sucked off their fingers or sopped up with…

She couldn't resist staring. She saw a heavy gardener dip meat into a bed of moss and rose petals and bring it up—*bloody*—to his lips. Goo, the consistency of a jelly, dripped from meat, pallid as if it had spoiled.

Instead of putting the meat directly in his mouth, he stuffed it in the soaked moss and chewed, bloody sauce streaming down his chin, then he packed rose petals in his cheeks like tobacco.

Sally's stomach churned. But—perversely—she craved that gray, mossy, bloody jelly.

She looked at Julio for reassurance, but his eyes were far away, pretending to stare at the menu. She reached for his hand, but he pulled it away. He was macho, and she knew he didn't want the men to see his woman hanging on him. The nature of their relationship hung in the air like cartoon-bubbles over their heads: *What's he doing here, in this mansion? Did she buy him that watch, those clothes?*

Julio approached the food window.

Out of the corner or her eye, Sally saw Guadalupe's worried face, shaped like an O, watching through one of the house's many windows.

"I'll have the special," Julio said with a nod at the list.

"No. Eh, eh, senora," said the heavy lady. Then she slammed the plastic window shut.

All the gardeners watched Julio.

"Hey! I'm not a senora!" Suddenly that seemed the most important thing.

The gardeners laughed.

Before Julio could say anything, he saw Senor Manuel's smile. His front teeth were gone now, where the windows had been.

There were black gums there, and they moved with the slow undulations of worms.

Julio ran.

––––––––

He told her he had to take a nap, then refused to talk.

She tried to work and couldn't.

Maybe Julio was right. He made bad jokes, but she was more scared of the Mexicans than they were of her. And why not? She was a woman. Twenty terror points right there. They must have guessed that Julio didn't live in the big house, that she didn't have a real husband. At best she was an anomaly. At worst she was a piece of pussy.

She called the company.

"I'm not happy with the gardeners. They, ah, destroyed some expensive plants. I *don't* want them to come back."

"What?"

"Well…they're fired. I'm sorry."

She took a breath and nuzzled Julio. You could never really understand another culture regardless of the politics you pretended to believe. And Julio could never understand her. But that was okay, she supposed.

She smiled and bit his brown neck.

––––––––

They were woken by the sound of a leaf blower.

Julio frowned. "I thought you were going to fire them."

"I did. I don't know what they—"

Enough, came an interrupting thought. She leaped from bed and stormed downstairs.

Signor Manuel greeted her: "Hola, senorita!"

He wasn't wearing his sunglasses and his pupils looked tight, constricted; he squinted as if he couldn't bear the sun.

She gave him a stiff nod.

"Today we finish the job."

"Oh, well. Thank you."

He pointed to the Ficus. His men were already circling it.

"Well, I appreciate that." She fished in her pocket for money as he turned away.

Julio suggested she look on the bright side. It was a good deal. And it was almost over.

She'd been assertive.

"That's quite a bargain! Worth the extra day. Awesome. Maybe they saw you wearing the purple skirt, hmm? The one I like, the tight one." He reached for her.

―――――――

It was a noisy affair, and Julio stayed out by the pool for most of it. Before it was over, unable, he said, to relax, Julio went home.

She watched from the upstairs window as the men shoveled and hacked and drilled; thick, arm-like pieces of root emerged like the tentacles of a squid.

Do those arms still live under the house?

Probably.

She shuddered.

She needed to talk to someone, but Guadalupe had claimed an emergency and taken the rest of the day off. Gardeners aside, she was alone. When Guadalupe had said "goodbye," Sally thought she heard a whispered, "*Be careful, Miss Sally.*" But she wasn't at all sure she wasn't going mad, hearing things.

The removal of the stump went on past sundown, the gardeners working and sweating under moonlight. Strange, the neighbors didn't complain.

The moon was high when they finally packed up and left.

She stepped outside barefoot and approached the hole where the stump had been. The excision was so clean she had to search hard find it. She peered at a neat trellis, pressed perfectly into the hole, the kind of thing you'd cover a foxhole with. By moonlight the hole seemed vast, bottomless. Carefully, she surveyed the lawn. Somehow, they'd cleared the entire mess.

Strange.

The next day Julio came over; he and Sally luxuriated in bed. For once they didn't talk about the gardeners, apart from his whistle of approval when she told him about all the work they'd done for a mere $50.

When he was asleep, she stuck her face out the window. The thick gardener stood below, scratching his hairy belly and beckoning . . .

Beckoning.

Sally screamed.

Julio jumped out of bed; but when he got to the window there was no one outside.

I'm seeing things. I'm going—

"You're just nervous," he said, as if reading her mind. "This has been stressful for you."

"Do you think the roots will die? I hope so."

"You *hope*?" He made "the-monster-will-get-you" noises: "The *roooooots*! They Live Inside! *Whoo-ooo*—"

"I heard something. A noise."

He tried to tickle her, but she pushed him away. "Really, I did."

He reached for her again. He didn't like to be put off. He grabbed her ass and screamed.

"Sally! My Jesus! What *is* that? Is that a . . . *tail*? A stub of a tail? Jesus God! You have a...*it's hairy*!"

She grinned, and her teeth looked sharp.

"Ka," was all she said.

He ran.

She looked down at him from the balcony. Outside, he was blinking, making vague, panicked calling sounds into the night air.

They were on him. A hand—no, a claw, something scaled—came down in front of his eyes. Another claw raked, closing his mouth forever. He struggled hard, but he couldn't stop them. Choking on wet rose petals they stuffed in his mouth, he tried to draw breath. No use. Moss pressed up and into his nostrils, cutting off his last gasps of life.

After ten minutes of silence, Sally stood. She touched the thing that grew out of her spine—gingerly at first, then with confidence, even affection. It had soft little hairs.

The night sky relaxed her eyes.

They crawled into the room, some of them on all fours, others leaning, the tips of their claws where fingers used to be, clacking at the air like mandibles. The stumps of their tails protruded from rags, teeth pushed from gray gums like spears. They had padded hands, like moles' paws.

She was dragged outside and pushed toward the hole. They pulled her down. And down.

Down.

Fresh earth tumbled around her.

Reaching a huge burrow, she saw Julio's body slumped in a corner. His mouth stuffed to suffocating with rosebuds, he wasn't breathing.

She had no more use for him.

But *they* had a use for her in their mole night-world.

She couldn't see much as they prepared her: wide black pupils, a pile of torn clothes, broken sunglasses, and tunnels that led to warrens.

She felt the press of stiff fur against her body.

Sharp claws raked her legs, and she smelled decay. Not human decay, or that of an animal—it was the sweet decay of roses long dead, and the waft of the unknown...

She was home.

When they were done making her right, she went to the handsome brown body and joined the feast.

They pulled the trellis shut. This was *their* world.

———

The neighbors' lights clicked on once, then went dead.

Amy Wallace is the author of more than fifteen books, including (with her family) the number-one *New York Times* bestselling *Book of Lists*, which has sold over eight million copies worldwide and spawned four additional bestselling editions. She also wrote *The Psychic Healing Book*, with Bill Henkin, now in print for more than thirty years. Family collaborations include *The Intimate Sex Lives of Famous People* (recently re-released in an updated edition by Feral House), *Significa* (based on a long-running *Parade* magazine column), and *The Book of Predictions*. She co-authored a biography, *The Two: The Story of the Original Siamese Twins*, with her father, the world-famous novelist Irving Wallace. Her second biography was *The Prodigy: A Biography of William James Sidis, the World's Greatest Child Prodigy*. She also wrote the acclaimed erotic novel, *Desire*. Among her most recent works are the controversial memoir *Sorcerer's Apprentice: My Life with Carlos Castaneda*, *The Official Punk Rock Book of Lists* (with Handsome Dick Manitoba), and *The Book of Lists: Horror* (with Del Howison and Scott Bradley), which earned her a nomination for the prestigious Bram Stoker Award. Amy shares her birthday, July 3, with Franz Kafka and Mississippi John Hurt. She lives in Los Angeles with two cats, Hank and Bella, who serve as her editors by lying across the keyboard at critical moments.

New Orleans' Best Beignets

Vic Kerry

Maurice Devereaux needed a job, and L'Enfant Bakery on Jackson Street was hiring. According to some of his sources, Denis L'Enfant would hire anyone as long as they were clean: both bathed and drug-free. Maurice could claim both, although he'd only been drug-free for a year.

The bakery looked nice. It sat between two microbreweries that popped up after Katrina. Before that, Maurice seemed to remember that an Irish pub took up one of the spaces. The other had been a cheap souvenir joint that sold Mardi Gras beads year 'round. L'Enfant Bakery had always been there. Before the storm, it was run down; the lettering on the windows had chipped off, and few people ate there. They called it "L'Infection Bakery." Even Maurice refused to eat there at his worst, which he thought was saying something, because he'd eaten out of the dumpsters at the Superdome and drank Hurricanes tourists abandoned on the street, even those with cigarette butts in them.

Now he, a cleaned-up man, stood outside the cleaned-up bakery. The words on the windows stared in festive New Orleans colors. The wrought iron posts out front were glossy black. All the neon in the signs glowed fresh. *Voted New Orleans' Best Beignets* was scrolled in gold letters across both windows.

Maurice caught his reflection. He looked darker than before he'd been shipped off to Angola. Some smart-alacky coon-ass might even tell him he looked like one of the freshly painted columns. In the old days, he'd have fought over that. But just like his city, he'd changed through time and hardship. He hoped he was better as he stepped into the cool, sugar-scented air of the bakery. Bells jingled as he walked in. The dining area was bereft of customers, but a stout man dressed in white stood behind the counter.

"Can I help you?" the man asked.

"I came because I heard that ya'll might be hiring," Maurice said, twisting his hands in front of his chest.

"I think I heard Mr. L'Enfant say something about that. He's in the back, at the soup kitchen. I'll step back there and get him."

"Ya'll serve soup here, too?"

"Naw, after the storm, when he got his huge insurance check, Mr. L'Enfant said he wanted to give something back. So he bought the store that opened up from our back onto the next street and turned it into a soup kitchen for the homeless." The man wiped his hands on his apron. "I'll go get him. Sit tight."

Maurice nodded and sat at a table near the door. Maybe his sources had been right. If Mr. L'Enfant ran a soup kitchen, he'd probably hire a convicted felon, too. As far as Maurice knew, the man he'd just talked to might have gotten out of Angola yesterday, just like him.

A red checked tablecloth covered the table where he sat. Powder sugar formed small hills all over the plastic cloth. Maurice remembered places—darker places—with small piles of white powder on tables. Most of the time he'd either sold the stuff on display or been stocking his supply-line. He never cared much for blow, and, as Whitney Houston had put it, "crack is whack." Maurice only smoked weed, but had been clean since arriving at Angola. He'd been sent up on dealing, plea-bargained down from trafficking. As much as the sirens of his old life called to him, a second chance lay before him, and he wanted to give life his best shot, even if it meant frying beignets for the tourists and staying free of the reefer.

"Sure hope I ain't been keeping you too long."

Maurice looked up from the sugar on the table and snapped back from his daydream. A plump man wearing a white apron over blue striped seersucker pants and a light blue shirt walked toward him from the counter. A broad white smile cut through his deep dark skin.

"Mr. L'Enfant?" Maurice asked, standing and extending his hand.

"The one and only. At least in this store."

The handshake was one good pump with a tight grip. L'Enfant's hands were hard as rocks. Maurice never imaged a pastry chef having such hard hands. The smile continued to beam at him and sincerity bloomed from it. Maurice had seen millions of insincere smiles in his time, and it was clear that L'Enfant sold his over the top grin as well as he did his beignets.

L'Enfant motioned for them to sit at the table. He brushed the sugar from the tablecloth with a quick sweep of his hand. "Beau tells me you're looking for a job."

"Yessir."

"As you can see, I need some help around here. I can't even keep the tables clean."

"I thought maybe you were having a dry spell seeing as how no one's here," Maurice said.

L'Enfant's laughter echoed around the empty bakery like thunder rolling over the bayou. "Everybody knows that I don't serve beignets at this time of the day. I devote this hour to my soup kitchen out back." He eyed Maurice. "Just get out of the joint?"

Maurice looked down at the pattern on the table cloth. The large red checks were in reality a series of smaller pink and red checks. "Yessir."

"Ain't no reason to be embarrassed around me, son. Everybody gets in a little trouble now and then. I hire all sorts— actually I like hiring ex-cons. Gives 'em the chance to start over."

"I heard you hire a lot of us." Maurice looked into L'Enfant's sparkling, dark brown eyes. "I heard you're a good man."

"Son, ain't got nothing to do with being good; got everything to do with being blessed. Katrina gave me a chance to start over and better myself. I took it. Now I offer the same to others, but without the trauma of that storm."

The man from earlier poked his head back into the bakery. "Mr. L'Enfant, I need you back here."

L'Enfant stood and held his hand back out to Maurice. "Congratulations, Mr....?"

"Devereaux. Maurice Devereaux."

"Mr. Devereaux, you've got a job cooking beignets for me on the graveyard shift. Show up tonight 'round midnight. I'll wait around and help get you started."

They shook, and L'Enfant hurried back to the soup kitchen. Maurice wanted to cheer. He'd not had a straight job since he worked at McDonald's as a teenager. The money wouldn't be anything like he made dealing, but the benefit of staying out of Angola was enough. He looked at his watch; he'd need some sleep before tonight. Maurice rushed out of the bakery, the bell on the door clattering loudly.

———————

Maurice walked into L'Enfant's Bakery through the front door. He couldn't hear the jangle of the door over the crowd of customers. Glasses and coffee mugs clinked as they hit the tables. The whole dining room buzzed with chatter. A baby squealed. He looked around at all the tourists enjoying a late night pastry. Plates of powdered sugar-laden beignets covered nearly every table. A line that stopped just short of the door ran to the check-out register.

The door to the kitchen burst opened, and L'Enfant hustled out a tray of what looked like ordinary donuts. Maurice didn't figure they sold much more than beignets. L'Enfant looked up as he placed the tray in the glass display counter.

"Maurice," he said. "Come on back."

Maurice broke between two people in line and walked behind the counter. L'Enfant shook his hand again with his signature firm, single pump, his thick palm sticky with donut glaze. They walked back to the kitchen. The smell of the baking pastries hit Maurice in the face like a soft punch. He didn't mind it because it meant honest work, although it was a bit overwhelming for his personal taste.

"The first thing is this," L'Enfant grabbed an apron from a hook and slung it at Maurice, "I don't care too much about what you wear to work as long as you wear an apron and hair net." He looked at Maurice's head. "I guess you don't need one."

"I keep it slick. It's cooler this way." Maurice rubbed his shaved head before pulling the apron's top loop over it. He crossed the side strings behind him then bow tied the front. "So what am I doing?"

L'Enfant led him to a large industrial mixer, then turned it on. It whirled with a loud mechanical noise. "You make sure the batter is nice and mixed." The mixer stopped, and L'Enfant dipped a long spoon into the bowl. "If this comes up without any dry mix on it, you're set. Easy enough."

Maurice nodded. "I think I can handle that. I worked in the kitchen some at Angola. We never had anything nice as this, though."

"All mixers pretty much work the same. What were you in Angola for?"

"Stupidity."

L'Enfant roared a laugh and slapped Maurice on the back with the same force as he shook hands. "Everybody ends up in there for that or being wrongfully accused. What kind of stupidity?"

Maurice didn't know if it was legal for L'Enfant to ask him that, but the baker had hired him with no other questions. "Dealing. Big-time dealing."

"All right. I've had a couple of big-time dealers. I want to introduce you to your supervisor." L'Enfant pointed at a small, wiry man sitting at a desk. "That's Bruce."

Bruce looked up with a blank expression and then back down at the *Times-Picayune*.

"Hey."

"Bruce isn't much for conversation. If you have any problems, bring them to him." L'Enfant led Maurice away and whispered, "He's not here as a dealer. He got out early for good behavior after murder one was brought down to manslaughter."

"How 'bout breaks or lunch?" Maurice asked.

"Bruce will tell you when to go. By the way, here it's all you can eat, so take advantage of it. We make the best beignets in New Orleans, maybe the world."

Maurice nodded and went back to this mixer. He switched it on and let it whirl. A few minutes later, he put the spoon into the batter to check the mixture, then passed the bowl down the line. Another bowl of ingredients awaited him. Before he realized it, he'd fallen into a pattern, and time passed quickly.

"Break time," Bruce called out. His voice was heavy like lead and thick with the bayou. "Make sure to eat some of the beignets."

Maurice looked over his shoulder. "I'm okay. I don't like them that well."

"Understand, on my shift you have to eat beignets." Bruce grabbed his arm with vice-like force.

Spikes of pain shot up his arm. He turned enough to see the small man's face; a smirk stretched his lips. Bruce meant business, and Maurice got the hint.

"I think I'm craving a beignet," Maurice said.

The pressure on his arm went away. "We understand each other, then," Bruce said. "I make sure Mr. L'Enfant has a certain amount of beignets eaten each night. It's how I stay the manager. Get it?"

Maurice rubbed his arm. "Yeah, got it."

Bruce handed Maurice a plate full of pastries. "Take it to the back in the soup kitchen's dining room. That's where we take all our breaks."

Maurice took the plate and walked through the door marked *Soup Kitchen*. He arrived in a large empty room full of long tables. The air felt stale and smelled of the homeless. He knew the smell well. A short time before getting shipped to Angola he'd spent some time living on the streets himself. L'Enfant was a good man to spend so much time and effort helping the down and out. Maybe Maurice would volunteer some of his free time to work the kitchen.

He sat at the first table and bit into one of the beignets. Why didn't he just throw them away instead of eating them? But that question quickly vanished from his mind when he realized how amazing they tasted. He shoved another in. If all the beignets he'd eaten tasted like these he would've eaten them twenty-four/seven. He shoved another in before swallowing. Then another. And another. Soon he needed something to drink. A scan of the room came up empty. But he noticed the place didn't look right. The area where the sink and counter should have been was blocked by a metal gate that looked like a garage door. Everything seemed clean, despite the smell. It looked more like a coffee house or an upscale café than any soup kitchen he'd seen while living on the streets. Maybe that was L'Enfant's idea. The homeless didn't enjoy their plight, and a standard soup kitchen did nothing but remind them of who they were.

The door to the kitchen burst opened, and Bruce hustled in. The noise of the door hitting the wall brought Maurice's focus back. He looked at Bruce. The ex-murderer looked put out, flexing his hand in and out of a fist.

"What are you doing?" Bruce asked.

"I'm on break. You forced me in here and made me eat these beignets."

"That was forty-five minutes ago. Get back in here, we're swamped."

Maurice wiped his mouth on his apron and hurried back into the kitchen. True to Bruce's words, everyone seemed to move faster and work harder. A red faced kid huffed as he moved a bowl from the mixer Maurice worked on. The boy's shirt under his apron was too tight, and a bit of his white belly hung from it.

"Let me help you with that," Maurice said, taking the bowl. "You look like you're about to pass out."

"I think I might be," the boy said. "I don't know when I got so out of shape. When I got out of juvie at the beginning of the summer, I could run two miles and barely be puffin'. Now I can't walk from one end of the kitchen to the other without a break."

It was hard to believe the pudgy kid could do anything without getting winded, but Maurice noticed that the boy's arms had ropy muscles in them like one accustomed to the gym. The weight around the boy's gut seemed out of place. No waddle hung from his chin like others with pronounced bellies.

"Simons," Bruce barked. "Break time. Get your plate of beignets and get to it."

The boy rubbed his hands on his apron and patted Maurice on the shoulder. Then Simons grabbed a plate piled with beignets and disappeared into the soup kitchen's dining room. Maurice kept staring at the door.

"Get that bowl over here," Bruce yelled.

Maurice shook off his thoughts and scurried across the kitchen with the bowl of batter. He passed it off to the next cook and headed back to his mixer. Bruce followed and stood behind him as Maurice started the paddles whirling in the bowl. The older man's breath reeked of coffee and cigarettes.

"Do you have to stand behind me like that?" Maurice asked not looking back.

"I'm your supervisor. I'm supervising."

"Am I doing an okay job?"

Bruce grabbed him by the upper arm. "Mr. L'Enfant doesn't like his workers getting buddy-buddy. Remember that. He hires a bunch of cons like us and doesn't need us planning out on how to knock the joint over or sell dope out of his soup kitchen."

"I promise those days are done for me, and I was just talking to Simons, trying to be friendly and such."

"Ain't no need to be 'friendly and such' with folks like Simons. Even by our standards he's trouble. Went up for rape, you see?"

Maurice knew that a hard con like Bruce didn't have time for rapists. He didn't either, but the kid looked so innocent. It was probably statutory. *Pity for a young guy to get that on his record.*

"How long has he been here?"

"A few weeks," Bruce said, "but don't get too into that. You got work to do so get to it."

The supervisor let go of his arm and walked back to his desk and *Times-Picayune*. Maurice stopped the spinning paddles and tested the batter with his spoon. No dry flour. He moved the bowl down the line. As he walked past the soup kitchen's door, he peered in at the teen gorging on beignets. If Simons had only been with the bakery a few weeks, he must have really put the pastries away. Maurice decided that he'd start throwing his out to keep from ending up with a saggy gut.

Maurice walked into the kitchen. Bruce sat at his desk reading his *Times-Picayune* as usual. L'Enfant stood by the mixing bowl area, a broad smile on his face.

"Maurice," L'Enfant said. "Guess what?"

"I don't know."

"You're getting a promotion and small raise."

"Really, to what?"

"It seems that Mr. Simons won't be coming back to us. Apparently, he's blown town."

Maurice's stomach sank. Simons had been his only friend in the kitchen. They talked a lot. Simons just got a new girlfriend who was of age. He was happy. Maurice couldn't image why he would blow town.

"Did he run off with his new girlfriend?" Maurice asked.

"Probably ran from the law," Bruce said, now standing beside Maurice. "Kid was stupid, started back into his old ways soon as he got out."

Maurice didn't like the coldness in his supervisor's voice. It seemed far too malicious. He also didn't understand how Simons could have gone back to his "old ways" since it had been statutory rape with his girlfriend. True, plenty who tried going straight ended back up in their crimes. But Simons was a different breed.

"So get to work," L'Enfant said. He poked Maurice's belly, a belly that had started to grow pudgy. "Been hitting the beignets?"

Maurice felt his face flush a little. His stomach had grown flabby from all the desserts he'd been eating. Although he'd tried to resist them, the beignets were irresistible. He dreamed about them and woke up wet and sticky like a teenager coming out of a wet dream.

L'Enfant left after patting Maurice on his back. Bruce guided him to his new position as shaper.

Maurice started rolling out the batter and putting the small balls on baking sheets. The stuff seemed stickier than it should. Years ago, he'd helped his grandmother make beignets for Christmas. They never seemed this sticky, but home cooking was not the same as industrial cooking. The ingredients had to be different.

The smell of the frying confections wafted toward Maurice. His mouth watered, and he felt aroused. Somehow the beignets were tapping into his sexual instincts, as well as his hunger. He was glad for the apron to hide his arousal.

"Boss," one of the others yelled across the kitchen. "We's running low on the shortening."

Bruce folded his paper and laid it on his desk. "We just got a new shipment in. Isn't it over there?"

"Nassir, it ain't."

"I'll go get it."

Bruce disappeared into the soup kitchen. Maurice never noticed a storage locker in that area. He rolled the dough and put it out on the sheets. A few minutes later, Bruce rolled a barrel in on a set of dollies. It was black with no writing on it. The top was off, and he could see into it. The shortening inside appeared too yellow. He'd never seen shortening that wasn't snow white.

"What is that?" he asked Bruce.

"Shortening."

"I've never seen shortening like that."

Bruce glared at him, cold and hard. "It's special shortening. It's what makes Mr. L'Enfant's beignets so special."

When his break came, Maurice hadn't even realized it. Time passed like a shot while he thought about his missing friend. Bruce pushed him away from the pans and handed him his plate of beignets. His trousers tightened when his thumb brushed one of the pastries, and he hurried into the soup kitchen.

The first bite made him groan. The sugar touched his tongue with an explosion of flavor. The next bite sent him into a full orgasm. The pastries seduced him. Each lounged on the plate like a wanton lover. He satisfied them all, and they he. By the time only powdered sugar remained on the plate, Maurice dripped with sweat. He'd climaxed at least twice. No sex had caused him that much pleasure in that quick of succession. He waited for his hands to quit shaking and his legs to finish wobbling before he went back to work.

The kitchen bustled when he stepped back into its sultry heat. Everything seemed to vibrate with energy. He felt like he'd taken a couple hits of X. The world glowed and shimmered. Even Bruce looked softer.

"What's your problem?" Bruce asked.

Maurice grinned. "Nothing's wrong. Everything's right."

Bruce clenched him around the arm. "Get back to work and wipe that stupid grin off your face."

Maurice tried, but it came right back. He felt the small muscles at the edge of his lips stretch and pull. "Sorry, I can't."

Bruce pinched the fat on Maurice's belly and twisted. Maurice quit smiling.

"That did it," Bruce said. "Getting a bit fatty, aren't you?"

Maurice wanted to curse his boss, but anger faded fast and his grin returned. He felt too good to let some screw like Bruce bring him down. Whatever had him so high, he needed it in pill form; he could make a million pushing the stuff.

"Whatever."

Bruce's expression didn't change. "I've got another shipment of shortening arriving first thing in the morning. I need you to stay behind and help me."

"Whatever."

———

Maurice followed Bruce into a stairwell behind the soup kitchen. It wound down to the storeroom below the bakery. Everything smelled like burnt bacon, and he almost wretched. Whatever took him up so high last night was now killing him, and he wondered if Bruce, to get him fired, had laced some of the beignets.

"So they're delivering down here? I don't see a door to the street," Maurice said as they walked into a large empty storage area.

"This is where the shortening arrives," Bruce said.

A chair sat in the middle of the floor. A plastic drop cloth lay across the floor and under the chair.

"Sit," Bruce said. "It's going to be a few minutes before it gets here, and you've been on your feet all night."

"I'm good," he said, but he wasn't. He couldn't seem to shake a feeling of vertigo. Everything swirled around him, and Bruce seemed weirder than usual.

"Nonsense. Mr. L'Enfant wants you taking care of yourself. Sit."

The world spun. Maurice wobbled to the chair and sat. He figured it was better to give in than fall. Bruce was up to something behind him, but Maurice didn't move lest be overtaken by the spinning world again.

"Hello, Maurice."

He looked up to see Mr. L'Enfant smiling at him.

"Good morning."

"Glad to see you looking so well." He brought out a plastic cup from behind his back. "Don't mind taking a pee test for me, do you?"

"What?"

"I've had a tip that you've gone back to your old ways, Maurice. Ex-cons are fine employees. Current cons aren't."

"I'll pee in your cup, but I've done nothing wrong."

L'Enfant handed him the cup. "Prove it."

Maurice took the cup and stood. "Where's the bathroom?"

"Right here."

He closed his eyes, unzipped his fly, and pissed in the cup. When he felt the warmth of urine touch his penis, he stopped. Opening his eyes, he handed the cup back to Mr. L'Enfant. "There."

L'Enfant took a plastic stick from his pocket and stirred it in the urine. A short moment later, he studied the dripping stick and shook his head.

"Positive."

"I've not done anything," Maurice protested.

"You're fired."

"I was set up. Was it Bruce? He's been after me. I've even been thinking about it. I think he may have something to do with Simons being gone."

L'Enfant's smile grew wider. "I know that."

Maurice turned and saw Bruce approaching him with an old fire ax. He tried to move away, but the world swirled again. The chair caught him when he fell.

"Simons is still around," L'Enfant said. "He's probably under your fingernails. We started using him last night."

"The shortening."

"After Katrina, it got hard to find shortening, but we were heavy on the homeless and dead. I rendered some hobo fat one day and used it for my beignets. They were magnificent. By the looks of you, I think you'll make a good batch," L'Enfant said. "I make the special ones for my employees. A little hoodoo makes them extra tasty and extra fat."

"But why us?"

"Less criminals in the world the better," L'Enfant said.

The last thing Maurice saw was L'Enfant waving his hand toward Bruce. The last thing he felt was the ax in his skull.

————

Jack read the article on L'Enfant's Bakery in the *Times-Picayune*. He was set to get out of Angola the next day and planned on heading back to New Orleans. Bruce, his probation officer, told him about the bakery. He read up on it because they hired cons who were clean. It sounded like a great place to work, and Jack was excited. The article ended with the owner, Mr. L'Enfant, talking about how everyone took part in making the best beignets in New Orleans.

There's a little bit of our cooks in each one.

Jack needed to take pride in something. He looked forward to getting that job.

Vic Kerry lives in Alabama with his wife, two cats, and six dogs (for right now). He's eaten a beignet or two in his lifetime but has never made one, so far. He's always looking for new friends on Facebook.

The Vessel

Jonah Quint stared, along with the rest of the congregation, at the kneeling form of Sister Helena as she laid hands on the fourth crippled man of the night. The split in her wrapped skirt exposed the left leg above the knee. His eyes locked on the exposed thigh for several seconds, staring at the glimpse of stocking top before finding the will to look away.

"All cameras," he said into the mic, "avoid Sister Helena's left leg. Angle for the cripple or above the waist." He watched everyone with him in the control room act as a single well-oiled machine.

On cue all monitors showed new angles, each avoiding the innocent exposure with surgical precision.

"Perfect."

He watched her body rock in time with the speaker's rhythmic beat. The televised audience was enthralled by the faith healings and him personally by the mane of blonde hair. Several strands fell forward, shielding her face from the camera.

"Camera two, tighten frame on the guy."

"Gotcha, Jonah."

One of the fifteen monitors fanned out and the cameraman zoomed in on the thirty-something praying with her wheelchair-bound ward. The man's twisted legs convulsed as Helena gripped his thighs. Tears flowed and his face screwed into a rictus of pain. One leg straightened, the unnatural angle of the joint hidden by her hand. A breath later the other leg followed suit and jutted forth rigid as stone. He jerked from the wheelchair and fell forward, leaning against the healer's shoulders for support. She grasped him and stood, lifting the healed man to full height.

"Arise," Helena shouted amidst a fury of cheers and amens.

Applause rang throughout the chapel and the chorus broke into one of the chosen hymns for the evening. Hands rose Heavenward, then attendees clasped each other as one unbroken chain and joined in the song. Three of the four camera crews paced the aisles catching tearful members in moments of prayer and rejoice while one shot up from waist level to get the inspiring "closer to God" angle. The fourth kept focus on the man, who bore the confused expression seen time and again after a healing. A white curtain, emblazoned with the words *The Vessel* in reflective royal blue, lowered.

"Roll credits." Jonah looked over at Karen Finch. "Get me archive footage from tonight's last fifteen minutes."

"Okay. Anything else?"

"Yeah. Fire the hairstylist."

Karen pushed back from the console, smoothed her skirt and stood. "I thought you liked Sister Helena's hair down."

"I do, and so does every other man out there, but she needs to be seen as the prophet we've built her to be."

"Prophet? You mean healer."

Jonah closed the distance between them, grasped the assistant producer by the arm and led her back into the sound booth, then slammed the door closed behind them. He jabbed a finger out like a weapon. "Listen...just close your mouth and listen. Sister Helena's bought out the entire hour and a half following the closing interviews with tonight's Saved. She's professed that we're on the verge of the End Times."

"Jonah," Karen took the finger that still jabbed at her and held it in between both palms, "prophets have been saying that for centuries. Many more popular than the great Sister Helena."

"No."

"No? What do you mean, no? By simple popularity standings, she has less viewers than the Seven Hundred Club."

"I mean, no." He pulled away. "She's healed the sick, professed—correctly I might add—to nine events in the last month alone."

"And that means she's on the level? We bought out two of the three network time slots for this. If she's wrong, it's the end for everything we've worked for."

"And if she's right?"

Karen rolled her eyes. "Speaking of that, the reporter from LQN is waiting on-line for you."

Jonah humphed a response.

Karen opened the door. "Your career's on the line, here. Be

sure what you're doing is right."

"Of course it's right. We purchased the time just like anyone else is able to."

Karen smirked. "Not right with the network," she pointed up with her pen, "right with Him. Are you serving the Lord or are you serving Sister Helena?" Karen stepped out and closed the door.

Below, Jonah watched the masses extricating themselves from pews and folding chairs, clogging the aisles like rainwater through a downspout. Grandparents, adults, teens, and children all wore varying shades of white, bringing to mind a white chocolate drink he'd tried on the last tour. Sister Helena's "Right Arm," as she'd dubbed Jonah, flopped down in one of the two seats and logged into his personal account. One small video camera icon flashed red in the upper right corner. He clicked it while running a comb through thinning hair. A shadowy image of himself popped up in a window. A few adjustments later the virtual doppelganger was bathed in light and he clicked the button to connect.

"Hello?" The deep voice came through the speakers just as the monitor showed a young man in a sweater vest.

"Thomas? Hello." Jonah reminded himself to smile since this wasn't one of the phone interviews he was used to.

Thomas picked up a legal pad and began scribbling. "Jonah. How're you doing?"

He sat back and tried to find a comfortable position in the office chair. "Well, the Lord's work is never done, so 'busy' seems to be answer of the day, my friend."

"Good, good." Thomas tapped his pen against the paper. "I only have a few questions for you."

"Whatever you need." Jonah regretted opening the door for whatever questions the reporter called about.

"Sister Helena's miraculous healings."

"What about them?"

"Have you ever done a follow-up on them?"

"On the healings? Why would we do that? It's been confirmed by seven hospitals that the afflicted were healed." Jonah felt his plastered grin falter a little.

"No, not the healings. The three tests at John Hopkins we witnessed were enough to concede that there are, in fact, healings being performed."

"Then what?"

Thomas leaned forward, head appearing too large for his body from the camera angle. "I mean on the people. Have you ever done a follow up on any of the people that Sister Helena's healed?"

A muffled knock came from the door and he looked up to see Karen, pointing emphatically at her watch.

"If I've caught you at a bad time—"

"No, no." Jonah waved her away and looked back at the monitor. "It's just a producer letting me know about the time. We *do* have a special event planned for this evening. I'm sure you've seen advertising for tonight."

Thomas laughed. "How could I not? It seems to be on every station across the country...prime time, even."

"Then you can understand that I'm a bit pressed for time. So," he said, taking control of the conversation, "let's get to these questions."

"Fair enough. As I said, I'd like to know if you've done a follow-up with any of the healed individuals or their families?"

"Not as of yet, but we are planning on doing a follow-up show later in the season. The Vessel," He smiled seeing the reporter wince at the name, "Sister Helena," he amended, "may heal the lame so they can walk, but the Saved still need exercise to rebuild their strength." Jonah made a mental note to have an intern map out an update show.

"You mention the healed as 'Saved.' Are you saying that the people who Sister Helena heals are touched by God?"

He clasped his hands together and sat in solemn repose at the desk. The leading question was obvious. "Sister Helena is simply the vessel for the Divine."

"Sir, that's not what I asked." Thomas quirked an eyebrow.

"I know. I'm happy to answer your questions, but let's not dance around while you grab for sensationalist headlines. My time, like yours, I'm sure, is limited."

"Fair enough." The reporter glanced at his notes. "Did you know that four of your 'Saved' people have committed felonies since being healed? One of which involved a teenage girl gutting her entire family while on a fishing trip?" An expectant stare waited for him to slip.

Jonah bowed his head, careful not to take the theatrics too far. "The thing about God is free will. At the time of their healing they were touched by God's vessel and returned whole. What they did afterward may or may not be of God." He pushed back from the desk and stood. "I really am pressed for time."

"One more question." Thomas didn't wait for a response, "We can't find reference to Sister Helena's appointment anywhere, or reference to where she studied."

"All of that information is on our website."

"Tonight's prophecy." The reporter shifted gears, realizing that he only had another few seconds. "She claims to know the exact date of—"

"I'm out of time, Mister Bradshaw."

"But, sir—"

"Thank you for your questions." Jonah clicked the escape key and broke the connection. "Son of a bitch!" He ripped the door open and stormed into the control room. "I need an updated list for Sister Helena's resume. You," he pointed at an intern too young for the mustache worn, "get updates on all of the people healed."

"This season?"

"From the beginning. Church tours as well." He bellowed, "I want them all! I want them on my desk tomorrow night!"

The eight people in the control booth sat stone-still in his presence, waiting for additional commands. When none came they nervously returned to their assigned tasks of monitoring the hallways, directing ushers to congested areas, and ensuring camera angles were optimum for viewers at home.

"Big J!"

Jonah jumped at the booming sound echoing from his earpiece. He keyed it and replied, "What?" Everyone in the control room looked up, and he turned away, putting a hand over the earpiece.

"Helena wants… "

"Sister Helena."

The tech cleared his throat. "Sorry, *sir. Sister* Helena requests your presence on stage."

"Ask her what for."

"Can't, sir. I have to try to get the parishioners back into the seats." An audible click sounded as the crew's newest technician changed channels. "Ladies and gentlemen, please take a moment for the needs of the body, but then return to your seats. Sister Helena has something special for each and every one of you."

A good portion of the crowd returned to their seats while others worked their way to the restrooms. The few that continued toward the exits were met by ushers who whispered something which convinced every person to remain for the upcoming event. In all, Jonah guessed there to be well over fifteen hundred attendees swirling around the chapel's floor.

"Bigger," he mumbled and exited the sound booth, stomping down the back stairs. "I told her we needed to build it bigger."

Jonah navigated the myriad of parishioners and through the "Staff Only" door which led below the floor and stage. The tunnel stood in direct contrast to the eggshell white walls and crystal chandeliers seen by the public. Here, not even whitewash splashed the concrete walls—only a rough gray cinder block and concrete maze of corridors wound their way under the Sonrise and Be Saved chapel. After two lefts and jogging along the fifty yard shaft leading stage left, he emerged through a tight opening only an anorexic could call an access point. A boom operator, nursing a cup of coffee before the next show, grasped an arm and helped extricate him from the makeshift stairway.

"Helena," he managed to blurt.

The operator finished another swallow of liquid caffeine and motioned with the half-empty cup to the layers of white curtains.

"Sister Helena?" Jonah shouted louder than intended, winning curious looks from the stage crew. Embarrassment flushed as he walked into the curtains. Slit after slit was found and stepped through, sending him closer to center stage. Thoughts of childhood, playing in his grandmother's laundry as it line-dried, flooded forth and brought a rare honest smile.

"Jonah…here."

Jonah turned left and made his way through three more gossamer layers and arrived center stage. With the main curtain down and no less than a dozen layers on either side and behind them, the draped fabric created a semblance of structure as he entered the stage proper. Two giant spots glowed on the front curtain and filled their space with a softer, but still pronounced, light. That's where he found her.

Helena stood behind a white glass-topped desk. She took off her earpiece and left the wire dangling along the V of her blouse. The plastic wire danced against the lace collar before its ear-hook snagged.

"We've got twenty minutes until you're back on-air. Shouldn't you be in makeup?"

Helena smiled. "Are you saying you think I need makeup?" With a gentle pull, she drew the leather chair, also dyed white, out and leaned forward, resting both arms on the seat's back. The mane of hair fell forward and framed not only her face, but a generous amount of cleavage visible from where he now stood.

"No…no." Jonah shifted his gaze, albeit reluctantly, away from his benefactor and squinted against the spotlight's illumination. "I mean that you're back on-air in just a few and everyone," he looked at her, straining to keep eye contact, "and I do mean *everyone*, needs a little help when on camera."

"Not after tonight." Helena said. The corners of her mouth broadened as she played with the coiled earpiece.

"There no time for this. Let's get you ready." Jonah walked over and started guiding her to one of the side curtains. She stopped short of stepping through and placed both hands on his chest.

"Do you remember when we first met?"

"Helena," his voice dropped to a whisper, "leave that for the P.R. to iron out."

"Do you?"

"Yes, Helena. I remember."

"Me barely out of my teens and doing whatever I could after that horrible marriage." She pushed against him, closing the foot of distance between them. "You taking me in, teaching me about everything from psychic cold readings to what most orbs actually are in spirit photography." Fingers massaged his chest, splaying then raking nails across his nipples. "Out of focus dust particles caught by the flash. Isn't that right?"

Jonah backed up another step, glancing at the front curtain, concerned about the congregation massing just a few yards beyond.

"You remember, right?" Taking another step forward, she pushed him back. Jonah first stumbled, then managed to maintain his footing by balancing against the edge of the desk. "You remember about the half a million in donations that disappeared two years ago?"

"A quarter million," he stammered.

"Oh no. It was a cool half million." She placed the hand on his chest again. "I *know* you took it."

Her smile appeared, to Jonah at least, more painted on at this close distance rather than actually there. "I…didn't…"

Helena caressed the side of this cheek. "Oh, but you did. I know because I took the other quarter million." An unexpected shove forced Jonah off balance and onto the desk. In pursuit, she opened the skirt's fold and straddled him. "It's okay," she soothed. "You swore you were with me in this 'til the end.'" Manicured hands fumbled with his trousers, fanning the belt and reaching into his now exposed green boxers.

"I..." Jonah looked around in a panic, grabbing at her only to have his half-hearted efforts slapped away. "No! We can't. Not with..."

"Just be quiet and hurry." Helena bent and delivered a kiss, her tongue snaking between Jonah's lips. She reached down and gripped hard, squeezing his member to arousal.

Jonah watched dumbfounded as the woman he'd known for years jerked the pants open and pulled his manhood free. She scooted forward to guide the rigid piece of flesh under the skirt and into her. Silky wetness enveloped him, and Helena took her time to draw out the moment. His hands found a life of their own and went to her thighs, fingertips stroking from stocking to bare skin. Her hips rolled and instinct took over where decorum left off. He thrust against the rocking, breathing in time with her and feeling the healer's own passion draw him closer to climax.

"Matheson," she purred.

He faltered, stopping mid-thrust.

Helena ground down hard, eliciting an uncontrolled buck from Jonah. "I didn't say stop." She went on, picking up speed. "I know you put the travel notes in his locker." Another pubic thrust returned him to sex's fluid motion.

"The police were getting too...*ohhh.*" He forgot what he was saying.

"...too close. I know. That was number nine."

Jonah grabbed onto her hips, animal tension overtaking him. "I...wha...?"

"Number nine." She grinned and matched his rhythm. "Thou shalt not bear false witness against your neighbor."

He stopped again only to have Helena's motions continue him along. "Stop." The grinding continued, pressing his butt cheeks down on what felt like the rings of her day planner.

"Oh, no. Not until we're done." She flexed, and Jonah clenched his teeth. "You know he was stomped to death while in lockup that first night. That was *my* doing." The muscles surrounding him fluttered. "I have...oh God damn it, that feels good." A chuckle escaped the healer. "There's number three."

"Helen," he switched to using her actual name, something he hadn't done in years. "Talking about that while we're..."

"Say it," Helena cooed," say it."

"Having sex."

"Fucking."

Jonah ignored the vulgarity of the word, though not the action. He found her rhythm, moving in time with her, and felt the telltale clenching of a forthcoming climax.

"Number three," she panted. "You know...about not taking God's name in vain."

Realization of the statement about orchestrating Greg Matheson's death struck home just as Helena's orgasm ripped through her. Short barks of passion loudly escaped and he tensed, imagining the hundreds of people, just a stone's throw away, stopping their conversations and preparations in recognition of their act.

"Five minutes!" echoed throughout the building as one of the producers called out for the final countdown to air.

"Five minutes and you..." she convulsed again, impaling herself against him, "you're making this possible."

Fear of being caught overcame passion. Jonah tried rolling onto his side to dislodge her, but she was firmly mounted and drawing him toward climax. Resigning to the inevitable, he gripped her waist and held tight as he spilled into her. Helena continued to move, though slowly now, draining everything he had to offer.

"Thank you," Helena whispered as she laid down on his chest. "Those were the final three."

"Huh?" He pushed her to the side, taking the time to make sure that no evidence of their act was visible on the front of her skirt. Jonah stood, tucked himself away, and began to straighten his clothes.

Helena lay on her back, legs open in an obscene mockery of the persona they'd worked for over fifteen years to perfect. "Four, obviously, seven and ten."

He ignored the statement and went about rearranging the desk while tapping his own headset. "Geri, Helena's at her stage desk. Get makeup here right away and touch her up. Micah, switch to camera three and tell the choir that there's a change, we want to start the show with 'Love's a River.'"

"Four's an easy one," Helena said.

He glared at her. "Helena, get your head in the game. We're on camera in just a few minutes. This…" he stumbled for an explanation and motioned at the desk, "was just too many years of working together. Nothing more than stress and nerves." Jonah grimaced while struggling not to catch himself in the zipper. "We'll…we'll get past this."

"Four's Keep the Sabbath Holy." She rolled onto her side and brought a knee forward, exposing the leg to the hip. "And you know today's Sunday."

"Damn it, Helena."

One of the six makeup artists stumbled through the same opening Jonah found, catching a low heel on the curtain's hem. The artist blushed when she saw Helena's disheveled appearance, certain of the cause. To her credit, she shook off the initial surprise, knelt and opened the modified tackle box, pulling a towel, brush, and base from the container. Only a single disapproving corner-of-the-eye glance came from the worker, darting from the healer to Jonah as she stood.

Without warning, Helena reached up, grabbed her blouse and ripped it open, exposing a lacy white bra tinged with red where the under-wire met ribcage. A little scream escaped as her stomach distended, grossly mimicking a hand pressed against a garbage bag. The internal thumb teased her belly button as one would a nipple. Helena rolled off the table, leaning against the desktop for balance as she stood. Her own hand reached up and caressed the depressions between the raised fingers. "I've waited years to know number seven…to know you." The statement came out in wet, ragged breaths. Bloody spittle fell, spattered the glass desk, and added a bruised shade of crimson to the peach lipstick she wore.

Jonah grabbed at the makeup artist's arm, fearful of being left alone in the waking nightmare.

"If Tom were dead tonight wouldn't be worth any—" Helena doubled over, breasts swung as the bra took on a decidedly redder tinge than seconds earlier. "*Oh*…I didn't expect it to hurt so much." She looked up at her audience of two. "You remember Tom…my husband. The bastard's in California under a bridge somewhere and stoned out of his ever-loving mind." Her body rocked back and forth, a marionette sans strings. "He has six months left at best. I just got...lucky." With the last word, she stared at Jonah's groin, fresh beads of sweat peppering her brow.

"Helena, what in hell—"

"*Hell?* You have no idea about Hell." The healer forced herself to stand upright, hand impressions doubled in number, one stretched itself between skin and ribs, pushing under the bra to cup her left breast in a fashion nature never intended. Skin darkened as it separated from the fascia and lifted. Helena's eyes rolled back into her head, though through ecstasy or agony was left to each of the onlookers to decide for themselves.

"AIDS," she spat between huffing gasps for air. "A stupid needle prick nearly ruined everything." More gasps followed as one of the impressions moved downward, disappearing under the skirt's waistline and doubling her over again a second later. "H...hard to believe it was a different needle prick that saved the day." She moaned, feet spreading to allow the hand its passage. "Number...seven...adultery." Helena moaned louder, letting out a long nasal tone. Blood trickled out and wept down the corner of her mouth. "The bastard actually wanted a divorce."

"You," Helena turned a now ashen face to her partner, "you were the key." Blood welled on her lips and she licked it away. "You watched me for years...played with that noodle while watching the security cams in my dressing room. I knew you could help me speed things up. You..." Her words choked off and she convulsed, hips rocking in an exaggerated mimic of what Jonah took part in only moments ago. A gush of blood dropped from under her skirt, chunks of organ matter splattered against white satin heels.

Jonah muttered, "Dear God."

"God, yes. But not...not..." Helena looked up, eyes bulging and bloodshot. One of the sub-dermal hands forced its way up from under the collarbone, across her throat, and came to rest along the side of her jaw, cutting off any further words or air. More hands pushed to the surface, stretching the skin everywhere visible, leaving the surface appearing bloated and writhing. A silent scream formed on an open mouth, denied the air needed for tone. One eye slipped free of the socket and a single red-slicked fingertip slid out, exploring the lashes in an obscene fashion.

All the hands spasmed within Helena. Every visible inch

contracted. The action repeated and the internal structure vanished from her front, leaving an upright sack of flesh bearing little resemblance to the faith healer but still managing to stand. Her torso concaved, drawing in where bones should be, but allowing the outer edges to remain. Impressions of hands gripped ribs, breaking them free. Skin stretched, then darkened beyond that of any surfacing bruise already welling. Dermal layers split, cracks opening further along the remains of breastbone, working down to the pubic bone. A crevice formed, starting at her belly button and slicing up to the neck. Flesh separated and opened with a sucking hiss. The effect appeared like dry leaves caught in an autumn breeze.

Helena's seized body shaking with epileptic fury, her one remaining eye looked over at them, weeping a viscous fluid while her mouth remained locked in an over-exaggerated O. Skin flapped along with hair against a breeze drawn into her from the room. Papers fluttered and two flew free, dancing briefly before they disappeared into the hole which had once been her chest. Slowly, ever so slowly, the healer turned, giving Jonah and the makeup artist a more direct view into her depths.

Light shone into the tunnel that was once Helena Crane. A well of bone and flesh bored deep, miles deep, then fell lost in a Stygian blackness beyond reason. The contrasting physical impossibility hurt Jonah's head.

Something in the void moved and the makeup artist blubbered, "Nuhnuhnuh…nuh nuh nuh…nuhnuhnuh nuhnuhnuh."

Jonah glanced over and saw the aid shaking her head, though her eyes never left the abomination before them.

A hissing sound came from the darkness within Helena. Inside, things moved just beyond the light's reach. Shadows shifted, creating shapes almost human, but not quite. More forms clustered at the edge of illumination, bordering on the choke point of the healer's body.

"God," he managed.

Helena blinked, and Jonah felt the artist flinch at the sight. Both arms opened wide and stuck straight out from her sides.

The first pulled itself from the darkness. No bigger than a child, it stared at them with three pairs of blue eyes, each blinking a different speed than the rest from atop the hairless, domed head. The jagged edges of a hole where its nose should be, flexed like that of a rabbit, testing the air. Pasty white skin covered the creature, showing every piece of filth clinging to it. Hands reached out of the healer and pushed against her hips in an attempt to free itself. Brown ichor stained the skirt and the creature fell to the floor. Bone spurs protruded in multiple directions, leaving angles and implied joints where no human had them. Flopping on the floor, it unsuccessfully tried to right itself as another followed through.

Appendages proved the best descriptive word as Jonah struggled to comprehend the second beast. The ropy mandibles went from cheekbone to underneath its chin, twitching with agitation. Its head pushed through Helena, tearing the opening wider and allowing a watermelon-sized pink cranium through. Though the basic features of a skull shone clear, the thing lacked actual eyes and nose, only the mouth appeared recognizable. A knot of tentacles roughly resembling an arm reached in their direction.

Survival instinct kicked in and he shoved the makeup artist at the groping monstrosity. The knot separated, slithering into her hair and entwining around the amber locks. A single pull launched the woman into the chasm, left leg snapping with a muffled crunch as she disappeared inside.

He waited for the scream and was rewarded, though the muffled voice sounded so distant he doubted anyone in the audience caught the shriek.

With the larger beast gone for the moment, Jonah saw a dull glow deep inside the rift. The void filled with things crawling toward them, things with segmented eyes and mandibles, legs bearing jutting signs of excited humanity, and hands, hands on arms, on legs, one even covering itself as a makeshift codpiece.

An army of insanity.

Madness.

Legion.

"...and we're on!"

The curtain rose to the audience's screams. White fabric turned red throughout the chapel and a new chorus, one of tortured pain, broke into a song as old as time itself.

Jonah was beyond screaming.

He bore witness, along with ten million viewers, to what The Vessel offered.

Henry Snider is a founding member of the award-winning Colorado Springs Fiction Writer's Group (http://www.csfwg.org). During the last two decades he's dedicated his time to helping others tighten their writing through critique groups, classes, lectures, prison prose programs, and high school fiction contests. He retired from the CSFWG presidency in December 2008. After a much needed vacation he returned to writing, this time for publication in mid-2010.

While still reserving enough time to pursue his own fiction aspirations, Henry continues to be active in the writing community through classes, editing services and advice.

Henry lives with his wife, fellow author and editor Hollie Snider, son—poet Josh Snider—and numerous neurotic animals, including, of course, Alexander, the black cat. Find out more about him at http://www.henrysnider.com.

Playing Blackjack with Mr. Paws

Craig Saunders

The building that housed the Fordham Town Herald offices was built in 1805. Originally it was a playhouse, holding productions of local theatre and travelling shows alike. Theatre had been big business back in the 19th century. That, and drinking.

Many a patron of the playhouse had come to see the shows, but the most popular of all was the famous gambling mouse, Mr. Paws.

The Marvelous Mr. Paws, the billing proclaimed. *The only card playing mouse in the world!*

But the sign sold the act a bit short. After all, Mr. Paws was always something more than a mere card playing mouse.

———

21 grand. That's what Clive Greenwood reckoned his life was worth after the government took its cut. It was all it would ever be worth. He stood no chance of promotion beyond junior editor. Ever.

"Morning," he grunted at the office, pulling himself awkwardly into an office chair that was too tall for one of such diminutive stature.

With a jaunty heave, he was in.

The senior editor sniggered behind his computer monitor. Clive knew they set his chair higher every night after he left. The chair needed weight on it to be lowered, so he had to climb up every morning. Just another in a long list of wounds he wished he could redress against his colleagues and the world in general.

He looked around the office. Senior editor, sub editor, assistant editor, and some cunt called Paul. Clive had no idea what Paul did. He thought he sold advertising space, but all he seemed to do was smoke and swear into the phone.

Neck aching already, feet dangling high above the floor, Clive switched the computer monitor on.

21 grand. That's what a life was worth.

21 grams. That's what a soul weighed. Some boffin called Dr. Duncan MacDougall weighed the departed and found they weighed 21 grams less dead than they had while living. Turned out he was full of shit.

He reached down and fiddled with the lever to lower his chair. It was difficult enough to lower an office chair with normal arms, and Clive could barely reach.

Would he sell his soul, all 21 grams of it, for a little more height? For normal arms and legs? For a body that matched his head?

Fucking right he would. Then these bastards wouldn't be able to take the piss out of him every day.

Like their insistence on calling him a little person. Clive wasn't a little person. A little person was a kid. He was nearly forty years old.

And he was also a dwarf, with Achondroplasia. The real deal. Not a "little person." Not some bearded axe-wielding manic, either. Just a plain old dwarf.

"Clive!"

He jumped and pulled the lever to raise his chair. His senior editor had somehow got behind him and shouted on purpose.

"David?" he said.

"Mouse, Clive. Mouse in the attic."

"And?"

"I want you to sort it out, young man."

"Young man" rankled, but Clive bit his tongue. He was used to it. Used to the insults and the jibes. His heart was protected by a layering of keloid scars that no bastard could penetrate, and certainly not David Corn, his senior editor and ultimate boss.

"I don't think that's appropriate," said Clive. "I'm a junior editor, not a mouse catcher."

"Troublesome little bugger," David continued as though he hadn't heard Clive's protest. "The attic space is too low for the rest of us. Just thought...you know..."

"Because I'm a dwarf."

"Ha. Little person, Clive. *Little person.*"

Clive couldn't believe his ears, but fuck it. What could he do? What could you do in the face of the endless torments but ride them?

"Here's a torch," said David with a smarmy smile, because he already knew that Clive wouldn't refuse. He never did.

But he kept tally, all right.

———

The old playhouse, once grandly titled the Theatre Royal, though no royalty had ever visited in its two hundred year history, had been renovated many times. The last was in 2003, when the Fordham Town Herald adopted it as their offices.

The first renovation began in 1849, six weeks after it almost burned to the ground.

1849 was also the year that Harris Jakes lost a game of cards to an old, white mouse named Mr. Paws.

———

Clive poked his head into the small attic space above the old playhouse. His colleagues gathered below the hatch, looking up as Clive swung the torch in wide arcs, into the dark corners, running the light over the beams and rafters.

"There's nothing up here," he said, knowing what the reply would be.

"Pesky buggers," said David. "Little blighters are sneaky."

Paul barked a laugh, and Clive bit his tongue once again.

"You'll have to get up there, in deep," said the sub-editor.

"Root around. Get to understand it. Get down to the mouse's level," said the assistant editor, kind of laughing, too, but held in check, even though Clive knew the laugh was there in the man's head, an actual laugh never more than a breath away.

Clive sighed and went up the last few steps of the ladder. The light from the torch let him see enough to know he didn't want to be up here among the cobwebs and giant spiders and bats and nesting birds and mice. All kinds of things to fall on his neck and make him scream and he really, really, didn't want to give the bastards below that kind of satisfaction.

Something skittered across the joists. He swung his torch toward the sound, and the mouse darted the other way. The torch flicked back and forth, until he finally caught the mouse in his sights.

It must have been the oldest rodent in the world. It was almost pure white, covered in thick hair, which he'd never seen on a mouse. The thing's whiskers were about six inches long, longer than the mouse's body. Its nose twitched, as though sniffing for

186 - Craig Saunders

intruders, but Clive got the impression that it could see perfectly well, because little red eyes fixed on him straight away. It was a bold stare.

Clive didn't return the stare. "I'm not getting into a staring contest with a fucking mouse," he muttered.

It was dead centre in the glare of the torch, and for some stupid reason Clive figured he could hit it and be done. So he threw the torch at it. The torch flipped end over end, then landed against an old oak beam, shattering the lens.

"Clive," said a voice that he didn't recognise.

The hatch banged shut and the darkness was total. And for some reason Clive thought the voice might just belong to the mouse.

———

"You there, Sir! Care to wager?"

Harris Jakes nodded, because all evening he'd been hoping he'd be the one to get the call. He was a drinking man, but, first and foremost, he was a gambling man. He had ten shillings in his pocket—the last of his money, all he owned in the world. He had no home since his wife had run off with a fat butcher. He had no kids. He didn't even have a dog.

Ten shillings was a lot of money to wager, but double that up...double it again...and...

"Yes, Sir, I would," he called out. Applause exploded from the eager audience.

He stepped carefully over the other patrons' legs in the cheap seats and worked his way to the front of the theatre. It wasn't a large theatre, housing roughly a hundred people, although sometimes more stood at the back.

The stage was lit with lanterns for atmosphere, and the only things on that stage were the mouse's handler, a round table with green baize on top, a pack of cards, and one small, wizened mouse. That mouse must have been ancient.

The mouse was sprightly enough, though. It ran down the handler's arm and hopped onto the table, then stood behind the pack of cards, nose twitching excitedly.

"What, Sir, is your name?"

"Harris Jakes," he said, smiling. The mouse was on its hind legs, sniffing. The air, or him, Harris didn't know.

"And what would you care to wager?"

"Ten shillings," he said, and an appreciative murmur spread through the crowd.

"The mouse is the house, ladies and gentlemen! Ten shillings it is...Mr. Jakes, shuffle away, blackjack's the game of the day!"

The crowd clapped politely, and Harris shuffled, tapped the deck, and, at the handler's nod, laid the cards before the happy old mouse.

Mr. Paws capered forward, so small that the people at the back of the theatre couldn't possibly see it. With its nose it pushed the first card toward Harris, the second toward itself.

Both turned at the same time, the handler turning the mouse's card for him.

"Mr. Harris has a ten of hearts, ladies and gentlemen. Mr. Paws holds a queen of spades!"

A gentle kind of excitement mounted, because the wager was high.

The mouse pushed the next card across the table, and with his clever nose, Mr. Paws dealt himself one next.

Harris turned his. The ace of spades.

The handler turned the next card. The ace of hearts.

"The house wins!"

Harris was suddenly very angry. It was the last of his money, and now he was destitute. He slammed his fist on the table, aiming for Mr. Paws, but the mouse was nimble. It ran up the handler's arm and down under his collar. Cards flew into the air and the table turned over.

"Cheat! Dirty bastard cheats!" Harris roared, and swung wildly at the handler, who stepped smartly to one side and rapped Harris on the head with a different kind of blackjack.

––––––––––

"Gambling man, Mr. Greenwood?" said the mouse, sitting up on its hind legs. It didn't look easy for the mouse to do it, either. It was ancient, looked older than a twenty year old dog.

He didn't wonder at a mouse talking. And he didn't think about the red glow that suffused the attic, the eerie light, the way it flickered, or the smell coming from below. None of that seemed important.

Just the green baize on the table, and the little old mouse, and a pack of cards.

Had the table been here before? He didn't remember, though it seemed to him perfectly reasonable that it was.

He stared dumbly at the mouse.

"No," he said. "Not really." He'd never gambled in his life.

"Know blackjack, though, right?"

Clive shook his head. "I played Rummy as a boy with my father." He shrugged and wanted to make the mouse happy, but he couldn't very well lie. If they were going to play cards he wouldn't be able to cover his ignorance.

He wasn't sure he did want to play cards, but the mouse was very old, and if cards made it happy...

More than anything he wanted to make the mouse happy.

But why?

It was so...

So old.

But more importantly the mouse was little.

Just like him. A strange reason to trust a talking mouse, but—

"Simple game," said the mouse. "Aiming for twenty-one. That's all there is to it. Five cards, bust. Over twenty one, bust. Stick on sixteen. Ace is one or eleven. Jack, Queen, King, ten. House rules, Mr. Greenwood, and believe me when I say, I am the house. Understand?"

"Not really," said Clive.

"Good," said the mouse with a laugh. You wouldn't think a mouse could laugh. But—what the hell?—this one talked, and you wouldn't expect that, either. Clive laughed right along with the mouse's joke, because it was a cute little thing, and Jesus, it wasn't just a talking, card playing mouse. It was a *laughing* mouse, too.

"What are we playing for?" Clive asked.

"What have you got?"

Clive shrugged again. "I don't know," he said, turning out his pockets. All he could think of was his watch, but even that wasn't worth much, and he didn't want to disappoint the mouse.

The mouse seemed amused.

"How 'bout...twenty-one grams?"

Clive almost laughed, but then he thought he saw the flicker of flames coming up through the ceiling, off to the right, between him and the eaves. A dim kind of daylight came in through the eaves where birds made their nests.

For a moment, looking at that sliver of daylight, his head seemed to clear.

This is dangerous, he thought, but then smoke swirled and the daylight was lost. All that remained was that flitting firelight and an old, old mouse, whiskers twitching, pushing a card toward him.

"One for you," said the mouse. "One for me. One for you. One for me."

The mouse turned first.

"That's ten, right?" it said. Clive shrugged and nodded. A king, could be ten...he didn't really know. The cards didn't seem quite as important to him as the mouse. He watched the mouse and forgot about his cards. Then the mouse coughed politely.

"Come along, Mr. Greenwood. I'm getting old waiting for that damn card, and in case you hadn't noticed," it said, flicking its head to the right, where flames were now leaping, "time's short for both of us."

Clive shrugged again. What did he care if his bastard colleagues burned to death below?

"You go first," he said. "Seems fair. Do them all at once."

"That's not the way the game's played," said the mouse. It seemed thoughtful, though. "Unfair advantage to you, you see?"

"No," admitted Clive.

The mouse was delighted at the answer and laughed again. "Oh, Mr. Greenwood, you are a card! Well, then, care to change the wager?"

Clive couldn't seem to remember what the wager was in the first place, so he just shook his head and coughed, smoke from the fire below tickling his nostrils.

The mouse flicked its second card over, an ace.

"Twenty-one," said the mouse. It sounded triumphant.

"Turn away," it said, so Clive did.

"Oh," said the mouse, because Clive held the jokers in the pack. Two of them with jester's hats adorned in bells.

In the distance, a little bell tinkled.

Clive reached up to find a jester's hat on his own head. He frowned.

"What's it mean?" he asked the mouse.

The mouse laughed again, full of good humour, even though the old playhouse was burning down around them.

"How much is that, then?" he said again, because the mouse just carried right on laughing.

"Joker's wild!" said the mouse, capering up Clive's jester suit to sit on his hat. The bells tinkled as Clive's head swayed, giddy from the smoke.

"Joker's wild," the mouse repeated, whispering in Clive's ear. "And they're worth whatever you want them to be..."

————————

Harris woke in the gutter bathed in the dim light of a street lamp. His head hurt like a bastard and when he felt around he found a knot the size of an egg just behind his right ear. He sat up with a groan and shivered, because someone had stolen his coat.

Mr. Harris Jakes was not only a gambling and drinking man, he was also a smoking man. Fortunately, he kept his matches in his trouser pocket.

He reached in and pulled out the matches, then walked unsteadily down a dirty alleyway where the light didn't reach, an alleyway that ran along the back of the Theatre Royal.

He tripped over a pile of rubbish and fell badly. He twisted his right hand and dropped the matches, but his left hand hit upon something hard. He felt around and discovered the object was a rolling pin.

Perfect.

He rummaged through the rubbish, swearing, until eventually he found his matches.

Then he smashed in a window and cleared away the glass and pulled himself with a groan over the sill.

"Bastard friggers," he said, setting fire to the curtains.

Mr. Harris Jakes died two weeks later in a bar fight over a tab. He didn't die easy. People said he was unlucky, the way he went, but then maybe luck had nothing to do with it.

Luck's not personal, but sometimes it can be, too. Like when you cross the wrong mouse, a mouse named Mr. Paws, and a mouse that maybe wasn't a mouse at all.

————————

Clive rapped his knuckles on the hatch, the bells on his jester costume jingle-jangling.

His colleagues giggled below, despite the fires licking at the ladder.

As he descended they all smiled and their smiles looked…
somehow…terrified.

"Saw old Mr. Paws, did you, young man?" said David, his
senior editor. "Good man. Good man."

Clive nodded.

"Join the club," said Paul. "Lost, of course, but won, too. Sold
my soul to that damn mouse, but I've got a sweet wife with big—"

"Never mind that now," said David. The sub editor giggled as
flames leapt around his feet.

The smell of charred flesh filled the offices of the Fordham
Town Herald, where the damned worked, sometimes for twenty-
one grand, and sometimes for twenty-one grams.

"What'd he offer for your soul, eh?" said the assistant editor.

"Nothing," said Clive. "Nothing at all."

"What do you mean?" said David.

"I didn't lose my soul in a game of cards. I've still got a soul."
Clive nodded madly, flicking his head side to side to set his bells
ringing.

"You won?" said David.

He kept nodding, bells going mad.

"Devious buggers, little people," said David sagely. The
assistant editor and the sub editor and the man named Paul all
nodded at this pearl of wisdom.

"What did you win?" asked Paul.

"Whatever I wanted," said Clive, "and I'm here to collect."

Craig Saunders lives in Norfolk, England with his wife and three
children. He used to have three black cats but they were unlucky.
Craig started out by writing fantasy, followed by science fiction,
then humor. It took eight novels before he figured out he was a
horror writer and he hasn't wasted any time since. With more than
a dozen published short stories, his first novel will soon be
published by the Library of Horror Press and his first novella will
soon be published by Blood Bound Books. He blogs at
www.petrifiedtank.blogspot.com. He's easy to follow, but a lazy
blogger.

Must Be Something in the Water

Mark Allan Gunnells

10:00 a.m.

I was sitting at my desk, typing up a report that was two days overdue, when the deliveryman brought in the new three-gallon jug for the water cooler. I didn't really pay the guy who wheeled the jug in on a handcart too much attention. I've never been much of a water drinker, and in the three years that I'd worked in the office, I don't think I ever drank from the water cooler. I spared the fellow only a cursory glance, and he made no impression on me. Tall and lanky, with a nondescript gray uniform, a name stenciled above the pocket, but I wouldn't have been able to pick him out of a lineup and later I couldn't recall what the name was on his shirt.

"Looks like we have a new company delivering water," Joyce said, coming up and leaning against the edge of my desk.

"What?" I said, not taking my eyes off the computer screen. If I didn't get the report finished by lunch, Mr. Griswald was going to have my sack.

"We usually get our water from Aqua Products, but this is a different company."

"Hmmm."

"The delivery guy from Aqua is cuter. Maybe—"

"Joyce," I snapped. Forcing myself to calm down, I continued in a more subdued tone of voice. "I'm sorry, but I'm really trying to concentrate on my work."

"Oh, of course, Marty. Yeah, I'll talk to you later."

Feeling like a shit, I watched Joyce walk away. There were six of us that worked together in the office, our desks sitting out in the open, not even cubicles to give us the illusion of privacy. Sometimes I thought of putting tape around my desk like that guy on *WKRP*, but I was afraid no one would get the joke. Our immediate supervisor, Mr. Griswald, was the only one with his own office, a space almost as large as the one we all shared with glass walls so that he could keep an eye on us.

The water cooler was in the far corner, next to the mini-fridge and microwave. Joyce, Carol, and Vic were gathered around it at the moment, waiting for the deliveryman to finish installing the new jug. It was just water, for Christ's sake; they could get the same stuff out of the faucet in the bathroom. Hardly something to start a line for.

Shaking my head and laughing to myself, I turned back to the report.

11:00 a.m.

By tuning out the rest of the office, I managed to finish the report in an hour. I quickly proofed what I'd written then printed it out. All done with an entire hour to spare. Not too shabby. Now I could get to all the other work I was behind on.

Leaning back in my chair and stretching, I noticed that everyone in the office—Joyce, Carol, Vic, Joel, Terri, even Mr. Griswald himself—was gathered around the water cooler, drinking from those little paper cups that came to points like ice cream cones. They were talking and laughing boisterously.

This was unprecedented. Mr. Griswald rarely partook in camaraderie with his employees, and he usually frowned upon socializing at work. Seeing him laughing it up by the water cooler, a hand clamped on Joel's shoulder in a friendly gesture, was like seeing a monkey in a tuxedo.

Intrigued, I headed for the water cooler, snagging the report from the printer on my way. I stood on the fringe of the group, listening to their laughter but having missed the source of their mirth. No one seemed to notice me there. I felt like a pauper standing outside an expensive restaurant with my nose pressed against the glass, fogging up the window with my need.

After being ignored for a full minute, I cleared my throat and said, "Hey guys, what's going on?"

The six turned toward me then. Smiles were stretched across their faces, wide and strained. It was like a half dozen Jokers staring back at me. It was a bit unnerving. "Oh, Marty," Terri said. "You've had your eyes glued to that computer screen for so long, we almost forgot you were here."

"What's so funny?"

"Oh, Ned was just telling us the most hilarious joke."

I was just about to ask who Ned was when I realized she was referring to Mr. Griswald. I had never heard anyone call him by his first name before. And who would have thought he had a sense of humor? He'd certainly never shown signs of having one in the three years I'd worked for him.

"Well, I have that report here for you, Mr. Griswald."

Mr. Griswald waved a dismissive hand. "Oh, forget about that, Marty. It can wait."

"Wait?" Mr. Griswald had been riding my ass since yesterday morning about finishing this report. He'd made it sound as if the world would spin off its axis if I didn't have it on his desk by noon today. "I thought you said it took precedence over everything."

Mr. Griswald drew close and put an arm over my shoulders, as if we were best buds. "You have to learn to take it easy now and then, my boy. All work and no play, you know how that goes."

Did Mr. Griswald really just call me *my boy*? I suddenly found myself wondering if I'd fallen asleep at the computer and was now in the grips of some bizarre dream.

"Here," Carol said, filling one of the paper cups from the water cooler and holding it out to me. "Have a drink with us."

"Uhm, no thanks. I'll just grab a soda."

I opened the mini-fridge and took out a frosty Pepsi.

"Soda's bad for you," Joel said, which was a joke. If there was one person in the office who was a bigger caffeine addict than me, it was Joel. "Have some nice, refreshing, *healthy* water."

"I'm fine, thanks." I started backing away toward my desk, and the group turned away from me, closing me out again. I glanced at the water cooler and wondered if maybe the water had been spiked. It seemed unlikely, but maybe the deliveryman had decided to have a little fun by slipping some alcohol in the water jug. Everyone in the office certainly seemed to be acting drunk.

I returned to my desk, the laughter trailing behind me. Maybe I was just overreacting. Perhaps Mr. Griswald was simply in a good mood and wanted to spread it around. Of course, in three years I had never seen him in a good mood, but the law of averages suggested it would have to happen sooner or later.

I pulled some files out of the two-drawer filing cabinet next to my desk and began going over them.

12:00 p.m.

At noon, I put aside the files and went to heat up my lunch. I'd brought leftover lasagna in a Tupperware bowl, and I took it out of the fridge and placed it in the microwave, setting it for two minutes then hitting the *Start* button.

"What're you doing, Marty?" Joyce asked, walking up to me.

"Lunch."

"Leftovers again?" Joyce took one of the paper cups and began filling it from the water cooler. I noticed that despite the constant trips my officemates had been making to the water cooler all day, the jug still seemed to be full.

"Waste not, want not, that's what my mother always taught me."

"Didn't you hear?" Joyce said with a tight smile. "Mr. Griswald has ordered in Chinese for everyone."

I stood there for a moment, just looking at Joyce. While I was friendly with everyone in the office, Joyce was the only one I would have really called a friend. About twice a month, we got together outside of work. A movie, dinner, once we went to see the Dixie Chicks in concert. She'd even set me up on a blind date with a guy in her ceramics class, although the resultant date had been a disaster of Katrina proportions. I felt I knew Joyce pretty well, and she just wasn't acting herself. It was nothing overt, nothing easily pinpointed. Her smile was forced, more of a grimace, and it didn't touch her eyes. She stood a little too rigidly, but her shoulders jerked now and then as if she were having muscle spasms. While I watched, she guzzled the water down, some of it dribbling down her chin. She made no move to wipe it away.

"Are you feeling okay, Joyce?"

"Never better. How about a drink of water?"

"You know I don't really like water. I'll stick with my soda."

"Well, are you going to join us for lunch? We're all going to eat in the conference room."

I found the idea of eating lunch with my officemates with their painted-on smiles and strangely cheerful demeanors rather unappetizing. "You know, I'm not really in the mood for Chinese. I think I'll just eat my lasagna at my desk."

Joyce's smile vanished in an instant, as if a magician had made it disappear. Her gaze darkened, storm clouds building up behind her eyes. In fact, the air suddenly seemed charged with an electrical current. I actually backed up a step, banging my ass into the front of the microwave.

"What, you think you're too good to eat with the rest of us?" Joyce said, her voice low and heated.

"Of course not. I just don't—"

"All day you've been at your desk, head down, just ignoring the rest of us. Like you think you're superior to us or something, like we're not worth your time."

I laughed uneasily, trying to hold to the belief that this was all a joke, but the rage I felt radiating from Joyce was quite real. "Come on, Joyce, you know I'm not like that. I'm just not feeling very sociable today."

Joyce said nothing for a moment, but her eyes sliced into my flesh like razor blades. Finally she said, her voice so soft it was almost inaudible, "Better be careful up there on your pedestal, Mr. My-Shit-Don't-Stink. Someone's liable to come along and knock it right out from under you."

Before I could respond, she turned and stalked off. As she approached the conference room, she shouted, "Marty won't be joining us for lunch! His Majesty is too good to dine with us common folk!"

The whole encounter had left me reeling. Was that really Joyce, the same woman whom I'd gossiped with since she began working in the office a year and a half ago? It looked like her, but that was where the similarities ended. And how quickly her mood had changed for chipper brightness to seething anger. Such a sudden mood swing, it had nearly given me whiplash.

Behind me, the microwave's timer went off. I took my bowl and a soda and returned to my desk, making a conscious effort to avoid looking in the direction of the conference room.

1:00 p.m.

Over the next hour, things appeared to be getting back to normal. No one was talking to me, but everyone seemed to return to their usual workday activities. I was actually beginning to believe that maybe the weirdness had passed, until I went to the restroom.

I stood at the urinal, staring at the tiled wall as I relieved my bladder. There was a black layer of grime coating the spaces between the tiles. I walked away, the sensor in the urinal letting it know that it was time to flush. I stepped over to the sink, sticking my hands under the faucet so the sensor would know to start the water. I was musing on how much of our lives were run off sensors when I heard the moan.

It was deep and drawn out, followed by a sudden intake of breath. I also thought I detected a sound like slurping. The noises were coming from one of the restroom's three toilet stalls. I knew what it sounded like; they were sounds I'd heard as a younger man in bathroom stalls in clubs I'd attended. Hell, they were sounds I'd *made* as a younger man in bathroom stalls in clubs I'd attended. But surely I was mistaken; this was an office, after all.

Crouching down, I ducked my head so that I could see under the stall doors. The stalls on either end were unoccupied, but in the middle stall were two pairs of legs. One pair belonging to someone standing, the other to someone kneeling. I recognized both pairs of shoes. The man standing in the polished black loafers was Vic; the man kneeling in the brown lace-ups was Joel.

I stood slowly, hearing the joints in my knees pop, wondering if Joel and Vic could hear it. If they had, the uninterrupted noises they made suggested they didn't care that they were no longer alone. I tried to wrap my mind around this, but it just wouldn't compute. Vic was a fifty-seven year old grandfather, and Joel was a newlywed.

I bolted from the restroom when I heard Vic hiss, "Here I come, boy." In the hallway, I almost collided with Carol. She gave me an annoyed look then continued on her way.

"Hey, Carol, have you seen Joyce?"

At first I thought she was just going to ignore me, but then she glanced over her shoulder and said, "Try the copier room."

"Thanks."

I hurried toward the copier room, eager to find Joyce and tell her about what I'd seen in the restroom. Not just out of a desire to gossip—although there was that, I had to admit—but so she could help me try to make sense of it. The door to the copier room was closed, which was unusual, but I didn't pause to consider it. I simply opened up the door and rushed inside. What I saw made me stop so abruptly I almost tripped over my own feet.

Joyce was on top of the table next to the copier, on all fours with her hair hanging over her face like a veil. Mr. Griswald was kneeling behind her, grabbing her hips as he thrust repeatedly. Both were naked and covered in sweat.

A tiny gasp escaped my lips, and both Joyce and Mr. Griswald looked up at me. Mr. Griswald did not stop thrusting, making throaty grunts with every stroke. Joyce smiled at me and said, "Hey there, Marty."

"Sorry, didn't mean to barge in," I said dumbly, edging back out the door.

"Nonsense. Why don't you join us?"

I felt like I was going to be ill and I quickly backpedaled out into the hallway, closing the door behind me.

Had everyone in the office gone insane? I had wondered earlier if the water had been spiked with alcohol; now I was wondering if it had been spiked with some kind of hallucinogenic drug. I wasn't sure what to do. I thought about leaving, but wasn't sure if I should. The workday didn't end until four, but surely when you found your boss fucking one of your coworkers in the copier room, standard workplace procedures were pretty much out the window.

In the end, I decided against leaving. I simply returned to my desk and tried to erase the image of Joyce and Mr. Griswald from my mind. I didn't have much success.

2:00 p.m.

"You goddamn cunt!"

At the sound of the angry words, I looked up. Carol and Terri were over by the water cooler. They had the stance of wrestlers about to start a match.

"I was here first," Terri said, taking a step toward the water cooler.

Carol snatched Terri by the hair and jerked her back. "The fuck you were. I was here first; you can just wait your turn."

Terri lashed out and smacked Carol across the cheek. The sound of flesh on flesh was loud in the office like a gunshot. Vic, Joel, and Mr. Griswald were making their way over to the fight. Joyce was nowhere to be seen.

"I got here before you, and I'm having the first drink," Terri said, taking a paper cup from the dispenser.

Carol punched Terri in the small of her back and then shoved her forward. Terri collided with the wall and slid to the floor.

Carol started for the water cooler, but Terri kicked out and tripped her. Carol fell to the floor, and suddenly the two women were rolling around, slapping and scratching at one another, spitting curses at each other that would have made Quentin Tarantino blush.

I pushed up from my desk and hurried over. Mr. Griswald grabbed me by the arm and said, "Where the fuck you think you're going, dickhead?"

"To put a stop to this."

"Oh, hell no!" Joel shouted at me. "This is good shit, and you ain't gonna ruin it!"

In the tumult, Terri ripped Carol's blouse open, revealing a bra that had a safety pin holding one of the straps. Vic, Joel, and Mr. Griswald hooted at the sight.

Suddenly, Joyce emerged from the conference room and bolted past the two women on the floor. Laughing like a mental patient, she yelled, "It's all mine!" Then she got down on her knees and stuck her head directly under the spigot of the water cooler, unleashing a flow into her mouth. Impossible as it seemed, she was laughing even as she gulped the water down.

Carol had bloodied Terri's nose, and the men started to chant as they watched the fight. Vic opened his pants and began masturbating. I retreated to my desk and decided to call corporate office to see if they could send any help. The phones weren't working.

3:00 p.m.

I was terrified. Following Carol and Terri's fight, I had tried to leave the office. Mr. Griswald had stopped me, informing me that no one left before the end of the workday. When I tried to leave anyway, he called over Vic and Joel, who physically escorted me back to my desk and deposited me in my chair. Joel was now standing guard by the door to make sure I didn't make another escape attempt.

Carol and Terri seemed to have made up. Carol was sitting on her desktop, legs spread, with Terri kneeling on the floor, her head hidden under Carol's skirt. Joyce, Vic, and Mr. Griswald were in Mr. Griswald's office, having what sounded like a very loud threesome.

Every so often, Joel would glance at Carol and Terri and play with himself.

Carol, a languid smile on her face, looked in my direction and said, "You know, Marty, you should really have some water."

"It really is yummy," Terri added, taking a break to peek out from under Carol's skirt then returning to business.

I cleared my throat and licked my lips. "Well, I am kind of thirsty."

"Then have some water," Joel said from the door. "You'll feel a lot better after having some water."

"You know, I think I'll do that," I said, standing. My legs felt weak, barely able to support my body, but I managed to walk across the office to the water cooler. It was still full. I took a paper cup and held it under the spigot. Then, instead of filling my cup, I grabbed the jug and toppled it.

It was made of heavy plastic, not glass, so it didn't shatter when it hit the floor, but it did made a loud noise, and the water began pouring out of the open end, forming a rapidly spreading puddle at my feet.

Carol let out a high-pitched scream that drilled into my eardrums like an ice pick. She pushed Terri away and started running for the water cooler. Terri looked confused for a moment, but when she spotted the overturned water jug, she too screamed and ran for the cooler.

"What's going on out here?" Mr. Griswald said, stepping out of his office. He was naked from the waist down.

"The sonofabitch knocked over the water jug," Joel said, on his knees next to Carol and Terri by the puddle. He was actually crying.

There was a wail from inside Mr. Griswald's office, and soon the threesome had joined the others by the spill. They were all crying and cursing me. Vic snatched up the now empty water jug and cradled it to his chest.

When all six of them leaned forward and started lapping up the spilled water from the floor, I took the opportunity to make a hasty exit.

Mark Allan Gunnells holds degrees in English and Psychology and is the author of the Sideshow Press titles *A Laymon Kind of Night*, *Whisonant/Creatures of the Light*, *Tales from the Midnight Shift Vol. I*, the Darkside Digital short "Dancing in the Dark," and the novella *Asylum* from The Zombie Feed, an imprint of Apex Books.

Like Riding a Bicycle

Marianne Halbert

Morrison stared slack-jawed from behind his desk at the coffee stain. It was blurred around the edges. Café-au-lait colored. He knew that aside from that stain, the proposal was impeccable. No typos. Formatting was beautiful. Even the placement of the staple was aesthetically pleasing.

"*Look* at me when I'm talking to you," came the growl.

Morrison raised his eyes. Rich Dickie's imposing frame filled the doorway. Scarlet blotches had bloomed on the man's cheeks, and were now spreading across his thick neck. On some level, Morrison was aware that his new boss was berating him, belittling him, and ordering him to provide a fresh copy of the proposal prior to the two o'clock board meeting. The floor vibrated as Mr. Dickie stomped away.

Morrison's gaze drifted back to the stain as it glared at him. Accusing him of sloppiness. *Slovenliness.* After he heard the door slam down the hall, he finally spoke out loud the words that had been swimming around his mind since the report had been flung onto his desk eight minutes ago. With only his pencil holder as a witness, he uttered his proclamation.

"But I don't even drink coffee."

"Second day on the job, and you've already managed to piss off the boss." The matronly woman from accounting pushed past him in the break room and reached into the freezer. She peeled the plastic off a portion of her meal, and popped the tray into the microwave. The crusty glass plate embarked on a lazy spin, uttering a distant hum. *What was her name? Beth? Bess?*

"Someone must've reviewed the proposal without telling me," Morrison said, sounding more defensive than he wished. "I don't even drink coffee," he mumbled, gleaning a slight satisfaction from the fact that human ears had now heard his defense.

"Well, watch yourself. Jack Ziegler got fired a few months back for the same thing. Mr. Dickie's not a fan of slop."

The microwave pinged, and the woman moved her lunch onto the table. While she was distracted, mixing a gray blob of goo into a measly helping of mystery meat, Morrison stole a glance at the ID badge dangling from a frayed lanyard around her neck. *Betsy Adkins.* They ate in silence. A couple of times, he thought about making conversation, but she had such an absent, glazed look in her eyes, he didn't think it would be worth the effort. Come to think of it, that's how all the employees here seemed. Vacant. After Morrison finished off his turkey on rye, he stood up from the table.

"What *is* that?" Betsy asked, white plastic fork in mid-air. She was staring at his shirt, shooting a scolding glance at it.

Morrison glanced down. He'd worn a butter-cream long-sleeved oxford with a royal blue and gold paisley tie. His jaw dropped when he saw the stain running in a diagonal across his torso. There was a nostalgic pattern to it, but he couldn't quite place it. He touched it, and a dark, oily, greasy smudge discolored his fingertips.

"My Lord," said Betsy. "If I didn't know better, I'd say that looks like it came from a bike chain. You *do* know bikes aren't allowed around here, right? Not since Drew Beamer's fell over and ruined the new office carpet." She whistled. "Whoo-hoo, did Mr. Dickie ever have a cow over that one. Took it out of Drew's pay. Poor Drew. Now he's traded in twenty miles a day on his hybrid for donut-laden train ride."

Morrison's mind was racing. He'd washed his hands right before coming to the break room. Surely he'd've noticed this in his reflection if it'd been there then. Blood rushed to his head, and all sound became a distant echo.

". . . in your office." Betsy was talking.

"What?" he asked, willing himself not to pass out. Her mouth was full now, her jowls bouncing as she chewed. It seemed as though she were speaking in slow motion.

"I said, I hope you have a spare in your office." She laughed, sending gray droplets showering over the table.

———————

The next morning, Morrison hung two fresh shirts and a new tie from the coat rack next to the silk fig tree behind his desk. Just in case.

He sat down and powered up his computer. He'd lain awake in the night, pondering how a coffee stain could appear on his report, and a bike chain track on his shirt. Around three a.m. he'd come to the conclusion that someone was trying to sabotage him. But who? And why?

At least no one can stain my emails, he thought as he read them and began sending out responses. He was halfway through listening to his voice mails when that bony blonde from HR swooped into his office, her horse-shaped jaw jacking away.

"What were you thinking? Mr. Dickie is going to have your head on a platter over this." She shook her head, and as she began to walk out the door, he could practically see the thought balloons floating about her. *Disgusting. Completely disgusting.* She paused, resting one hand on the frame. "I never figured you for a porn guy. You seemed so *normal*." There was a sense of betrayal in her eyes, like he'd made her a promise during the interview. *I'm always on time. I'm a people person. And I'm so* normal.

The increasingly familiar tightening of his chest sensation overcame him. *Porn?* Morrison's fingers hesitated as he searched for his sent emails. He scrolled through them.

7:57. Subject: Next Quarter's Projection. To: S.Levine@...

8:01. Subject: Brainstorming mtg pushed back to 11:30. To: A.Peters@..., M.Knoble@...

8:04. Subject: Fuzzy dice meet Tu-Lips. Who wants to play!!?? To: All@...

Don't click on the attachment. Do *not* click on the attachment. But his hand seemed to have found a mind of its own. The uber-megapixel detail would have been impressive had the image not been so utterly revolting as it unfurled across his monitor.

To: All.

All.

Everyone in the office. In his mind's eye he could imagine everyone in the firm opening the attachment. Even those who hadn't received the upgraded monitors would be in for quite a show. Big-bossomed Betsy, playing with the strands of her lanyard, after placing her three-hundred calorie lunch in the freezer. Drew Beamer licking his donut-glazed fingertips as he leered at the fuzzy dice, leaving a glazy smudge on his cordless mouse. That red-headed vixen, Amy Mc'Something, would never agree to lunch with him now. And Mr. Dickie...

Morrison tried to delete it. Delete ALL. To take it back.

The screen politely disobeyed him. *Internet is not responding.* The little hour-glass figure, sexy, sassy little vixen that she was, hovered. He could touch her, but he'd never reach her.

I've got to hide. Hide, and figure this out.

Morrison stepped into the hallway, the few people gathered there whispering conspiratorially, averting his gaze. He took the stairs two flights up, to the balcony. He kicked the cigarette urn, scaring away a few pigeons, and then gripped the railing. He was now seven stories above ground level. Traffic was slower now than at rush hour, but was still at a steady stream. He tightened his grip so much that his knuckles whitened. What to do?

Morrison leaned over, wondering if he would vomit. Pretty sure based on the clenching in his gut that he would. Imagining how his half-digested sunnyside-up egg and blueberry bagel would look splattering onto the heads of the pedestrians below. He knew this feeling. The helplessness. The anxiety. The hopelessness.

He watched people swarming in and out of the corner coffee shop. The barista was surely smiling. Cha-ching! He watched bike messengers and cycling commuters zipping up and down the street. An arm out to signal a turn. A helmeted head tucked to signal a speed burst. He watched for twenty minutes, but couldn't discern the signal for *I'm going to drop my chain across your shirt*. Can't shout that one out!

Morrison closed his eyes. His voice was pleading. "I don't drink coffee. I haven't ridden a bicycle since I was ten."

"And you've n-e-v-e-r looked at porn." The voice was in complete agreement with him.

He spun and saw the waif-like girl looking over the railing about ten feet away. She was people-watching, her dark shaggy hair blowing in the breeze. "Although," she spoke, as though debating with herself, "Jack Ziegler drank coffee." She paused, squinting her eyes a bit, focusing on the coffee shop. "Got it from that place right down there. Every day. Extra crème. Always extra crème. Poor Jack couldn't stand anything bitter. He gave his heart and soul to this place. I tried to convince him to use a coaster, but..."

A sideways grin spread across her face and her gaze slid to Morrison. "I guess we both know how that worked out."

"But Ziegler was fired. What're you saying? That he snuck back in and damaged my report?"

The girl threw her head back and giggled.

"So you think he's in cahoots with Beamer?" She might as well have said, *Silly Boy*. "Beamer sold his bike in a garage sale. Needed the money to make up for what Dick Dickie was scalping from his check to pay for the carpet." She let that comment float between them for a moment. A few blocks away, someone honked their horn. Her voice was softer, less sarcastic when she spoke again. She tilted her head slightly forward, her dark gaze boring into him. "Beamer gave his soul to this place too."

Morrison knew how they felt. He worked his first job out of college for nine years. Up the ladder. Was loyal. Did things right. Then his boss called him in one day, and patiently explained about the economy. How it had nothing to do with the quality of his work. How he was sure Morrison would bounce back and get scooped up right away.

"I'd given my heart and soul to that job," he whispered.

"I know." She stood, facing him now, one arm on the railing. Her eyes were beautiful. She understood.

"I found out, in the months following, he did it to a lot of us. Firing us before our ten years. Hiring in college grads for half the salary. It wasn't fair. We didn't do anything wrong." He moved closer to her, within arms' reach. "*I* didn't do anything wrong."

"No," she said. Complete empathy rippled from her voice. "But you suffered. The pointless interviews. The disgrace of cashing those unemployment checks. And finally, two years later," her free arm swept over the building rooftop, "*this*."

"Someone's trying to sabotage me," he said, the desperation in his trembling voice palpable.

"No," she said, raising a delicate finger and hushing his lips. "Even they don't know it, but they are trying to warn you. Ziegler moved his family to Sandusky after getting a new job. I've no doubt he's leaving his coffee stains all along Lake Erie, from Toledo to Cleveland. He hasn't touched your report. But this place," and at this, for the first time her confidence seemed to waiver. She shuddered, loathing thick in her voice, "this place sucks the spirit out of people. Jack's long gone, but his spirit remains."

"But Beamer," Morrison muttered, "he's still here. His office is four doors down from mine."

The girl's fawn-colored skirt fluttered in the breeze, revealing a tattoo'd anklet. She shook her head patiently. "Drew Beamer still comes to work, each week gaining another pound or two. But his spirit, his soul, belonged to the guy who did the Hilly Hundred six years running. He may be four doors down, but his spirit haunts this place."

He didn't want to accept it, but it was beginning to make sense. "If this place is so awful, that it drains the life and soul, what are you doing here?"

The waif smirked. "Dick Dickie caught me one morning. Thought I was alone with my vice." She bit her rosebud lip as though stifling something that wanted to fly free, but that she didn't want him to hear. "Anyway, I couldn't tell my parents I'd lost my first job. Especially since I'd lost it to porn. So, I ran up here, and jumped."

Morrison drew in a breath, looking her up and down. She looked so...unscathed. "Jumped? From here?" His gaze was drawn to the traffic seven stories below.

"My bad luck. Didn't realize the fruit vendor was delivering to the juice bar downstairs. The crates of mango and papaya in the bed of the truck broke my fall." She waivered. "Somewhat. I'm in a coma, hooked up to a bunch of tubes in Mercy Hospital half a mile away." She seemed a little put out. "You know, I don't think those nurses have even washed my hair? My mom swears I still smell like a tropical smoothie every time she kisses my forehead."

Morrison looked across town. Past the quad apartments and the art district, he could see the hospital rising against the mid-morning sun.

"So what do I do?" he asked.

"What did you do last time?" She tugged on the hem of her sleeveless emerald lace shirt, a move that seemed modest for a girl who fancied fuzzy dice and tu-lips.

Morrison threw his hands into the air. "I spent about a year fantasizing about murdering my boss. All sorts of creative ways. Over and over." He looked at her, but saw no judgment in her dark eyes. "Then moved past the anger and depression. Eventually got this job. Was so excited, and incredibly nervous."

"Nervous because?"

"It had been a long time. But I got right back in the flow of it. I drew on my experience."

"Just like riding a bike," she said. She raised her eyebrows. "And those dreams you had over and over. The whole boss-killing scenario." Normally Morrison wasn't a fan of air quotes, but when she did them, they were kind of adorable. Especially when placed around *boss-killing scenario* and her lower lip got a little pouty. "You're pretty experienced at that, too?"

Morrison took a step back.

"No, that was just fantasy."

"So was you getting another job—until you got it." She crossed her arms in front of her. *So determined, for such a little thing.*

"But this is different, I couldn't begin to imagine—"

"Dicky Dickie always comes up to smoke a cigar after his ten o'clock constitution." She looked at her vintage watch. "Which means he'll be here in about four minutes. And the fruit vendor won't pull up for at least another ten." She tossed a glance down the street. "Trust me, I know. Draw on all your experience. All your fantasies. You won't forget. You've done it before. I promise. It's just like riding a bicycle."

––––––––––

The fruit truck smashed into a light pole in its attempt to avoid the body, spilling everything from grapefruit to guava into three lanes. Morrison was surprised the next evening, strolling around the balcony at sunset, at the scent that still lingered in the air. And as he looked out over the shimmering skyline, he envied the waif's mother, who was able to smell the fruit smoothie with every kiss.

Marianne Halbert is an attorney from central Indiana, her practice focused on advocacy for clients with mental health diagnoses; in that capacity, she helped develop the first mental health diversion program in the U.S. in 1996. Her stories have appeared in *Thuglit, Midnight Screaming, Coach's Midnight Diner, Necrotic Tissue, Bedlam at the Brickyard,* numerous Pill Hill Press anthologies (*Love Kills: My Bloody Valentine, Silver Moon Bloody Bullets, Haunted, Patented DNA, Back to the Middle of Nowhere, Flesh & Bone: Rise of the Necromancers, Bloody Carnival, Daily Flash 2011,* and *ePocalypse*), as well as the Wicked East Press anthologies *Ransom* and *Hannibal's Manor.*

A Hundred Bucks is a Hundred Bucks

Will Huston

"Had to lay off two more of my guys last Friday. Didn't want ta do it but times are tough," old Melvin says. "I don't know." Old Melvin is always stating the obvious. He also always follows up on the obvious with the same self-doubting phrase of "I don't know." He feels this lends balance to his observations. Either that or he really doesn't know. He always says it the same way, too, trailing off at the end.

Yes, times are tough. Fuzzy knows this all too well as he finishes blocking the back of the old man's gray head. "Yes they are, Melvin, indeed they are," he answers back. He grabs the big hand mirror on the shelf behind the barber chair and steps in front of Melvin, holding it so the customer can admire Fuzzy's tonsorial talents.

"That's right nice. There's not a better barber in all of Clarksville...I don't know..."

Fuzzy unfastens the snap on Melvin's smock and with a fluid sweep removes it to shake the hair onto the floor.

"On that note," Fuzzy says, "I've got to close early this evening."

"Ya'do? Why's that?"

"I've got extra work, a special client. And I need to be there as soon as I can. Tell you what. You sweep up for me and it's no charge."

"That's a deal, Mister. I don't know..."

"I appreciate it, Melvin. Just be sure the door's locked behind you."

And with that, Bob "Fuzzy" Manes walks out of his little barber shop.

———

The drive across Buggs Island Lake reminds Fuzzy why he loves it so much in Clarksville. The crystal lake waters, the verdant rolling hills—little mountains really—and the azure blue sky with the perfectly placed cotton ball clouds all made for an idyllic summer evening. Fuzzy has always enjoyed driving through this countryside, often aimlessly. But tonight is different, no aimlessness allowed. He has somewhere he has to be. And like Melvin said, "times are tough." Folks are waiting longer between haircuts these days, so Fuzzy's cash flow has been reduced to more of a cash trickle. The state had cut back on full-time help in some areas, so he was glad this one time opportunity had come his way when it did. And it's easy money. In and out. The extra cash will come in handy. A hundred bucks is a hundred bucks. Or, at least, it used to be. And besides, Fuzzy is the kind of man who likes meeting new people, likes getting to know them, likes to hear about their hopes and dreams. He likes to think of himself as a kind of therapist, a bartender without the booze, a psychiatrist minus the angst. It's not that he cares about their hopes and dreams. He doesn't. He just likes the idea of people confiding in him. This makes Fuzzy feel good about himself, feel good about the drive across southern Virginia, feel good about life in general His one regret right now is that the drive to Jarratt isn't long enough to completely unwind and bask in his feel-goodness. Eighty minutes goes by in a flash.

He pulls up to the gate. "Good evening. How are ya?" Fuzzy asks the guard.

But Fuzzy's neighborly overture meets a terse one-word response. "Name?"

"Manes, Robert."

The starched, stone-faced officer checks his clipboard, nods, hands Fuzzy a clip-on *Visitor* badge, then dryly instructs him to park in lot C and wait for the shuttle to take him to where he needs to go. Fuzzy isn't used to such indifference. He's thankful he's not the type that treats others the way he's just been treated. *Hell, this guy's no better'n me*, he thinks to himself. *Who the hell does he think he is?*

Eight minutes later Fuzzy comes to the stark realization that the guard at the front gate was no different than the one presently patting him down for weapons, drugs, or anything else not allowed to be brought into prison. Yet another guard steps up and instructs Fuzzy to, "Follow me, sir."

The guard leads the barber down a brightly lit hallway, turns a corner, and stops at a door. "Do not engage the prisoner in conversation. No talking." The loud buzz of the door lock disengaging, then the guard opens the door. "Step in, sir. I'll be right out here. Knock when you're finished."

Fuzzy walks into the little windowless room to find everything already prepared for him: a small table with electric clippers, a brush, and a smock. He circles around to the front of the chair Lester's sitting in, shackled to the seat back and the chair's legs. He picks up the smock and lays it over the prisoner's chest and arms, then reaches around his neck and snaps the fastener to hold it in place

"Good evening, young man. How are ya?"

Lester smirks, bemused by such an inane question. "You're kidding, right? How do you think I am, mister?"

Fuzzy steps behind Lester, picks up the clippers, presses the on button, and starts cutting the prisoner's hair. "My name's Bob, but you can call me Fuzzy. Everybody does. Last name's Manes. Fuzzy Manes? I'm a barber. Get it? What's your name?"

"Mister, are you just stupid, or do you not pay attention to the world around you?"

Fuzzy knows the prisoner's name all right. Everybody in Virginia knows his name. And everybody in Virginia knows that in twenty-seven minutes Lester will be dead. Anybody who rapes and strangles two teenagers, a young girl and a young boy, to death will die in the state of Virginia. Not a matter of if, a matter of when. Fuzzy can't help but notice how young Lester looks. A boy, actually. A boy who has twenty-six minutes of life left in him. Fuzzy also can't help but feel a touch of empathy.

"Just trying to be friendly."

"Really? You want to be friendly with me? A little late for me to be making new friends, don't ya think."

Fuzzy doesn't know what to say so he doesn't say anything. The hum of the clippers seems to grow louder as he continues to cut off Lester's long blond locks. Lester can't help but notice the clippings of his hair cascading onto the spotless concrete floor.

"Mister, you say you want to be my friend?"

"I guess, yeah."

"Okay. You can be my friend but on one condition."

"What condition is that?"

Minutes later, Fuzzy can't drive away from Greensville Correctional Center fast enough. The sun's down now but the summer night air hasn't quite cooled from the heat of the day.

And Fuzzy's mood makes him feel even hotter than it is. *Get away, just get away from this God-awful place*, his inner voice tells him. *Get away and you can put all this behind you.* He pulls into the southbound traffic on I-95, feeling a little better. He feels even better a few miles on as he gets off on U.S. Highway 58 and heads west, back to the sanctuary of his beloved little barbershop in Clarksville. No murderers or indifferent prison guards there. The smells of impending rain mix with the freshness of the Christmas tree farms he passes; that and the far off sheet lightning have a soothing effect on Fuzzy's mood. He can think good thoughts now. He turns on the radio and tunes it to a station that plays his favorite country tunes, tunes he likes to sing along with. And why not? He's got a pretty good voice. Fuzzy's enjoying his duet with Hank on "Long Gone Lonesome Blues" and when it ends he's pleased that he's done Hank, and the song, proud. Fuzzy is feeling good about himself, about the drive back across southern Virginia, about life in general.

And then his feel-goodness is brought to a quick end when he hears the country radio deejay say that it's nine o'clock and that this portion of the program is sponsored in part by Gold Bond medicated foot powder.

Nine o'clock. Lester is being strapped into the electric chair about now. The metal skullcap clamped down on his cleanly shaven head. In a few seconds 1800 volts at 7.5 amps will flow through Lester's body for 30 seconds followed by 60 seconds of 240 volts at 1.5 amps. And the same thing will happen again for the next 90 seconds after that. Then the boy will be dead.

Fuzzy turns the radio up full, hoping that the loud music will drown out the gruesome thoughts screaming inside his head. *Did I contribute to Lester's death? Am I somehow responsible? Hell, if it wasn't me that cut his hair it would have been somebody else. A hundred bucks is a hundred bucks. And I need it. He was a rapist and a killer. What he got, he deserves. Screw that scumbag.*

Merle is halfway through the first verse of "Mama Tried" when Fuzzy joins in, perfectly harmonizing at the top of his lungs, right along with the country music legend.

The gas gauge is reading about a quarter of a tank as Fuzzy approaches the outskirts of Lawrenceville. He figures it's best to pull over now and fill up rather than take a chance on finding another station open on down the road. His throat had a little tickle in it, too, so a bottle of water would hit the spot.

He puts the bottle on the counter.

"This and twenty dollars on pump two." Fuzzy pulls out the crisp hundred-dollar bill and hands it to the sleepy-eyed clerk. A moment later the clerk gives him back his seventy-eight dollars in change. He pockets it and when he takes his hand out he is again reminded of the man he met a little over an hour ago. The man who is now dead. He's reminded because there, in his hand, is a clump of blond hair. He is also reminded again because he is in Lawrenceville.

"Mister, something wrong?" Sleepy-eyes asks.

"No, no. Everything's fine. Why are you asking?"

"Because, you've been standing there for five minutes."

"I have?"

"Yes, you have."

Fuzzy sheepishly sticks the hair back in his pocket, grabs the bottle of water, and heads for his car.

The barber takes a long drink from his water bottle and turns the radio down before he pulls back onto Highway 58 running through the middle of town. He stops at the light at the intersection with 6th Avenue and waits for it to turn green. He reaches back into his pocket and takes the blond locks out again. It all comes rushing back.

"Mister, you say you want to be my friend?"

"I guess, yeah."

"Well, then, there's something I'd like you to do for me."

"If I can. What do you want me to do?"

"Well…my mama can't be here and it would mean an awful lot to her if you could maybe make sure she got something to remember me by."

"I don't know what you mean."

"She used to always brag on my hair. How much she liked it. Maybe you could take some and see that she gets it. It ain't much but it's about the only good thing I've got to offer. Besides, the prison ain't going ta do anything with it but throw it out."

"I…uh…I suppose I could. I mean, where does she live?"

"On 6th Avenue, off of Highway 58 in Lawrenceville. Could you send it to her?"

"I can go you one better. I'm from Clarksville. That's right on my way home."

"Thanks, mister. You're all right…Fuzzy."

"Sure, no trouble...Lester."

The light turns green. Fuzzy ponders a moment, then the loud horn blast from the car behind him helps him make up his mind. He steps on the gas, crosses 6th Avenue, and heads for home less than an hour away. "Screw that murderin' rapist." Fuzzy feels embarrassed for having had empathy for Lester, for agreeing to carry out a mission of sentimental gesture. "What the hell was I thinking anyway?" The tickle comes back. He clears his throat. Once. Twice. No help. Another drink of water. "Aah, that's better."

The miles melt away over the next fifty minutes. The street lights of Clarksville dot the silken darkness in the distance, flickering like a hovering swarm of fireflies. The occasional flash of sheet lightning in the background lends a certain majesty to Fuzzy's vision of the safe haven he calls home. It's starting to sprinkle as he closes in on the turn-off to cross the lake and on into town. The sprinkle turns to rain. In no time it's coming down in buckets. Fuzzy rolls up his window and hits the wiper switch. "Dang, almost made it before the rain." He can see no more than twenty feet in front of him as the ka-chooka swish, ka-chooka swish of the wipers and the pounding rain combine to compose a grand symphony, playing up the drama of the long last mile of Fuzzy's journey across southern Virginia and back.

Fuzzy's sedan crosses the last few yards of the bridge and enters downtown. His is the only car driving on the street. That's a small town for you, though. They roll the sidewalks up at eight every weeknight. It occurs to him that old Melvin doesn't always have the best of memories. One evening just last year he forgot to close the door on the coop after feeding his chickens. He came out the next morning to get some eggs for breakfast and there were none to be had. And there were none to be had because old Melvin had forgotten to close the door on the coop and all of his chickens were dead. Probably a fox, but no one's really sure. Anyway, Fuzzy figures he better stop by the shop to make sure all's well and that Melvin has locked the door as promised. Only problem is that there are no places near the shop to park and Fuzzy doesn't have an umbrella. But what the heck? It's just a little rain.

He jumps out of the car and walks the two blocks to his shop as fast as he can. By the time he gets there he is drenched to the bone. He tries the door and his suspicions of old Melvin are confirmed as he turns the knob and the door opens. He gives the place a once over. "Well, Melvin, at least you swept up." Fuzzy makes a beeline for the back room, taking off his smock and unbuttoning his shirt as he goes. He coughs, then sits down on the folding chair and takes off his shoes, socks, pants, and underwear. He throws the clothes into a pile in a corner. Buck naked, he coughs again. And again.

"Dang, I hope this isn't a summer cold. Nothing worse than a summer cold." His throat tickles. No water. He coughs. "Ha-hulk. Uh-hum, uh-hum." It's not getting any better. "Ah-choo." That's one violent sneeze. "AAAA-CHOO!" This one's even more violent. Fuzzy grabs a rag off the nearby shelf to blow his nose. "Hooonk!" He looks at the rag. "What the heck?" He blows his nose a second time. "What's going on here?" His throat tightens. "HA-HULK! HA-HULK! HA-HULK! HA-HULK! HA-HULK!" Something is wrong, very wrong. He can barely stop coughing, and when he can he gasps for air in desperation.

He stumbles into the bathroom, clicks on the light, then looks into the mirror above the sink. *This can't be happening. This is not real.* Thick strands of long blond hair sprout from his nostrils, spew from his mouth, grow out of his ears. He starts to scream but all the comes out is a gagging plea for life.

"ALK! ALK!…ALK!…ALK!…ALK!…alk…"

———————

Melvin sits alone at his kitchen table, sipping his morning coffee as he scans the morning paper. "Two and a half inches of rain overnight. That's some storm, I don't know…" Suddenly, something occurs to him. "Oh shoot."

Melvin approaches the front door of Fuzzy's barbershop. He grabs the door knob and confirms that he forgot to lock it last night. "Well, at least no chickens got killed. But Fuzzy'd kill me if he knew I forgot to lock up. I don't know…"

He walks into the shop to make sure everything's in order. "Anybody here? Hello."

Silence.

He steps into the back room, looks it over. "Looks okay to me." Then he notices the light coming from the bathroom. "I thought I turned that off. I don't know…"

He goes into the bathroom. "I thought I swept up all the hair in this place," Melvin tells himself as he looks at the two-foot high pile of blond hair on the floor beneath the sink. "Better clean this up 'fore Fuzzy comes to open up. He'd skin me alive if he saw this…I don't know…"

Will Huston is primarily a filmmaker, having written and produced the award winning film *Vic* as well as directing movies and commercials in the U.S. and Europe over the past twenty years. He's also an actor, having appeared in a number of motion pictures, most notably as one of the Knox brothers, alongside Kane Hodder, in *Pumpkinhead 2*. He's pretty sure he's the only actor in cinematic history who meets his end by being pecked to death by a pair of angry chickens. Will is from Branson, Missouri (yes, that Branson!) and credits growing up there as the number one reason he finds solace in the less frightening world of horror.

The Pipes

Trevor Denyer

I must admit that I wasn't feeling at my best when Debs came up from the basement and complained about ringing in the pipes.

"What?"

"Howie, it drives you crazy down there. It's like torture."

My attention was always diverted when Debs appeared; those fulsome hips, large breasts, and dark curly hair. I secretly relished the way she referred to me by my first name, which strictly speaking was Howard, not Howie. Even so, today was "one of those days," and it was only 9:00 a.m. I'd already had complaints from the Head Bitch, admonishing me for not letting her know that the contractors were coming to replace her old computer monitor and keyboard.

"What *are* you talking about?" I growled.

"The pipes. They're ringing."

"What, wet?"

She smiled, despite herself. "No, Howie. Ringing, as in making a noise."

I sighed, exasperated and feeling stupid. "Okay, I'll look into it," I said dismissively, and promptly pushed it from my mind. I knew that today would be busy, what with contractors changing monitors and keyboards and inspectors due to arrive at any moment to check that Health and Safety rules were being properly followed.

As Debs grunted and swayed away towards her office, I consoled myself by imagining the things I'd like to do with her, given half a chance.

———

It was always a relief to escape to the privacy of my office, high up on the fourth floor, overlooking the car park. The building had been a Magistrates' Court before being occupied by the Council. Its Victorian gables overlooked the main road that led to the centre of

Castlebridge, the small market town where I was born and had always lived.

My office was light and airy. I'd secretly christened it "The Eagle's Nest," a rather dubious title, I know, but I did feel it was the seat of my power. I resisted the urge to look in the small mirror by the coat-stand. It always led to me examining my dark hair for streaks of grey and mithering over how much it was receding. Then I'd examine the dark spaces beneath my slightly bloodshot eyes, frown at the bags residing there and the creases of aging skin.

I sat down and entered the password to unlock my computer terminal. I felt depressed, mulling over the opportunities I'd never taken over the forty-eight years of my life. If only I'd done this, been bolder then, followed a different course at that time…Fuck! If I'd not married when I did. Another disaster well and truly on the rocks. A fake partnership for the sake of the children who were not children anymore, but still reliant on Mum and Dad, for God's sake!

My mind strayed, remembering the time I'd bedded the Head Bitch. Caroline Mortlake was one of those women that present a challenge to a man. A tough nut to crack. She presented herself as austere, taking no prisoners when it came to dealing with staff. She wasn't a "people person," though good at the more practical aspects of managing a Borough Council.

The memory was tinged with regret. The sex had happened after a long, frustrating car trip home from a National Conference on how best to utilize resources in the public sector. She had attended as Chief Executive and me as Premises Manager. We had travelled together in my car, mainly because we needed to show how we were best utilizing our *own* resources as a public organization.

Caroline, recently divorced, weakened, probably because she was tired and lonely. She invited me in to her flat for a coffee. I remember thinking that it was a place to scurry away to, rather than having the personal trappings that would make it a home. There were no photographs or pictures on the walls and nothing that connected with Caroline on a personal level. It was as though she had decided to reject her old life, leaving only a shell, devoid of genuine personality, because her own emotional zeitgeist had shifted too far from her memories of, maybe, a happier past.

At that moment, she was vulnerable and I took advantage. Unfortunately, I came far too soon and she never climaxed. A fucking disaster, in other words!

The screen in front of me filled with a list of emails, all needing urgent attention, or so the senders liked to think. *Bureaucratic arseholes,* I thought, *I'll put them back in their little boxes.* Thoughts of Caroline slid regretfully away. If only things had been different. If only the sex had been better. I could have been her rock. Instead, my creaking marriage continued relentlessly...

A knock startled me from my bitter reverie. I turned to the open door and saw Patricia standing there. I smiled, the sight of her reviving me like an unexpected burst of sunlight through cloud.

I stood clumsily, turning at the same time and catching my foot in the chair. I shook the offending furniture off, suppressing a curse of frustration.

"Hi there, Patricia. Come in, please."

She moved into the room, her fine blonde hair framing a round baby-face, her eyes a startling, hypnotic blue. I knew she was half my age and there was no chance of intimacy, but I found myself, as often happened, admiring the upthrust of her tight little breasts.

"I'm sorry to bother you, Mr. Courtland, but I've just come from the basement and there's a hell of a noise down there."

She smiled disarmingly. I invited her to take a seat. She sat down, crossing her pale legs demurely. I wondered for an instant what it would be like to touch her up there. I felt myself starting to perspire and had to reign in the arousal that was threatening to embarrass me.

"Um...okay, Patricia, shall we take a look?" The clumsy phrase echoed in my mind, imagining a very different association.

"Please, Mr. Courtland," she said, standing and walking towards the door.

I followed her, like a sick puppy, forgetting to reinstate my terminal's security screen—a disciplinary offence, if discovered but, at that moment, the last thing on my mind.

"Mr. Courtland, the Health people have arrived." Andria's thin, disinterested voice called from behind the Reception screen.

"Health people?"

"Yeah."

"You mean *Health and Safety*, Andria?" I replied, with a tinge of sarcasm.

"Yeah."

"Right, where are they at the moment."

"Waiting in the small interview room."

Bollocks, I thought. I'd hoped to descend to the slightly creepy basement with Patricia. Maybe offer a crumb of comfort... Impossible, of course. The legislation prohibited any suggestion of intimacy between members of staff. I'd worked for the Council for twenty years, trapped there by the promise of a decent pension one day. I was surprised that the incident with the Head Bitch hadn't leaked out. I guess it was in both of our interests to keep quiet.

I turned to Patricia. "Leave it with me. I'll check it out later."

She smiled disarmingly and I wasn't sure if I imagined a flirty flick of the eyebrows. "Okay, Mr. Courtland. Thanks."

By the time I'd dealt with the Health and Safety inspectors and checked and responded to the most urgent of my email messages, it was almost 11:30. I needed a break from the computer, so decided to venture down to the basement.

Accessing it by swipe card, I found the light switch, flicking it on. A series of stone steps descended towards a fire door. The light cast a yellow glow against the cream coloured brick walls. I began descending, pushing open the fire door and making sure I ducked my head to avoid cracking it on the lintel above. A faded sign exclaimed MIND YOUR HEAD! above the door. I made a mental note to replace it with something more prominent and less faded. The residue of my encounter with the Health and Safety nerds still lingered like a bad taste.

Beyond the fire door was a short corridor, swathed in gloom. I switched the second light on and the cream coloured brickwork became visible, curving upwards and creating a tunnel. The feeling of claustrophobia increased with the light, which seemed a contradiction; but, I reasoned, in the darkness, there was no detail to confound the senses.

There were two alcoves on the left side of the corridor. These were hidden in shadow, but I knew that they were entrances to store rooms where the detritus from the organization above ended up. There were discarded files, old diaries, boxes of out-of date manuals, filing trays, and other "stuff" that people wanted to hide away. The smell of decaying, dusty paper pervaded these spaces. Again, I resolved to sort through it all, maybe circulating a vitriolic message about keeping work areas tidy and uncluttered...*especially* storage areas.

A further fire door at the far end of the corridor accessed the main file storage area. A further light switch illuminated an average sized room containing four large metal cabinets filled with bloated, buff covered files hanging in card cradles that slid along metal runners. Here were the records of the dead, the dispossessed, and the unloved. Here were the stories of rejection, humiliation, and abuse. They hung in orderly rows, like mummified corpses awaiting burial.

Though all records were now stored on a database, the council had decided not to destroy these old files. I supposed that it was because of the requirement to retain information and the fear of putting all their rotten eggs in one electronic basket (so to speak).

Vertically attached to the end of these cabinets were wheels with turning handles. These allowed the storage units to be moved along tramlines sunk into the floor, thereby easing access to parts of the records and saving space within the confines of the room.

I listened. There was no sound. I realized that I had never noticed any pipes down here and as soon as I thought that, I noticed two pipes, camouflaged with cream paint, running horizontally across the length of the back wall. The pipes were thick, appearing to be sewage pipes from the facilities above.

"Well fuck me," I muttered, surprised that their presence had eluded me for all these years. "Well I can't hear anything."

Then it began; a thin whistle, like a vibration through water. The sound drilled into my head, setting my teeth on edge. I covered my ears, but the sound penetrated, seeping through until I felt my temples start to pound and the dull inevitability of a headache begin to rise.

There was something else, though. As I adapted to the sound, a subtle hiss prevailed. The whistle faded and the hiss resolved itself into something more coherent.

Somewhere, deep in my mind, something was whispering.

There had been something strange about that night with Caroline. Although we were both willing, I was over-enthusiastic and she *almost* held back. It's difficult to describe and there was a point at which I felt it shouldn't have continued. As it turned out, I was right. The whole thing had been a disaster.

As I've said, she was recently divorced from her husband, so the only infidelity was on my part, and I suppose there was a trace of guilt which I ameliorated with bitter thoughts about how unsuccessful my own marriage was.

The strangeness was in her eyes as I came. They were glazed, unblinking, suffused with icy blue.

"You bastard," she groaned, as if in pain.

I assumed it was because of my lack of control, but as I stood in the basement, I wasn't so sure. The whispers had resolved themselves into identifiable words.

"You bastard," they said.

―――――――

"What do you want?" snapped Caroline as I burst into her office. A techie was in the process of replacing various parts of her desktop computer.

"Sorry, I..." My mutterings did not impress an already irascible Head Bitch. She stared at me and, as she began to notice my shocked state, the hardness in her eyes softened and she moved towards me.

"What's wrong, Howie? You look like you've seen a ghost."

"Well I don't know. I might have *heard* one."

"What?"

"In the basement…from the pipes."

She faltered and the colour drained from her face. Now it was my turn to be concerned. I moved across to her, grabbing her arm and easing her into the office chair. The techie registered a fleeting interest and then carried on as if nothing had happened. After all, it was none of *his* business and these Council types were an odd lot.

"Let's go into the other room," she muttered.

"Okay. Are you sure you can walk there all right?" It was a stupid, patronizing question and some of the hardness glinted in her eyes once more.

"Yes, I'm sure," was all she said.

―――――――

"What was it you thought you heard?" Caroline sipped the water I had hurriedly fetched upon her command.

"Whispering."

"From the pipes." There was a vagueness to her words, as if her thoughts were elsewhere. Her face appeared gaunt in the shadows, framed by the silky darkness of her shoulder-length hair.

"Yes. Do you know anything about it?"

"Why would you think so?"

"Because of what the voices said to me."

"What did they say to you?"

I hesitated, then knew that I had to tell her and wondered if she would make the connection. "You bastard," I said.

It was as if I had slapped her. She recoiled, raising her hands to her face in horror. "No, it's impossible!" she cried.

Alarmed, I instinctively moved away. "What is?"

"He's come back, the bastard! He's come back and I thought I'd got rid of him for good!"

"Who? What do you mean?"

She stood, knocking the chair over, and ran from the room. I followed downstairs to the Reception area, past a startled receptionist, and, after swiping her card at the entrance to the basement, she descended into the darkness.

I fumbled for the switch, flooding the stairway with insipid light. Caroline had flung open the door at the bottom and run into the tunnel.

"Fuck," I muttered, my body shaking and a barely contained nausea filling my throat. I followed, illuminating the tunnel and then the main storage room as I went.

Caroline was standing under the pipes, staring up defiantly. "What do you want?" she cried.

"Caroline..." I began.

She whipped her body around, and I recoiled from the sight of her blazing, bloodshot eyes. "Fuck off!" she screamed at me, then returned her gaze to the pipes.

"No, I won't. I want to know what all this is about. I *deserve* to know!" I wasn't sure why I felt I deserved to know; it was a feeling that linked back to squandered passion and a wasted opportunity. As I stood there I realized that, despite everything, despite my amorous, some might call it perverse, nature, I actually loved the Chief Bitch.

I moved forward, encircling her in my arms and pulling against her resistance. She turned. Her eyes had softened again and her cheeks were wet with tears, her makeup tracing black rivulets through the haunted landscape of her face.

"Please," she said pleadingly. "I can't tell you. I just can't."

Then the basement was plunged into darkness.

We stood there, frightened and holding tight to each other. My mind was a whirl of conflicting emotions. There was something malevolent down here and it was coming for us. My logical mind dismissed this melodramatic thought as nonsense, but underneath, I felt the uncertainty of a trapped animal. Fight or flight; which should it be? But what was I *actually* fighting or running away from?

"We should get out of here," I said, my voice low and uneven.

Caroline kissed me hard, with a passion that, despite our circumstances, encouraged an immediate and obvious reaction.

"I'll tell you why this is happening," she said. "It's because that big fat fuck has come back. That piece of shit that raped me in my *own office!*"

She wrenched herself from my arms and turned once more to the pipes. "Come on then, why don't you do this thing properly. You've haunted me for long enough and now, at last, they'll find your rotten carcass in the pipes!"

I stood, shocked and frozen to the spot, my heart beating heavily as a thin, yellow glow began to emanate from the pipes. Gradually, the glow resolved itself into a grey ectoplasmic shroud that oozed towards Caroline, hovering in front of her. From deep within its depths an angry red glow began to spread outwards. The air in the room felt desert dry as the heat increased.

"Caroline," I managed to say, "we've got to get out. This is..." Something bore down upon me. Invisible hands pushed hard against my shoulders. *"Stay,"* it whispered.

"You bastard! Yes, those were the last words, weren't they? You remember, do you? Why have you waited so long? Did you think I hadn't suffered enough?" Caroline was raging at the entity, gesticulating frantically.

The heat in the room was increasing and I was finding it harder to breath. I sensed the first wisps of burning as the files within their rolling tombs began to smoulder.

Panic engulfed me. "Let me go!" I screamed at the invisible hands. The weight lifted and I bolted towards where I thought the door should be. I turned, ashamed at my cowardice, as the glowing entity engulfed Caroline and the files burst into flames.

———————

It's been a year since then. For many months, my mind closed the memories off, as though remembering would infect me like a virus. Only recently has it come back and I've been able to cope with what still seems to be an impossible event. My psychiatrist is ambivalent. Aren't they always? I don't think he really believes me, and the suspicion that I am an arsonist remains. The only thing that prevented me being prosecuted was the testimony of James Mortlake, Caroline's divorced husband.

His confession that he and Caroline had murdered Bill Drinkwater, a fat, lonely, red-faced, bullying arsehole employed by the Council as a junior executive. That led to the discovery of bones and the leathery remains of flesh in the pipes. It transpired that the pipes had been disconnected from the main sewer system many years before and were accessible from above by removing the metal discs capping them.

Caroline had told James of the rape a week after it happened, following his insistence that something wasn't right. He had met her at work, after hours. The building was empty except for the two of them and Bill, who had been contrite, begging Caroline not to tell her husband. Needless to say, James went wild, storming into Bill's office. There had been a very frank verbal exchange and an assault.

The assault had proved fatal as Bill reeled under the hammering blows delivered by the fit, muscular James. Eventually, Bill had stopped breathing. The last words that his dying brain heard were the spittle flecked barbs, filled with hate like poison: "You bastard!"

Using his skills as a butcher, James had returned home and collected the appropriate butchery tools and a large sheet of plastic. He and Caroline had moved the body to the basement before dismembering it. They had cleaned Bill's office, removing all trace of the blood spatters.

The pipes provided the ideal concealment. Once sealed again, there was no smell as the pieces of Bill dried out like jerky and his bones shed the flesh like old clothes.

Quite how they knew about the pipes and how to access them, I don't know. All I do know is that Caroline was always very resourceful. You don't become a Chief Executive by not being so.

So, there it is. Out at last. I've retired on medical grounds, living off a meagre pension that I seemed to pay into forever. Pamela left me, bewailing the fact that I couldn't be trusted; a weak excuse, I suspect, for being unable to sustain our wreck of a marriage. I do still see the kids occasionally, but they treat me as though I'm some sort of pariah.

The last I heard, James had hung himself in prison. That's what I heard, anyway. Whether there was any supernatural agency involved remains unclear. There were unexplained scorch marks in his cell, rising from the pipes to the radiator and culminating in a sooty exclamation, like a pointing finger, beneath his fouled body.

The Council arranged for the basement to be cleared out and refurbished. The pipes remain, for some reason. I think it's to do with the structural integrity of the room or some such bullshit. The files are returning already. They fill up the space like bodies in a graveyard.

No trace of Caroline was ever found, but the last I heard, when Debs contacted me (which she has been doing more and more recently), the pipes were silent.

I often wake in the night, my heart constricted, labouring to beat as I try to drag air into my lungs, feeling the heat of something malevolent. The voices are very near. Like dust in a desert they whisper: *"You bastard..."*

Trevor Denyer has been published in magazines including *Scheherazade*, *Nasty Piece of Work*, *Enigmatic Tales*, *Symphonie's Gift* and *Night Dreams*. He received an Honourable Mention in the *Year's Best Fantasy & Horror* and has appeared on-line at *Time Out Net Books* and *Gathering Darkness*. His work has appeared in several collections including *Nasty Snips* and *Gravity's Angels*. He is the creator and editor of the critically acclaimed *Roadworks*, *Legend*, and currently *Midnight Street* magazines (www.midnightstreet.co.uk).

Deadline

Matt Kurtz

Sydney watched from the darkness as a zombie lumbered across the shadowy street to chase the vampire. She clicked the pause button on the viewer and shuffled the footage back a few frames to trim her edit.

Alone in the advertising office, she was burning the midnight oil while huddled around her computer in the dimly lit editing suite. The raw footage of the undead monsters had been delivered earlier that day to be assembled for a local costume shop's Halloween commercial. Unfortunately for her, the person who shot the original footage had no concept of editing, let alone filmmaking. What she had put together so far was nothing but a series of jarring edits—known in her industry as jump cuts—that would completely confuse the viewer as to what was taking place onscreen.

And to make matters worse, her deadline was approaching fast—nine hours and counting. Since the client's Halloween sale was only a few days away, they were paying extra to expedite the production and Sydney promised that it would be edited and delivered for their approval first thing in the morning.

With her foot tapping a mile a minute, she exhaled and leaned back in her chair. Although she had quit smoking cold turkey (six weeks, two days, twelve hours, and forty-eight...forty-nine...fifty seconds ago), she could've really gone for one at that moment. It always got her creative juices flowing whenever she hit a road block. But, even if she hadn't quit, she still would have been too afraid to step outside the office to burn one off since the building wasn't located in the best part of town. During the daytime, when the guys were all there, the place wasn't bad. But after hours, the office was downright spooky. Her boss was extremely apprehensive of her staying alone after dark even with her assurance that she would be just fine. He knew that the commercial had to get done and she reminded him that the client was depending on them. She was hoping to rack up enough of these "take one for the team" jobs to ask for a substantial raise (especially since money was about to get real tight in the near future). But presently, she wasn't afraid to admit that being the only living soul in such a large place made her a little jittery.

Once a doctor's office decades earlier, the building sat vacant for years until Paul, the owner of Magic Cable Advertising, snapped it up for a steal, buying it outright instead of haggling over a lease. The entire one-story complex was far too large for the company's five employees, who (for obvious reasons) chose to set up shop in the smallest suite while Paul planned to lease the remaining wings once renovated. Sydney had wandered over there a few times while he was cleaning and saw the vast array of dusty medical equipment left behind. It was all outdated stuff that Paul kept confined to a couple of the back rooms. He hoped to make some extra cash selling the items on eBay, figuring there had to be some sort of niche for odd medical nostalgia.

Sydney pushed away from the desk and slowly spun in her chair. She fought her overwhelming desire to fetch a pack of smokes from the corner convenience store. Maybe if she whirled fast enough it would provide the same euphoria she always felt taking the first drag on her morning cigarette. The one that spiked her adrenaline. Raced her heart.

Spinning faster, she closed her eyes and felt like a kid on a merry-go-round, playing in a time when life was much simpler. Moments later, her lids fluttered open and she caught someone standing in her doorway, backlit by the bright hall light.

Sydney gasped and leaped from the chair. Stumbling to the opposite wall, she spun back to the open door.

No one was there.

She felt a tremor of fear race up her spine and explode along her scalp.

The front door…? It's locked, right?! Yes, you triple checked it after Paul left.

Could it be one of the boys trying to spook her for a laugh? But the figure she saw appeared bald and all the guys at the office had full heads of hair.

She snatched the brass letter opener off her desk and held it in front of her. Maybe she should call 911? Maybe—

She took a calming breath. The only way into the office was through the front door and it was locked. If someone shattered the glass to gain entrance, she would have heard the commotion, no matter how loud she had the audio cranked while editing.

It's all in your head. You were spinning around, getting dizzy, and things blurred to form a shape. That's all. Now go and prove to yourself that no one's here so you can get back to work. Remember your deadline?

Sydney forced herself to step forward and peek into the hall. It was empty. She continued on until her view became a straight shot into the well-lit lobby. The glass door and windows were completely intact, easing her frazzled nerves considerably. She just had to check, yet again, to make sure the entrance was still locked.

She cautiously inched her way into the reception area. The lobby's bright fluorescent lights blocked all visibility beyond the glass and reflected only her frightened image. Outside, a black void pressed against the window panes where anything could be lurking—waiting to grab her—if the door was (somehow) unlocked. Sydney slid forward and pushed on it.

The door didn't move. She pushed again, and again, just to make sure it wouldn't pop open. Staring into the murky abyss outside, her scalp prickled from the odd sensation of being watched. What made it even more unnerving was she didn't feel it originating from somewhere out in the parking lot, but from just over her shoulder. From within the office.

Remaining frozen, her eyes quickly refocused on the glass, using its reflection to scan the hallway behind her.

No one was there.

Okay, you're totally giving yourself the heebie jeebies.

To put herself at ease (so she could get back to work), Sydney quickly searched all the rooms, closets, and areas under the desks. While at the rear of the office, she paused in front of the thick metal door with the glowing EXIT sign above it.

She had been wrong. Apparently, there were *two* possible ways in.

Used as a fire exit, the door opened into a back hallway that led to the outside. The other suites also funneled into the same hall used in case of an emergency and acted as hub to the entire building.

Sydney moved closer and inspected its handle. It was one that had to be pushed for the door to open and locked when shut behind you. Without a handle or knob on the opposite side, it was impossible to get in. An *Exit* only, just as the sign above stated.

She pressed against the door anyway, just to make sure.

When it didn't budge, she decided that she was done letting her imagination get the best of her, having already wasted enough of her precious time.

Sydney entered the small kitchen and checked the mini-fridge for something to drink, finding it stocked with energy drinks. Wanting to avoid the caffeine, she remembered seeing a box of decaffeinated tea somewhere in one of the cabinets and found it in the bottom drawer. Closing it, there was a clacking sound like paper or cardboard catching on something. Sydney reopened the drawer and closed it, hearing the distinct sound again. Kneeling, she removed it from its slider and stared into the opening. Finding nothing, she flipped the drawer over and discovered a dog-eared manila file folder taped underneath.

She wondered what weird item it might contain, obviously left behind by the doctor. While his general practice was in the west wing, Paul informed his employees that the doctor used what was now their suite as secondary living quarters. Once moved in, the Magic staff kept discovering remnants of the man's morbid collection in odd places. Sydney found a wax-sealed Coke bottle stuffed with (what appeared to be) human hair in the tank of her toilet. While running an Ethernet cable above the ceiling tiles, the IT guy Dan came across a series of filthy rag dolls placed in the dark crawlspace. Paul unearthed a pouch full of extracted teeth under a loose floorboard in his office.

Such disgusting things made Sydney leery to check the contents of the folder but she unfastened it and flipped it open so her imagination wouldn't go into overdrive. Thankfully, it only contained a few blank pages from the doctor's prescription tablet. Written on the back of one of the forms was a list of items. Among the many entries that stood out were Belladonna, Mandrake, Nightshade, Toad's skin…Virgin's Blood…

Fetus Tissue.

Sydney gasped and threw the papers on the counter as if they were diseased. She stared down at the doctor's name printed on the stationary and wondered what this sicko's story was all about.

A few minutes later, while waiting for the water to heat for her tea, Sydney stared at a photograph of Dr. Bowden on the internet. He was even creepier than she imagined with his deep-set, piercing blue eyes, wolfish grin, and quarter-sized port-wine birthmark on top his bald head. For decades, he had been a respected physician in the community, until his scandal broke. Accused of secretly performing abortions on underage girls without parental consent, he was arrested and thrown in jail. Once arraigned on bail—fearful of a conviction and possible prison time—Bowden returned to his office and committed—

Sydney's stomach dropped.

Did Paul know the history of this place before buying it? Or was that the reason he got such a good deal on it?

She returned to what little remained of the doctor's story. Bowden's lawyer discovered his body while doing a welfare check on his client after repeated phone calls went unanswered. The police reported various items of an occult nature surrounding his corpse. His method of suicide was never officially revealed, becoming fodder for the local gossip. Even more sensational was the mystery surrounding where the corpses of the aborted fetuses had been discarded, since no remains were found on the premises.

Fetus Tissue.

"Jesus…" Sydney said, exhaling. She noticed her hand had subconsciously moved to cover her belly, protecting what was growing inside her for the past eight weeks. "Unbelievable."

She wanted to get the hell out of there. Wished that she had never pushed for the rush job on the Halloween spot. Even with all the lights on, knowing that some guy killed himself in the building made being there, all alone, downright unbearable.

But she had to stay. She had a job to finish. Needed to impress Paul. Needed that raise in order to squirrel away as much money as possible. She didn't even want to think about discussing a maternity leave yet, which was really going to put Paul in a quandary. With Sydney as the company's sole editor, he would either have to suspend production, not accepting any more gigs (not likely), or he was going to hire someone else to do the job (temporarily, she could only hope) in her absence. Sydney prayed that he'd be understanding, especially when informed that she planned to raise the baby alone, without the father (whom she hadn't heard from since he was first told about the pregnancy).

Look, stupid, she thought, tearing her eyes away from the creepy gaze of the doctor's picture on the internet, *the sooner you get back to work, the sooner you'll be outta here and safe at home.*

She minimized the internet window and expanded the editing program. Maybe she'd spent enough time being distracted that she'd have a fresh take on how to make the Halloween commercial work.

A wet gurgle—like something gelatinous being sucked through a tube—came from somewhere outside her room. Sydney lurched back in her chair then slowly rose and peeked into the hallway, finding it empty.

She crept forward with a letter opener, ready to slash at any potential threats. Approaching the two rooms nearest the fire exit, she heard the gurgling noise to her left.

In the kitchen.

Where the coffeemaker had just finished heating the last of the water for her tea, *gurgling* it out into the glass pot.

Sydney lowered her head and exhaled. *Oh. My. God. You're such a dork. You're gonna give yourself a freakin' heartatta—*

The lights in the entire office suddenly went out.

Sydney gasped; her first instinct was to widen her eyes to make sure they were still open. As if stricken blind, she felt for the wall and slid against it, keeping her back flush to it and raising the letter opener for protection. Being at the rear of the suite (where there weren't any windows), a wall of black pressed against her from all sides. She would have to maneuver her way through the darkness in order to get to the front lobby where the streetlights outside might provide illumination.

It's gonna be okay.

Trying to step forward, her feet refused to budge, telling her that she still needed a moment to gather her nerves.

It's probably just a blackout. Don't overreact. Nobody cut the power. She took a deep breath. *Wait…doesn't Paul have the lights on some sort of timer?*

Because of the somewhat rough area, he had previously mentioned leaving all the lights on to ward off burglars and vandals. What was the time? If it was exactly at one of the quarterly intervals, then it must be some sort of timer. Sydney searched her pockets for her cell phone—to use its light and check the hour.

She came up empty. The phone was probably in her purse, back in the editing suite.

Okay. Then maybe—

There was creak. Then a loud thud. Both noises came from somewhere just outside the kitchen.

Somebody's in here!

Using the wall as her guide, she crouched and duck-walked sideways until reaching a corner and wedged herself into it. She clutched the letter opener in both hands, aiming it into the black void.

Another thud in the hall. Closer.

With adrenaline flushing her body and thunderous heartbeats pounding her ribcage, Sydney felt on fire. Without sight, she felt submerged in some sensory depravation tank. Her quickening breaths flooded her eardrums, practically muting all other sounds. The room felt like it dropped twenty degrees.

She had to move. Now! She refused to sit there and wait for someone to grab her and do God knows what. If she could find some sort of light then she would make a mad dash to the lobby and escape. She racked her brain about searching the drawers earlier, trying to remember if there were any matches mixed with the condiment packages, plastic utensils, and round peppermints. What about a lighter? Damn, if she still smoked there'd be a Bic in her pocket right now.

The refrigerator! But do mini-fridges have lights inside? She couldn't recall ever seeing one, but who the hell pays attention to things like that? Maybe it did. It was worth a shot.

She stuck her hand out into the blackness to feel for it when…something licked her fingers.

Sydney gasped and jerked back, slamming her spine against the wall. She stifled a cry of pain with a palm over her mouth.

Eyes bulging, staring into the abyss, she felt a cold caress against her belly. Sydney shrieked and swung the sharp opener back and forth, slicing only the air. Still feeling the touch, she ripped the frigid hand off her stomach and stabbed at the ground in front of her. Someone *had* to be lying there, reaching up for her. But the metal tip only poked the bare linoleum floor.

She felt an icy breath against her scalp, raising gooseflesh over every inch of her body.

Something was *on* the wall. Above her.

Then came an exhale of excitement that reeked of rotting meat as it descended upon her.

Sydney screamed and sprang to her feet. She whirled around to face the intruder in the darkness while shuffling backwards into the hallway.

A maniacal laugh sounded from somewhere within the void.

Sydney whimpered and jabbed the letter opener in (what she thought was) its direction. In her blind panic, she attempted to recall which way it was to the front door. With her eyes refusing to adjust to the darkness, she still couldn't see an inch in front of her face.

Then it hit her. Making it to the lobby was pointless without her keys to unlock the front door. They were in her purse, somewhere in her office.

She needed to get out now!

The fire exit. But which way was it? She was completely turned around, lost in an alien setting so familiar during the daylight hours.

The green EXIT sign suddenly flickered on.

Sydney took off toward it. The sign went black again but the door's location was already seared in her mind like a ghost image from a camera flash. She sliced through the darkness with arms raised.

Sydney felt the metal door and turned sideways, her hips slamming into its handle. The lock released and it swung open.

Stumbling into a much colder darkness, Sydney fought to remember which direction the exit was to the outside. A moment later, the door swung shut over her shoulder, making her jump. She spun toward the noise and realized that the intruder could've followed her through. Cursing that she hadn't slammed the door immediately behind her to prevent him from doing so, she could now only pray that he wasn't silently standing next to her.

The thought made her skin practically crawl off her bones.

Shivering in fear, Sydney turned around and slowly shuffled forward, hoping she was heading in the right direction. She was too terrified to extend a hand into the darkness after her last experience, choosing instead to grasp the letter opener tightly against her chest—sharp end pointing out.

The metallic click of a door opening came from behind her. Sydney froze in her tracks. Then the surrounding darkness dissipated as a faint illumination filled the hall. She spun around and saw a glow outlining her office's fire exit. The door was slightly ajar. The lights were back on in the advertising suite, beckoning her to return—to get out of the cold darkness and away from what might be lurking within it.

But Sydney refused to go back. The exit leading outside was only inches away.

A shadow suddenly moved under her office door, causing the light to flicker. Keeping her eyes glued to the opposite end of the hall, Sydney pushed the handle to the outside exit and stepped forward then...bounced back.

The door didn't open.

She shoved again. Harder.

If she couldn't get outside, she'd be cornered. Trapped in the dimly lit hallway. Sydney slammed against it once more then came to the bleak conclusion that it wasn't going to open.

The shadow suddenly swallowed the light under the door at the end of the hall. Someone was just on the other side. And about to come through.

Sydney ran to the next available door, a fire exit from one of the empty suites. Without a handle to grab and pull, she wedged her fingers into the door's half-inch seam and tried to pry it open in order to escape. Clawing at the metal, her fingertips turned white. Her nails started to bend.

Then she lost her grip. Her taut muscles snapped her arms back to her body. Whimpering, Sydney glanced toward her office.

Its door started to slowly open, spilling light into the hall.

As Sydney clawed at the seam again, a shadow fell over her. A bald man, silhouetted by the bright office lights, stood at the end of the hallway. The only discernible feature of his shadowy face was his piercing blue eyes that seemed to glow in their sockets.

Dr. Bowden.

Sydney screamed and wedged her fingers deeper into the door seam, pulling so hard her nails started to split and peel back.

The door suddenly released, swinging open with such velocity, it knocked Sydney into the wall behind her. She bounced off and crashed to the hard linoleum floor. With her adrenaline racing into overdrive, she scrambled to her feet and glanced at the man standing in the distance at the end of the hallway.

The lights went off, encasing her in a pitch black void. A heartbeat later, she felt a cold breath in her ear.

"The Doctor is in," the man whispered.

Sydney screeched as icy hands clamped over her shoulders, pushing her forward into the abandoned suite. She blindly swung the letter opener through the air, hoping to stab her attacker, but only impaled it into the plaster wall. As she was pushed, her feet drug across the polished floor then left the ground completely. She landed on hard tile then was yanked across it by her hair.

Pulled through the pitch-black corridors, she zigzagged back and forth across the linoleum, kicking and screaming.

When she finally skidded to a stop, her attacker released her hair then clamped his frigid grasp around her throat. Lifted into the air, Sydney gasped and attempted to claw at the hands throttling her but only swung at empty space. She reached behind her and felt nothing. Where was he, God damn it!? How was he holding her?

Before her windpipe could be crushed, she was thrown through the darkness, landing face down on some sort of bed; its cool, slick surface made of either leather or vinyl. The cold hands flipped her onto her back and choked her again.

Fighting for breath, Sydney's scream transformed into gargling gasps. As the hands squeezed tighter, the blackness around her somehow grew darker.

When she awoke, she was lying on her back, naked below the waist. Her legs were spread and held up in the air by the stirrups attached to the end of the exam table. Although the domed examination light blasted her face, she was still able to make things out beyond its intense beam. Things like the old medical equipment. And the familiar style and layout of the cabinets.

She was next door in the west wing. In one of the rooms containing the doctor's abandoned items.

Wincing, she fought to break free from the leather straps restraining her wrists, ankles, and chest.

"Struggling accelerates the heartbeat," the voice from the murky corner told her. "Which will only make you bleed more."

Sydney turned in its direction and watched the man with the port wine-stained scalp materialize from the shadows.

Stepping closer, he lifted the exam light and repositioned it.

Sydney failed to notice that the beam was now aimed at her crotch. In fact, she was too terrified to notice anything except for the piercing blue eyes that stared down and, seemingly, through her.

"You-you-you….you're…" she babbled.

"Dead?" he said then shrugged. "In due time..." Dr. Bowden placed his frigid hand on her warm belly, "...that will all change."

Sydney recoiled at his touch. "Please! Please let me go!"

Bowden smiled, ignoring her pleas. "I've been watching you. Patiently waiting."

Sydney shook her head as tears streaked her face.

"And now that the lunar cycle is right..." he said, walking to the end of the exam table, "and you carry child..." he positioned himself in-between her spread-eagled legs, "the time is absolutely perfect."

"Please don't! Please don't hurt my baby!"

"Not my plan at all...*Mommy*," he said, smiling. His face looked more canine than human. He disrobed until completely naked.

"Oh God! Please don't do this!"

Bowden simply shot her a wink then stooped lower, moving closer to her pubic area.

At first mumbling, Bowden gradually spoke louder, then more defined, chanting something in another language.

Sydney winced and felt his index finger violate her. "Please! No! No! No!!"

Bowden seemed to be glowing, illuminating from within.

Then his middle finger penetrated. Sydney wailed in agony as he kept adding more fingers. Then his thumb. She passed out once his entire hand was inside her, snaking its way toward her womb.

Sydney woke with a start, bolting up and out of her desk chair, sending it crashing on its side. Heart racing. Gasping for breath. Drenched in sweat. She shuffled in reverse, slamming her back against her office wall for some sense of security.

Her hands wrapped around her stomach. She was fully clothed. The lights were on—dim in her suite and bright in the hall. The letter opener sat on her desk. The sun was rising outside her window, its warm rays penetrating the mini-blinds.

She leaned against the wall and fought to catch her breath.

Her hands moved between her legs. There was no pain. She caressed her belly. All was fine. She just fell asleep. That was all.

Dissolves.

Her head slowly rose.

"Yeah, dissolves," she said, chuckling. She could get around the jump cuts in the commercial by using a series of dissolves between the edits. Its cutting wouldn't be nearly as jarring.

Why hadn't she thought of that earlier? As horrible as that nightmare was, maybe she needed the sleep in order to clear her mind and find the answer.

The clock on the wall read six a.m. Her deadline was three hours away. She could still pull it off if she got moving. Sydney picked up her chair at the editing bay and plopped into it.

She exhaled a slight sigh of relief. Everything was going to be just fine.

───────────

But less than eight months later, Sydney realized things were far from fine when she caught the first glimpse of her baby boy in the delivery room. Although he was strong and healthy, it was the mere sight of the port-wine stain on his peach-fuzzed head that made her stomach drop. It sunk even further when the boy's lids fought to open and what stared back were the most piercing blue eyes.

"Not my plan at all…Mommy."

Knowing that most newborns had light blue eyes before turning slightly darker over time, Sydney could only pray that the child's eye color would eventually transform to brown or green…anything besides that cold blue that stared up and, seemingly, through her.

Originally a part-time independent filmmaker and screenwriter, **Matt Kurtz** decided to narrow his creative energy to focus more on short stories and future novels. He writes twisted tales for fun when not working at a small advertising company somewhere within the large state of Texas. His fiction can be found in anthologies from Pill Hill Press, Blood Bound Books, Comet Press and *Necrotic Tissue* Magazine.

The Little Church of Safe Crossing

Joe McKinney

For Rudyard Kipling

It was Christmas Eve, and Eddie and Bobby and I were driving on a rock-strewn dirt road that ran along a ridge line in the Bullis Gap Range, looking for a group of illegals one of our helicopters had spotted walking through the badlands. There was a little town called Sandersville about twenty-five miles to the north of us, and Eddie figured they were probably headed that way. There were lots of places to hide if they could get there.

We hadn't really expected to get any activity, and to tell the truth, we weren't really all that worried about a few extra Mexicans getting through the border. Working for the U.S. Customs and Border Patrol is a lot like standing in the middle of a river and being told you have to drink every drop that comes your way. You do what you can, you blow off the rest.

Our sector covers some of the roughest country along the whole Texas-Mexico border, and during the winter the cold and the shear size of the desert makes it practically impossible to pass through it on foot. Most who try end up food for the buzzards. So what we were really worried about was having to go into the desert and look for their dead bodies on Christmas Day. Working ghoul duty when you should be rolling in the covers with your best girl just sucks. There's no other way to put it.

And since we weren't really expecting to get any activity, we let Bobby talk us into cracking open the case of homemade Coahuila tequila we'd seized off a goat truck a few weeks earlier. Eddie and I weren't regular drinkers—not anything like Bobby, who routinely knocked back a six pack after the end of every shift—but it was Christmas Eve, and our girlfriends were both with their families, so we figured a little tequila wouldn't bother anybody.

But of course by the time the helicopter reported the illegals, it was well after dark and we were all thoroughly shitfaced. So I tossed a cooler of beer into the back of our Chevy Tahoe and Eddie took the wheel and Bobby the shotgun seat and we took off across the range to find the Mexicans before the desert killed them.

We had been tearing across the desert for more than twenty minutes when Eddie suddenly slammed on the brakes.

"What the...?" Bobby yelled. His beer had slopped into his lap and all over the dashboard.

Eddie ignored him and motioned for me to look out his side of the truck. "Jason, look down there along that line. You see them? Go around back and grab the night scope."

"Why me?" I said.

"Because you're the junior man."

"Eddie, come on. It's like ten degrees out there."

"Yeah?"

I rolled my eyes at him. "Fine," I said, and climbed out.

The winter winds coming down from the Chisos Mountains are like a cold from another world. It reaches through your clothes and clutches at your heart, and it can steal the breath from your lungs. When I stepped from the Tahoe my boots crunched through the white powder of ice that had formed in the dirt. Bolts of icy pain shot up my shins with every step. I looked out across the desert and saw a fine white frosting had covered everything. I heard the limbs of nearby hackberry trees cracking under the weight of accumulated ice. And there was the constant wailing of the wind coming down from the mountains, haunting in its beauty and loneliness.

I got the night scope from the back and went up to the driver's side window and stood there next to Eddie, shivering as I tried to blow some warmth onto my hands. He rolled down his window and we both looked out across the range. I didn't see anything, though. Just rocks and dirt.

Most people think the whole Texas-Mexico border is hot and dusty and flat and desolate. Well, it isn't flat. At least it isn't around the part of the border we patrolled. The Bullis Gap has got so many ridge lines and pocket canyons it looks like an unmade bed sheet on the topographical maps; and when you get down in it and start wandering around you can smell the acacia trees and feel the wind ripping at your ears and the whole thing is so savagely beautiful you just know it hasn't changed a hitch since the days when it was the northern frontier of the Aztec empire.

And, during the deepest part of winter, it can get cold enough to kill a man in no time flat. Standing there next to Eddie, I was shivering so hard that when I did finally catch sight of the Mexicans, it was all I could do to steady the reticule long enough to count them.

"Nine, looks like."

"Eleven," Eddie corrected me. "The other two are over there to the right, behind that clump of acacia."

I lowered the scope and tried to spot the group with my naked eye. "You can see that? How can you see that?"

"I say fuck 'em," Bobby offered. He had managed to get a lot drunker than either of us. "Turn us around, Eddie. I didn't see nothing if you didn't."

"Shut up, Bobby," Eddie said. He turned to me and said, "Get in, Jason. That ridge cuts back northwest for another two hundred yards. We can come across the line and catch 'em when it opens back up."

I looked again, this time with the night scope, to see if I could spot the other two, then gave up.

"Okay," I said. "You're the boss."

Eddie tore off down the dirt road, then cut down an embankment at full speed. Bobby was hollering like a loon for him to go faster and I was holding on to the roll cage for dear life and praying that Eddie really did know where he was taking us.

When we stopped I looked around and saw that the ridge line had opened up just like Eddie promised it would. We parked out of the way and killed the engine and waited.

We waited in the dark, cold and sullen, our buzzes fading to headaches, listening to the wind as it whistled through the truck. We waited 'til at last even Eddie's patience gave out and he admitted they must have slipped out of the ridge at some spot even he didn't know about.

"There's no way we can get our vehicle in there," he said, more to himself than to either of us. "We're gonna have to go in on foot."

"You sure you don't want to call the helicopter out again?" I asked.

"Why bother? We saw 'em go in. All we got to do is go in and get 'em."

"Yeah, but it's really cold out there."

"Don't be such a pussy. Get the flashlights."

————————

I got three flashlights out of the toolbox and we started off into the pocket. It was hard to tell how far we walked, but when we came up on the ridge line where the Mexicans had gone in, even I could tell we had gone too far.

"Double back," Eddie said. "We missed something."

On our way back we found where they slipped off. There was a section of the ridge wall that folded in on itself and was all covered over with wild tosora grass and cat's paw cactus. If we hadn't been looking for it we never would have seen it.

It was pretty clever the way whoever hid it did it. The helicopter probably flew over it every day and never saw the opening, but from right up close we could see the hidden pocket for what it really was. One section of the ridge wall had been dug out and reformed so that it bowled up at a shallow, but natural enough looking angle. Below that was what appeared to be some sort of structure.

It might have been more obvious in the daytime, but with only our flashlights to guide us it was hard to tell where the front wall started and the ridge walls stopped. The fit was seamless. Everything about it was a perfect blend with the surroundings. The only thing that really made it stand out at all was the dark, angular cut of the door and the rough-hewn mesquite wood cross embedded in the wall next to it.

But the longer I studied it, the more uncomfortable it made me. For such a small, primitive looking structure, it felt powerful and dignified, like it was some kind of dividing line—though what it was dividing me from I couldn't have said at the time. What I remember more than anything else about standing in front of that door was the feeling that we were absolutely unwelcome there. I've never felt anything else like it. The feeling was so strong, so undeniably clear in its meaning, that it was all I could do to hold my ground and not run away. As I stared at that door, a very distinct sense came over me that someone or something had looked into my heart and recognized me as one of the unclean.

"Somebody's god lives in there," I said.

Eddie turned around and looked at me like I had just said something every fourth grader knew by heart. "It's a church," he said.

"How do you know that?"

"Those pictures on the cross."

"What pictures?" I turned my light on the cross and saw there really were pictures on it—small, roughly carved pictures of birds and men dressed like animals and some wavy lines that sort of looked like a stream. I had to squint to see them, they were so small.

"It's picture writing. That part right there means 'sanctuary,' and that part there means 'safe crossing.'"

"And you didn't know this was here?"

He shook his head.

"So how do you know so much about it?"

"I grew up in Coahuila, remember? These are my people."

Bobby made an impatient coughing. Eddie and I turned back to look at him. He took a swig of his beer and pointed at the door. "You guys mind if we go inside," he said. "I'm fucking freezing out here."

"Get rid of that," Eddie told him. "Jesus. What the hell's wrong with you? And give me that shotgun. Jason, let's go."

Eddie held the door to the church open with the shotgun and we all went inside. We stepped into a narrow corridor with a low ceiling so that we had to stoop over and walk doubled over for about twenty feet before the passage opened up on a round room. The room was lit by a big pit fire in the middle and there were several smaller fires in lamps hanging from the ceiling.

The place was a lot bigger on the inside than it looked from the outside. All eleven illegals were there, sitting on their haunches along the wall. They were praying softly when we walked in, but one by one they stopped and grew silent.

Eddie told them who we were. He said something to them in the pidgin blend of Spanish and Indian dialects of the Coahuila farmers. It took them by surprise, I could tell. Two of them along the far wall were partially obscured in shadow, but I could see the whites of their eyes as they stared at Eddie.

On the other side of the fire I saw a large wooden statue of a man. The man's skin was painted sky blue and he was wearing the traditional eagle feather cloak and headdress of an Aztec god. There was a rough cut stone altar at his feet and the farmers must have been praying to it because there was a pile of gold and silver coins and desert flowers on it, placed there with obvious care, like an offering.

Bobby came around my right side while I was looking at the altar and told two of the Mexicans to get up.

"They don't speak English," Eddie said to him. "They're farmers."

Bobby either didn't hear him or didn't care. "Come on, you little piece of shit. Get up!" He yelled at them, and when that didn't work, he kicked dirt in their faces.

"Cut it out," Eddie snapped.

It was too late for that, though. Bobby was drunk and stewed for a fight. When none of the Mexicans would get up, he turned on their statue, grabbed it by the head, and yanked on it 'til it came loose and fell over into the fire.

Suddenly everybody was on their feet. I pulled my pistol and Eddie leveled his shotgun at the crowd and together we kept them from attacking Bobby, but only barely.

"Come on, you assholes," Bobby roared. "Come on, I'll beat all your asses."

"Shut up, you idiot!" Eddie said. He grabbed Bobby by the shoulder and pushed him toward the door. "Get out of here."

I kept my eyes on the ring of hostile faces closing in on us. In all the confusion none of us had noticed there was another corridor behind the statue, and while we were busy trying to put the peace back together, a naked man came running out of it and jumped on Bobby. He knocked Bobby down and the two of them rolled into the fire light. The naked man's entire body was covered with what had to be some sort of bluish-green lichen. Bobby pulled at him and threw a couple of useless punches into the air, but he was too drunk to do any damage, and the other man was a zealot. Bobby ended up on his back with the naked man on top of him, clawing and biting at his chest.

By the time we got to him, the naked man had torn open Bobby's winter gear and clamped down on Bobby's skin with his teeth. I kicked the naked man in the head and Eddie grabbed his neck with both hands and pulled at him until we heard something tear and the man came loose with a big chunk of Bobby's skin still clenched in his teeth. Bobby screamed as they came apart, and then passed out.

Eddie punched the naked man in the face with the butt of the shotgun and sent him tumbling back into the wall. When he hit he fell down into a crouch and growled at us like a cat.

I stood next to Eddie and we put ourselves between the naked man and Bobby. The bluish-green lichen covering his skin made him shine in the fire light, and it had done something to his face, too. His ears and his nose and his lips seemed to have rotted most of the way off. Bobby's blood was all over his cheeks and his chin, but beneath that, where the lichen had yet to spread, the skin was blistered and cracked like burned linoleum. His eyes were perfectly round and yellow and feral looking.

"What's that on his skin? He looks sick." I looked at my hands. Some of it had rubbed off there. "I got it on my hands."

"Me too," Eddie said.

Then, before either of us could get off a shot, he jumped sideways toward the back corridor and was gone. Bobby moaned softly at our feet, but he was still unconscious.

"Help me with him," Eddie said.

"What about them?" I asked, pointing at the illegals.

"Leave 'em. We need to get Bobby out of here."

We brought Bobby back to the station and put him in his cot and cleaned the wound the best we could. The wound looked bad, but it wasn't all that deep. The edges turned pink while we were working on him and stayed that way even after the bleeding stopped. He stayed unconscious through the whole thing.

"You want me to call a doctor?" I asked.

"No."

"He's hurt bad, Eddie."

"I know. And if we get a doctor out here we'll have to make a report on the injury. And when the doctor tells the Patrol the three of us were stinking drunk we'll all be looking for work." He shook his head. "No. We've got stuff here to help him. He'll be all right."

The next morning was Christmas and we decided to let Bobby sleep it off. Eddie and I went out to the kennel to feed the dogs and while we were putting out the food bowls I asked Eddie what he thought about the man who attacked Bobby.

"I don't know," was all he said, though if you know Eddie the way I do, you know that faraway look he gets when he's got a lot on his mind but isn't ready to share it yet. He was wearing that look as he put out the last of the dog food and wiped his hands. "Come on. Let's go eat."

We went back inside and Eddie fried up some chorizo while I cooked the eggs and heated up the tortillas. A few minutes later Bobby stumbled into the kitchen and yawned and stretched himself wide. He looked hung over, but more or less healthy.

Eddie and I traded a look and Eddie asked him if he was feeling hungry.

"I'm starved," he said. "Jesus, how much did we drink yesterday? I feel like a fucking goat took a crap in my mouth. What's there to eat, anyway?"

"Chorizo and eggs," Eddie said.

Bobby made a face. "Is that what that is?"

"It's good."

"I want meat," Bobby said.

"Chorizo is meat," I said. "Meat and pork together, actually."

"Don't we have any real meat? I want meat. Maybe a steak or something like that?"

"There should be some steaks out in the cooler," Eddie said. "You'll have to cook it yourself, though. We're eating this."

Bobby stumbled outside toward the cooler. Eddie and I sat down to eat, and I started to feel better about our decision not to call the doctor. Bobby's appetite seemed to be back, and I took that as a good sign.

But as we ate we heard the dogs making some awful noises outside. It didn't sound right, so Eddie and I went outside to see what was going on.

Bobby was standing outside the gate to their kennel and the dogs on the other side were barking at him. His breath was coming in little puffs of steam from between the thin line of his lips. Oscar, our big black shepherd mix, was standing opposite Bobby with his fur all bristled up and a fat rope of slobber hanging from his muzzle. The two of them were locked in a stare and both were growling.

"What the hell's going on?" Eddie demanded.

"Your dogs are going nuts."

"I can see that. What the hell did you do to 'em?"

"I ain't done nothing," Bobby said, still staring Oscar right in the eyes. "I was just walking by and they decided they wanted to fuck with me."

Oscar looked like he was ready to eat his way through the cage and Bobby looked like he wanted him to do it. Eddie pushed Bobby out of the way and slipped inside the gate.

"Easy boy. Easy," he said, and he grabbed Oscar by his collar and whispered to him and rubbed his ears 'til he started to calm down a little. "Go and get your steak, Bobby."

Bobby walked off to the cooler while Eddie talked softly with Oscar and I got the other dogs under control. Eddie was still whispering to Oscar and rubbing his ears when Bobby came back down the walkway.

Oscar had calmed down a lot while Eddie was holding him, but as soon as Bobby passed the gate, Oscar jumped out of Eddie's hands and ran full speed into the gate, barking and growling like something out of hell. Bobby kicked the gate and growled back at him.

"Keep your fucking mutt in line," Bobby said between his teeth.

"Get out of here, Bobby," Eddie said. "Go on back inside."

Bobby walked away, carrying an armful of steaks wrapped up in white butcher's paper.

When we were all back inside Bobby was smiling again like nothing had happened and even whistled while he unwrapped his steaks. He took out two good-sized rib eye cuts and dropped them in the same pan Eddie had used for the chorizo. He let them fry for about two minutes without bothering to flip them over and dropped them onto his plate.

He sat down next to us and cut into his steaks like he hadn't eaten in weeks. Eddie and I glanced at each other doubtfully and watched him dig in.

"Bobby," Eddie said, "are you sure you want to eat it that raw? I mean, with a hangover and all, isn't that a little much for your stomach to handle?"

Bobby just grunted at him and finished off both steaks like he couldn't eat them fast enough. He made a smacking, gulping noise as he ate.

"Still hungry," he grumbled. "Anybody else want some?"

"No thanks," Eddie said.

Bobby grunted, got up, and cooked three more steaks just like the first two. While he ate them, Eddie and I pushed our plates away. When he was done he got up and picked at his teeth with his fingers.

"I'm gonna take a nap," he said.

"We were going into Sandersville in a little bit to give our Christmas presents to the girls," Eddie said. "You wanna come?"

"No. I want to take a nap. Wake me up when you get back. Or I'll wake myself up if I get hungry."

Bobby went off for his nap and Eddie and I cleaned up and then drove into town to see our girlfriends. We spent most of the day in Sandersville and drove back around three so there'd be time to take care of some chores around the station and still have some time to just sit and hang out before nightfall.

Bobby was eating when we came home. The garbage can in the kitchen was full of a lot of white butcher paper and crushed bones that looked like they'd been gnawed to splinters and all the marrow sucked out.

"How many steaks did you eat?" I asked him.

"Don't know. We need more."

"What do you mean we need more?" Eddie asked. "We had twenty pounds of meat in there."

Bobby just grunted and then got up from the table and said he was going to his room for another nap.

About an hour later we heard Bobby banging around in his room and it sounded like he was moving furniture. He was making a lot of noise, and when we heard something crash we both got up and went to his room.

"You okay in there?" Eddie asked through the door.

"Go away."

I looked at Eddie and he at me. Bobby's voice didn't sound right. "Hey, Bobby," Eddie said, "open the door."

There was no answer that time.

"What do you want to do?" I whispered.

"Open it," Eddie said. "Hey, Bobby, I'm gonna open your door, okay? We're just making sure you're all right."

But he didn't have to force it open. Bobby opened it himself and walked away from the door to the middle of his room, where he turned around and faced us. He was wearing jeans and nothing else, not even shoes and socks. The first thing I saw was the wound on his chest. It had gotten a lot worse and turned black around the edges.

"It started hurting about an hour or so ago," he said when he noticed me looking at it. "Something's wrong with it, isn't it?"

"It's starting to bruise up probably," said Eddie, though not very convincingly. "That's probably why it's black around the edges."

"You think so?"

The wound was so nasty it took me a second to notice something was wrong with his face, too. I had expected to see worry there, maybe a need for reassurance, but what I saw instead was something more primitive, almost animal. His features looked wrong, like they had been stretched out at the mouth and the nose chiseled to a point. The chin, too. I thought maybe it was the light playing tricks on me or something, but then I looked at Eddie and realized he had noticed it too.

"Bobby, why don't you lay down for a bit. Try not to worry yourself too much. Jason and I will get the first aid kit and we'll clean that wound again."

"Yeah, okay," Bobby said, and climbed into his cot.

Eddie sent me to get some rubbing alcohol and he got the first aid kit and we met back in the rec room. He put the kit on the pool table and looked through it, making sure he had what he needed.

"I'm thinking he needs a doctor," I said.

"No."

"Eddie, come on. That wound on his chest looks really bad. There's no way that can be normal."

"It's not normal—and I wasn't thinking about the wound. You saw his face. Did that look like something a doctor could fix to you?"

"Eddie, he really needs a doctor."

"Let's see what we can do first. If we can't help him, we'll call a doctor."

Something made a huge crashing noise in Bobby's room and we both ran that way. It sounded like he was throwing stuff around and when we got to his door something heavy hit it from the other side—hit it so hard the whole wall shook.

I banged on the door with my fists and yelled for him to open it. The noises in his room stopped for a moment, but then they came back even louder. There's something in there with him, I thought, something animal. I heard a growl like the kind cougars make out in the desert at night.

"Bust it open," Eddie said.

I took a running start at the door and plowed into it with my shoulder. It flew open. I brought myself to a stop on the other side of the threshold and nearly lost my breath. There, on the ground, crouched and ready to strike, was something awful, something that had to have been Bobby at one time.

All the furniture in the room had been thrown against the walls and the thing was alone in the middle of the room. There was enough of Bobby left in that thing to recognize the shell of the man, but he was horribly changed. His mouth was wide open, filled with jagged teeth, and his face looked grotesquely stretched to make room for it. The nose and chin were even more pointed than when I saw them last, and it made his mouth look diamond shaped when it was all the way open. When he closed it I could see his eyes were closer together than normal, perfectly round and piercingly yellow.

The body still seemed to be that of a man, but only vaguely. It was lithe and sinewy, more predatory. My sense was that it was a being caught midway between man and cat, and every part of it was poised to strike.

"Bobby?" I asked it.

He growled at me and gathered up for the kill. His eyes narrowed and his teeth flashed. When he jumped for my throat it was so fast I didn't even have time to stagger back. I just stood there stupidly, bewildered by his speed and fierceness. The thing was still in the air when Eddie hit it with his baton. He came around my right side just as the thing leaped for me and hit it on the side of its head. All I saw was a flash of metal and the next thing I knew the thing was on its side up against the wall and Eddie was standing over it with blood dripping from the tip of his baton.

"What in the hell is that? Jesus, Eddie, is that supposed to be Bobby?"

Eddie didn't answer. He walked out and I followed him into the hallway. He closed the door and stuck his baton through the handle so that thing couldn't open it if it somehow got up.

"You didn't kill him, did you?"

"No."

"What the hell was that?"

Eddie didn't answer. He was looking into space over my shoulder, his mind somewhere else.

"Eddie?"

"Build a fire," he said, and went over to the ready lockers and put on his coat and took the keys to the Bronco.

"What?"

"Go outside," he said. "I'll be back in about an hour. I want you to build a fire. A big one. One that'll burn all night. Have it burning big by the time I get back." And then he reached over the door to the dorm rooms and took down the antique branding iron we found the previous summer while out on patrol. "Toss this in the fire. Make sure it's good and hot."

I put a hand on his shoulder, meaning to make him stop and explain himself. "Where are you going? Tell me what's going on."

He brushed my hand away.

"Just do what I ask, Jason. Be ready when I get back."

I had a raging fire six feet high by the time he returned. He backed the truck up to the rec room door and went to the kennel. When he came back he had a dog pole in his hand, the kind with the leather noose at the end to secure rabid animals.

"What did you do?" I asked him.

"Help me," he said, and handed me a pair of blue surgical gloves. "Put these on first."

He had the lichen priest stuffed into a dog crate in the back of the Bronco. He was handcuffed and leg cuffed and it looked like Eddie had beaten the living crap out of him to get him in that position. There was still plenty of fight left in him, though, because as soon as Eddie opened the tailgate, the lichen priest lunged at us.

Eddie punched him in the face 'til he wilted. He put the rope end of the dog pole around the priest's neck and then dragged him into the rec room.

He handed me the pole. "Hold him down," he said.

Eddie went out to the yard and came back with the branding iron in his hand.

He got on top of the lichen priest and went to work with the branding iron. The rec room started to smell. When the lichen priest stopped moving, I got up and went over to the trash can so I could throw up. Then I came back and grabbed the priest's legs so Eddie could start in on him again.

The two of them fought a strange kind of battle long into the night, but just before daybreak, they reached some kind of accord. I speak fluent Spanish, but they said things I didn't understand.

They spoke that pidgin language Eddie used when he spoke to the farmers from the Indian parts of Coahuila, and to this day I have never been able to get Eddie to tell me what went on between them. I only know that Eddie understood the lichen priest. And more importantly, the lichen priest understood Eddie.

When Eddie finally let him up, the lichen priest stood slowly, painfully, like he had a broken back, and then limped out our door, out into our yard, and off into the desert without ever looking back.

Eddie and I watched him walk off and then we stayed there to watch the sunrise.

"So what about Bobby?" I asked.

Eddie wet his lips, like he was tasting the cold morning air. "Help me with the dogs," he said. "After that, we eat some breakfast."

Later that afternoon the events of the previous two days seemed a million miles away. Eddie and I had finished the day's chores and were sitting down to lunch when Bobby appeared in the doorway, holding his head. There was dried blood on his forehead and his fingers, and he looked profoundly tired.

"What the hell happened? Jesus, what did I hit my head on? It feels like it's about to bust open."

"You don't remember?" Eddie asked him.

"No. The last thing I remember was you driving us down that embankment last night. Jesus, what a headache. Terrible way to spend Christmas."

"Yesterday was Christmas, Bobby," Eddie told him. "You missed it. You got so drunk after we came back here that you fell and hit your head on the pool table and passed out. You were out the whole day. Don't worry, though. I carried you on-duty on the pay sheets."

"That freaking Mexican tequila is from the devil," Bobby said. "You guys do me a favor and stop me before I get into that junk again."

I looked from Eddie to Bobby and back to Eddie. Eddie was staring off into space, his coffee cup poised at his lips, and I knew he was thinking about souls, and the horrible things we do to fight for them. My own mind was racing for a rational explanation, but all I could say for sure was that the rec room still smelled like something was burning.

Joe McKinney is a sergeant in the San Antonio Police Department who has been writing professionally since 2006. He is the Bram Stoker-nominated author of *Dead City, Quarantined, Apocalypse of the Dead, Dodging Bullets, Flesh Eaters* and *Dead Set*. His upcoming books include *The Zombie King, St. Rage, Lost Girl of the Lake,* and *The Red Empire*. As a police officer, he's received training in disaster mitigation, forensics, and homicide investigation techniques, some of which finds its way into his stories. He lives in the Texas Hill Country north of San Antonio.

Visit Joe at joemckinney.wordpress.com for news and updates.

Expulsion

1.

What we do is, we expel.

Air from our gut pockets. Piss, shit, and come by way of boiling glands. Babies from God-knows-where, by way of deflated wombs.

Up comes the pressure, out comes the force.

Such is why the gun holds such appeal. It's not the kind of thing you can put on an ad. But in our tissues, in our crevices, somewhere where we can't explain, we understand its build-build-build-release logic.

Which is why it satisfies so deep.

Which is why, if you think about it, all of us owe our survival to the gun.

Tear down the statues and houses of worship. I pray before the steel on my palm.

Or at least, that is, I did. Until last Wednesday.

2.

The mirror, in the morning, showed not a handsome man. Not a charismatic man. Not a man worthy of a second look.

But the mirror, what it did was, the mirror lied.

For whatever fibs my outside tells, my inside can knock you dead.

3.

I went into the office prepared to issue mayhem on two rungs. Rung one was essential: the pres, the vice, their secretaries, Larry from accounting. Rung two was optional: the interns, the front desk receptionist, the guy who updates the water cooler.

What interested me, then as now, was *force*. An adrenal situation was developing inside of me, in places where the mirror can't see. Let me put it this way: if you took a living stallion's adrenal glands and implanted them within the living body of an ether-addicted gorilla, you'd have something resembling my minute-to-minute mind-frame.

In line at the post office, stirring, it was like, "Let me make these fucking people bleed."

On the subway, it was always like, "These men and women would look better minus faces."

Street corners, alleyways, crowded restaurants, and I'm like, "Too much air in these people's lungs. Two many blinks in their eyes.

"An excess of thoughts within their heads."

None of this said out loud, of course. Who would stand still for such rabid constructions? Particularly from the mouth of one as bland as myself.

And besides, no volume of mine could compare to the volume of the gun.

4.

In my pocket.

As I paced, sloppy-haired, toward the boardroom.

Heart acting like the experiments done by the gods when creating thunder. Throat so dry it's like the same gods forgot to make water.

But this release was overdue.

Let me, at last, be lightning. Let me be people's destinies articulated.

Let me be anything but the vanilla pudding seen by you.

5.

Way back when, for me, it was all weakness. It was us 'round the dinner table; me catching sneers from my parents. One would say, "He's not the brightest," and the other would seal the deal with "He's not even close."

But, goddamn it, I had thoughts inside of me.

Good ones. Big ones. Ones that could block out a rural sky.

6.

Rung one, or most of it, was in the boardroom. Only Larry from accounting was missing. But he was two doors down, and not fast enough to run. Gut hung so low it would no doubt get in front of his feet.

The gun was plain at that moment, a fact that I loved. In other words, if you could see me, you could see it.

And then the steel pellets aligned within its curves.

7.

The thing is, there's a crust over everything. We spend our whole lives trying to crack it open.

The crust is the glass we look through, darkly. It's the lie lain like fresh snowfall upon all we perceive. Only unlike snow, it never melts in the sun.

No season has arrived yet to loosen this crust.

Perhaps, though, acting God-like, *I* can usher one in.

Pierce the veil; isn't that what we want? What artists want. What revolutionaries want. Narrowing the distance between the seen and unseen, praying for a train wreck of revelation once that distance is nil.

Such is why, at last, we desire expulsion.

Release the shit from our intestines. The come from our scrotums. The life from our wombs.

Crack it open. Shed the waste. Expel, at last, the *force*.

8.

But I'm so stupid.

An error grabbed me.

Story of my goddamn life.

I am, after all, the guy who goes to the gym without his sneakers. The guy who can't memorize the dates when his bills are due. The guy who, one time, given bad directions, spent four hours in a gay bar awaiting women.

9.

The error I made—which to all but me was fortunate—was to contemplate the nature of the first rung before entering the room.

Looking in upon them, I peeled back some crust.

Only this layer was inside of me, and beneath it was the nature of these people…

10.

The pres, before then, was a parasitic being, a man for whom waking up was only worth it if it meant sucking in more money.

At that moment, though, gun in my hand, he became a creature of persistence, somebody who never backed down from a fight, somebody whose tenacity could spur humility in most living others.

11.

As for the vice, his prior, ill status as a perverse mouth-breather got replaced by an immodest standing as a creature of solidity. Day in, day out, as steady as the moon and sun. To be sure, his titty jokes fell flat, but was the man not entitled to his own releases?

12.

The secretaries, formerly bitches or brats, got upgraded to a baker of a mean pear pie (the pres's) and the owner of a gorgeous face (the vice's).

13.

Larry from accounting…he…

14.

What was it that I had against him?

15.

Still, however, was all that adrenaline. Dark as the moment of night when it's farthest from day. Pumping so hard it may as well have been motionless.

Making my soul want to split from this shitty chrysalis.

16.

By the time I lowered the gun, it was too late. One of the interns had spied me from behind. The phone got dialed—two digits/three key strokes—and I then had men in ironed cloth grabbing toward my love handles.

Since I shot nobody, I may go home someday.

And between you and me, the beautiful things that I saw might have just been worth it...

17.

City behind me. Chatter behind me. Horns and screeches and metal and fumes, all behind me.

Above me, spinning-spinning-spinning, red lights, blue lights, patriotic essentially but candy-apple-psychotic in actuality.

Biting steel about my wrists, causing a click in all the blood that passes that way.

Ahead of me, a future without my clothes. Without my things. My apartment, gone. Wallet, hidden somewhere else. Refrigerator, manned by people in hairnets.

Gun in a cellophane bag where no breath can leave it.

Mirror only in the bathroom, where a hard and permanent fog keeps me from knowing what I look like (but is the fogged reflection any sharper than the real one?).

Brain, however, still in my head. Lit up like a nuclear Christmas on the moon's lonely surface.

18.

And it's hard to be like I am inside of a cage. Mind stretching outward, ripping and expanding in the ways of a scream. But like a scream, it touches nothing—save, of course, for the source from which it emanates.

Which undergoes a sweetish char of pain.

19.

Humans aren't only expelled when born. Schools expel them. Jobs expel them.

Society shakes its head and says, "Come *on*—get out of here."

Some of us don't fit within the grid. Try to put us there and it gets all bent.

We, however? We're bent to begin with.

20.

Me to the guard:

"Some water, you think?"

But the guy's already turned the corner.

The featurelessness of his back defying me.

Though certainly he, like all others, is possessed of useful things.

21.

Certainly whatever's beneath the crust is only dark when encrusted.

And yet it gets light when the crust is gone.

Certainly our expulsions can be marked by dankness.

And yet carry its opposite, too…

22.

And certainly I, as I pace the concrete, have a most novel nature to contemplate.

For I'd like nothing more than to expel this grand force.

But I'm afraid, goddamn it, that it's made of love.

I'd be such a good killer if only I hated people.

Eric Shapiro's acclaimed 2005 novella, *It's Only Temporary*, was on the preliminary ballot for the Bram Stoker Award in Long Fiction. He directed and produced the motion picture *Rule of Three* (2010), which had its world premiere at the Fantasia Festival and its U.S. Premiere at Fantastic Fest before being released on DVD and Netflix Instant. In 2010, Permuted Press published an omnibus collection of Eric's three short novels and a handful of selected short stories called *Stories for the End of the World*. Eric lives in Los Angeles with his wife and producing partner Rhoda Jordan.

Career Day

Scott Bradley

"It's career day!" shrilled Mrs. Greenwood. "You must behave yourselves for our guests!"

The children, excited and purple, tried to contain themselves and mostly did.

They drank juice.

They gobbled sweets.

They whispered amongst themselves during the morning lessons until Mrs. Greenwood's steely gaze froze them back into silence.

Career Day was a very special day.

This was the day the Grown-Ups told them all about what they did for a living out in the World.

The Grown-Up World.

So secret, so mysterious.

The children whispered at recess about the Grown-Up World.

At 1:00 p.m. exactly (because Mrs. Greenwood was never anything but punctual), Career Day began.

"My name is Mr. Tanner and I sell Real Estate!" The large, wheezing, mustachioed man grinned ominously. "Do any of you know what that is?"

None of them did.

But one pale girl named Emma—who liked music and her cat and sometimes wondered why the sky was blue—ventured: "Something real?"

After a big "HA-HA" from Mr. Tanner, Emma was jerked harshly out of her seat by Mrs. Greenwood, rushed into the hallway, and never seen again.

It went on like that for another two hours.

It took some of the children very little time, all things considered, to understand when they should speak and when they shouldn't.

For the other children—those too smart and those not smart enough—the less said, the better.

By the time the 3 p.m. bell rang, even Mrs. Greenwood—who had been through this on so many days for so many years—was taking little stabs at herself with one of the classroom's crisply sharpened Ticonderoga #2 pencils.

There were ten children (out of the original eighty-seven) still in the classroom.

Mrs. Greenwood looked at them.

They looked through her.

Mrs. Greenwood, as she had for so many years, after so many Career Days, unleashed the monsters on the world.

She nodded and said: "Class dismissed."

Scott Bradley was born on July 25, 1972 in Springfield, Missouri, the birthplace of serial killer Francis Dolarhyde in *Red Dragon* by Thomas Harris. Scott considers himself generally better-adjusted than Mr. Dolarhyde, however, and even earned a bachelor's degree in English from the University of Missouri-Kansas City. In 2008, he co-edited *The Book of Lists: Horror* (HarperCollins) which earned him a nomination for the prestigious Bram Stoker Award. He is the co-author of "The Better Half: A Love Story," appearing in the anthology *Werewolves and Shapeshifters: Encounters With the Beast Within*, edited by John Skipp, and his critical essay on the 1986 cult film "The Hitcher" appears in *Butcher Knives and Body Counts*, edited by Vince Liaguno. His criticism and journalism have appeared in *Film Quarterly*, *The Kansas City Star*, *Creative Screenwriting*, among other publications. He is working on a novel, a screenplay, and (with Jason Aaron) on the literary biography of the legendary Vietnam War author Gustav Hasford.

Scott lives in Los Angeles and suggests you join him on Facebook at www.facebook.com/SBradley1972.

Acknowledgements

For everyone who submitted to this anthology, thank you. Great authors worked hard to create the tales in this tome, but other, equally talented scribes, toiled with different results. Could I have accepted every story, my job might have seemed easier at times, but then this collection would be larger than a New York City phonebook and scheduled for release some time next decade. Alas, an editor must make decisions and I stand by mine. A grateful thanks to all who tried. I hope you will do it again.

A special debt of gratitude is due to Charles Day. Those who know Charlie know he's a jubilant spirit with an unwavering sense of commitment. When Charlie shared his dream of opening a small press that specialized in speculative fiction, he gained my attention. But when he asked me to launch and run the press, he caught me by surprise. After delivering a tentative series of "maybes" and "we'll-sees," I finally gave in, but with one caveat. "Later," I said, "I'm too busy writing right now." A few days passed and I couldn't write. I became anxious, Blofeldian delusions of world domination dancing in my head. Before the knowledge of my actions set in, I had posted a submission call for *Help! Wanted: Tales of On-the-Job Terror*. Charlie laughed at me and pointed out, "We're a lot alike." He was right. I'm grateful for his enthusiasm, trust, and effective (often selfless) carnival barking. Without him this endeavor would never have been as much fun or as fruitful. Gracias, you evil little jester!

For putting up with all my bullshit, I thank my wife, Karen. And to our three glorious cats—Cup, Baby, and Bert—I offer thanks for the comfort of soft pelts at moments of frustration. The cats don't read very well, but Karen, our resident "Cat Whisperer," will read this to them, and they'll understand...or so I'm told.

To my dear friend and collaborator, Scott Bradley, who encouraged me to reach out to Stephen Volk, I can't begin to properly express my appreciation. When Scott—the bona fide E.F. Hutton of the horror genre—speaks, I listen. Thanks, amigo.

I'm indebted to all the members at the EJP Forum. Their humor, suggestions, and words of encouragement have helped me through many rough patches. Thank you, all!

And last, but certainly not least, thank *you*. Yes, you, the person holding this book or e-book. You not only bought the anthology, you took the time to read the Acknowledgements. Wow! I hope that means you're hungry for more.

—*Peter Giglio*
August, 2011

Join the

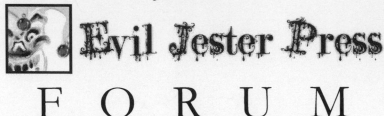

F O R U M

Interact with authors and readers!
Stay informed about upcoming projects!
Tell us what you'd like to see from EJP!

It's Fun!
It's Free!
And The Jester's waiting for *you*!

Join the forum at:
www.eviljesterpress.lefora.com
And visit us at:
www.eviljesterpress.com

78592981R00163

Made in the USA
Middletown, DE
03 July 2018